Quatermain

Quatermain
The Complete Adventures: 6

Heu-Heu or, the Monster
★
The Treasure of the Lake

H. Rider Haggard

LEONAUR

Quatermain : the Complete Adventures: 5—
Heu-Heu or, the Monster & The Treasure of the Lake
by H. Rider Haggard

Leonaur is an imprint of Oakpast Ltd

ISBN: 978-1-84677-605-2 (hardcover)
ISBN: 978-1-84677-606-9 (softcover)

http://www.leonaur.com

Publisher's Notes

The views expressed in this book are not necessarily
those of the publisher.

Contents

Publisher's Note

Suggested reading sequence for the Allan Quatermain stories:

Heu–Heu, or
the Monster

Author's Note

The author wishes to state that this tale was written in its present form some time before the discovery in Rhodesia of the fossilized and immeasurably ancient remains of the proto-human person who might well have been one of the Heuheua, the *hairy wood-folk*, of which it tells through the mouth of Allan Quatermain.
(1923)

CHAPTER 1

The Storm

Now I, the Editor, whose duty it has been as an executor or otherwise, to give to the world so many histories of, or connected with, the adventures of my dear friend, the late Allan Quatermain, or Macumazahn, Watcher-by-Night, as the natives in Africa used to call him, come to one of the most curious of them all. Here I should say at once that he told it to me many years ago at his house called The Grange, in Yorkshire, where I was staying, but a little while before he departed with Sir Henry Curtis and Captain Good upon his last expedition into the heart of Africa, whence he returned no more.

At the time I made very copious notes of a history that struck me as strange and suggestive, but the fact is that afterwards I lost them and could never trust my memory to reproduce even their substance with the accuracy which I knew my departed friend would have desired.

Only the other day, however, in turning out a box-room, I came upon a hand-bag which I recognized as one that I had used in the far past when I was practising, or trying to practise, at the Bar. With a certain emotion such as overtakes us when, after the lapse of many years, we are confronted by articles connected with the long-dead events of our youth, I took it to a window and with some difficulty opened its rusted catch. In the bag was a small collection of rubbish: papers connected with cases on which once I had worked as "devil" for an eminent and learned friend who afterwards became a judge, a blue pencil with a broken point, and so forth.

I looked through the papers and studied my own marginal notes made on points in causes which I had utterly forgotten, though doubtless these had been important enough to me at the time, and, with a sigh, tore them up and threw them on the floor. Then I reversed the bag to knock out the dust. As I was doing this there slipped from an inner pocket, a very thick notebook with a shiny black cover such as used to be bought for sixpence. I opened that book and the first thing that my eye fell upon was this heading:

Summary of A. Q.'s strange story of the Monster-God, or fetish, Heu-Heu, which he and the Hottentot Hans discovered in Central South Africa.

Instantly everything came back to me. I saw myself, a young man in those days, making those shorthand notes late one night in my bedroom at the Grange before the impression of old Allan's story had become dim in my mind, also continuing them on the train upon my journey south on the morrow, and subsequently expanding them in my chambers at Elm Court in the Temple whenever I found time to spare.

I remembered, too, my annoyance when I discovered that this notebook was nowhere to be found, although I was aware that I had put it away in some place that I thought particularly safe. I can still see myself hunting for it in the little study of the house I had in a London suburb at the time, and at last giving up the quest in despair. Then the years went on and many things happened, so that in the end both notes and the story they outlined were forgotten. Now they have appeared again from the dust-heap of the past, reviving many memories, and I set out the tale of this particular chapter of the history of the adventurous life of my beloved friend, Allan Quatermain, who so long ago was gathered to the Shades that await us all.

* * * * * * * *

One night, after a day's shooting, we—that is, old Allan, Sir Henry Curtis, Captain Good, and I—were seated in the smoking room of Quatermain's house, The Grange, in Yorkshire, smoking and talking of many things.

I happened to mention that I had read a paragraph, copied from an American paper, which stated that a huge reptile of an antediluvian kind had been seen by some hunters in a swamp of the Zambezi, and asked Allan if he believed the story. He shook his head and answered in a cautious fashion which suggested to me, I remember, his unwillingness to give his views as to the continued existence of such creatures on the earth, that Africa is a big place and it was possible that in its recesses prehistoric animals or reptiles lingered on.

"I know that this is the case with snakes," he continued hurriedly as though to avoid the larger topic, "for once I came across one as large as the biggest Anaconda that is told of in South America, where occasionally they are said to reach a length of sixty feet or more. Indeed, we killed it—or rather my Hottentot servant, Hans, did—after it had crushed and swallowed one of our party. This snake was worshipped as a king of gods, and might have given rise to the tale of enormous reptiles. Also, to omit other experiences of which I prefer not to speak, I have seen an elephant so much above the ordinary in size that it might have belonged to a prehistoric age. This elephant has been known for centuries and was named Jana.

"Did you kill it?" inquired Good, peering at him through his eyeglasses in his quick, inquisitive way.

Allan coloured beneath his tan and wrinkles, and said, rather sharply for him, who was so gentle and hard to irritate, "Have you not learned, Good, that you should never ask a hunter, and above all a professional hunter, whether he did or did not kill a particular head of game unless he volunteers the information? However, if you want to know, I did not kill that elephant; it was Hans who killed it and thereby saved my life. I missed it with both barrels at a distance of a few yards!"

"Oh, I say, Quatermain!" ejaculated the irrepressible Good. "Do you mean to tell us that *you* missed a particularly big elephant that was only a few yards off? You must have been in a pretty fright to do that."

"Have I not said that I missed it, Good? For the rest, perhaps you are right, and I was frightened, for as you know, I never set myself up as a person remarkable for courage. In the circumstances of the encounter with this beast, Jana, any one might have been frightened; indeed, even you yourself, Good. Or, if you choose to be charitable, you may conclude that there were other reasons for that disgraceful—yes, disgraceful exhibition of which I cannot bear to think and much less to talk, seeing that in the end it brought about the death of old Hans—whom I loved."

Now Good was about to answer again, for argument was as the breath of his nostrils, but I saw Sir Henry stretch out his long leg and kick him on the shin, after which he was silent.

"To return," said Allan hastily, as one does who desires to escape from an unpleasant subject, "in the course of my life I did once meet, not with a prehistoric reptile, but with a people who worshipped a Monster-god, or fetish, of which perhaps the origin may have been a survival from the ancient world."

He stopped with the air of one who meant to say no more, and I asked eagerly: "What was it, Allan?"

"To answer that would involve a long story, my friend," he replied, "and one that, if I told it, Good, I am sure, would not believe; also, it is getting late and might bore you. Indeed, I could not finish it tonight."

13

"There are whisky, soda, and tobacco, and whatever Curtis and Good may do, here, fortified by these, I remain between you and the door until you tell me that tale, Allan. You know it is rude to go to bed before your guests, so please get on with it at once," I added, laughing.

The old boy hummed and hawed and looked cross, but as we all sat round him in an irritating silence which seemed to get upon his nerves, he began at last:

* * * * * * * *

Well, if you will have it, many years ago, when by comparison I was a young man, I camped one day well up among the slopes of the Drakensberg. I was going up Pretoria way with a load of trade goods which I hoped to dispose of among the natives beyond, and when I had done so to put in a month or two game-shooting towards the north. As it happened, when we were in an open space of ground between two of the foothills of the Berg, we got caught in a most awful thunderstorm, one of the worst that ever I experienced. If I remember right, it was about mid-January and you, my friend (this was addressed to me), know what Natal thunderstorms can be at that hot time of the year. It seemed to come upon us from two quarters of the sky, the fact being that it was a twin storm of which the component parts were travelling towards each other.

The air grew thick and dense; then came the usual moaning, icy wind followed by something like darkness, although it was early in the afternoon. On the peaks of the mountains around us lightnings were already playing, but as yet I heard no thunder, and there was no rain. In addition to the driver and *voorlooper* of the wagon I had with me Hans, of whom I was speaking just now, a little wrinkled Hottentot who, from my boyhood, had been the companion of my journeys and adventures. It was he who came with me as my after-rider when as a very young man I accompanied Piet Retief on that fatal embassy to Dingaan, the Zulu king, of whom practically all except Hans and myself were massacred.

He was a curious, witty little fellow of uncertain age and of his sort one of the cleverest men in Africa. I never knew his equal in resource or in following a spoor, but, like all Hottentots, he had his faults; thus, whenever he got the chance, he would drink like a fish and become a useless nuisance. He had his virtues, also, since he was faithful as a dog and—well, he loved me as a dog loves the master that has reared it from a blind puppy. For me he would do anything—lie or steal or commit murder, and think it no wrong, but rather a holy duty. Yes, and any day he was prepared to die for me, as in the end he did.

14

* * * * * * * *

Allan paused, ostensibly to knock out his pipe, which was unnecessary, as he had only just filled it, but really, I think, to give himself a chance of turning towards the fire in front of which he was standing, and thus to hide his face. Presently he swung round upon his heel in the light, quick fashion that was one of his characteristics, and went on:

* * * * * * * *

I was walking in front of the wagon, keeping a lookout for bad places and stones in what in those days was by courtesy called the road, though in fact it was nothing but a track twisting between the mountains, and just behind, in his usual place—for he always stuck to me like a shadow—was Hans. Presently I heard him cough in a hollow fashion, as was his custom when he wanted to call my attention to anything, and asked over my shoulder, "What is it, Hans?"

"Nothing, Baas," he answered, "only that there is a big storm coming up. Two storms, Baas, not one, and when they meet they will begin to fight and there will be plenty of spears flying about in the sky, and then both those clouds will weep rain or perhaps hail."

"Yes," I said, "there is, but as I don't see anywhere to shelter, there is nothing to be done."

Hans came up level with me and coughed again, twirling his dirty apology for a hat in his skinny fingers, thereby intimating that he had a suggestion to make.

"Many years ago, Baas," he said, pointing with his chin towards a mass of tumbled stones at the foot of a mountain slope about a mile to our left, "there used to be a big cave yonder, for once when I was a boy I sheltered in it with some Bushmen. It was after the Zulus had cleaned out Natal and there was nothing to eat in the land, so that the people who were left fed upon one another."

"Then how did the Bushmen live, Hans?"

"On slugs and grasshoppers, for the most part, Baas, and buck when they were lucky enough to kill any with their poisoned arrows. Fried caterpillars are not bad, Baas, nor are locusts when you can get nothing else. I remember that I, who was starving, grew fat on them."

"You mean that we had better make for this cave of yours, Hans, if you are sure it's there?"

"Yes, Baas, caves can't run away, and though it is many years ago, I don't forget a place where I have lived for two months."

I looked at those advancing clouds and reflected. They were uncommonly black and evidently there was going to be the devil of a

15

storm. Moreover, the situation was not pleasant for we were crossing a patch of ironstone on which, as I knew from experience, lightning always strikes, and a wagon and a team of oxen have an attraction for electric flashes.

While I was reflecting a party of *Kaffirs* came up from behind, running for all they were worth, no doubt to seek shelter. They were dressed in their finery—evidently people going to or returning from a wedding-feast, young men and girls, most of them—and as they went by one of them shouted to me, whom evidently he knew, as did most of the natives in those parts, "Hurry, hurry, Macumazahn!" as you know the Zulus called me. "Hurry, this place is beloved of lightnings," and he pointed with his dancing stick first to the advancing tempest and then to the ground where the ironstone cropped up.

That decided me, and running back to the wagon I told the *voor-looper* to follow Hans, and the driver to flog up the oxen. Then I scrambled in behind and off we went, turning to the left and heading for the place at the foot of the slope where Hans said the cave was. Luckily the ground was fairly flat and open—hard, too; moreover, although he had not been there for so many years, Hans's memory of the spot was perfect. Indeed, as he said, it was one of his characteristics never to forget any place that he had once visited.

Thus, from the driving box to which I had climbed, suddenly I saw him direct the *voorlooper* to bear sharply to the right and could not imagine why, as the surface there seemed similar to that over which we were travelling. As we passed it, however, I perceived the reason, for here was a ground spring which turned a large patch of an acre or more into a swamp, where certainly we should have been bogged. It was the same with other obstacles that I need not detail.

By now a great stillness pervaded the air and the gloom grew so thick that the front oxen looked shadowy; also it became very cold. The lightning continued to play upon the mountain crests, but still there was no thunder. There was something frightening and unnatural in the aspect of nature; even the cattle felt it, for they strained at the yokes and went off very fast indeed, without the urgings of whips or shouts, as though they too knew they were flying from peril. Doubtless they did, since instinct has its voices which speak to everything that breathes. For my part, my nerves became affected and I hoped earnestly that we should soon reach that cave.

Presently I hoped it still more, for at length those clouds met and from their edges as they kissed each other came an awful burst of fire—perhaps it was a thunderbolt—that rushed down and struck the earth with a loud detonation. At any rate, it caused the ground to shake and me to wish that I were anywhere else, for it fell within fifty yards of the wagon, exactly where we had been a minute or so before. Simultaneously there was a most awful crash of thunder, showing that the tempest now lay immediately overhead.

This was the opening of the ball; the first sudden burst of music. Then the dance began with sheets and forks of flame for dancers and the great sky for the floor upon which they performed.

It is difficult to describe such a hellish tempest because, as you, my friend, who have seen them, will know, they are beyond description. Lightnings, everywhere lightnings; flash upon flash of them of all shapes—one, I remember, looked like a crown of fire encircling the brow of a giant cloud. Moreover, they seemed to leap upwards from the earth as well as downwards from the heaven, to the accompaniment of one continuous roar of thunder.

"Where the deuce is your cave?" I yelled into the ear of Hans, who had climbed on to the driving box beside me.

He shrieked something in answer which I could not catch because of the tumult, and pointed to the base of the mountain slope, now about two hundred yards away.

The oxen *skrecked* and began to gallop, causing the wagon to bump and sway so that I thought it would overset, and the *voorlooper* to leave hold of the *reim* and run alongside of them for fear lest he should be trodden to death, guiding them as best he could, which was not well. Luckily, however, they ran in the right direction.

On we tore, the driver plying his whip to keep the beasts straight, and as I could see from the motion of his lips, swearing his hardest in Dutch and Zulu, though not a word reached my ears. At length they were brought to a halt by the steep slope of the mountain and proceeded to turn round and tie themselves into a kind of knot after the fashion of frightened oxen that for any reason can no longer pull their load.

We leapt down and began to outspan them, getting the yokes off as quickly as we could—no easy job, I can tell you, both because of the mess in which they were and for the reason that it must be carried out literally under fire, since the flashes were falling all about us. Momentarily I expected that one of them would catch the wagon and make an end of us and our story. Indeed, I was so frightened that I was sorely tempted to leave the oxen to their fate and bolt to the cave, if cave there were—for I could see none.

However, pride came to my aid, for if I ran away, how could I ever expect my *Kaffirs* to stand again in a difficulty? Be as much afraid as you like, but never show fear before a native; if you do, your influence over him is gone. You are no longer the great White Chief of higher blood and breeding; you are just a common fellow like himself; inferior to himself, indeed, if he chances to be a brave specimen of a people among whom most of the men are brave.

So I pretended to take no heed of the lightnings, even when one struck a thorn tree not more than thirty paces away. I happened to be looking in that direction and saw the thorn in the flare, every bough of it. Next second all I saw was a column of dust; the thorn had gone and one of its splinters hit my hat.

With the others I tugged and kicked at the oxen, getting the thongs off the *yoke-skeis* as best I could, till at length all were loose and galloping away to seek shelter under overhanging rocks or where they could in accordance with their instincts. The last two, the pole oxen—valuable beasts—were particularly difficult to free, as they were trying to follow their brethren and strained at the yokes so much that in the end I had to cut the *rimpis*, as I could not get them out of the notches of the *yoke-skeis*. Then they tore off after the others, but did not get far, poor brutes, for presently I saw both of them—they were running together—go down as though they were shot through the heart. A flash had caught them; one of them never stirred again; the other lay on its back kicking for a few seconds and then grew as still as its yoke-mate.

* * * * * * * *

"And what did you say?" inquired Good in a reflective voice.

"What would you have said, Good?" asked Allan severely, "if you had lost your best two oxen in such a fashion, and happened not to have a sixpence with which to buy others? Well, we all know your command of strong language, so I do not think I need ask you to answer."

"I should have said——" began Good, bracing himself to the occasion, but Allan cut him short with a wave of his hand.

"Something about *Jupiter Tonans*, no doubt," he said.

Then he went on.

* * * * * * * *

Well, what I said was only overheard by the recording angel, though perhaps Hans guessed it, for he screamed at me, "It might have been *us*, Baas. When the sky is angry, it will have *something*; better the oxen than us, Baas."

18

"The cave, you idiot!" I roared. "Shut your mouth and take us to the cave, if there is one, for here comes the hail."

Hans grinned and nodded, then hastened by a large hailstone which hit him on the head, began to skip up the hill at a surprising rate, beckoning to the rest of us to follow. Presently we came to a tumbled pile of rocks through which we dodged and scrambled in the gloom that now, when the hail had begun to fall, was denser than ever between the flashes. At the back of the biggest of these rocks Hans dived among some bushes, dragging me after him between two stones that formed a kind of natural gateway to a cavity beyond.

"This is the place, Baas," he said, wiping the blood that ran down his forehead from a cut in the head made by the hailstone.

As he spoke, a particularly vivid flash showed me that we were in the mouth of a cavern of unknown size. That it must be large, however, I guessed from the echoes of the thunder that followed the flash, which seemed to reverberate in that hollow place from unmeasured depths in the bowels of the mountain.

CHAPTER 2

The Picture in the Cave

We did not reach the cave too soon, for as the boys scrambled into it after us the hail began to come down in earnest, and you fellows know, or at any rate have heard, what African hail can be, especially among the mountains of the Berg. I have known it to go through sheets of galvanized iron like rifle bullets, and really I believe that some of the stones which fell on this occasion would have pierced two of them put together, for they were as big as flints and jagged at that. If anybody had been caught in that particular storm on the open veldt without a wagon to creep under or a saddle to put over his head, I doubt whether he would have lived to see a clear sky again.

The driver, who was already almost weeping with distress over the loss of Kaptein and Deutchmann, as the two pole oxen were named, grew almost crazed because he thought that the hail would kill the others, and actually wanted to run out into it with the wild idea of herding them into some shelter. I told him to sit still and not be a fool, since we could do nothing to help them. Hans, who had a habit of growing religious when there was lightning about, re-marked sententiously that he had no doubt that the "Great-Great" in the sky would look after the cattle since my Reverend Father (who had converted him to the peculiar faith, or mixture of faiths, which, with Hans, passed for Christianity) had told him that the cattle on a thousand hills were His especial property, and, here in the Berg, were they not among the thousand hills? The Zulu driver who had not "found religion," but was just a raw savage, replied with point that if that were so the "Great-Great" might have protected Kaptein and Deutchmann, which He had clearly neglected to do. Then, after the fashion of some furious woman, by way of relieving his nerves, he fell to abusing Hans, whom he called "a yellow jackal," adding that the tail of the worst of the oxen was of more value than his whole body, and that he wished his worthless skin were catching the hailstones instead of their inestimable hides.

These nasty remarks about his personal appearance irritated Hans, who drew up his lips as does an angry dog, and replied in suitable language, which involved reflections upon that Zulu's family, and especially on his mother. In short, had I not intervened there would have been a very pretty row that might have ended in a blow from a *kerry* or a knife thrust. This, however, I did with vigour, saying that he who spoke another word should be kicked out of the cave to keep company with the hail and the lightning, after which peace was restored.

That storm went on for a long while, for after it had seemed to go away it returned again, travelling in a circle as such tempests sometimes do, and when the hail was finished, it was followed by torrential rain. The result was that by the time the thunder had ceased to roar and echo among the mountain-tops darkness was at hand, so it became evident that we must stop where we were for the night, especially as the boys, who had gone out to look for the oxen, reported that they could not find them. This was not pleasant, as the cave was uncommonly cold and the wagon was too soaked with the rain to sleep in.

Here, however, once more Hans's memory came in useful. Having borrowed my matches, he crept off down the cave and presently returned, dragging a quantity of wood after him, dusty and worm-eaten-looking wood, but dry and very suitable for firing.

"Where did you get that?" I asked.

"Baas," he replied, "when I lived in this place with the Bushmen, long before those black children" (this insult referred to the driver and the *voorlooper*, Mavoon and Induka by name) "were begotten of their unknown fathers, I hid away a great stock of wood for the winter, or in case I should ever come back here, and there it is still, covered with stones and dust. The ants that run about the ground do the same thing, Baas, that their children may have food when they are dead. So now if those *Kaffirs* will help me to get the wood we may have a good fire and be warm."

Marvelling at the little Hottentot's foresight that was bred into his blood by the necessities of a hundred generations of his forefathers, I bade the others to accompany him to the cache, which they did, glowering, with the result that presently we had a glorious fire. Then I fetched some food, for luckily I had killed a Duiker buck that morning, the flesh of which we toasted on the embers, and with it a bottle of Square-face from the wagon, so that soon we were eating a splendid dinner. I know that there are many who do not approve of giving spirits

21

to natives, but for my part I have found that when they are chilled and tired a "tot" does them no harm and wonderfully improves their tempers. The trouble was to prevent Hans from getting more than one, to do which I made a bedfellow of that bottle of Square-face.

When we were filled I lit my pipe and began to talk with Hans, whom the grog had made loquacious and therefore interesting. He asked me how old the cave was, and I told him that it was as old as the mountains of the Berg. He answered that he had thought so because there were footprints stamped in the rock floor farther down it, and turned to stone, which were not made by any beasts that he had ever heard of or seen, which footprints he would show me on the morrow if I cared to look at them. Further, that there were queer bones lying about, also turned to stone, that he thought must have belonged to giants. He believed that he could find some of these bones when the sun shone into the cave in the early morning.

Then I explained to Hans and the *Kaffirs* how once, thousands of thousands of years ago, before there were any men in the world, great creatures had lived there, huge elephants and reptiles as large as a hundred crocodiles made into one, and, as I had been told, enormous apes, much bigger than any gorilla. They were very interested, and Hans said that it was quite true about the apes, since he had seen a picture of one of them, or of a giant that looked like an ape.

"Where?" I asked. "In a book?"

"No, Baas, here in this cave. The Bushman made it ten thousand years ago." By which he meant at some indefinite time in the past.

Now I bethought me of a fabulous creature called the *Ngoloko* which was said to inhabit an undefined area of swamps on the East Coast and elsewhere. This animal, in which, I may add, I did not in the least believe, for I set it down as a native bogey, was supposed to be at least eight feet high, to be covered with gray hair and to have a claw in the place of toes. My chief authority for it was a strange old Portuguese hunter whom I had once known, who swore that he had seen its footprints in the mud, also that it had killed one of his men and twisted the head off his body. I asked Hans if he had ever heard of it. He replied that he had, under another name, that of *Milhoy*, I think, but that the devil painted in the cave was larger than that.

Now I thought that he was pitching me a yarn, as natives will, and said that if so he had better show me the picture forthwith.

"Best wait until the sun shines in the morning, Baas," he replied, "for then the light will be good. Also this devil is not nice to look at at night."

"Show it me," I repeated with asperity; "we have lanterns from the wagon."

So, somewhat unwillingly, Hans led the way up the cave for fifty paces or more, for the place was very big, he carrying one lantern and I another, while the two Zulus followed with candles in their hands. As we went I saw that on the walls there were many Bushmen paintings, also one or two of the carvings of this strange people. Some of these paintings seemed quite fresh, while others were faded or perhaps the ochre used by the primitive artist had flaked off. They were of the usual character, drawings of elands and other buck being hunted by men who shot at them with arrows; also of elephants and a lion charging at some spearmen.

One, however, which oddly enough was the best preserved of any of the collection, excited me enormously. It represented men whose faces were painted white and who seemed to wear a kind of armour and queer pointed caps upon their heads, of the sort that I believe are known as Phrygian, attacking a native *kraal* of which the reed fence was clearly indicated, as were the round huts behind. Moreover, to the left some of these men were dragging away women to what from a series of wavy lines, looked like a rude representation of the sea.

I stared and gasped, for surely here before me was a picture of Phoenicians carrying out one of their women-hunting raids, as ancient writers tell us it was their habit to do. And if so, that picture must have been painted by a Bushman who lived at least two thousand years ago, and possibly more. The thing was amazing. Hans, however, did not seem to be interested, but pushed on as though to finish a disagreeable task, and I was obliged to follow him, fearing lest I should be lost in the recesses of that vast cave.

Presently he came to a crevice in the side of the cavern which I should have passed unnoticed, as it was exactly like many others.

"Here is the place, Baas," he said, "just as it used to be. Now follow me and be careful where you step, for there are cracks in the floor."

So I squeezed myself into the opening where, although I am not very large, there was barely room for me to pass. Within its lips was a narrow tunnel, either cut out by water or formed by the rush of explosive gases hundreds of thousands of years ago—I think the latter, as the roof, which was not more than eight or nine feet from the floor, had sharp points and roughnesses that showed no water-wear. But as I have not the faintest idea how these great African caves were formed, I will not attempt to discuss the matter. This floor, however, was quite smooth, as though for many generations it had been worn by the feet of men, which no doubt was the case.

When we had crept ten or twelve paces down the tunnel, Hans called to me to stand quite still—not to move on any account. I obeyed him, wondering, and by the light of my lantern saw him lift his own, which had a loop of hide fastened through the tin eye at the top of it for convenience in hanging it up in the wagon, and set it, or rather the hide loop, round his neck, so that it hung upon his back. Then he flattened himself against the side of the cavern with his face to the wall as though he did not wish to see what was behind him, and cautiously crept forward with sidelong steps, gripping the roughnesses in the rock with his hands. When he had gone some twenty or thirty feet in this crab-like fashion, he turned and said, "Now, Baas, you must do as I did."

"Why?" I asked.

"Hold down the lantern and you will see, Baas."

I did so, and perceived that a pace or two farther on there was a great chasm in the floor of the tunnel of unknown depth, since the lamplight did not penetrate to its bottom. Also I noted that the ledge at the side that formed the bridge by which Hans had passed, was nowhere more than twelve inches, and in some places less than six inches wide.

"Is it deep?" I asked.

By way of answer Hans found a bit of broken rock and threw it into the gulf. I listened, and it was quite a long while before I heard it strike below.

"I told the Baas," said Hans in a superior tone, "that he had better wait until tomorrow when some light comes down this hole, but the Baas would not listen to me and doubtless he knows best. Now would the Baas like to go back to bed, as I think wisest, and return tomorrow?"

If the truth were known there was nothing that I should have liked better, for the place was detestable. But I was in such a rage with Hans for playing me this trick that even if I thought that I was going to break my neck I would not give him the pleasure of mocking me in his sly way.

"No," I answered quietly, "I will go to bed when I have seen this picture you talk about, and not before."

Now Hans grew alarmed and begged me in good earnest not to try to cross the gulf, which reminded me vaguely of the parable of Abraham and Dives in the Bible, with myself playing the part of Dives, except that I was not thirsty, and Hans did not in any way resemble Abraham.

"I see how it is," I said, "there is not any picture and you are simply playing one of your monkey tricks on me. Well, I'm coming to look, and if I find you have been telling lies I'll make you sorry for yourself."

"The picture is there or was when I was young," answered Hans sullenly, "and for the rest, the Baas knows best. If he breaks every bone in his body presently, don't let him blame me, and I pray that he will tell the truth, all of it, to his Reverend Father in the sky who left him in my charge, saying that Hans begged him not to come but that because of his evil temper he would not listen. Meanwhile, the Baas had better take off his boots, since the feet of those Bushmen whose spooks I feel all about me have made the ledge very slippery."

In silence I sat down and removed my boots, thinking to myself that I would gladly give all my savings that were on deposit in the bank at Durban, to be spared this ordeal. What a strange thing is the white man's pride, especially if he be of the Anglo-Saxon breed, or what passes by that name. There was no need for me to take this risk, yet, rather than be secretly mocked at by Hans and those *Kaffirs*, here I was about to do so just for pride's sake. In my heart I cursed Hans and the cave and the hole and the picture and the thunderstorm that brought me there, and everything else I could remember. Then, as it had no strap like that of Hans, although it smelt horribly, I took the tin loop of my lantern in my teeth because it seemed the only thing to do, put up a silent but most earnest prayer, and started as though I liked the job.

To tell the truth, I remember little of that journey except that it seemed to take about three hours instead of under a minute, and the voices of woe and lamentation from the two Zulus behind, who insisted upon bidding me a tender farewell as I proceeded, amidst other demonstrations of affection, calling me their father and their mother for four generations.

Somehow I wriggled myself along that accursed ridge, shoving my stomach as hard as I could against the wall of the passage as though this organ possessed some prehensile quality, and groping for knobs of rock on which I broke two of my nails. However, I did get over all right, although just towards the end one of my feet slipped and I opened my mouth to say something, with the result that the lantern fell into the abyss, taking with it a loose front tooth. But Hans stretched out his skinny hand, and, meaning to catch me by the coat collar, got hold of my left ear, and, thus painfully supported, I came to firm ground and cursed him into heaps. Although some might have thought my language pointed, he did not resent it in the least, being too delighted at my safe arrival.

"Never mind the tooth, Baas," he said. "It is best that it should be gone without knowing it, as it were, because you see you can now eat crusts and hard biltong again, which you have not been able to do for months. The lantern, however, is another matter, though perhaps we can get a new one at Pretoria or wherever we go."

Recovering myself, I peered over the edge of the abyss. There, far, far below, I saw my lantern, which was a sort that burns oil, flaring upon a bed of something white, for the container had burst and all the oil was on fire.

"What is that white stuff down there?" I asked. "Lime?"

"No, Baas, it is the broken bones of men. Once when I was young, with the help of the Bushmen I let myself down by a rope that we twisted out of rushes and buckskins, just to look, Baas. There is another cave underneath this one, Baas, but I didn't go into it because I was frightened."

"And how did all those bones come there, Hans? Why, there must be hundreds of them!"

"Yes, Baas, many hundreds, and they came this way. Since the beginning of the world the Bushmen lived in this cave and set a trap here by laying branches over the hole and covering them with dust so that they looked like rock, just as one makes a game pit, Baas—yes, they did this until the last of them were killed not so long ago by the Boers and Zulus, whose sheep and beasts they stole. Then when their enemies attacked them, which was often, for it has always been right to kill Bushmen—they would run down the cave and into the cleft and creep along the narrow edge of rock, which they could do with their eyes shut. But the silly *Kaffirs*, or whoever it might be, running after them to kill them would fall through the branches and get killed themselves. They must have done this quite often, Baas, since there are such a lot of their skulls down there, many of them quite black with age and turned to stone.

"One might have thought that the *Kaffirs* would have grown wiser, Hans."

"Yes, Baas, but the dead keep their wisdom to themselves, for I believe that when all the attackers were in the passage, then other Bushmen, who had been hiding in the cave, came up behind and shot them with poisoned arrows and drove them on into the hole so that none went back; indeed, the Bushmen told me that this used to be their father's plan. Also, if any did escape, in a generation or two all was forgotten, and the same thing happened again because, Baas, there are always plenty of fools in the world and the fool who comes after is just as big as the fool who went before. Death spills the water of wisdom upon the sand, Baas, and sand is thirsty stuff that soon grows dry again. If it were not so, Baas, men would soon stop falling in love with women, and yet even great ones—like you, Baas—fall in love."

Having delivered this thrust, in order to prevent the possibility of answer Hans began to chat with the driver and the *voorlooper* on the other side of the gulf.

"Be quick and come over, you brave Zulus there," he said, "for you are keeping your Chief waiting and me also."

The Zulus, holding their candles forward, peered into the pit below.

"*Ow!*" said one of them, "are we bats that we can fly over a hole like that or baboons that we can climb on a shelf no wider than a spear, or flies that we can walk upon a wall? *Ow!* we are not coming, we will wait here. That road is only for yellow monkeys like you or for those who have the white man's magic like the *Inkoos* Macumazahn."

"No," replied Hans reflectively, "you are none of these creatures which are all of them good in their way. You are just a couple of low-born *Kaffir* cowards, black skins blown up to look like men. I, the 'yellow jackal,' can walk the gulf, and the Baas can walk the gulf, but you, Windbags, cannot even float over it for fear lest you should burst in the middle. Well, Windbags, float back to the wagon and fetch the coil of small rope that is in the *voorkissie*, for we may want it."

One of them replied in a humbled voice that they did not take orders from him, a Hottentot, whereon I said, "Go and fetch the rope and return at once."

So they went with a dejected air, for Hans's winged words had gone home, and again they learned that at the end he always got the best of a quarrel. The truth is that they were as brave as men can be, but no Zulu is any good underground and least of all in the dark in a place that he thinks haunted.

"Now, Baas," said Hans, "we will go and look at the picture—that is, unless you are quite sure I am lying and that there is no picture, in which case it is not worth while to take the trouble, and you had better sit here and cut your broken nails until Mavoon and Induka come back with the rope."

"Oh, get on, you poisonous little vermin!" I said, exasperated by his jeers, emphasizing my words with a tremendous kick.

Here, however, I made a great mistake, since I had forgotten that at the moment I lacked boots, and either Hans carried a collection of hard articles in the seat of his filthy trousers or his posterior was of a singularly stonelike nature. In short, I hurt my toes most abominably and him not at all.

"Ah, Baas," said Hans with a sweet smile, "you should remember what your Reverend Father taught me: always to put on your boots before you kick against the thorn pricks. I have a gimlet and some nails in my pistol pocket, Baas, that I was using this morning to mend that box of yours."

Then he bolted incontinently lest I should experiment on his head and see if there were nails in that also, and as he had the only lantern, I was obliged to limp, or rather to hop, after him.

The passage, of which the floor was still worn smooth by thousands of dead feet, went on straight for eight or ten paces and then bent to the right. When we came to this elbow in it I saw a light ahead of me which I could not understand till presently I found myself standing in a kind of pit or funnel—it may have measured some thirty feet across—that rose from the level at which we stood, right through the strata to the mountain-side eighty or a hundred feet above us. What had formed it thus I cannot conceive, but there it was—a funnel, as I have said, in shape exactly like those that are used when beer is poured into barrels or port wine into a decanter, the place on which we were, being, of course, its narrower end. The light that I had seen came, therefore, from the sky, which, now that the tempest had passed away, was clean-washed and beautiful, sown with stars also, for at the moment a dense black cloud remaining from the storm hid the moon, now just past its full.

For a little way, perhaps five-and-twenty feet, the sides of this tunnel were almost sheer, after which they sloped outwards steeply to the mouth of the pit in the mountain flank. One other peculiarity I noticed—namely, that on the western face of the tunnel which, as it chanced, was in front of us as we stood, just where it began to expand, projected a sloping ridge of rock like to the roof of a lean-to shed, which ridge ran right across this face.

"Well, Hans," I said, when I had inspected this strange natural cavity, "where is your picture? I don't see it."

"*Wacht een beetje*" (that is, "Wait a bit"), "Baas. The moon is climbing up that cloud; presently she will get to the top of it and then you will see the picture, unless someone has rubbed it out since I was young."

I turned to look at the cloud and to witness a sight of which I never have grown tired: the uprising of the glorious African moon out of her secret halls of blackness. Already silver rays of light were shooting across the vastness of the firmament, causing the stars to pale. Then suddenly her bent edge appeared and with extraordinary swiftness grew and grew till the whole splendid orb emerged from a bed of inky vapour and for a while rested on its marge, perfect, wonderful! In an instant our hole was filled with light so strong and clear that by it I could have read a letter.

For a few moments I stood thrilled with the beauty of the scene, and forgetting all else in its contemplation, till Hans said with a hoarse cackle, "Now turn round, Baas, and look at the pretty picture."

I did so, and followed the line of his outstretched hand, which pointed to that face of the rock with the pent roof that looked towards the east. Next second—my friends, I am not exaggerating—I nearly fell backwards. Have any of you fellows ever had a nightmare in which you dreamed you were in hell and suddenly met the devil *tete-a-tete*, all by your little selves? At any rate, I have, and there in front of me was the devil, only much worse than fond fancy can paint him even with the brush of the acutest indigestion.

Imagine a monster double life size—that is to say, eleven or twelve feet high—brilliantly portrayed in the best ochres of which these Bushmen have always had the secret, namely, white, red, black, and yellow, and with eyes formed apparently of polished lumps of rock crystal. Imagine this thing as a huge ape to which the biggest gorilla would be but a child, and yet not an ape but a man, and yet not a man, but a fiend.

It was covered with hair like an ape, long gray hair that grew in tufts. It had a great, red, bushy beard like a man; its limbs were tremendous, the arms being of abnormal length like to the arms of a gorilla, but, mark this, it had no fingers, only a great claw where the thumb should be. The rest of the hand was all grown together into one piece like a duck's foot, although what should have been the finger part was flexible and could grip like fingers, as shall be seen.

At least, that is what the picture suggested, though it occurred to me afterwards that it might represent the creature as wearing fingerless gloves such as men in this country use when cutting fences. The feet however, which were certainly shown as bare, were the same; I mean that there were no toes, only one terrible claw where the big toe should be. The carcass was enormous; supposing it to have been drawn from life, the original, I should guess, would have weighed at least thirty stone; the chest was vast, indicating strength, and the paunch beneath wrinkled and protuberant. But—and here came one of the human touches—about its middle the thing wore a *moocha* or, rather, a hide tied round it by the leg skins, which hide seemed to have been dressed.

So much for the body. Now for the head and face. These I know not how to describe, but I will try. The neck was as that of a bull, and perched horribly on the top of it was quite a small head, which—notwithstanding the great red beard whereof I have spoken that grew upon the chin, and a wide mouth from whose upper jaw projected yellow tusks like to those of a baboon that hung over the lower lip—was curiously feminine in appearance; indeed, that of an old, old she-devil with an aquiline nose. The brow, however, was disproportionate to the rest of the face, being prominent, massive, and not unintellectual, while set deep in it and unnaturally far apart were those awful glaring crystal eyes.

That was not all, for the creature seemed to be laughing cruelly, and the drawing showed by it laughed. One of its feet was set upon the body of a man into which the great claw was driven deep. One of its hands held the head of the man, that evidently it had just twisted from the body. The other hand grasped by the hair a living naked girl badly drawn, as though this detail had not interested the artist, whom apparently it was about to drag away.

"Isn't it a pretty picture, Baas?" sniggered Hans. "Now the Baas will not say that I tell lies, no, not for quite a week."

CHAPTER 3

The Opener-of-Roads

I stared and stared, then was overcome with faintness and sat down upon the ground.

I see you laughing at me, young man (this was addressed to me, the recorder of the tale) who no doubt have already decided that this drawing was the work of some imaginative Bushman who had gone mad and set down upon the rock the hellish dream of a mind diseased. Of course, that was the conclusion I came to myself next morning, but at the time it did not strike me like that.

The place was lonesome and eerie, a horrible place with the pit full of bones near by; heavily silent also except for a distant hyena or jackal howling at the moon, and I had gone through some trials that day—the passage of the death-pit, for instance, which reminded me of the oubliettes in ancient Norman castles that I have read of down which prisoners were hurled to doom. Also, as you may have observed, even in your short career, moonlight differs from sunlight and we, or some of us, are much more affected by horrible things at night than we are by day. At any rate, I sat down because I felt faint and thought that I was going to be ill.

"What is it, Baas?" queried the observant Hans, still mocking. "If you want to be sick, Baas, please don't mind me, for I'll turn my back. I remember that I was sick myself when first I saw Heu-Heu—just there," he added reminiscently, pointing to a certain spot.

"Why do you call that thing 'Heu-Heu,' Hans?" I asked, trying to master the reflex action of my interior arrangements.

"Because that is his nice name, Baas, given him by his Mammie when he was little, perhaps."

(Here I nearly *was* sick, the idea of that creature with a mother almost finished me—like the sight and smell of a bit of fat bacon in a gale at sea.)

"How do you know that?" I gurgled.

"Because the Bushmen told me, Baas. They said that their fathers, a thousand years ago, knew this Heu-Heu far away, and that they left that part of the country because of him as they never slept well at night there, just like a Boer when another Boer comes and builds a house within six miles of him, Baas. I think they meant that they heard Heu-Heu when he talked, for they told me that their great-great-grandfathers could hear him doing it and beating his breast when he was miles away. But I daresay they lied, for I don't believe they really knew anything about Heu-Heu, or who painted his portrait on the rock, Baas."

"No," I answered, "nor do I. Well, Hans, I think I have had enough of your friend Heu-Heu for this evening, and should like to go back to bed."

"Yes, Baas, so should I, Baas. Still, take another good look at him before you leave. You don't see a picture like that every night, Baas, and you know you wanted to come."

Now I would have kicked Hans again, but luckily I remembered those nails in his pocket in time, so, after one lingering glance, I only rose and loftily motioned to him to lead on.

This was the last that I saw of the likeness of Heu-Heu or Beelzebub, or whoever the monster may have been. Somehow, although I intended to return to examine it more closely by the light of day, when morning came I thought that I would not risk another scramble over that ledge but would be satisfied with the memory of first impressions. These they say, are always the best—like first kisses, as Hans added when I explained this to him.

Not that I could forget Heu-Heu; on the contrary, it is not too much to say that this devilish creature haunted me. I could not dismiss that picture as some mere flight of distorted savage imagination. From a hundred characteristics I knew or thought I knew it, erroneously as I now believe, to be Bushmen's work and was certain that no Bushman, even if he had *delirium tremens*—not a complaint from which these people ever suffered, because they lacked the opportunity of doing so, could have evolved this monstrous creation out of his own soul—if a Bushman has a soul. No, Bushman or not, that artist was drawing something that he had seen, or thought that he had seen.

Of this there were several indications. Thus, on Heu-Heu's right arm the elbow joint was much swollen as though he had once suffered an injury there. Again, the claw of one of his horrible hands—the left, I think—was broken and divided at the point. Further, there was a wart or protuberance upon the brow, just beneath where the long iron-gray tufts of hair parted in the middle and hung down on each side of the demoniacal, womanish face. Now the painter must have remembered these blemishes and set them down faithfully, copying from some original, real or imagined. Certainly, I reflected, he would not have invented them.

Where, then, did he get his model? I have mentioned that I had heard rumours of creatures called *Ngolokos*, which I took it, if they existed at all, were peculiarly terrific apes of an unknown variety. Heu-Heu, then, might be a most distinguished and improved specimen of these apes. Yet that could scarcely be, for this beast was more man than monkey, notwithstanding his huge claws where the thumbs and big toes should be. Or perhaps I should say that he was more devil than either.

Another idea occurred to me: he might have been the god of these Bushmen, only I never heard that they had any god except their own stomachs. Afterwards I questioned Hans on this point but he replied that he did not know, as the Bushmen he lived with in the cave had never told him anything to that effect. It was true, however, that they did not go to the place where the picture was except through fear of enemies, and that when they did they would not look or speak about it more than they could help. Perhaps, he suggested with his usual shrewdness, Heu-Heu might be the god of some other people with whom the Bushmen had nothing to do.

Another question—when was this work executed? Owing to its sheltered position the colours were still fairly bright, but it must have been a long while ago. Hans said that the Bushmen told him that they did not know who painted it or what it represented, but that it was *"old, old, old!"* which might mean anything or nothing, since to a people without writing five or six generations become remote antiquity. One thing was certain, however, that another of the paintings in the cave was undoubtedly old, that of the Phoenicians raiding a *kraal* of which I have spoken, which can scarcely have been executed since the time of Christ. Of this I am sure, for I examined it carefully on the following morning and it was not more faded than that of the Monster. Further, in this picture a piece of the rock had scaled off just above the left knee, and I had noticed that the surface thus exposed seemed as much weathered as that of the surrounding rock outside the limits of the painting.

On the other hand, it must be remembered that the Phoenician picture was under cover, while that of Heu-Heu was exposed to the air and would therefore age more rapidly.

Well, all that night I dreamed of this horrid Heu-Heu, dreamed that he was alive and challenging me to fight him, dreamed that someone was calling to me to rescue her—it was certainly her—not him—from the power of the beast; dreamed that I did fight him and that he got me down and was about to twist my head off as he had done to the man in the picture, when something happened—I do not know what—and I woke up covered with perspiration and in a most pitiable fright.

* * * * * * * *

Now at the time I visited this cave I was not far from the borders of Zululand on one of my trading expeditions, the wagon being laden with blankets, beads, iron pots, knives, hoes, and such other articles as the simple savage loves, or in those days loved to pay for in cattle. Before the storm overtook us, however, I was contemplating leaving the Zulus alone on this trip and trying to break new ground somewhere north of Pretoria among less sophisticated natives who might put a higher value on my wares. After seeing Heu-Heu, as it chanced, I changed my mind for two reasons. The first of these was that the lightning had killed my two best oxen and I thought that I could replace these without cash expenditure in Zululand, where debts were owing to me that I might collect in kind. The second was connected with that confounded and obsessing Heu-Heu. I felt convinced that only one man in the world could tell me about this monster, if, indeed, there were anything to tell, namely, old Zikali, the wizard of the Black Kloof, the *Thing-that-should-never-have-been-born*, as Chaka, the great Zulu king, named him.

I think that I have told you all about Zikali before, but in case I have not, I will say that he was the greatest witch doctor who ever lived in Zululand and the most terrible. No one knew when he was born, but undoubtedly he was very ancient and under his native name of "Opener-of-Roads" had been known and dreaded in the land for some generations. For many years, since my boyhood, indeed, he and I had been friends in a fashion, though of course I was aware that from the first he was using me for his own ends, as, indeed, became very clear before all was done and he had triumphed over and brought about the fall of the Zulu Royal House, which he hated.

However, Zikali, like a wise merchant, always paid those who served him with a generous hand, in one coin or another, as he paid those he hated. My coin was information, either historical or concerning the hidden secrets of the strange land of Africa, of which, for all our knowledge, we white men really understand so little. If any one could give

34

information about the picture in the cave and its origin, it would be Zikali, and therefore to Zikali I would go. Curiosity about such matters, as perhaps you have guessed, was always one of my besetting sins.

* * * * * * * *

We had great trouble in recovering our remaining fourteen oxen since some of them had wandered far to find cover from the storm. At last, however, they were found uninjured except for some bruises from the hailstones, for it is wonderful, if they are left alone, how cattle manage to protect themselves against the forces of nature. In Africa, however, they seldom take shelter beneath trees during a thunderstorm, as is their habit here in England, perhaps because, such tempests being so frequent, they have inherited from their progenitors an instinctive knowledge that lightning strikes trees and kills anything that happens to be underneath them. At least, that is my experience.

Well, we inspanned and trekked away from that remarkable cave. Many years afterwards, by the way, when Hans was dead, I tried to find it again and could not. I thought that I reached the same mountain slope in which it was, but I suppose that I must have been mistaken, since in that neighbourhood there are multitudes of such slopes and on the one that I identified I could discover no trace of the cave.

Perhaps this was because there had been a landslide and, with the funnel-like shaft in the mountain side down which the moonlight poured on to the picture of Heu-Heu, the orifice that, it will be remembered, was very small, had been covered up with rocks. Or it may be that I was searching the wrong slope, not having taken my bearings sufficiently when I visited the place at a time of tempest and hurry.

Further, I was pressed and, desiring to reach a certain outspan before night fell, could only give about an hour to the quest and when it failed was obliged to get on. Nor have I ever met any one who was acquainted with this cave, so I suppose that it must have been known to the Bushmen and Hans only, dead now all of them, which is a pity because of the wonderful paintings that it contains or contained.

You will remember I told you that just before the storm broke we were overtaken by a party of *Kaffirs* going to or returning from some feast. When we had gone about half a mile we found one of those *Kaffirs* again quite dead, but whether he (the body was that of a young man) had been killed by the lightning or by the hail, I was not sure. Evidently his companions were so frightened that they had left him where he lay, proposing, I suppose, to return and bury him later. So you will see that when it gave us shelter, this cave did us a good turn.

Now I will skip all the details of my trek into Zululand, which was as are other treks, only slower, because it was a hard job to get that heavily laden wagon along with but fourteen oxen. Once, indeed, we stuck in a river, the White Umfolozi, quite near to the Nongela Rock or Cliff which frowns above a pool of the river. I shall never forget that accident because it caused me to be the unwilling witness of a very dreadful sight.

Whilst we were fast in the drift a party of men appeared upon the brow of this Nongela Rock, about two hundred and fifty yards away, dragging with them two young women. Studying them through my glasses, I came to the conclusion from the way they moved their heads and stared wildly about them, that these young women were blind or had been blinded. As I looked at them, wondering what to do, the men seized the women by the arms and hurled them over the edge of the cliff. With a piteous wail the poor creatures rolled down the stratified rock into the deep pool below and there the crocodiles got them, for distinctly I saw the rush of the reptiles. Indeed, in this pool they were always on the look-out, as it was a favourite place of execution under the Zulu kings.

When their horrible business was finished the party of *slayers*—there were about fifteen of them—came down to the ford to interview us. At first I thought there might be trouble, and to tell the truth, should not have been sorry, for the sight of this butchery had made me furious and reckless. As soon as they found out, however, that the wagon belonged to me, Macumazahn, they were all amiability, and wading into the water, tackled on to the wheels, with the result that by their help we came safe to the farther bank.

There I asked their leader who the two murdered girls might be. He replied that they were the daughters of Panda, the King. I did not question this statement although, knowing Panda's kindly character, I doubted very much whether they were actually his children. Then I asked why they were blind, and what crime they had committed. The captain replied that they had been blinded by the order of Prince Cetywayo, who even then was the real ruler of Zululand, because "they had looked where they should not."

Further inquiry elicited the fact that these unhappy girls had fallen in love with two young men, and run away with them against the King's orders, or Cetywayo's, which was the same thing. The party were overtaken before they could reach the Natal border, where they would have been safe; the young men were killed at once and the girls brought up for judgment, with the result that I have described. Such was the end of their honeymoon!

Moreover, the captain informed me cheerfully that a body of soldiers had been sent out to kill the fathers and mothers of the young men and all who could be found in their *kraals*. This kind of free love must be put a stop to, he said, as there had been too much of it going on; indeed, he did not know what had come to the young people in Zululand, who had grown very independent of late, contaminated, no doubt, by the example of the Zulus in Natal, where the white men allowed them to do what they liked without punishment.

Then with a sigh over the degeneracy of the times, this crusted old conservative took a pinch of snuff, bade me a hearty farewell, and departed, singing a little song which I think he must have invented, as it was about the love of children for their parents. If it had been safe I should have liked to let him have a charge of shot behind to take away as a souvenir, but it was not. Also, after all, he was but an executive officer, a product of the iron system of Zululand in the day of the kings.

Well, I trekked on, trading as I went, and getting paid in cows and heifers, which I sent back to Natal, but could come by no oxen that were fit for the yoke, and much less any that had been broken in, since in those days such were almost unknown in Zululand. However, I did hear of some that had been left behind by a white trader because they were sick or footsore, I forget which, who took young cattle in exchange for them. These were said now to be fat again, but no one seemed to know exactly where they were. One friendly chief told me, however, that the Opener-of-Roads, that is, old Zikali, might be able to do so, as he knew everything and the oxen had been traded away in his district.

Now by this time, although I was still obsessed about Heu-Heu, I had almost made up my mind to abandon the idea of visiting Zikali on this trip, because I had noticed that whenever I did so, always I became involved in arduous and unpleasant adventures as an immediate consequence. Being, however, badly in need of more oxen, for, not to mention the two that were dead, others of my team seemed never to have recovered from the effects of the hailstorm and one or two showed signs of sickness, this news caused me to revert to my original plan. So after consultation with Hans, who also thought it the best thing to be done, I headed for the Black Kloof, which was only two short days' trek away.

Arriving at the mouth of that hateful and forbidding gulf on the afternoon of the second day, I outspanned by the spring and, leaving the cattle in charge of Mavoon and Induka, walked up it accompanied by Hans.

The place, of course, was just as it had always been, and yet, as it ever did, struck me with a fresh sense of novelty and amazement. In all Africa I scarcely know a gorge that is so eerie and depressing. Those towering cliffsides that look as though they are about to fall in upon the traveller, the stunted, melancholy aloe plants which grow among the rocks; the pale vegetation; the jackals and hyenas that start away at the sound of voices or echoing footsteps; the dense dark shadows; the whispering winds that seem to wail about one even when the air is still over-head, draughts, I suppose, that are drawing backwards and forwards through the gulley; all of these are peculiar to it. The ancients used to declare that particular localities had their own genii or spirits, but whether these were believed to be evolved by the locality or to come thither because it suited their character and nature, I do not know.

In the Black Kloof and some other spots to which I have wandered, I have often thought of this fable and almost found myself accepting it as true. But, then, what kind of a spirit would it be that chose to inhabit this dreadful gorge? I think some embodiment—no, that word is a contradiction—some impalpable essence of Tragedy, some doomed soul whereof the head was bowed and the wings were leaded with a weight of ineffable and unrepented crime.

Well, what need was there to fly to fable and imagine such an invisible inhabitant when Zikali, the *Thing-that-should-never-have-been-born*, was, and for uncounted years had been, the Dweller in this tomb-like gulf? Surely he was Tragedy personified, and that hoary head of his was crowned with ineffable and unrepented crime. How many had this hideous dwarf brought down to doom and how many were yet destined to perish in the snares that year by year he wove for them? And yet this sinner had been sinned against and did but pay back his sufferings in kind, he whose wives and children had been murdered and whose tribe had been stamped flat beneath the cruel feet of Chaka, whose House he hated and lived on to destroy. Even for Zikali allowances could be made; he was not altogether bad. Is any man *altogether* bad, I wonder.

Musing thus, I tramped on up the gorge, followed by the dejected Hans, whom the place always depressed, even more than it did myself.

"Baas," he said presently, in a hollow whisper, for here he did not dare to speak aloud, "Baas, do you think that the Opener-of-Roads was once Heu-Heu himself who has now shrunk to a dwarf with age, or at any rate, that Heu-Heu's spirit lives in him?"

"No, I don't," I answered, "for he has fingers and toes like the rest of us, but I do think that if there is any Heu-Heu he may be able to tell us where to find him."

"Then, Baas, I hope that he has forgotten, or that Heu-Heu has gone to heaven where the fires go on burning of themselves without the need for wood. For, Baas, I do not want to meet Heu-Heu; the thought of him turns my stomach cold."

"No, you would rather go to Durban and meet a gin bottle that would turn your stomach warm, Hans, and your head, too, and land you in the Trunk for seven days," I replied, improving the occasion.

Then we turned the corner and came upon Zikali's *kraal*. As usual, I appeared to be expected, for one of his great silent body servants was waiting, who saluted me with uplifted spear. I suppose that Zikali must have had a look-out man stationed somewhere who watched the plain beneath and told him who was approaching. Or possibly he had other methods of obtaining information. At any rate, he always knew of my advent and often enough why I came and whence, as, indeed, he did on this occasion.

"The Father of Spirits awaits you, Lord Macumazahn," said the body servant. "He bids the little yellow man who is named Light-in-Darkness, to accompany you and will see you at once."

I nodded and the man led me to the gate of the fence that surrounded Zikali's great hut, on which he tapped with the handle of his spear. It was opened, by whom I did not see, and we entered, whereon someone slipped out of the shadows and closed the gate behind us, then vanished. There in front of the door of his hut, with a fire burning before him, crouched the dwarf wrapped in a fur *kaross*, his huge head, on either side of which the gray locks fell down much as they did in the picture of Heu-Heu, bent forward, and the light of the fire into which he was staring shining in his cavernous eyes. We advanced across the shiny beaten floor of the courtyard and stood in front of him, but for half a minute or more he took no notice of our presence. At length, without looking up, he spoke in that hollow, resounding voice which was unlike to any other I ever heard, saying:

"Why do you always come so late, Macumazahn, when the sun is off the hut and it grows cold in the shadows? You know I hate the cold, as the aged always do, and I was minded not to receive you."

"Because I could not get here before, Zikali," I answered.

"Then you might have waited until tomorrow morning unless,

perhaps, you thought that I should die in the night, which I shall not do. No, nor for many nights. Well, here you are, little white Wanderer who hops from place to place like a flea."

"Yes, here I am," I replied, nettled, "to visit you who do not wander but sit in one spot like a toad in a stone, Zikali."

"Ho, ho, ho!" he laughed—that wonderful laugh of his which echoed from the rocks and always made me feel cold down the back, "Ho, ho, ho! how easy it is to make you angry. Keep your temper, Macumazahn, lest it should run away with you as your oxen did before the storm in the mountains the other day. What do you want? You only come here when you want something from him whom once you named the Old Cheat. So I don't wander, don't I, but sit like a toad in a stone? How do you know that? Is it only the body that wanders? Cannot the spirit wander also, far, oh, far, even to the 'Heaven Above' sometimes, and perhaps to that land which is under the earth, the place where they say the dead are to be found again? Well, what do you want? Stay, and I will tell you, who explain yourself so badly, who, although you think that you speak Zulu like a native, have never really learned it properly because to do that you must think in it and not in your own stupid tongue, that has no words for many things. Man, my medicines."

A figure darted out of the hut, set down a cat-skin bag before him, and was gone again. Zikali plunged his claw-like hand into the bag and drew out a number of knuckle bones, polished, but yellow with age, which he threw carelessly on to the ground in front of him, then glanced at them.

"Ha," he said, "something about cattle, I see; yes, you want to get oxen, broken oxen, not wild ones, and think that I can tell you where to do it cheap. By the way, what present have you brought for me? Is it a pound of your white man's snuff?" (As a matter of fact, it was a quarter of a pound.) "Now am I right about the oxen?"

"Yes," I replied, rather amazed.

"That astonishes you. It is wonderful, isn't it, that the poor Old Cheat should know what you want? Well, I'll tell you how it is done. You lost two oxen by lightning, did you not? You therefore, naturally would want others, especially as some of those which remain"—here he glanced at the bones once more—"were hurt, yes, by hailstones, very large hailstones, and others are showing signs of sickness, red-water, I think. Therefore, it isn't strange that the poor Old Cheat should guess that you needed oxen, is it? Only a silly Zulu would put such a thing down to magic. About the snuff, too, which I see you have taken from your pocket—a very little parcel, by the way. You've brought me snuff before, haven't you? Therefore, it isn't strange that I should guess that you would do so again, is it? No magic there."

"None, Zikali, but how did you learn of the lightning killing the cattle and of the hailstorm?"

"How did I learn that the lightning killed your pole-oxen, Kaptein and Deutchmann? Why, are you not a very great man in whom all are interested, and is it wonderful that I should be told of accidents that happen a hundred miles or so away? You met a party going to a wedding, did you not, just before the storm, and found one of them dead afterwards? By the way, he wasn't killed either by lightning or by hail. The flash fell near and stunned him, but really he died of the cold during the night. I thought that you might like to know that, as you are curious on the point. Of course, those *Kaffirs* would have told me about it, would they not? No magic, again you see. That's how we poor witch doctors gain repute, just by keeping our eyes and ears open. When you are old you might set up in the trade yourself, Macumazahn, since you do the same thing, even at night, they say."

Now while he went on mocking me he had gathered up the bones out of the dust and suddenly threw them again with a curious spiral twist that caused them to fall in a little heap, perched on one another. He looked at them, and said, "Why, what do these silly things remind me of? They are some of the tools of my trade, you know, Macumazahn, used to impress the fools that come to see us witch doctors, who think that they will tell us secrets, and to take off their attention while we read their hearts. Somehow or other they remind me of rocks piled one on another as on a mountain slope, and look! there is a hollow in the middle like the mouth of a cave.

"Did you chance to take refuge from that storm in a cave, Macumazahn? Oh, you did! Well, see how cleverly I guessed it. No magic there again, only just a guess. Isn't it likely that you would go to a cave to escape from such a tempest, leaving the wagon outside? Look at that bone there, lying a little distance off the others, that's what made me think of the wagon being outside. But the question is, what did you see in the cave? Anything out of the way, I wonder? The bones can't tell me that, can they? I must guess that somehow else, mustn't I? Well, I'll try to do so, just to give you, the wise white man, another lesson in the manner that we poor rascals of witch doctors do our work and take in fools. But won't you tell me, Macumazahn?"

"No, I won't," I answered crossly, who knew that the old dwarf was making a butt of me.

"Then I suppose that I must try to discover for myself, but how,

how? Come here, you little yellow monkey of a man, and sit between me and the fire so that its light shines through you, for then perchance I may be able to see something of what is going on in that thick head of yours, Light-in-Darkness, as you are called, and get some light in my darkness."

Hans advanced unwillingly enough and squatted down at the spot that Zikali indicated with his bony finger, being very careful that none of the magic bones should touch any portion of his anatomy, for fear lest they should bewitch him, I suppose. There he sat, holding his ragged felt hat upon the pit of his stomach as though to ward off the gimlet-like glances of Zikali's burning eyes.

"Ho-ho! Yellow Man," said the dwarf after a few seconds of inspection, which caused Hans to wriggle uncomfortably and even to colour beneath his wrinkled skin, like a young woman being studied by her prospective husband, who desires to ascertain whether she will or will not do for a fifth wife. "Ho-ho! it seems to me that you knew this cave before you went there in the storm, but of course I should guess that, for how otherwise would you have found it in such a hurry; also that it had something to do with Bushmen, as most caves have in this land.

"The question is, what was in it? No, don't tell me. I want to find out for myself. It is strange that the thought comes to me of pictures. No, it isn't strange, since the Bushmen often used to paint pictures in caves. Now, you shouldn't nod your head, Yellow Man, because it makes the riddle too easy. Just stare at me and think of nothing at all. Pictures, lots of them, but one principal picture, I think; something that was difficult to come at. Yes, dangerous, even. Was it perchance a picture of yourself that a Bushman drew long ago when you were young and handsome, Yellow Man?

"There, again you are shaking your head. Keep it quite still, will you, so that the thoughts in it don't ripple like water beneath a wind. At least it was a picture of something hideous, but much bigger than you. Ah! it grows and grows. I am getting it now. Macumazahn, come and stand by me, and you, Yellow Man, turn your back so that you face the fire. Bah! it burns badly, does it not, and the air is so cold, so cold! I must make it brighter.

"Are you there, Macumazahn? Yes. Now look at this stuff of mine; see what a fine blaze it causes," and putting his hand into the bag, he drew out some kind of powder, only a little of it, which he threw on to the embers. Then he stretched his skinny fingers over them as though for warmth, and slowly lifted his arms high into the air. It is a fact that after him the flames sprang up to a height of three or four feet. He dropped his arms again and the flames sank down. He lifted them once more and once more they rose, only this time much higher. A third time he repeated this performance, and now the sheet of flame sprang fully fifteen feet into the air and so remained burning steadily, like the flame of a lamp.

"Look at that fire, Macumazahn, and you also, Yellow Man," he said, in a strange new voice, a sort of dreamy far-off voice, "and tell me if you see anything in it, for I can't—I can't."

I looked, and for a moment perceived nothing. Then some shape began to grow upon the blazing background. It wavered; it changed; it became fixed and definite, yes, clear and real. There before me, etched in flame, I saw Heu-Heu—Heu-Heu as he had been in the painting on the cave wall, only, as it seemed to me, alive, for his eyes blinked—Heu-Heu, looking like a devil in hell. I gasped but stood firm. As for Hans, he ejaculated in his vile Dutch, *"Allemaghte! Da is die leeliker auld deil!"* (that is, "Almighty! There is the ugly old devil!") and having said this, rolled over on to his back and lay still, frozen with terror.

"Ho, ho, ho!" laughed Zikali. "Ho, ho, ho!" and from a dozen places the walls of the kloof echoed back, "Ho, ho, ho!"

CHAPTER 4

The Legend of Heu-Heu

Zikali stopped laughing and contemplated us with his hollow eyes.

"Who was it who first said that all men are fools?" he asked. "I do not know, but I think it must have been a woman, a pretty woman who played with them and found that it was so. If so, she was wise, as all women are in their narrow way, which the saying shows, since they are left out of it. Well, I will add to the proverb; all men are cowards also in one matter or another, though in the rest they may be brave enough. Further, they are all the same, for what is the difference between you, Macumazahn, wise White Man who have dared death a hundred times, and yonder little yellow ape?" Here he pointed to Hans lying upon his back, with rolling eyes and muttering prayers to a variety of gods between his chattering teeth. "Both of you are afraid, one as much as the other; the only difference being that the White Lord tries to conceal his fear, whilst the Yellow Monkey chatters it out, as monkeys do.

"Why are you so frightened? Just because by a common trick I show to your eyes a picture of that which is in the minds of both of you. Mark you again, not by magic but by a common trick which any child could learn, if somebody taught it to him. I hope that you will not behave like this when you see Heu-Heu himself, for if you do I shall be disappointed in you and soon there will be two more skulls in that cave of his. But then, perhaps, you will be brave; yes, I think so, I think so, since never would you like to die remembering how long and loud I should laugh when I heard of it."

Thus the old wizard rambled on, as was his fashion when he wished to combine his acrid mockery with the desire to gain space for thought, till presently he grew silent and took some of the snuff which I had brought him, for he had been engaged in opening the packet while he talked, all the while continuing to watch us as though he would search out our very souls.

Now, because I thought that I must say something, if only to show that he had not frightened me with his accursed manifestations, or whatever they were, I answered, "You are right, Zikali, when you say that all men are fools, seeing that you are the first and biggest fool among them."

"I have often thought it, Macumazahn, for reasons that I keep to myself. But why do you say so? Let me hear, who would learn whether yours are the same as my own."

"First, because you talk as though there were such a creature as Heu-Heu, which, as you know well, does not live and never did; and secondly, because you speak as though Hans and I would meet it face to face, which we shall never do. So cease from such nonsense and show us how to make pictures in the fire—an art, you tell us, any child could learn."

"If they are taught, Macumazahn, *if* they are taught how. But were I to do this, I should indeed be the first of fools. Do you think that I wish to establish two rival cheats—you see, between ourselves, I give myself my right name—in the land to trade against me? No, no, let each keep the knowledge he has gained for himself, for if it becomes common to all, who will pay for it? But why do you believe that you will never stand face to face with Heu-Heu except in pictures on rock or fire?"

"Because he doesn't exist," I answered with irritation; "and if he does, I suppose his home is a long way off and I cannot trek without fresh oxen."

"Ah!" said Zikali, "that reminds me of how you refuged in the cave from the storm and the rest said that you wanted more oxen. So, knowing that you would be in as great a hurry to get to Heu-Heu as a young man is to find his first wife, I made ready. The story you heard was quite true. A white trader did leave a very fine team of footsore oxen in this neighbourhood, salted, every one of them, which after three moons' rest, are now fat and sound. I will have them driven up tomorrow morning and take care of yours while you are away."

"I have no money to pay for more oxen," I said.

"Is not the promise of Macumazahn better than any money, even the red English gold? Does not the whole land know it? Moreover," he added slowly, "when you return from visiting Heu-Heu you ought to have plenty of money—or, rather, of diamonds, which is the same thing—and perhaps of ivory, though of that I am not so sure. No, I am not sure whether you will be able to carry the ivory. If I do not speak truth I will pay for the oxen myself."

Now at the word "diamonds" I pricked up my ears, for just then all Africa was beginning to talk about these stones; even Hans rose from the ground and began once more to take interest in earthly things.

"That's a fair offer," I said, "but stop blowing dust" (*i.e.* talking nonsense) "and tell me straight out what you mean before it grows dark. I hate this kloof in the dark. Who is Heu-Heu? And if he or it lives, or lived, where is Heu-Heu, dead or alive? Also, supposing that there was or is a Heu-Heu, why do you, Zikali, wish me to find him, as I perceive you do, who always have a reason for what you wish?"

"I will answer the last question first, Macumazahn, who, as you say, always have a reason for what I want you or others to do."

Here he stopped and clapped his hands, whereon instantly one of his great serving men appeared from the hut behind, to whom he gave some order. The man darted away and presently was back with more of the skin bags such as witch doctors use to carry their medicines. Zikali opened one of these and showed me that it was almost empty, there being in it but a pinch of brown powder.

"This stuff, Macumazahn," he said, "is the most wonderful of all drugs, even more wonderful than the herb called *taduki* that can open the paths of the past, with which herb you will become acquainted one day. By means of it—I speak not of *taduki*, but of the powder in the bag—I do most of my tricks. For instance, it was with a dust of it that I was able to show you and the little yellow man the picture of Heu-Heu in the flames just now."

"You mean that it is a poison, I suppose."

"Oh, yes, among other things, by adding another powder it can be made into a very deadly poison; so deadly that as little of it as will lie upon the point of a thorn will kill the strongest man and leave no trace. But it has other properties also that have to do with the mind and the spirit; never mind what they are; if I tried to tell you, you would not understand. Well, the Tree of Visions from the leaves of which this medicine is ground grows only in the garden of Heu-Heu and nowhere else in Africa, and I got my last supply of it thence many years ago, long before you were born, indeed, Macumazahn; never mind how.

"Now I must have more, of those leaves, or what these Zulus call my magic, which wise white men like you know to be but my tricks, will fail me, and the world will say that the Opener-of-Roads has lost his strength and turn to seek wiser doctors."

"Then why do you not send and get some, Zikali?"

"Whom can I send that would dare to enter the land of Heu-Heu and rob his garden? No one but yourself, Macumazahn. Ah! I read your mind. You are wondering now if that be so, why I do not order that the leaves should be brought to me from the place of Heu-Heu. For this reason, Macumazahn. The dwellers there may not leave their hidden land; it is against their law. Moreover, if they might they would not part even with a handful of that drug, except at a great price. Once, a hundred years ago" (by which, I suppose, he meant a long time), "I paid such a price and bought a quantity of the stuff of which you see the last in that bag. But that is an old story with which I will not trouble you. Oh! many went and but two returned, and they mad, as those are apt to be who have looked on Heu-Heu and left him living. If ever you see Heu-Heu, Macumazahn, be sure to destroy him and all that is his, lest his curse should follow you for the rest of your days. Fallen, he will be powerless, but standing, his hate is very strong and reaches far, or that of his priests does, which is the same thing."

"Rubbish!" I said. "If there is any Heu-Heu, he is but a big ape, and living or dead, I am not afraid of any ape."

"I am glad to hear that, Macumazahn, and hope that you will always be of the same mind. Doubtless it is only his picture painted on rock or in the fire that frightens you, just as a dream is more terrible than anything real. Some day you shall tell me which was the worse, Heu-Heu's picture or Heu-Heu himself. But you asked me other questions. The first of them was, Who is Heu-Heu?

"Well, I do not know. The legend tells that once, in the beginning, there was a people white, or almost white, who lived far away to the north. This people, says the old tale, were ruled over by a giant, very cruel and very terrible; a great wizard also, or cheat, as you would call him. So cruel and terrible was he, indeed, that his people rose against him, and strong as he might be, forced him to fly southwards with some who clung to him or could not escape him.

"So south he came with them, thousands of miles, until he found a secret place that suited him to dwell in. That place is beneath the shadow of a mountain of a sort that I have heard spouted out fire when the world was young, which even now smokes from time to time. Here this people, who are named Walloo, built them a town after their northern fashion out of the black stone which flowed from the mountain in past ages. But their king, the giant wizard, continued his cruelties to them forcing them to labour night and day at his city and Great House and a cave in which he was worshipped as a god, till at last they could bear no more and murdered him by night.

"Before he died, however, which he took long to do because of

47

his magic, he mocked them, telling them that not thus would they be rid of him since he would come back in a worse shape than before and still rule over them from generation to generation. Moreover, he prophesied disaster to them and laid this curse upon them, that if they strove to leave the land that he had chosen, and to cross the ring of mountains by which it is enclosed, they should die, every one of them. This, indeed, happened, or so I have heard, since if even one of them travels down the river, by which alone that country can be approached from the desert, and sets foot in the desert, he dies, sometimes by sudden sickness, or sometimes by the teeth of lions and other wild beasts that live in the great swamp where the river enters the desert, whither the elephants and other game come to drink from hundreds of miles around."

"Perhaps fever kills them," I suggested.

"Maybe so, or poison, or a curse. At least, soon or late they die, and therefore it comes about that now none of them leaves that land."

"And what happened to the Walloos after they had finished off this kind king of theirs?" I asked, for Zikali's romantic fable interested me. Of course, I knew that it was a fable, but in such tales, magnified by native rumour, there is sometimes a grain of truth. Also Africa is a great country, and in it there are very queer places and peoples.

"Something very bad happened, Macumazahn, for scarcely was their king dead when the mountain began to belch out fire and hot ashes, which killed many of them and caused the rest to fly in boats across the lake that makes an island of the mountain, to the forest lands that lie around. There they live to this day upon the banks of the river which flows through the forest, the same that passes through the gorge of the mountains into the swamp, and there loses itself in the desert sands. So, at least, my messengers told me a hundred years ago, when they brought me the medicine that grows in Heu-Heu's garden."

"I suppose that they were afraid to go back to their town after the eruption was over," I said.

"Yes, they were afraid, at which you will not wonder when you see it, for when the mountain blew up the gases killed very many of them and what is more, turned them to stone. Aye, there they sit, Macumazahn, to this day, turned to stone, and with them their dogs and cattle."

Now at this amazing tale I burst out laughing, and even Hans grinned.

"I have noted, Macumazahn," said Zikali, "that in the beginning it is you who always laugh at me, while in the end it is I who laugh at you, and so I believe it will be in this case also. I tell you that there those people sit turned to stone, and if it is not so, you need not pay me for the oxen that I bought from the white man even should you come back with your pockets full of diamonds."

Now I bethought me of what happened at Pompeii, and ceased to laugh. After all, the thing was possible.

"That is one reason why they did not return to their town, even when the mountain went to sleep again, but there was another, Macumazahn, that was stronger still. Soon they found that it was haunted."

"Haunted! By what? By the stone men?"

"No, they are quiet enough, though what their spirits may be I cannot tell you. Haunted by their king who they had killed, turned into a gigantic ape, turned into Heu-Heu."

Now at this statement I did not laugh, although at first sight it seemed much more absurd than that of the dead people who had been petrified. For this reason: as I knew well, it is the commonest of beliefs among savages, and especially those of Central Africa, that dead chiefs, notably if they have been tyrants during their life, are metamorphosed into some terrible animal, which thenceforward persecutes them from generation to generation. The animal may be a rogue elephant or a man-killing lion, or perhaps a very poisonous snake. But whatever shape it takes, it always has this characteristic, that it does not die and cannot be killed—at any rate, by any of those whom it afflicts. Indeed, in my own experience I have come across sundry examples of this belief among natives. Therefore, it did not strike me as strange that these people should imagine their country to be cursed by the spirit of a legendary tyrant turned into a monster.

Only in the monster itself I put no faith. If it existed at all probably it would resolve itself into a large ape, or perhaps a gorilla living upon an island in the lake where it had become marooned, or drifted upon a tree in a flood.

"And what does this spirit do?" I asked Zikali incredulously. "Throw nuts or stones at people?"

"No, Macumazahn. According to what I have been told, it does much more. At times it crosses to the mainland—some say on a log, some say by swimming, some say as spirits can. There, if it meets any one, it twists off his or her head" (here I bethought me of the picture in the cave), "for no man can fight against its strength, or woman either, because if she be old and ugly, it serves her in the same fashion, but if she be young and well favoured, then it carries her away. The island is said to be full of such women who cultivate the garden of

Heu-Heu. Moreover, it is reported that they have children who cross the lake and live in the forest—terrible, hairy creatures that are half human, for they can make fire and use clubs and bows and arrows. These savage people are named Heuheua. They dwell in the forests, and between them and the Walloos there is perpetual war."

"Anything else?" I asked.

"Yes, one thing. At a certain time of the year the Walloos must take their fairest and best-born maiden and tie her to an appointed rock upon the shore of the island upon a night of full moon. Then they go away and leave her alone, returning at sunrise."

"And what do they find?"

"One of two things, Macumazahn; either that the maiden has gone, in which case they are well pleased, except those of them to whom she is related, or that she has been torn to pieces, having been rejected by Heu-Heu, in which case they weep and groan, not for her but for themselves."

"Why do they rejoice, and why do they weep, Zikali?"

"For this reason. If the maiden has been taken, Heu-Heu, or his servants, the Heuheua, will spare them and his priests for that year. Moreover, their crops will prosper and they be free from sickness. If she has been killed, he or his servants haunt them, snatching away other women, and they will have bad harvests; also fever and other ills fall upon them. Therefore, the Offering of the Maiden is their great ceremony, which, should she be taken, is followed by the Feast of Rejoicing, and should she be rejected and slain, by the Fast of Lamentation and the sacrifice of her parents or others."

"A pleasant religion, Zikali. Tell me, is it one that pleases these Walloos?"

"Does any religion please any man, Macumazahn, and do tears, want, sickness, bereavement, and death please those who are born into the world? For example, like the rest of us, you white people suffer these things, or so I have heard; also you have your own Heu-Heu or devil who claims such sacrifices and yet avenges himself upon you. You are not pleased with him, still you go on making your sacrifices of war and blood and all wickedness in return for what he did to you, thereby binding yourselves to him afresh and confirming his power over you, and as you do, so do we all. Yet if you and the rest of us would but stand up against him, perhaps his strength might be broken, or he might be slain. Why, then, do we continue to sacrifice our maidens of virtue, truth, and purity to him, and how are we better than those who worship Heu-Heu, who do so to save their lives?"

I considered his argument, which was subtle for a savage, however old and instructed, to have evolved from his limited opportunities of observation, and answered rather humbly, "I do not suppose that we are better at all." Then to change the subject to something more practical, I added, "But what about those diamonds?"

"The diamonds! Oho! the diamonds, which, by the way, I believe are one of the offerings that you white people make to your own Heu-Heu. Well, these people seem to have plenty of them. Of course, they are useless to them, as they do not trade. Still, the women know that they are pretty, and fasten them about themselves in little nets of hair after polishing them upon stone, because they do not know how to make holes in them, being so hard, and cannot set them in metals. Also they stick them in the clay of their eating dishes before these are dried, making pretty patterns with them. It seems that these stones and others that are red, are washed down by the river from some desert across which it flows above, through a tunnel in the mountains, I believe. At any rate, they find them in plenty in the gravel on its banks, which they set the children to sift in a closely woven sieve of human hair, or in some such fashion. Stay, I will show you what they are like, for my messengers brought me a fistful or two many years ago," and he clapped his hands.

Instantly, as before, one of his servants appeared, to whom he gave certain instructions. The man went, and presently returned with a little packet of ancient, wrinkled skin that looked like a bit of an old glove. This he untied and gave to me. Within were a quantity of small stones that looked and felt like diamonds, very good diamonds, as I judged from their colour, though none of them were large. Also among them was a sprinkling of other stones that might have been rubies, though of this I could not be sure. At a guess I should have estimated the value of the parcel at 200 or 300 pounds. When I had examined them, I offered them back to Zikali, but he waved his hand and said:

"Keep them, Macumazahn, keep them. They are no good to me, and when you come to the land of Heu-Heu, compare them with those you will find there, just to show yourself that in this matter I do not lie."

"When I come to the land of Heu-Heu!" I exclaimed indignantly. "Where, then, is this land, and how am I to reach it?"

"That I propose to tell you tomorrow, Macumazahn, not tonight, since it would be useless to waste time and breath upon the business until I know two things: first, whether you will go there, and secondly, whether the Walloos will receive you if you do go."

"When I have heard the answer to the second question, we will talk of the first, Zikali. But why do you try to make a fool of me? These Walloos and the savage Heuheuas with whom they fight, I understand, dwell far away. How, then, can you have the answer by tomorrow?"

"There are ways, there are ways," he answered dreamily, then seemed to go into a kind of doze with his great head sunk upon his breast.

I stared at him for a while, till, growing weary of the occupation, I looked about me and noted that of a sudden it was growing dusk. Whilst I did so I began to hear screechings in the air: sharp, thin screechings such as are made by rats.

"Look, Baas," whispered Hans in a frightened voice, "his spirits come," and he pointed upwards.

I did look, and far above, as though they were descending from the sky, saw some wide-winged, flittering shapes, three of them. They descended in circles very swiftly, and I perceived that they were bats, enormous and evil-looking bats. Now they were wheeling about us so closely that twice their outstretched wings touched my face, sending a horrid thrill through me; and each time that a creature passed, it screeched in my ear, setting my teeth on edge.

Hans tried to beat away one of them from investigating him, whereon it clung to his hand and bit his finger, or so I judged from the yell he gave, after which he dragged his hat down over his head and plunged his hands into his pockets. Then the bats concentrated their attention upon Zikali. Round and round him they went in a dizzy whirl which grew closer and closer, till at last two of them settled on his shoulders just by his ears, and began to twitter in them, while the third hung itself on to his chin and thrust its hideous head against his lips.

At this point in the proceedings Zikali seemed to wake up, for his eyes opened and grew bright, also with his skinny hands he stroked the bats upon his shoulders as though they were pet birds. More, he seemed to speak with the creature that hung to his chin, talking in a language which I could not understand, while it twittered back the answers in its slate-pencil notes. Then suddenly he waved his arms and all three of them took flight again, wheeling outwards and upwards, till presently they vanished in the gloom.

"I tame bats and these are quite fond of me," he said by way of explanation, then added, "Come back tomorrow morning, Macumazahn, and perhaps I shall be able to tell you whether the Walloos wish for a visit from you, and if so, to show you a road to their country."

So we went, glad enough to get away, since the Opener-of-Roads, with his peculiar talk and manifestations, as I believe they call them in spiritualistic circles, was a person who soon got upon one's nerves, especially at nightfall. As we stumbled down that hateful gorge in the gloom, Hans asked, "What were those things that hung to Zikali's shoulders and chin?"

"Bats, very large bats. What else?" I answered.

"I think a great deal else, Baas. I think that they are his familiars whom he is sending to those Walloos, just as he said."

"Do you believe in the Walloos and the Heuheua then, Hans? I don't."

"Yes, I do, Baas, and what is more, I believe that we shall visit them, because Zikali means that we should, and who is there that can fight against the will of the Opener-of-Roads?"

CHAPTER 5

Allan Makes a Promise

I never could sleep well in the neighbourhood of the Black Kloof. It always seemed to me to give out evil and disturbing emanations, nor was this night any exception to the rule. For hour after hour, cogitating the old wizard's marvellous tale of the Walloos and Heu-Heu, their devil-ghost, I lay in the midst of the intense silence of that lonely place which was broken only by the occasional scream of a nighthawk, or perhaps of the prey that it gripped, or the echoing bark of some baboon among the rocks.

The story was foolishness. And yet—and yet there were so many strange peoples hidden away in the vast recesses of Africa, and some of them had these extremely queer beliefs or superstitions. Indeed, I began to wonder whether it is not possible for these superstitions, persisted in through ages, to produce something concrete, at any rate to the minds of those whom they affect.

Also there were odd circumstances connected with this tale or romance that might, in a way, be called corroborative. For instance, the picture of Heu-Heu in the cave which Zikali, by his infernal arts or tricks, reproduced in the flame of fire; for instance, the diamonds and rubies, or crystals and spinels, whichever they might be, that at present reposed in the pocket of my shooting coat. These, presuming them to be the former, must have come from some very far-off or hidden spot, since I had never seen or heard of such in any place that I had visited, as they were entirely unlike those which, at that time, they were beginning to find at Kimberley, being, for one thing, much more water-worn.

Still, the presence of diamonds in a certain district had nothing to do with the possible existence of a Heu-Heu. Therefore, they proved nothing, one way or the other.

And if there were a Heu-Heu, did I wish to meet him face to

face? In one sense, not at all, but in another, very much indeed. My curiosity was always great, and it would be wonderful to behold that which no white man's eyes had ever seen, and still more wonderful also to struggle with and kill such a monster. A vision rose before my eyes of Heu-Heu stuffed in the British Museum with a large painted placard underneath:

Shot in Central Africa by Allan Quatermain, Esq.

Why, then I, the most humble and unknown of persons, would become famous and have my likeness published in the *Graphic*, and probably the *Illustrated London News* also, perhaps with my foot set upon the breast of the prostrate Heu-Heu.

That, indeed, would be glory! Only Heu-Heu looked a very nasty customer, and the story might have a wrong ending; his foot might be set upon *my* breast, and he might be twisting off my head, as in the cave picture. Well, in that case the illustrated papers would publish nothing about it.

Then there was the story of the town full of petrified men and animals. This must either be true or false, since it lacked ghostly implications. Although I had never heard of anything of the sort, there might be such a place, and if so, it would be splendid to be its discoverer.

Oh, of what was I thinking? Zikali's yarn must be nonsense, and rank fiction. Yet it reminded me of something I had once heard in my youth, which for a long while I could not recall. At last, in a flash, it came back to me. My old father, who was a learned scholar, had a book of Grecian legends, and one of these about a lady called Andromeda, the daughter of a king who, in obedience to popular pressure and in order to avert calamities from his country, tied her up to a rock, to be carried off by a monster that rose out of the sea. Then a magically aided hero of the name of Perseus arrived at the critical moment, killed the monster and took away the lady to be his wife.

Why, this Heu-Heu story was the same thing over again. The maiden was tied to a rock; the monster came out of the sea, or rather, the lake, and carried her off, whereby calamities were duly averted. So similar was it, indeed, that I began to wonder whether it were not an echo of the ancient myth that somehow had found its way into Africa. Only hitherto there had been no Perseus in Heuheua Land. That role, apparently, was reserved for me. And if so, what should I do with the maiden? Restore her to a grateful family, I suppose, for certainly I had no intention of marrying her. Oh, I was growing silly with thinking! I would go to sleep; I *would*, I wo——

A minute or two later, or so it seemed, I woke up thinking, not of Andromeda, but of the prophet Samuel, and for a while wondered what on earth could have put this austere patriarch and priest into my head. Then, being a great student of the Old Testament, I remembered that autocratic seer's indignation when he heard the lowing of the oxen which Saul spared from the general *eating up* of the Amalekites, as the Zulus would describe it, by divine command. (What was the use of cutting the throats of all that good stock, personally, I could never understand.)

Well, in my ears also was the lowing of oxen, which, of course, formed the connecting link. I marvelled what they could be, for our own were grazing at a little distance, and poked my head out under the wagon-hood to perceive a really beautiful team of trek cattle, eighteen of them, for there were two spare beasts, which had just been driven up to my camp by two strange *Kaffirs*. Then, of course, I remembered about the oxen which Zikali had promised to sell me upon easy terms, or under certain circumstances to give me, and thought to myself that in this matter, at any rate, he had proved a wizard of his word.

Slipping on my trousers, I descended from the wagon to examine them, and with the most satisfactory results. They had quite recovered from their poverty and footsoreness that had caused their former owner to leave them behind in Zikali's charge, and were now as fat as butter, looking as though they would pull anything anywhere. Indeed, even the critical Hans expressed his unqualified approval of the beasts which, as he pointed out from various indications, really seemed to be *salted*, and inoculated also, some of them, as could be seen from the loss of the ends of their tails.

Having sent them to graze in charge of the *Kaffirs* who had brought them, for I did not wish them to mix with my own beasts, which showed signs of sickness, I breakfasted in excellent spirits, as wherever I might go I was now set up with draught beasts, and then bethought me of my undertaking to revisit Zikali. Hans tried to excuse himself from accompanying me, saying that he wanted to study the new oxen which those strange Zulus might steal, etc.; the fact being, of course, that he was afraid of the old wizard, and would not go near him again unless he were obliged. However, I made him come, since his memory was first rate, and four ears were better than two when Zikali was concerned.

Off we trudged up the kloof, and as before, without delay, were admitted within the fence surrounding the witch doctor's hut, to find the Opener-of-Roads seated in front of it, as usual with a fire burning before him. However hot the weather, he always kept that fire going.

"What do you think of the oxen, Macumazahn?" he asked abruptly.

I replied with caution that I would tell him after I had proved them.

"Cunning as ever," said Zikali. "Well, you must make the best of them, Macumazahn, and as I told you, you can pay me when you get back."

"Get back from where?" I asked.

"From wherever you are going, which at present you do not know."

"No, I don't, Zikali," I said, and was silent.

He also was silent for a long while, so long that at last he outwore my patience, and I inquired sarcastically whether he had heard from his friend Heu-Heu, by bat-post.

"Yes, yes, I have heard, or think that I have heard—not by bats, but perchance by dreams or visions. Oho! Macumazahn, I have caught you again. Why do you always walk into my snare so easily? You see some bats, which in truth, as I told you, are but creatures that I have tamed by feeding them for many years, flitter about me and fly away, and you half believe that I have sent them a thousand miles to carry a message and bring back an answer, which is impossible.

"Now I will tell the truth. Not thus do I communicate with those who are afar. Nay, I send out my thought and it flies everywhere to the ends of the earth, so that the whole earth might read it if it could. Yet perchance it is attuned to one mind only among the millions, by which it can be caught and interpreted. But for the vulgar—yes, and even for the wise White Man who cannot understand—there remains the symbol of the bats and their message. Why will you always seek the aid of magic to explain natural things, Macumazahn?"

Now I reflected that my idea of nature and Zikali's differed, but knowing that he was mocking me after his custom, and declining to enter into argument as though it were beneath me, I said, "All this is so plain that I wonder you waste breath in setting it out. I only desired to know if you have any answer to your message, however it was sent, and if so—what answer."

"Yes, Macumazahn, as it happens I have; it came to me just as I was waking this morning. This is its substance; that the chief of the Walloos, with whom my heart talked, and, as he believes, most of his people, will be very glad to welcome you in their land, though, as he believes again, the priests of Heu-Heu, who worship him as a god and are sworn to his service, will not be glad. Should you choose to come, the chief will give you all that you desire of the river diamonds or aught else that he possesses, and you can carry away with you, also, the medicine that *I* desire. Further, he will protect you from dangers so far as he is able. Yet for these gifts he requires payment."

"What payment, Zikali?"

"The overthrow of Heu-Heu at your hands."

"And if I cannot overthrow Heu-Heu, Zikali?"

"Then certainly you will be overthrown and the bargain will fall to the ground."

"Is it so? Well, if I go, shall I be killed, Zikali?"

"Who am I that I should dispense life or death, Macumazahn? Yet," he added slowly, separating his words by deliberate pinches of snuff— "yet I do not think that you will be killed. If I did I should not trust you to pay me for those oxen on your return. Also I believe that you have much work left to do in the world—my work, some of it, Macumazahn, that could not be carried out without you. This being so, the last thing I should wish would be to send you to your death."

I reflected that probably this was true, since always the old wizard was hinting of some great future enterprise in which we should be mixed up together; also I knew that he had a regard for me in his own strange way, and therefore wished me no evil. Moreover, of a sudden a great longing seized me to undertake this adventure in which perchance I might see remarkable new things—I who was wearying of the old ones. However, I hid this, if anything could be hid from Zikali, and asked in a businesslike fashion, "Where do you want me to go, how far off is it, and if I went, how should I get there?"

"Now we begin to handle our assegais, Macumazahn" (by which he meant that we were coming to business). "Hearken, and I will tell you."

Tell me he did indeed for over an hour, but I will not trouble you fellows with all that he said, since geographical details are wearisome and I want to get on with my story. You, my friend (this was addressed to me, the Editor, are only stopping here over tomorrow night, and it will take me all that time to finish it—that is, if you wish to hear the end.

It is enough to say, therefore, that I had to trek about three hundred miles north, cross the Zambezi, and then trek another three hundred miles west. After this I must travel nor'west for a rather indefinite distance till I came to a gorge in certain hills. Here I must leave the wagon, if by this time I had any wagon, and tramp for two days through a waterless patch of desert till I came to a swamp-like oasis. Here the river of which Zikali had spoken lost itself in the sands of the desert, whence I could see on a clear day the smoke of the volcano of which he had also spoken. Crossing the swamp, or making my way round it, I must steer for this slope, till at length I came to a second gorge in the mountains, through which the river ran from Heuheua Land out into the desert. There, according to Zikali, I should find a party of Walloos waiting for me with canoes or boats, who would take me on into their country, where things would go as they were fated.

Before you leave, my friend, I will give you a map[1] of the route, which I drew after travelling it, in case you or anybody else should like to form a company and go to look for diamonds and fossilized men in Heuheua Land, stipulating, however, that you do not ask me to share in the venture.

"So that's the trek," I said, when at last Zikali had finished. "Well, I tell you straight out that I am not going to make it through unknown country. How could I ever find my way without a guide? I'm off to Pretoria with your oxen or without them."

"Is it so, Macumazahn? I begin to think that I am very clever. I thought that you would talk like that and therefore have made ready by finding a man who will lead you straight to the House of Heu-Heu. Indeed, he is here, and I will send for him," and he summoned a servant in his usual way and gave an order.

"Whence does he come, who is he, and how long has he been here?" I asked.

"I don't quite know who he is, Macumazahn, for he does not talk much about himself, but I understand that he comes from the neighbourhood of Heuheua Land, or out of it, for aught I know, and he has been here long enough for me to be able to teach him something of our Zulu language, though that does not matter much since you know Arabic well, do you not?"

"I can talk it, Zikali, and so can Hans, a little."

"Well, that is his tongue, Macumazahn, or so I believe, which will make things easier. I may tell you at once that he is a strange sort of man, not in the least like any one you would expect, but of that you will judge for yourself."

I made no answer, but Hans whispered to me that doubtless he was one of the children of the Heu-Heu and just like a great monkey. Although he spoke in a low voice, and at a distance Zikali seemed to

---

1. If Allan ever gave me this map, of which, after the lapse of so many years, I am not sure, I have put it away so carefully that it is entirely lost, nor do I propose to hunt for it amidst the accumulated correspondence of some five-and-thirty years. Moreover, if it were found and published, it might lead to foolish speculation and probable loss of money among maiden ladies, the clergy, and other venturesome persons.—Editor.

overhear him, for he remarked, "Then you will feel as though you had found a new brother, is it not so, Light-in-Darkness?" which, if I have not said so before, was a title that Hans had earned upon a certain honourable occasion.

Thereon Hans grew silent, since he dared not show his resentment of this comparison of himself to a monkey to the mighty Opener-of-Roads. I, too, was silent, being occupied with my own reflections, for now, in a flash, as it were, I saw the whole trick laid bare of its mysterious and pseudo-magical trappings. A messenger from some strange and distant country had come to Zikali, demanding his help for reasons that I did not know.

This he had determined to give through me, whom he thought suited to the purpose. Hence his bribe of the oxen, the news of which he had conveyed to me while I was still far off, having in some way become acquainted with my dilemma. Indeed, it looked as though everything had been part of a plan, though of course this was not possible, since Zikali could not have arranged that I should take shelter in a particular cave during a thunderstorm.

The sum of it was, however, that I should serve his turn, though what exactly that might be I did not know. He said that he wanted to obtain the leaves of a certain tree, which perhaps was true, but I felt sure that there was more behind.

Possibly his curiosity was excited and he desired information about a distant, secret people, since for knowledge of every kind he had a perfect lust. Or perhaps in some occult fashion this Heu-Heu, if there were a Heu-Heu, might be a rival who stood between him and his plans, and therefore was one to be removed.

Allowing ninety per cent. of Zikali's supernatural powers to be pure humbug, without doubt the remaining ten per cent. were genuine. Certainly he lived and moved and had his being upon a different plane from that of ordinary mortals, and was in touch with things and powers of which we are ignorant. Also as I have reason to know, though I do not trouble you with instances, he was in touch with others of the same class or hierarchy throughout Africa—yes, thousands of miles distant—of whom some may have been his friends and some his enemies but all were mighty in their way.

While I was reflecting thus and old Zikali was reading my thoughts—as I am sure he did, for I saw him smile in his grim manner and nod his great head as though in approval of my acumen—the servant returned from somewhere, ushering in a tall figure picturesquely draped in a fur *kaross* that covered his head as well as his body.

Arrived in front of us, this person threw off the *kaross* and bowed in salutation, first to Zikali and then to myself. Indeed, so great was his politeness that he even honoured Hans in the same way, but with a slighter bow.

I looked at him in amazement, as well I might, since before me stood the most beautiful man that I had ever seen. He was tall, something over six feet high, and superbly shaped, having a deep chest, a sinewy form, and hands and feet that would have done credit to a Greek statue. His face, too, was wonderful, if rather sombre, perfectly chiselled and almost white in colour, with great dark eyes, and there was something about it that suggested high and ancient blood. He looked, indeed, as though he had just stepped straight out of the bygone ages. He might have been an inhabitant of the lost continent of Atlantis or a sun-burned old Greek, for his hair, which was chestnut brown, curled tightly, even where it hung down upon his shoulders, though none grew upon his chin or about the curved lips. Perhaps he was shaven. In short, he was a glorious specimen of mankind, differing from any other I had seen.

His costume, too, was striking and peculiar, although dilapidated; indeed, it might have been rifled from the body of an Egyptian Pharaoh. It consisted of a linen robe that seemed to be twisted about him, which was broidered at the edges with faded purple, a tall and battered linen headdress shaped like the lower half of a soda-water bottle reversed and coming to a point, a leather apron narrow at the top but broadening towards the knees, also broidered, and sandals of the same material.

I stared at him amazed, wondering whether he belonged to some people unknown to me, or was another of Zikali's illusions, and so did Hans, for his muddy little eyes nearly fell out of his head and he asked me in a whisper, "Is he a man, Baas, or a spirit?"

For the rest the stranger wore a plain torque or necklet apparently of gold, and about him was girdled a cross-hilted sword with an ivory handle and a red sheath.

For a while this remarkable person stood before us, his hands folded and his head bent in a humble fashion, though it was really I who should have been humble, owing to the physical contrast between us. Apparently he did not think it proper to speak first, while Zikali squatted there grimly, not helping me at all. At last, seeing that something must be done, I rose from the stool upon which I was seated and held out my hand. After a moment's hesitation the splendid stranger took it, but not to shake in the usual fashion, for he bent his head and gently touched my fingers with his lips, as though he were a French courtier and I a pretty lady. I bowed again with the best grace I could command, then putting my hand in my trouser pocket, said, "How do you do?" and as he did not seem to understand, repeated it in the Zulu word, "*Sakubona.*" This also failing, I greeted him in the name of the Prophet in my best Arabic.

Here I struck oil, as an American friend of mine named Brother John used to say, for he replied in the same tongue, or something like it. Speaking in a soft and pleasing voice, but without alluding to the Prophet, he addressed me as "Great Lord Macumazahn, whose fame and prowess echo across the earth," and a lot of other nonsense, with which I could see that Zikali had stuffed him, that may be omitted.

"Thank you," I cut in, "thank you, Mr.——?" and I paused.

"My name is Issicore," he said.

"And a very nice name, too, though I never heard one like it," I replied. "Well, Issicore, what can I do for you?" An inadequate remark, I admit, but I wanted to come to the facts.

"Everything," he answered fervently, pressing his hands to his breast. "You can save from death a most beautiful lady who will love you."

"Will she?" I exclaimed. "Then I will have nothing to do with that business, which always leads to trouble."

Here Zikali broke in for the first time, speaking very slowly to Issicore in Zulu, which I remembered he said he had been teaching him, and saying, "The Lord Macumazahn is already full of woman's love and has no room for more. Speak not to him of love, O Issicore, lest you should anger the ghost of one who haunts this spot, a certain royal Mameena whom once he knew too well."

Now I turned upon Zikali, promising to give him a piece of my mind, when Issicore, smiling a little, repeated, "Who will love you—as a brother."

"That's better," I said, "though I don't know that I want to take on a sister at my time of life, but I suppose you mean that she will be much obliged?"

"That is so, O Lord. Also the reward will be great."

"Ah!" I replied, really interested. "Now be so good as to tell me exactly what you want."

Well, to cut a long story short, with variations he repeated Zikali's tale. I was to travel to his remote land, bring about the destruction of a nebulous monster, or fetish, or system of religion, and in payment to be given as many diamonds as I could carry.

"But why can't you get rid of your own devil?" I asked. "You look a warrior and are big and strong."

"Lord," he replied gently, spreading out his hands in an appealing fashion, "I am strong and I trust that I am brave, but it cannot be. No man of my people can prevail against the god of my people, if so he may be called. Even to revile him openly would bring a curse upon us; moreover, his priests would murder us——"

"So he has priests?" I interrupted.

"Yes, Lord, the god has priests sworn to his service, evil men as he is evil. O Lord, come, I beseech you, and save Sabeela the beautiful."

"Why are you so interested in this lady?" I asked.

"Lord, because she loves me—not as a brother—and I love her. She, the great Lady of my land and my cousin, is my betrothed and, if the god is not overthrown, as the fairest of all our maidens she will be taken by the god." Here emotion seemed to overcome him, very real emotion, which touched me, for he bowed his head and I saw tears trickle down from his dark eyes.

"Hearken, Lord," he went on, "there is an ancient prophecy in my land that this god of ours, whose hideous shape hides the spirit of a long-dead chief, can only be destroyed by one of another race who can see in the night, some man of great valour destined to be born in due season. Now through our dream-doctors I caused enquiry to be made of this Master of Spirits, who is named Zikali, for I was in despair and knew what must happen at the appointed time. From him I learned that there lived in the south such a man as is spoken of in the prophecy and that his name meant Watcher-by-Night. Then I dared the journey and the curse and came to seek you, and lo! I have found you."

"Yes," I answered, "you have found one whose native name means Watcher-by-Night, but who cannot see in the dark better than any one else, and is not a hero or very brave, but only a trader and a hunter of wild beasts. Yet I tell you, Issicore, that I do not wish to interfere with your gods and priests and tribal matters, or to give battle to some great ape, if it exists, on the chance of earning a pocketful of bright stones should I live to take them away, and of getting a bundle of leaves that this doctor desires. You had better seek some other white man with eyes like a cat's and more strength and courage, Issicore."

"How can I see another when, without doubt, you are the one appointed, Lord? If you will not come, then I return to die with Sabeela, and all is finished."

He paused a few moments, and continued, "Lord, I can offer you little, but is not a good deed its own reward, and will not the memory of it feed your heart through life and death? Because you are noble I beseech you to come, not for what you may gain, but just because you are noble and will save others from cruelty and wrong. I have spoken—choose."

"Why did you not bring Zikali his accursed leaves yourself?" I asked furiously.

"Lord, I could not come to the place where that tree grows in the garden of Heu-Heu; nor, indeed, did I know that this Master of Spirits needed that medicine. Lord, be noble according to your nature, which is known afar."

Now I tell you fellows when I heard this I felt flattered. We all think that we are noble at times, but there are precious few who tell us so, and therefore the thing came as a pleasant surprise from this extraordinarily dignified, handsome and, if it would appear in his own fashion, well-educated son of Ham—if he were a son of Ham. To my mind, he looked more like a prince in disguise, somebody of unknown but highly distinguished race who had walked out of a fairy book. But when I came to think of it, that was exactly what he said he was. Anyway, he was a most discriminating person with a singular insight into character. (It did not occur to me at the moment that Zikali was also a discriminating person with an insight into character which had induced him to bring us two together for secret purposes of his own. Or that, in order to impress me, he had stuffed Issicore with the story of a predestined white man, told of in prophecy, who could see in the dark, as, without doubt, he had done.)

Also the adventure proposed was of an order so wild and unusual that it drew me like a magnet. Supposing that I lived to old age, could I, Allan Quatermain, bear to look back and remember that I had turned down an opportunity of that sort and was departing into the grave without knowing if there was or was not a Heu-Heu who snatched away lovely Andromedas—I mean Sabeelas—off rocks, and combined in his hideous personality the qualities of a god or fetish, a ghost, a devil, and a super-gorilla?

Could I bury my two humble talents of adventure and straight shooting in that fashion? Really, I thought not, for if I did, how could I face my own conscience in those last failing years? And yet there was so much to be said on the other side into which I need not enter. In the end, being unable to make up my mind, I fell into weakness and determined to refer the matter to fate. Yes, I determined to toss up, using Hans for the spinning coin.

"Hans," I said in Dutch, a tongue which neither of the other two understood, "shall we travel to this man's country, or shall we stay in our own? You have heard all; speak and I will accept your judgment. Do you understand?"

"Yes, Baas," said Hans, twirling his hat in his vacant fashion, "I understand that the Baas, as is usual when he is in a deep pit, seeks the wisdom of Hans to get him out—of Hans who has brought him up from a child and taught him most of what he knows; of Hans upon whom his Reverend Father, the Predikant, used to lean as upon a staff, that is, after he had made him into a good Christian. But the matter is important, and before I give my judgment that will settle it one way or another, I would ask a few questions."

Then he wheeled round, and, addressing the patient Issicore in his vile Arabic, said, "Long Baas with a hooked nose, tell me, do you know the way back to this country of yours, and if so, how much of it can be travelled in a wagon?"

"I do," answered Issicore, "and all of it can be travelled in a wagon until the first range of hills is reached. Also along it there is plenty of game and water, except in the desert of which you have been told. The journey should take about three moons, though, myself alone, I accomplished it in two."

"Good, and if my Baas, Macumazahn, comes to your country, how will he be received?"

"Well by most of the people, but not well by the priests of Heu-Heu, if they think he comes to harm the god, and certainly not well by the Hairy Folk who live in the forest, who are called the Children of the god. With these he must be prepared to war, though the prophecy says that he will conquer all of them."

"Is there plenty to eat in your country, and is there tobacco, and something better than water to drink, Long Baas?"

"There is plenty of all these things. There is wealth of every kind, O Counsellor of the White Lord, and all of them shall be his and yours, though," he added with meaning, "those who have to deal with the priests of the god and the Hairy Folk would do well to drink water, lest they should be found asleep."

"Have you guns there?" Hans asked, pointing to my rifle.

"No, our weapons are swords and spears, and the Hairy Folk shoot with arrows from bows."

Hans ceased from his questions and began to yawn as though he were tired, as he did so, staring up at the sky where some vultures were wheeling.

"Baas," he said, "how many vultures do you see up there? Is it seven or eight? I have not counted them but I think there are seven."

"No, Hans, there are eight; one, the highest, was hid behind a cloud."

"You are quite sure that there are eight, Baas?"

"Quite," I answered angrily. "Why do you ask such silly questions when you can count for yourself?"

Hans yawned again and said, "Then we will go with this fine, hook-nosed Baas to the country of Heu-Heu. That is settled."

"What the deuce do you mean, Hans? What on earth has the number of vultures got to do with the matter?"

"Everything, Baas. You see, the burden of this choice was too heavy for my shoulders, so I lifted my eyes and put up a prayer to your Reverend Father to help me, and in doing so saw the vultures. Then your Reverend Father in the heaven above seemed to say to me, 'If there are an even number of vultures, Hans, then go; if an odd number, then stop where you are. But, Hans, do not count the vultures. Make my son, the Baas Allan, count them, for then he will not be able to grumble at you if things turn out badly whether you go or whether you stay behind, and say that you counted wrong or cheated.' And now, Baas, I have had enough of this, and should like to return to our outspan and examine those new oxen."

I looked at Hans, speechless with indignation. In my cowardice I had left it to his cunning and experience to decide this matter, virtually tossing up, as I have said. And what had the little rascal done? He had concocted one of his yarns about my poor old father and tossed up in his turn, going odd or even on the number of the vultures which he made *me* count! So angry was I that I lifted my foot with meaning, whereon Hans, who had been expecting something of the sort, bolted, and I did not see him again until I got back to the camp.

"Oho! Oho!" laughed Zikali, "Oho!" while the dignified Issicore studied the scene with mild astonishment.

Then I turned on Zikali, saying, "A cheat I have called you before, and a cheat I call you again, with all your nonsense about bat-messengers and the tale you have taught to this man as to a prophecy of his people, and the rest. *There* is the bat who brought the message, or the dream, or the vision, or whatever you like to call it, and all the while he was hidden beneath your eaves," and I pointed to Issicore. "And now I have been tricked into saying that I will go upon this fool's errand, and as I do not turn my back upon my word, go I must."

"Have you, Macumazahn?" asked Zikali innocently. "You talked with Light-in-Darkness in Dutch, which neither I nor this man understood, and therefore we did not know what you said. But, as out of the honesty of your heart you have told us, we understand now, and of course we know, as everyone knows, that your word once spoken is worth all the writings of the white men put together, and that only death or sickness will prevent you from accompanying Issicore to his own country. Oho ho! It has all come about as I would have it, for reasons with which I will not trouble you, Macumazahn."

Now I saw that I was doubly tricked, hit, as it were, with the right barrel by Hans and with the left by Zikali. To tell the truth, I had quite forgotten that he did not understand Dutch, although I remembered it when I began to use that tongue, and that therefore it did not in the least matter what I had said privately to Hans. But if Zikali did not understand Dutch, of which after all I am not so sure, at any rate he understood human nature, and could read thoughts, for he went on:

"Do not boil within yourself, like a pot with a stone on its lid, Macumazahn, because your crafty foot has slipped and you have repeated publicly in one tongue what you had already said secretly in another, and therefore made a promise to both of us. For all the while, Macumazahn, you had made that promise and your white heart would not have suffered you to swallow it again just because we could not hear it with our ears. No, that great white heart of yours would have risen in your throat and shut it fast. So kick away the burning sticks from beneath the water of your anger and let it cease from boiling, and go forth as you have promised, to see wonderful things and do wonderful deeds and snatch the pure and innocent out of the hands of evil gods or men."

"Yes, and burn my fingers, scooping your porridge out of the blazing pot, Zikali," I said with a snort.

"Perhaps, Macumazahn, perhaps, for if I had no porridge to be saved, should I have taken all this trouble? But what does that matter to you, to the brave White Lord who seeks the truth as a thrown spear seeks the heart of the foe? You will find plenty of truth yonder, Macumazahn, new truth, and what does it matter if the spear is a little red after it has reached the heart of things? It can be cleaned again, Macumazahn, it can be cleaned, and amidst many other services, you will have done one to your old friend, Zikali the Cheat."

* * * * * * * *

Here Allan glanced at the clock and stopped.

"I say—do you know what time it is?" he said. "Twenty minutes past one—by the head of Chaka. If you fellows want to finish the story tonight, you can do so for yourselves according to taste. I'm off, or out shooting tomorrow I shan't hit a haystack sitting."

CHAPTER 6

The Black River

On the following evening, pleasantly tired after a capital day's shooting and a good dinner, once more the four of us—Curtis, Good, myself (the Editor) and old Allan—were gathered round the fire in his comfortable den at The Grange.

"Now then, Allan," I said, "get on with your tale."

"What tale?" he asked, pretending to forget, for he was always a bad starter where his own reminiscences were concerned.

"That about the monkey-man and the fellow who looked like Apollo," answered Good. "I dreamt about it all night, and that I rescued the lady—a dark girl dressed in blue—and that just as I was about to receive a well-earned kiss of thanks, she changed her mind and turned into stone."

"Which is just what she would have done if she had any sense in her head and you were concerned, Good," said Allan severely, adding, "Perhaps it was your dream that made you shoot more vilely than usual today. I saw you miss eight cock pheasants in succession at that last corner."

"And I saw you kill eighteen in succession at the first," replied Good cheerily, "so you see the average was all right. Now then, get on with the romance. I like romance in the evening after a dose of the hard facts of life in the shape of impossible cock pheasants."

"Romance!" began Allan indignantly. "Am I romantic? Pray do not confuse me with yourself, Good."

Here I intervened imploring him not to waste time in arguing with Good, who was unworthy of his notice, and at last, mollified, he began.

* * * * * * *

Now I am in a hurry and want to be done with this job that dries up my throat—who, having lived so much alone, am not used to talking like a politician—and makes me drink more whisky and water than I ought. You are in a hurry, too, all of you, especially Good, who wants to get to the end of the story in order that he may argue about it and try to show that he would have managed much better, and you, my friend, because you have to leave tomorrow morning early and must see to your packing before you get to bed. Therefore, I am going to skip a lot, all about our journey, for instance, although, in fact, it was one of the most interesting treks I ever made, and for much of the way through a country that was quite new to me, about which one might write a book.

I will simply say, therefore, that in due course after some necessary delay to re-pack the wagon, leaving behind all articles that were not wanted in Zikali's charge, we trekked from the Black Kloof. The oxen that I had bought—on credit—from Zikali were in the yokes, and we drove with us his two extra beasts as well as four of the best of my old team to serve as spares.

Also I took, in addition to my own driver and *voorlooper*, Mavoon and Induka, two other Zulus, Zikali's servants, who I knew would be faithful because they feared their terrible master, although I knew also that they would spy upon me and, if ever they returned alive, make report of everything to him.

Well, leaving out all the details of this remarkable trek in which we met with no fighting, disasters, or great troubles and always had plenty to eat, game being numerous throughout, I will take up the tale on our arrival, safe and sound, at the first line of hills that I show upon the map, of which Zikali had spoken as bordering the desert. Here we were obliged to leave the wagon, for it was impossible to get it over the hills or through the desert beyond.

This, fortunately, we were able to do at a little village of peaceable folk who lived in a charming and well-watered situation, and, having no near neighbours, were able to cultivate their lands unmolested. I placed it in the charge of Mavoon and Induka, whom I could trust and who would not run away, also the oxen, of which, by good fortune, we had only lost three. With them, as Issicore declared that we must go on alone, I left Zikali's servants, knowing that they would keep an eye on my men, and my men on them, and promised the headman of the village a good present if we found everything safe on our return.

He said that he would do his best, but added impressively—he was a melancholy person—that if we were going to the country of Heu-Heu we never should return, as it was a land of devils. In that event he asked what was to happen to the wagon and goods. I replied that

I had given orders that if I did not reappear within a year, it was to trek back to whence we came and announce that we were gone, but that he need not be afraid as, being a great magician, I knew that we should be back long before that time.

He shrugged his shoulders, looking doubtfully at Issicore, and there the conversation ended. However, I persuaded him to lend us three of his people to guide us across the mountains and to carry water through the desert on the understanding that they should be allowed to return as soon as we sighted the swamp. Nothing would induce them to go nearer to the country of Heu-Heu.

****

So in due course off we started, leaving Mavoon and Induka almost in tears, for the gloom of the headman had spread to them and they too believed that they would see us no more. Hans, it is true, they never would have missed, since they hated him as he hated them, but in my case the matter was different because they loved me in their own way.

Our baggage was light: rifles (I took a double-barrelled Express), as much ammunition as we could manage, some medicines, blankets, etc., a few spare clothes and boots for myself, a couple of revolvers and as many vessels of one sort or another as possible to carry water, including two paraffin tins slung at either end of a piece of wood after the fashion of a milkman's yoke. Also we had tobacco, a good supply of matches, candles, and a bundle of dried biltong to eat in case we found no game. It doesn't sound much, but before we got across that desert I felt inclined to throw away half of it; indeed, I don't think we could have got the stuff over the mountain pass, which proved to be precipitous, without the assistance of the three water-bearers.

It took us twelve hours to reach and cross that mountain's crest, just beneath which we camped, and another six to descend the other side next day. At its foot was thin, tussocky grass with occasional thorn trees growing in a barren veldt that by degrees merged into desert. By the last water we camped for the second night; then, having filled up all our vessels, started out into the arid, sandy wilderness.

Now, you fellows know what an African desert is, for we went through a worse one than this on our journey to Solomon's Mines. Still, the particular specimen I am speaking of was pretty bad. To begin with, the heat was tremendous. Then, in parts, it consisted of rolling slopes or waves of sand, up which we must scramble and down which we must slide—a most exhausting process. Further, there grew in it a variety of thick-leaved plant with sharp spines that, if touched, caused a painful soreness, which abominable and useless growths made it impossible to travel at night, or even if the light were low, when they could not be seen and avoided.

We spent three days crossing that wretched desert, that had another peculiarity. Here and there in its waste, columns of stones, polished by blowing sand, stood up like obelisks, sometimes in one piece, monoliths, and sometimes in several, piled on each other. I suppose that they were the remains of strata: hard cores that had resisted the action of wind and water, which in the course of thousands or millions of years had worn away the softer rock, grinding it to dust.

Those obelisk-like columns gave a very strange appearance to that wilderness, suggesting the idea of monuments; also, incidentally, they were useful, since it was by them that our water-bearing guides, who were accustomed to haunt the place to kill ostriches or to steal their eggs, steered their path. Of these ostriches we saw a good number, which showed that the desert could not be so very wide, since in it there seemed to be nothing for them to live on, unless they ate the prickly plants. There was no other life in the place.

Fortunately, by dint of economy and self-denial, our water held out, until on the afternoon of the third day, as we trudged along parched and weary, from the crest of one of the sand waves we saw far off a patch of dense green that marked the end, or, rather, the beginning, of the swamp. Now our agreement with the guides was that when they came in sight of this swamp they should return, for which purpose we had saved some of the water for them to drink on their homeward journey.

After a brief consultation, however, they determined to come on with us, and when I asked why, wheeled round and pointed to dense clouds that were gathering in the heavens behind us. These clouds, they explained, foretold a sand tempest in which no man could live in the desert. Therefore they urged us forward at all speed; indeed, exhausted as we were, we covered the last three miles between us and the edge of the swamp at a run. As we reached the reeds the storm burst, but still we plunged forward through them, till we came to a spot where they grew densely and where, by digging pits in the mud with our hands, we could get water which, thick as it was, we drank greedily. Here we crouched for hours while the storm raged.

It was a terrific sight, for now the face of the desert behind was hidden by clouds of driven sand, which even among the reeds fell upon us thickly, so that occasionally we had to rise to shake its weight off us. Had we still been in the desert, we should have been buried alive. As it was we escaped, though half choked and with our skins fretted by the wear of the particles of sand.

So we squatted all night till before dawn the storm ceased and the sun rose in a perfectly clear sky. Having drunk more water, of which we seemed to need enormous quantities, we struggled back to the edge of the swamp and from the crest of a sand wave looked about us. Issicore stretched out his arm towards the north and touched me on the shoulder. I looked, and far away, staining the delicate blue of the heavens, perceived a dark, mushroom-shaped patch of vapour.

"It is a cloud," I said. "Let us go back to the reeds; the storm is returning."

"No, Lord," he answered, "it is the smoke from the Fire Mountain of my country."

I studied it and said nothing, reflecting, however, that in this particular, at any rate, Zikali had not lied. If so, was it not possible that he had spoken truth about other matters also? If there existed a volcano as yet unreported by any explorer, might there not also be a buried city filled with petrified people, and even a Heu-Heu? No, in Heu-Heu I could not believe.

Here, after they had filled themselves and their gourds with water, the three natives from the village left us, saying that they would go no farther and that they could now depart safely as the sandstorm would not return for some weeks. They added that our magic must be very strong, since had we delayed even for a few hours we should certainly all have been killed.

So they departed, and we camped by the reeds, hoping to rest after our exhausting journey. In this, however, we were disappointed, for as soon as the sun went down we became aware that this vast area of swampy land was the haunt of countless game that came thither, I suppose, from all the country round in order to drink and to fill themselves with its succulent growths.

By the light of the moon I saw great herds of elephants appearing out of the shadows and marching majestically towards the water. Also there were troops of buffalo, some of which broke out of the reeds showing that they had hidden there during the day, and almost every kind of antelope in plenty, while in the morass itself we could hear sea cows wallowing and grunting, and great splashes which I suppose were caused by frightened crocodiles leaping into pools.

Nor was this all, since so much animal life upon which they could prey attracted many lions that coughed and roared and slew according to their nature. Whenever one of them sprang on to some helpless buck, a stampede of all the game in the neighbourhood would follow. The noise they made crashing through the reeds was terrific, so much so that sleep was impossible. Moreover, there was always a possibility that the lions might be tempted to try a change of diet and eat us, especially as we had no bushes with which to form a *boma*, or fence. So we made a big fire of dry, last year's reeds, of which, fortunately, there were many standing near, and kept watch.

Once or twice I saw the long shape of a lion pass us, but I did not fire for fear lest I should wound the beast only and perhaps cause it to charge. In short, the place was a veritable sportsman's paradise, and yet quite useless from a hunter's point of view, since, if he killed elephants, it would be impossible to carry the ivory across the desert, and only a boy desires to slaughter game in order to leave it to rot. At dawn, it is true, I did shoot a reed buck for food, which was the only shot I fired.

As amidst all this hubbub the idea of sleep must be abandoned, I took the opportunity to question Issicore about his country and what lay before us there. During our journey I had not talked much to him on the matter, since he seemed very silent and reserved, all his energies being concentrated upon pushing forward as quickly as possible; also, there was no object in doing so while we were still far away. Now, however, I thought that the time had come for a talk.

In answer to my queries, he said that if we travelled hard, by marching round the narrow western end of the swamp, in three days we should arrive at the mouth of the gorge down which the river ran that flowed through the mountains surrounding his country. These mountains, I should add, we had sighted as a black line in the distance almost as soon as we entered the desert, which showed that they were high. Here, if we reached it without accident, he hoped to find a boat waiting in which we could be paddled to his town, though why anybody should be expecting us I could not elicit from him.

Leaving that question unsolved, I asked him about this town and its inhabitants. He replied that it was large and contained a great number of people, though not so many as it used to do in bygone generations. The race was dwindling, partly from intermarriage and partly because of the terror in which they lived, that made the women unwilling to bear children lest these should be snatched away by the Hairy Folk who dwelt in the surrounding forest, or perhaps sacrificed to the god himself. I inquired whether he really believed that there was such a god, and he replied with earnestness that certainly he did, as once he had seen him, though from some way off, and he was so awful that description was impossible. I must judge of him for myself when we met—an occasion that I began to wish might be avoided.

I cross-examined him persistently about this god, but with small result, for the subject seemed to be one on which he did not care to dwell. I gathered, however, that he, Issicore, had been in a canoe when he saw Heu-Heu on a rock at dawn, surrounded by women, upon the occasion of some sacrifice, and that he had not looked much at him because he was afraid to do so. He noted, however, that he was taller than a man and walked stiffly. He added that Heu-Heu never came to the mainland, though his priests did.

Then, dropping the subject of Heu-Heu, he went on to tell me of the system of government amongst the Walloos, which, it appeared, was an hereditary chieftainship that could be held either by men or women. The present chief, an old man, like the people was named Walloo, as indeed were all the chiefs of the tribe in succession, for "Walloo" was really a title which he thought had come with them from whatever land they inhabited in the dark, forgotten ages. He had but one child living, a daughter, the lady Sabeela, of whom he had spoken to me at the hut of the Opener-of-Roads, she who was doomed to sacrifice. He, Issicore, was her second cousin, being descended from the brother of her grandfather, and therefore of the pure Walloo blood.

"Then if this lady died, I suppose you would be the chief, Issicore?" I said.

"Yes, Lord, by descent," he answered; "yet perhaps not so. There is another power in the land greater than that of the kings or chiefs—the power of the priests of Heu-Heu. It is their purpose, Lord, should Sabeela die, to seize the chieftainship for themselves. A certain Dacha, who is also of the pure Walloo blood, is the chief priest, and he has sons to follow him."

"Then it is to this Dacha's interest that Sabeela should die?"

"It is to his interest, Lord, that she should die and I also, or, better still, both of us together, for then his part would be clear."

"But what of her father, the Walloo? He cannot desire the death of his only child."

"Nay, Lord, he loves her much and desires that she should marry me. But, as I have said, he is an old man and terror-haunted. He fears the god, who already has taken one of his daughters; he fears the priests, who are the oracles of the god, and, it is said, murdered his son as they have striven to murder me. Therefore, being frozen by fear, he is powerless, and without his leadership none can act, since all must be done in the name of the Walloo and by his authority. Yet it was he also who sent me to seek for help from the great wizard of the South with whom he and his fathers have had dealings in bygone years. Yes, because of the ancient prophecy that the god could only be over-thrown and the tyranny of the priests be broken by a white man from the South, he sent me, who am the betrothed of his daughter, secretly and without the knowledge of Dacha, and because of Sabeela I dared the curse and went, for which deed perchance I must pay dearly. He it is also who watches for my return."

"And if he exists, which you have not proved to me, how am I to kill this god, Issicore? By shooting him?"

"I do not know, Lord. It is believed that he cannot be harmed by weapons, over whom only fire and water have power, since legend tells that he came out of the fire and certainly he lives surrounded by water. The prophecy does not say how he will be killed by the stranger from the South."

Now, listening to this weird talk in that wild-beast-peopled wil-derness from the mouth of a man who evidently was very frightened, and wearied as I was, I confess that I grew frightened also, and wished most heartily that I had never been beguiled into this adventure. Prob-ably the terrible god, of whom I could learn no details, question as I would, was nothing but an invention of the priests, or perhaps one of their number disguised. But, however this might be, no doubt I was travelling to a fetish-ridden land in which witchcraft and murder were rampant; in short, one of Satan's peculiar possessions. Yes, I, Allan Quatermain, was brought here to play the part of a modern Hercules and clean out this Augean stable of bloodshed and superstitions, to say nothing of fighting the lion in the shape of Heu-Heu, always supposing that there was a Heu-Heu, a creature taller than a man that "walked stiffly," whom Issicore believed he had once seen from a distance at dawn.

However, I was in for it, and to show fear would be as useless as it was undignified, since, unless I turned and ran back into the desert, which my pride would never suffer me to do, I could see no escape. Having put my hand to the plough I must finish the furrow. So I sat silent, making no comment upon Issicore's rather nebulous informa-tion. Only after a while I asked him casually when this sacrifice was to take place, to which he replied with evident agitation, "On the night of the full harvest moon, which is this moon, fourteen days from now; wherefore we must hurry, since at best it will take us five days to reach the town of Walloo, three in travelling round the swamp and two upon the river. Do not delay, Lord, I pray you do not delay, lest we should be too late and find Sabeela gone."

"No," I answered, "I shall not be late, and I can assure you, my friend Issicore, that the sooner I am through with this business one way or another, the better I shall be pleased. And now that all those beasts in the swamp seem to have grown a little quieter I will try to go to sleep."

Happily I was successful in this effort and obtained several hours' sound rest, which I needed sorely, before the sun appeared and Hans woke me. I rose, and, taking my rifle, shot a fat reed-buck, which I selected out of a number which stood quite close by, a young female off which we breakfasted, for, as you know, if the meat of antelopes is cooked before it grows cold it is often as tender as though it had been hung for a week. The odd thing was that the sound of the shot did not seem to disturb the other beasts at all; evidently they had never heard anything of the sort before, and thought that their companion was just lying down.

An hour later we started on our long tramp round the edge of that swamp. I did not like to march before for fear lest we should get into complications with the herds of elephants and other animals that were trekking out of it in all directions with the light, though where they went to feed I am sure I do not know. In all my life I never saw such quantities of game as had collected in this place, which probably furnished the only water for many miles round.

However, as I have said, it was of no use to us, and therefore our object was to keep as clear of it as possible. Even then we stumbled right on to a sleeping white rhinoceros with the longest horn that ever I saw. It must have measured nearly six feet, and anywhere else would have been a great prize. Fortunately the wind was blowing from it to us, so it did not smell us and charged off in another direction, for, as you know, the rhinoceros is almost blind.

Now I am not going to give all the details of that interminable trudge through sand, for in the mud of the swamp we could not walk at all. During the day we were scorched by the heat and at night we were tormented by mosquitoes and disturbed by the noise of the game and the roaring of lions, which fortunately, being so full fed, never molested us. By the third night, bearing always to the right, we had come quite close to the mountain range, which, although it was not so very lofty, seemed to be absolutely precipitous, faced, indeed, by sheer cliffs that rose to a height of from five to eight hundred feet.

To what extraordinary geological conditions these black cliffs and the desert by which they were surrounded owe their origin, I am sure I do not know, but there they were, and no doubt are.

Before sunset on this third day, by Issicore's direction, we collected a huge pile of dried reeds, which we set upon the crest of a sand mound, and after dark fired them, so that for a quarter of an hour or so they burned in a bright column of flame. Issicore gave no explanation of this proceeding, but as Hans remarked, doubtless it was a signal to his friends. Next morning, at his request, we started on before the dawn, taking our chances of meeting with elephants or buffaloes, and at sunrise found ourselves right under the cliffs.

An hour later, following a little bay in them where there was no swamp, because here the ground rose, of a sudden we turned a corner and perceived a tall, white-robed man with a big spear standing upon a rock, evidently keeping a look-out. As soon as he saw us he leapt down from his rock with the agility of a *klip-springer* and came towards us.

After one curious glance at me he went straight to Issicore, knelt down and, taking his hand, pressed it to his forehead, which showed me that our guide was a venerated person. Then they conversed together in low tones, after which Issicore came to me and said that so far all was well, as our fire had been seen and a big canoe awaited us. We went on, guided by the sentry, and after one turn suddenly came on quite a large river, which had been hidden by the reeds. To the left appeared this deep, slow-flowing river; to the right, within a hundred paces, indeed, it changed into swamp or morass, of which the pools were fringed with very tall and beautiful papyrus plants, such open water as there was being almost covered by every kind of wild fowl that rose in flocks with a deafening clamour. This stream, the Black River, as the Walloos called it, was bordered on either side by precipices through which I suppose it had cut its way in the course of millenniums, so high and impending that they seemed almost to meet above, leaving the surface of the water nearly dark. It was a stream gloomy as the Roman Styx, and, glancing at it, I half expected to see Charon and his boat approaching to row us to the Infernal fields. Indeed, into my mind there floated a memory of the poet's lines, which I hope I quote correctly:

In Kubla Khan a river ran
Through caverns measureless to man,
Down to a sunless sea.

I confess honestly that the aspect of the place filled me with fear: it was forbidding—indeed, unholy—and I marvelled what kind of a sunless sea lay beyond this hell gate. Had I been alone, or with Hans only, I admit that I should have turned tail and marched back round that swamp, upon which, at any rate, the sun shone, and, if I could, across the desert beyond to where I had left the wagon. But in the presence of the stately Issicore and his myrmidon, this I could not do because of my white man's pride. No, I must go on to the end, whatever it might be.

If I was frightened, Hans was much more so, for his teeth began to chatter with terror.

"Oh, Baas," he said, "if this is the door, what will the house beyond be like?"

"That we shall learn in due course," I answered, "so there is no good in thinking about it."

"Follow me, Lord," said Issicore, after some further talk with his companion.

I did so, accompanied by Hans, who stuck to me as closely as possible. We advanced round the rock and discovered a little indent in the bank of the river where a great canoe, hollowed apparently from a single huge tree, or rather its prow, was drawn up on the sandy shore. In this canoe sat sixteen rowers or paddle-men—I remember there were sixteen of them because at the time Hans remarked that the number was the same as that of a wagon team and subsequently called these paddlers "water oxen."

As we approached they lifted their paddles in salute, apparently of Issicore, since of me and my companion, except by swift, surreptitious glances, they took no notice.

With a kind of silent, unobtrusive haste Issicore caused our small baggage, which consisted chiefly of cartridge bags, to be stowed away in the prow of the canoe that for a few feet was hollowed out in such a fashion that it made a kind of cupboard roofed with solid wood, and showed us where to sit. Next he entered it himself, while the lookout man ran down the canoe and took hold of the steering oar.

Then at a word all the paddlers back-watered and the craft slid off the sandy beach into the river which was full to the banks, almost in flood indeed. It seemed that here the rain had been nearly incessant for some months and the lowering sky showed that ere long there was much more to come.

CHAPTER 7
The Walloo

In perfect stillness, except for the sound of the dipping of the paddles in the water, we glided away very swiftly up the placid river. I think that nothing upon this strange journey, or at any rate during the first part of it, struck me more than its quietness. The water was still, flowing peacefully between its rocky walls towards the desert in which it would be lost, just as the life of some good man flows towards death. The rocky precipices on either side were still; they were so steep that on them nothing which breathed could find a footing, except bats, perhaps, that do not stir in the daytime. The riband of grey sky above us was still, though occasionally a draught of air blew between the cliffs with a moaning noise, such as one might imagine to be caused by the passing wind of spiritual wings. But stillest of all were those rowers who for hour after hour laboured at their task in silence, and with a curious intentness, or, if speak they must, did so only in a whisper.

Gradually an impression of nightmare stole over me; I felt as though I were a sleeper taking part in the drama of a dream. Perhaps, in fact, this was so, since I was very tired, having rested but little for a good many nights and laboured hard during the day trudging through the sand with a heavy rifle and a load of cartridges upon my back. So really I may have been in a doze, such as is easily induced in any circumstances by the sound of lapping water. If so, it was not a pleasant dream, for the titanic surroundings in which I found myself and the dread possibilities of the whole enterprise oppressed my spirit with a sensation of departure from the familiar things of life into something unholy and unknown.

Soon the cliffs grew so high and the light so faint that I could only just see the stern, handsome faces of the rowers appearing as they bent forward to their ordered stroke, and vanishing into the gloom as they leant back after it was accomplished. The very regularity of the effort produced a kind of mesmeric effect which was unpleasant. The faces looked to me like those of ghosts peeping at one through cracks of the curtains round a bed, then vanishing, continually to return and peep again.

I suppose that at last I went to sleep in good earnest. It was a haunted sleep, however, for I dreamed that I was entering into some dim Hades where all realities had been replaced by shadows, strengthless but alarming.

At length I was awakened by the voice of Issicore, saying that we had come to the place where we must rest for the night, as it was impossible to travel in the dark and the rowers were weary. Here the cliffs widened out a little, leaving a strip of shore upon either side of the river, upon which we landed. By the last light that struggled to us from the line of sky above we ate such food as we had, supplemented by biscuits of a sort that were carried in the canoe, for no fire was lighted. Before we had finished, dense darkness fell upon us, for the moonbeams were not strong enough to penetrate into that place, so that there was nothing to be done except lie down upon the sand and sleep with the wailing of the night air between the cliffs for lullaby.

The night passed somehow. It seemed so long that I began to think or dream that I must be dead and waiting for my next incarnation, and when occasionally I half woke up, was only reassured by hearing Hans at my side muttering prayers in his sleep to my old father, of which the substance was that he should be provided with a half-gallon bottle of gin! At last a star that shone in the black riband far above vanished and the riband turned blue, or, rather, grey, which showed that it was dawn. We rose and stumbled into the canoe, for it was impossible to see where to place our feet, and started. Within a few hundred yards of our sleeping place suddenly the cliffs that hemmed in the river widened out, so that now they rose at a distance of a mile or more from either bank of flat, water-levelled land.

These banks, which here were steep, were clothed with great, dark-coloured, spreading trees of which the boughs projected far over the water and cut off the light almost as much as the precipices had done lower down the stream. Thus we travelled in gloom, especially as the sun was not yet up. Presently through this gloom, to which my trained eyes had grown accustomed, I thought that I caught sight of tall, dark-hued figures moving between the trees. Sometimes these figures seemed to stand upright and walk upon their feet, and sometimes to run swiftly upon all fours.

"Look, Hans," I whispered—everyone whispered in that place—"there are baboons!"

"Baboons, Baas!" he answered. "Were ever baboons such a size? No, they are devils."

Now from behind me Issicore also whispered, "They are the Hairy Men who dwell in the forest, Lord. Be silent, I pray you, lest they should attack us."

Then he began to consult with the rowers in low tones, apparently as to whether we should go on or turn back. Finally we went on, paddling at a double pace. A moment later a sound arose in that dim forest, a sound of indescribable weirdness that was half an animal grunt and half a human cry, which to my ears shaped itself into the syllables, *"Heu-Heu!"* In an instant it was taken up upon all sides, and from everywhere came this wail of *"Heu-Heu!"* which was so horrid to hear that my hair stood up even straighter than usual. Listening to it, I understood whence came the name of the god I had travelled so far to visit.

Nor was this all, for there followed heavy splashes in the water, like to those made by plunging crocodiles, and in the deep shadow beneath the spreading trees I saw hideous heads swimming towards us.

"The Hairy Folk have smelt us," whispered Issicore again, in a voice that I thought perturbed. "Do nothing, Lord; they are very curious. Perhaps when they have looked they will go away."

"And if they don't?" I asked—a question to which he returned no answer.

The canoe was steered over towards the left bank and driven forward at great speed with all the strength of the rowers. Now in the space of open water, upon which the light began to shine more strongly, I saw a beast-like, bearded head that yet undoubtedly was human, yellow-eyed, thick-lipped, with strong, gleaming teeth, coming towards us at the speed of a very strong swimmer, for it had entered the water above us and was travelling downstream. It reached us, lifted up a powerful arm that was completely covered with brown hair like to that of a monkey, caught hold of the gunwale of the boat just opposite to where I sat, and reared its shoulders out of the water, thereby showing me that its great body was for the most part also covered with long hair.

Now its other hand was also on the gunwale, and it stood in the water, resting on its arms, the hideous head so close to me that its stinking breath blew into my face. Yes, there it stood and jabbered at me. I confess that I was terrified who never before had seen a creature like this. Still, for a while I sat quiet.

Then of a sudden I felt that I could bear no more, who believed that the brute was about to get into the boat, or perhaps to drag me out of it. I lost control of myself, and drawing my heavy hunting-knife—the one you see on the wall there, friends—I struck at the hand that was nearest. The blow fell upon the fingers and cut one of them right off so that it fell into the canoe. With an appalling yell the man or beast let go and plunged into the water, where I saw him waving his bleeding hand above his head.

Issicore began to say something to me in frightened tones, but just then Hans ejaculated, "*Allemaghter!* here's another!" and a second huge head and body reared itself up, this time on his side.

"Do nothing!" I heard Issicore exclaim. But the appearance of the creature was too much for Hans, who drew his revolver and fired two shots in rapid succession into its body. It also tumbled back into the water, where it began to wallow, screaming, but in a thinner voice. I thought, and rightly, that it must be female.

Before the echo of the shots had died away there rose another hideous chorus of *Heu-Heus* and other cries, all of them savage and terrible. From both banks more of the creatures precipitated themselves into the water, but luckily not to attack us because they were too much occupied with the plight of their companion. They congregated round her and dragged her to the shore. Yes, I saw them lift the body out of the stream, for by this time I was sure from its hanging arms and legs that it was dead, an act which showed me that although they had the shape and the covering of beasts, in fact they were human.

****

"Elephants will do as much," interrupted Curtis.

"Yes," said Allan, "that is true. Sometimes they will; I have seen it twice. But everything about the behaviour of those Hairy Men was human. For instance, their wailing over the dead, which was dreadful and reminded me of the tales of banshees. Moreover, I had not far to look for proof. At my feet lay the finger that I had cut off. It was a human finger, only very thick, short, and covered with hair, having the nail worn down, too, doubtless in climbing trees and grubbing for roots."

****

Even then with a shock I realized that I had stumbled on the Missing Link, or something that resembled it very strongly. Here in this unknown spot still survived a people such as were our forefathers hundreds of thousands or millions of years ago. Also I reflected that I ought to be proud, for I had made a great discovery, although, to tell the truth, just then I should have been quite willing to resign its glory to someone else.

After this I began to reflect upon other things, for a large jagged stone whizzed within an inch of my head, and presently was followed by a rude arrow tipped with fish bone that stuck in the side of the canoe.

Amidst a shower of these missiles, which fortunately, beyond a bruise or two, did us no harm, we headed out into mid-stream again where they could not reach us, and as no more of the Hairy People swam from the banks to cut us off, soon were pursuing our way in peace. For once, however, the imperturbable Issicore was much disturbed. He came forward and sat by me and said:

"A very evil thing has happened, Lord. You have declared war upon the Hairy Men and the Hairy Men never forget. It will be war to the end."

"I can't help it," I answered feebly, for I was sick with the sight and sound of those creatures. "Are there many of them, and are they all over your country?"

"A good many, perhaps a thousand or more, Lord, but they only live in the forests. You must never go into the forest, Lord, at any rate, not alone; or on to the island where Heu-Heu lives, for he is their king and keeps some of them about him."

"I have no present intention of doing so," I answered.

Now, as we went, the cliffs receded farther and farther from the river, till at length they ceased altogether. We were through the lip of the mountains, if I may so call it, and had entered a stretch of unbroken virgin forest, a veritable sea of great trees that occupied the rich land of the plain and grew to an enormous size and tallness. Moreover, before us appeared clearly the cone of the volcano, broad but of no great height, over which hung the mushroom-shaped cloud of smoke.

All day long we travelled up this tranquil river, rejoicing in the comparative brightness in its centre, although, of course, the trees upon either edge overhung it much.

Late in the afternoon a bend of the banks brought us within sight of a great sheet of water from which apparently the river issued, although, as I learned afterwards, it flowed into it upon the other side, from I know not whence. This lake—for it was a big lake many miles in circumference—surrounded an island of considerable size, in the centre of which rose the volcano, now a mere grey-hued mountain that looked quite harmless, although over it hung that ominous cloud of smoke which, oddly enough, one could not see issuing from its crest. I suppose that it must have gone up in steam and condensed into smoke above. At the foot of the mountain, upon a plain between it and the lake, with the help of my glasses I could see what looked like buildings of some size, constructed of black stone or lava.

"They are ruins," said Issicore, who had observed that I was examining them. "Once the great city of my forefathers stood yonder until the fire from the mountain destroyed it."

"Then does nobody live on the island now?" I asked.

"The priests of Heu-Heu live there, Lord. Also Heu-Heu himself lives there in a great cave upon the farther side of the mountain, or so it is said, for none of us has ever visited that cave, and with him some of the Hairy People who are his servants. My grandfather did so, however, and saw him there. Indeed, as I have told you, once I saw him myself; but what he looked like you must not ask me, Lord, for I do not remember," he added hastily. "In front of the cave is his garden, where grows the magic tree of which the Master of Spirits yonder in the South desires leaves to mix with his medicines; the tree that gives dreams with long life and vision."

"Does Heu-Heu eat of this tree?" I asked.

"I do not know, but I know that he eats the flesh of beasts, because of these we must make offerings to him, and sometimes of men, or so it is said. Near the foot of the garden burn the eternal fires, and between them is the rock upon which the offerings are made."

Now I thought to myself I should much like to see this place of which it was evident that Issicore knew or would tell very little, where there was a great cave in which dwelt a reputed demon with his slaves and hierophants; and where too grew a tree supposed to be magical, flanked by eternal fires. What were these eternal fires, I wondered. I could only suppose that they had something to do with the volcano.

As it happened, however, whilst I was preparing to question Issicore upon the subject, we passed round a tree-clad headland, for here the river had widened into a kind of estuary, and on the shore of the bay beyond it discovered a town of considerable size, covering several hundred acres of ground. The houses of this town, most of which stood in their own gardens, though some of the smaller ones were arranged in streets, had an Eastern appearance, inasmuch as they were low and flat-roofed.

Only there was this difference: Eastern houses of the primitive sort as a rule are whitewashed, but these were all black, being built of lava, as I discovered afterwards. All round the town also, except on the lake side, ran a high wall likewise of black stone, the presence of which excited my curiosity and caused me to inquire its object.

"It is to defend us from the Hairy Folk who attack by night," answered Issicore. "In the daylight they never come, and therefore our fields beyond are not walled," and he pointed to a great stretch of cultivated land that I suppose had been cleared of trees, which extended for miles into the surrounding forest.

Then he went on to explain that they laboured there while the sun was up and at nightfall returned to the town, except certain of them who slept in forts or blockhouses to guard the crops and cattle *kraals*.

Now I looked at this place and thought to myself that never in my life had I seen one more gloomy, especially in the late afternoon under a sullen, rain-laden sky. The black houses, the high black walls that reminded me of a prison, the black waters of the lake, the outlook on to the black volcano and the black mass of the forest behind, all contributed to this effect.

"Oh, Baas, if I lived here I should soon go mad!" said Hans, and upon my word, I agreed with him.

Now we paddled towards the shore, and presently ran alongside a little jetty formed of stones loosely thrown together, on which we landed. Evidently our approach had been observed, for a number of people—forty or fifty of them, perhaps—were collected at the shore end of the jetty awaiting us. A glance showed me that although of varying ages and both sexes, in type they all resembled our guide, Issicore. That is to say, they were tall, well-shaped, light-coloured and extremely handsome, also clothed in white robes, while some of the men wore hats of the Pharaonic type that I have described. The women's headdress, however, consisted of a close-fitting linen cap with lappets hanging down on either side, and was extraordinarily becoming to their severe cast of beauty. From what race could this people have sprung, I wondered. I had not the faintest idea; to me they looked like the survivals of some ancient civilization.

Conducted by Issicore, we advanced, carrying our scanty baggage, a forlorn and battered little company. As we drew near, the crowd separated into two lines, men to the right and women to the left, like the congregation in a very high church, and stood quite silent, watching us intently with their large, melancholy eyes. Never a word did they say as we passed between them, only watched and watched till I felt quite nervous. They did not even offer any greeting to Issicore, although it seemed to me that he had earned one after his long and dangerous journey.

I observed, however, although at the time I took little notice of the matter, and afterwards forgot all about it until Hans brought the circumstance back to my mind, that a certain dark man of austere countenance, clothed rather differently from the rest, approached Issicore, addressed him, and thrust something into his hand. Issicore glanced at this object, whatever it might be, and distinctly I saw him tremble and turn pale. Then he hid it away, saying nothing.

Turning to the right, we marched along a roadway that bordered the lake, which was constructed about twelve feet above its level, perhaps to serve as a protection against inundation, till we came to a wall in which was a door built of solid balks of wood. This door opened as we approached, and, passing it, we found ourselves in a large garden cultivated with taste and refinement, for in it were beds of flowers, the only cheerful thing I ever saw in this town that, it appeared, was named Walloo after the tribe or its ruler. At the end of the garden stood a long, solid, flat-roofed house built of the prevailing lava rock.

Entering, we found ourselves in a spacious room which, as dusk was gathering, was lit with cresset-like lamps of elegant shape placed upon pedestals cut from great tusks of ivory.

In the centre of this room were two large chairs made of ebony and ivory with high backs and footstools, and in these chairs sat a man and a woman who were well worth seeing. The man was old, for his silver hair hung down upon his shoulders, and his fine, sad face was deeply wrinkled.

At a glance I saw that he must be the king or chief, because of his dignified if somewhat senile appearance. Moreover, his robes, with their purple borders, had a royal look, and about his neck he wore a heavy chain of what seemed to be gold, while in his hand was a black staff tipped with gold, no doubt his sceptre. For the rest, his eyes had a rather frightened air, and his whole aspect gave an idea of weakness and indecision.

The woman sat in the other chair with the light from one of the lamps shining full upon her, and I knew at once that she must be the Lady Sabeela, the love of Issicore. No wonder that he loved her, for she was beautiful exceedingly; tall, well developed, straight as a reed, great-eyed, with chiselled features that were yet rounded and womanly, and wonderfully small hands and feet. She, too, wore purple-bordered robes. About her waist hung a girdle thickly sewn with red stones that I took to be rubies, and upon her shapely head, serving as a fillet for her abundant hair, which flowed down her in long waving strands of a rich and ruddy hue of brown or chestnut, was a simple golden band. Except for a red flower on her breast she wore no other ornament, perhaps because she knew that none was needed.

Leaving us by the door of the chamber, Issicore advanced and knelt before the old man, who first touched him with his staff and then laid a hand upon his head. Presently he rose, went to the lady and knelt before her also, whereon she stretched out her fingers for him to kiss, while a look of sudden hope and joy, which even at that distance I could distinguish, gathered on her face. He whispered to her for a while, then turned and began to speak earnestly to her father. At length he crossed the room, came to me and led me forward, followed by Hans at my heels.

"O Lord Macumazahn," he said, "here sit the Walloo, the Prince of my people, and his daughter, the Lady Sabeela. O Prince my cousin, this is the white noble famous for his skill and courage, whom the Wizard of the South made known to me and who at my prayer, out of the goodness of his heart, has come to help us in our peril."

"I thank him," said the Walloo in the same dialect of Arabic that was used by Issicore. "I thank him in my own name, in that of my daughter who now alone is left to me, and in the name of my people."

Here he rose from his seat and bowed to me with a strange and foreign courtesy such as I had not known in Africa, while the lady also rose and bowed, or rather curtseyed. Seating himself again, he said, "Without doubt you are weary and would rest and eat, after which perchance we may talk."

Then we were led away through a door at the end of the great room into another room that evidently had been prepared for me. Also there was a place beyond for Hans, a kind of alcove. Here water, which I noticed had been warmed—an unusual thing in Africa—was brought in a large earthenware vessel by two quiet women of middle age, and with it an undershirt of beautiful fine linen which was laid upon a bed, or cushioned couch, that was arranged upon the floor and covered by fur rugs.

I washed myself, pouring the warm water into a stone basin that was set upon a stand, and put on the shirt, also the change of clothes that I had with me, and, with the help of Hans and a pair of pocket scissors, trimmed my beard and hair. Scarcely had I finished when the women reappeared, bringing food on wooden platters—roast lamb, it seemed to be—and with it drink in jars of earthenware that were of elegant shape and powdered all over with the little rough diamonds of which Zikali had given me specimens, that evidently had been set in it in patterns before the clay dried. This drink, by the way was a kind of native beer, sweet to the taste but pleasant and rather strong, so that I had to be careful lest Hans should take too much of it.

After we had finished our meal, which was very welcome, for we had eaten no properly cooked food since we left the wagon, Issicore arrived and took us back to the large room, where we found the Walloo and his daughter seated as before, with several old men squatting about them on the ground. A stool having been set for me the talk began.

I need not enter into all its details, since in substance they set out what I had already heard from Issicore; namely, that there dwelt Something or Somebody on the island in the lake who required annually the sacrifice of a beautiful virgin. This was demanded through the head priest of a college, also established on the island which acknowledged the being, real or imaginary, that lived there as its god or fetish. Further, that creature (if he existed) was said to be the king of all the Hairy Folk who inhabited the forest. Lastly, there was a legend that he was the reincarnation of some ancient monarch of the Walloo folk, who had come to a bad end at the hands of his indignant subjects at some date undefined. Walloo, it seemed, was their correct name, that of Heuheua applying only to the Hairy Men of the woods.

This story I dismissed at once, being quite convinced that it was only a variant of a very common African fable. Doubtless Heu-Heu, if there really were a Heu-Heu, was the ruler of the savage hairy aboriginals of the place that once in the far past had been conquered by the invading Walloo, who poured into the country from the north or west, being themselves the survivors of some civilized but forgotten people. This conclusion, I may add, I never found any reason to doubt. Africa is a very ancient land, and in it once lived many races that have vanished, or survive only in a debased condition, dwindling from generation to generation until the day of their extinction comes.

Here I may state briefly the final opinions at which I have arrived about this people.

Almost certainly these Walloos were such a dying race, hailing, as names among them seemed to suggest from some region in West Africa, where their forefathers had been highly civilized. Thus, although they could not write, they had traditions of writing and even inscriptions graven upon stones, of which I saw several in a character that I did not know, though to me it had the look of Egyptian hieroglyphics. Also they still had knowledge of certain cultured arts such as the weaving of fine linen, the carving of wood and marble, the making of pottery, and the smelting of metals with which their land abounded, including gold that they found in little nuggets in the gravel of the streams.

Most of these crafts, however, were dying out except those that were necessary to life, such as the moulding of pottery and the building of houses and walls, and particularly agriculture, in which they were very proficient. When I saw them all the higher arts were practised only by the very old men. As they never intermarried with any other blood, their hereditary beauty, which was truly remarkable, remained to them, but owing to the causes I have mentioned already, the stock was dwindling, the total population being now not more than half of what it was within the memory of the fathers of their oldest men. Their melancholy, which now had become constitutional, doubtless was induced by their gloomy surroundings and the knowledge that as a race they were doomed to perish at the hands of the savage aboriginals who once had been their slaves.

Lastly, although they retained traces of some higher religion, since they made prayer to a Great Spirit, they were fetish-ridden and believed that they could continue to exist only by making sacrifice to a devil who, if they neglected to do so, would crush them with misfortunes and give them over to destruction at the hands of the dreadful Forest-dwellers. Therefore they, or a section of them, became the priests of this devil called Heu-Heu, and thereby kept peace between them and the Hairy Men.

Nor was this the end of their troubles, since, as Issicore had told me, these priests, after the fashion of priests all the world over, now aspired to the absolute rule of the race, and for this reason plotted the extinction of the hereditary chief and all his family.

Such, in substance, was the lugubrious story that the unhappy Walloo poured into my ears that night, ending it in these words:

"Now you will understand, O Lord Macumazahn, why in our extremity and in obedience to the ancient prophecy, which has come down to us from our fathers, we communicated with the great Wizard of the South, with whom we had been in touch in ancient days, praying him to send us the helper of the prophecy. Behold, he has sent you and now I implore you to save my daughter from the fate that awaits her. I understand that you will require payment in white and red stones, also in gold and ivory. Take as much as you want. Of the stones there are jars full hidden away and the fences of some of my courtyards at the back of this house are made of tusks of ivory, though it is black with age, and I know not how you would carry it hence. Also there is a quantity of gold melted into bars, which my grandfather caused to be collected, whereof we make little use except now and again for women's ornaments, but that, too, would be heavy to carry across the desert. Still, it is all yours. Take it. Take everything you wish, only save my daughter."

"We will talk of the reward afterwards," I said, for my heart was touched at the sight of the old man's grief. "Meanwhile, let me hear what can be done."

"Lord, I do not know," he answered, wringing his hands. "The third night from this is that of full moon, the full moon which marks the beginning of harvest. On that night we must carry my daughter, on whom the lot has fallen, to the island in the lake where stands the smoking mountain and bind her to the pillar upon the Rock of Offering that is set between the two undying fires. There we must leave her, and at the dawn, so it is said, Heu-Heu himself seizes her and carries her into his cavern, where she vanishes for ever. Or, if he does not come, his priests do, to drag her to the god, and we see her no more."

"Then why do you take her to the island? Why do you not call your people together and fight and kill this god or his priest?"

"Lord, because not one man among us, save perhaps Issicore yonder, who can do nothing alone, would lift a hand to save her. They believe that if they did the mountain would break into flames, as happened in the bygone ages, turning all upon whom the ashes fell into stone; also, that the waters would rise and destroy the crops, so that we must die of starvation, and that any who escaped the fire and the water and the want would perish at the hands of the cruel Wood-devils. Therefore, if I ask the Walloos to save the maiden from Heu-Heu, they will kill me and give her up in accordance with the law."

"I understand," I said, and was silent.

"Lord," went on the old Walloo presently, "here with me you are safe, for none of my people will harm you or those with you. But I learn from Issicore that you have stabbed a Hairy Man with a knife, and that your servant slew one of their women with the strange weapons that you carry. Therefore, from the Wood-devils you are not safe, for, if they can, they will kill you both and feast upon your bodies."

"That's cheerful," I thought to myself, but made no further answer, for I did not know what to say.

Just then the Walloo rose from his chair, saying that he must go to pray to the spirits of his ancestors to help him, but that we would talk again upon the morrow. After this he bade us good-night and departed without another word, followed by the old men, who all this while had sat silent, only nodding their heads from time to time like porcelain images of Chinese mandarins.

CHAPTER 8

The Holy Isle

When the door had closed behind him, I turned to Issicore and asked him straight out if he had any plan to suggest. He shook his noble-looking head and answered, "None," as it was impossible to resist both the will of the people and the law of the priests.

"Then what is the use of your having brought me all this way?" I inquired with indignation. "Cannot you think of some scheme? For instance, would it not be possible for you and this lady to fly with us down the river and escape to a land which is not full of demons?"

"It would not be possible," he answered in a melancholy voice. "Day and night we are watched and would be seized before we had travelled a mile. Moreover, could she leave her father, and could I leave all my relations to be murdered in payment for our sacrilege?"

"Have you no thought in your mind at all?" I asked again. "Is there nothing that would save the Lady Sabeela?"

"Nothing, Lord, except the end of Heu-Heu and his priests. It is to you, great Lord, that we look to find a way to destroy them, as the prophecy declares will be done by the White Deliverer from the South."

"Oh, dash the prophecy! I never knew prophecies to help anybody yet," I ejaculated in English, as I contemplated that beautiful but helpless pair. Then I added in Arabic, "I am tired and am going to bed. I hope that I shall find more wisdom in my dreams than I do in you, Issicore," I added, staring at the man in whom I seemed to detect some subtle change, some access of fatalistic helplessness, even of despair.

Now Sabeela, seeing that I was angry, broke in, "O Lord, be not wrath, for we are but flies in the spider's web, and the threads of that web are the priests of Heu-Heu, and the posts to which it is fixed are the beliefs of my people, and Heu-Heu himself is the spider, and in my breast his claws are fixed."

Now, listening to her allegory, I thought to myself that a better one might have been drawn from a snake and a bird, for really, like the rest of them, this poor girl seemed to be mesmerized with terror and to have made up her mind to sit still waiting to be struck by the poisoned fangs.

"Lord," she went on, "we have done all we could. Did not Issicore make a great journey to find you? Yes, did he not even dare the curse which falls upon the heads of those who try to leave our country, and travel south to seek the counsel of the Great Wizard, who once sent messengers here to obtain the leaves of the tree that grows in Heu-Heu's garden, the tree that makes men drunk and gives them visions?"

"Yes," I answered, "he did that, Lady, and might I say to you that his health seems none the worse. Those curses of which you speak have not yet hurt him."

"It is true they have not hurt his body—yet," she said in a musing voice, as though a new thought had struck her.

"Well, if that is true, Sabeela, may it not be true also that all this talk about the power of Heu-Heu is nonsense? Tell me, have you ever spoken with or seen Heu-Heu?"

"No, Lord, no, though unless you can save me I shall soon see him."

"Well, and has any one else?"

"No, Lord, no one has ever spoken with him, except, of course, his priests, such as my distant cousin, Dacha, who is the head of them, but whom I used to know before he was chosen by Heu-Heu to be one of their company."

"Oh! So no one has seen him? Then he must be a very secret kind of god who does not take exercise, but lives, I understand, in a cave with priests."

"I did not say that no one had ever seen Heu-Heu, Lord. Many say that they have seen him, as Issicore has done, when he came out of the cave on a Night of Offering, but of what they saw it is death to speak. Ask me and Issicore no more of Heu-Heu, Lord I pray you, lest the curse should fall. It is not lawful that we should tell you of him, whose secrets are sacred even to his priests," she added with agitation.

Then in despair I gave up asking questions about Heu-Heu and inquired how many priests he had.

"About twenty, I believe, Lord," she answered, ceasing from evasions, "not counting their wives and families, and it is said that they do not live with Heu-Heu in the cave, but in houses outside of it."

"And what do they do when they are not worshipping Heu-Heu, Sabeela?"

"Oh, they cultivate the land and they rule the Wild People of the Woods, who, it is believed, are all Heu-Heu's children. Also they come here and spy on us."

"Do they indeed?" I remarked. "And is it true that they hope to rule over you Walloos also?"

"Yes, I believe that it is true. At least, should my father die and I die, it is said that Dacha means to make war upon the Walloos and take the chieftainship, setting aside or killing my cousin and betrothed Issicore. For Dacha was always one who desired to be first."

"So you used to know Dacha pretty well, Lady?"

"Yes, Lord, when I was quite young before he became a priest. Also," she added, colouring, "I have seen him since he became a priest."

"And what did he say to you?"

"He said that if I would take him for a husband perhaps I should escape from Heu-Heu."

"And what did you answer, Lady?"

"Lord, I answered that I would rather go to Heu-Heu."

"Why?"

"Because Dacha, it is reported, has many wives already. Also I hate him. Also from Heu-Heu at the last I can always escape."

"How?"

"By death, Lord. We have swift poison in this country, and I carry some of it hidden in my hair," she added with emphasis.

"Quite so. I understand. But, Lady Sabeela, as you have been so good as to ask my advice about these matters, I will give you some. It is that you should not taste that poison till all else has failed and there is no escape. While we breathe there is hope, and all that seems lost still may be won, but the dead do not live again, Lady Sabeela."

"I hear and will obey you, Lord," she answered, weeping. "Yet sleep is better than Dacha or Heu-Heu."

"And life is better than all three of them put together," I replied, "especially life with love."

Then I bowed myself off to bed, followed by Hans, also bowing— like a monkey for pennies on a barrel-organ. At the door I looked back, and saw these two poor people in each other's arms, thinking, doubtless, that we were already out of sight of them. Yes, her head was upon Issicore's shoulder, and from the convulsive motions of her form I guessed that she was sobbing, while he tried to console her in the ancient, world-wide fashion. I only hope that she got more comfort from Issicore than I did. To me he now seemed to be but a singularly unresourceful member of a played-out race, though it is true that he had courage, since otherwise he would not have attempted the journey to Zululand. Also, as I have said, quite suddenly he had changed in some subtle fashion.

When we were in our own room with the door bolted (it had no windows, light and ventilation being provided by holes in the roof) I gave Hans some tobacco and bade him sit down on the other side of the lamp, where he squatted upon the floor like a toad.

"Now, Hans," I said, "tell me all the truth of this business and what we are to do to help this pretty lady and the old chief, her father."

Hans looked at the roof and looked at the wall; then he spat upon the floor, for which I reproved him.

"Baas," he said at length, "I think the best thing we can do is to find out where those bright stones are, fill our pockets with them, and escape from this country which is full of fools and devils. I am sure that Beautiful One would be better off with the priest Dacha, or even with Heu-Heu, than with Issicore, who now has become but a carved and painted lump of wood made to look like a man."

"Possibly, Hans, but the tastes of women are curious, and she likes this lump of wood, who, after all, is brave, except where ghosts and spirits are concerned. Otherwise he would not have journeyed so far for her sake. Moreover, we have a bargain to keep. What should we say to the Opener-of-Roads if we returned, having run away and without his medicine? No, Hans, we must play out this game."

"Yes, Baas, I thought that the Baas would say that because of his foolishness. Had I been alone, by now, or a little later, I should have been in that canoe going down-stream. However, the Baas has settled that we must save the lady and give her to the Lump of Wood for a wife. So now I think I will go to sleep, and tomorrow or the next day the Baas can save her. I don't think very much of the beer in this country, Baas—it is too sweet; and all these handsome fools who talk about devils and priests weary me. Also, it is a bad climate and very damp. I think it is going to rain again, Baas."

Having nothing else at hand, I threw my tobacco-pouch at Hans's head. He caught it deftly, and in an absent-minded fashion, put it into his own pocket.

"If the Baas really wishes to know what I think," he said, yawning, "it is that the medicine man named Dacha wants the pretty lady for himself; also to rule alone over all these dull people. As for Heu-Heu, I don't know anything about him, but perhaps he is one of those Hairy Men who came here at the beginning of the world. I think that the best thing we can do, Baas, would be to take a boat tomorrow morning and go to that island, where we can find out the truth for ourselves. Perhaps the Lump of Wood and some of his men can row us there. And now I have nothing more to say, so, if the Baas does not mind, I will go to sleep. Keep your pistol ready, Baas, in case any of the Hairy People wish to call upon us—just to talk about the one I shot."

Then he retired to a corner, rolling himself up in a skin rug, and presently was snoring, though, as I knew well enough, with one eye open all the time. No Hairy Man, or any one else, would have come near that place without Hans hearing him, for his sleep was like to that of a dog who watches his master.

As I prepared to follow his example, I reflected that his remarks, casual as they seemed, were full of wisdom. These folk were superstition-riddled fools and useless; probably the only ones that had wits among them became priests. But the Hairy aboriginals were an ugly fact, as the priests knew, since apparently they had obtained rule over them. For the rest, the only thing to do was to visit the Holy Island and find out the truth for ourselves, as Hans had said. It would be dangerous, no doubt, but at the least it would also be exciting.

Next morning I rose after an excellent night's rest and found my way into the garden, where I amused myself by examining the shrubs and flowers, some of which were strange to me. Also I studied the sky, which was heavy and lowering, and seemed full of rain. I could study nothing else because the high wall cut off the view upon every side so that little was to be seen except the top of the volcano, which rose from the lake at a distance of several miles, for it was a large sheet of water. Presently the door of the garden opened and Issicore appeared, looking weary and somewhat bewildered. It occurred to me that he had been sitting up late with Sabeela. As they were to be parted so soon, naturally they would see as much as they could of each other. Or for aught I knew, he might have been praying to his ancestral spirits and trying to make up his mind what to do, no doubt a difficult process under the circumstances. I went to the point at once.

"Issicore," I said, "as soon as possible after breakfast, will you have a canoe ready to take me and Hans to the island in the lake?"

"To the island in the lake, Lord!" he exclaimed, amazed. "Why, it is holy!"

"I daresay, but I am holy also, so that if I go there it will be holier."

Then he advanced all kinds of objections, and even brought out the Walloo and his grey-heads to reinforce his arguments. Hans and Sabeela also joined the party; the latter, I noted, looking even more beautiful by day than she did in the lamplight. Sabeela, indeed, proved my only ally, for presently, when the others had talked themselves hoarse, she said, "The White Lord has been brought hither that we, who are bewildered and foolish, may drink of the cup of his wisdom. If his wisdom bids him visit the Holy Isle, let him do so, my father."

As no one seemed to be convinced, I stood silent, not knowing what more to say. Then Hans took up his parable, speaking in his bad coast-Arabic:

"Baas, Issicore, although he is so big and strong, and all these others are afraid of Heu-Heu and his priests. But we, who are good Christians, are not afraid of any devils because we know how to deal with them. Also we can paddle, therefore let the Chief give us quite a small canoe and show us which way to row, and we will go to the island by ourselves."

In sporting parlance, this shot hit the bull in the eye, and Issicore, who, as I have said, was a brave man at bottom, fired up and answered, "Am I a coward that I should listen to such words from your servant, Lord Macumazahn? I and some others whom I can find will row you to the island, though on it we will not set our foot because it is not lawful for us to do so. Only, Lord, if you come back no more, blame me not."

"Then that is settled," I replied quietly, "and now, if we may, let us eat, for I am hungry."

* * * * * * * *

About two hours later we started from the quay, taking with us all our small possessions, down to some spare powder in flasks which we had brought to reload fired cartridge cases, for Hans refused to leave anything behind with no one to watch it. The canoe which was given to us was much smaller than that in which we had come up the river, though, like it, hollowed from a single log; and its crew consisted of Issicore, who steered, and four other Walloos, who paddled, stout and determined-looking fellows, all of them. The island was about five miles away, but we made a wide circuit to the south, I suppose in the hope of avoiding observation, and therefore it took us the best part of two hours to reach its southern shore.

As we approached I examined the place carefully through my glasses, and observed that it was much larger than I had thought— several miles in circumference, indeed, for in addition to the central volcanic cone there was a great stretch of low-lying land all round its base, which land seemed not to rise more than a foot or two above the level of the lake. In character, except on these flats by the lake, it was stony and barren, being, in fact, strewn with lumps of lava ejected from the volcano during the last eruption.

Issicore informed me, however, that the northern part of the island where the priests lived, which had not been touched by the lava stream, was very fertile. I should add that the crater of the volcano seemed to bear out his statement as to the direction of the flow, since on the south it was blown away to a great depth, whereas the northern segment rose in a high and perfect wall of rock.

The day was very misty—a circumstance which favoured our approach—and the sky, which, as I have said, was black and pregnant with coming rain, seemed almost to touch the crest of the mountain. These conditions, until we were quite close, prevented us from seeing that a stream of glowing lava, not very broad, was pouring down the mountain-side. When they discovered this, the Walloos grew much alarmed, and Issicore told me that such a thing had not been known "for a hundred years," and that he thought it portended something unusual, as the mountain was supposed to be "asleep."

"It is awake enough to smoke, anyway," I answered, and continued my examination.

Among the stones, and sometimes half-buried by them, I saw what appeared to be the remains of those buildings of which I have spoken. There, Issicore said, had once been part of the city of his forefathers, adding that, as he had been told, in some of them the said forefathers were still to be seen turned to stone, which, you will remember, exactly bore out Zikali's story.

Anything more desolate and depressing than the aspect of this place seen on that grey day and beneath the brooding sky cannot be imagined. Still I burned to examine it, for this tale of fossilized people excited me, who have always loved the remains of antiquity and strange sights.

Forgetting all about Heu-Heu and his priests for the moment, I told the Walloos to paddle to the shore, and, after a moment of mute protest, they obeyed, running into a little bay. Hans and I stepped easily on to the rocks and, carrying our bags and rifles, started on our search. First, however, we arranged with Issicore that he should await our return and then row us back round the island so that we might have a view of the priests' settlement. With a sigh he promised to do so, and at once paddled out to about a hundred yards from the shore, where the canoe was anchored by means of a pierced stone tied to a cord.

Off went Hans and I towards the nearest group of ruins. As we approached them, Hans said, "Look out, Baas! There's a dog between those rocks."

I stared at the spot he indicated, and there, sure enough, saw a large grey dog with a pointed muzzle, which seemed to be fast asleep. We drew nearer, and as it did not stir, Hans threw a stone and hit it on the back. Still it did not stir, so we went up and examined it.

"It is a stone dog," I said. "The people who lived here must have made statues," for as yet I did not believe the stories I had heard about petrified creatures, which, after all, must be very legendary.

"If so, Baas, they put bones into their carvings. Look," and he touched one of the dog's front paws which was broken off. There, in the middle of it, appeared the bone fossilized. Then I understood.

The animal had been fleeing away to the shore when the poisonous gases overcame it at the time of the eruption. After this, I suppose, some rain of petrifying fluid had fallen on it and turned it into stone. It was a marvellous thing, but I could not doubt the evidence of my own eyes. All the tale was true, and I had made a great discovery.

We hurried on to the houses, which, of course, now were roofless, and in some instances choked with lava, though the outer walls, being strongly built of rock, still stood. On certain of these walls were the faint remains of frescoes; one of people sitting at a feast, another of a hunting scene, and so forth.

We passed on to a second group of buildings standing at some distance against the flank of the mountain and more or less protected by an overhanging ledge or shelf of stone. These appeared to have been a palace or a temple, for they were large, with stone columns that supported the roofs. We went on through the great hall to the rooms behind, and in the furthermost, which was under the ledge of rock and probably had been used as a store chamber, we saw an extraordinary sight.

There, huddled together, and in some instances clasping each other, were a number of people, twenty or thirty of them—men, women, and children—all turned to stone. Doubtless the petrifying fluid had flowed into the chamber through the cracks in the rock above and done its office on them. They were naked, every one, which suggested that their clothing had either been burnt off them or had rotted away before the process was complete. The former hypothesis seemed to be borne out by the fact that none of them had any hair left upon their heads. The features were not easy to distinguish, but the general type of the bodies was certainly very similar to that of the Walloos.

Speechless with amazement, we emerged from that death chamber and wandered about the place. Here and there we found the bodies of others who had perished in the great catastrophe and once came across an arm projecting from a mass of lava, which seemed to show that many more were buried underneath. Also we found a number of fossilized goats in a *kraal*. What a place to dig in! I thought to myself. Given some spades, picks, and blasting-powder, what might one not find in these ruins?

All the relics of a past civilization, perhaps—its inscriptions, its jewellery, the statues of its gods; even, perhaps, its domestic furniture buried beneath the lava and the dust, though probably this had rotted. Here, certainly, was another Pompeii, and perhaps beneath that another Herculaneum.

Whilst I mused thus over glories passed away and wondered when they had passed, Hans dug me in the ribs and, in his horrible Boer Dutch, ejaculated a single word, *"Kek!"* which, as perhaps you know, means "Look!" at the same time nodding towards the lake.

I did look, and saw our canoe paddling off for all it was worth, going "hell for leather," as my old father used to say, towards the Walloo shore.

"Now why is it doing that?" I asked.

"I expect because something is behind it, Baas," he replied with resignation, then sat down on a rock, pulled out his pipe, filled it, and lit a match.

As usual, Hans was right, for presently from round the curve of the island there appeared two other canoes, very large canoes, rowing after ours with great energy and determination, and, as I guessed, with malignant intent.

"I think those priests have seen our boat and mean to catch it, if they can," remarked Hans, spitting reflectively, "though as Issicore has got a long start, perhaps they won't. And now, Baas, what are we to do? We can't live here with dead men, and stone goat is not good to eat."

I considered the situation, and my heart sank into my boots, for the position seemed desperate. A moment before I had been filled with enthusiasm over this ruined city and its fossilized remains. Now I hated the very thought of them, and wished that they were at the bottom of the lake. Thus do circumstances alter cases, and our poor variable human moods. Then an idea came to me, and I said boldly, "Do! Why, there is only one thing to do. We must go to call on Heu-Heu, or his priests."

"Yes, Baas. But the Baas remembers the picture in the cave on the Berg. If it is a true picture, Heu-Heu knows how to twist off men's heads!"

"I don't believe there is a Heu-Heu," I said stoutly. "You will have noticed, Hans, that we have heard all sorts of stories about Heu-Heu, but that no one seems to have seen him clearly enough to give us an accurate description of what he is like or what he does—not even Zikali. He showed us a picture of the beast on his fire, but after all it was only what we had seen on the wall of the cave, and I think that he got it out of our own minds. At any rate, it is just as well to die quickly without a head, as slowly with an empty stomach, since I am sure those Walloos will never come back to look for us."

"Yes, Baas, I think so, too. Issicore used to have courage, but he seems to have changed, as though something had happened to him since he got back into his own country. And now, if the Baas is ready, I think we had better be trekking, unless, indeed, he would like to look at a few more stone men first. It is beginning to rain, Baas, and we have been much longer here than the Baas thinks, since it is a slow business crawling about these old houses. Therefore, if we are to get to the other side of the island before nightfall, it is time to go."

So off we went, keeping to the western side of the volcano, since there it did not seem to project so far into the flat lands. A while later we turned round and looked at the lake. There in the far distance our canoe appeared a mere speck, with two other specks, those of the pursuers, close upon its heels. As we watched, out of the mists on the Walloo shore came yet other specks, which were doubtless Walloo boats paddling to the rescue, for the priests' canoes gave up the chase and turned homewards.

"Issicore will have a very nice story to tell to the Lady Sabeela," said Hans; "but perhaps she will not kiss him after she has heard it."

"He was quite wise to go. What good could he have done by staying?" I answered, as we trudged on, adding, "Still, you are right, Hans, Issicore has changed."

It was a hard walk over rough ground, at least at first, for so soon as we got round the shoulder of the volcano the character of the country altered and we found ourselves in fertile, cultivated land that appeared to be irrigated.

"These fields must lie very low, Baas," said Hans, "since otherwise how do they get the lake water on to them?"

"I don't know," I replied crossly, for I was thinking of the sky water, which was beginning to descend in a steady drizzle upon ourselves. But all the same, the remark stuck in my mind and was useful afterwards. On we marched, till at length we entered a grove of palm trees that was traversed by a road.

Presently we came to the end of the road and found ourselves in a village of well-built stone houses, with one very large house in the middle of it, of which the back was set almost against the foot of the mountain. As there was nothing else to be done, we walked on into the village, at first without being observed, for everybody was under cover because of the rain. Soon, however, dogs began to bark, and a woman, looking out of the doorway of one of the houses, caught sight of us and screamed. A minute later men with shaven heads and wearing white, priestly-looking robes, appeared and ran towards us flourishing big spears.

"Hans," I said, "keep your rifle ready, but don't shoot unless you are obliged. In this case, words may serve us better than bullets."

"Yes, Baas, though I don't believe that either will serve us much."

Then he sat down on the trunk of a fallen tree that lay by the roadside, and waited, and I followed his example, taking the opportunity to light my pipe.

CHAPTER 9

The Feast

When they were within a few paces of us the men halted, apparently astonished at our appearance, which certainly did not compare favourably with their own, for they were all of the splendid Walloo type. Evidently what astonished them still more was the match with which I was lighting my pipe, and indeed the pipe itself, for although these people grew tobacco, they only took it in the form of snuff.

That match went out and I struck another, and at the sight of the sudden appearance of fire they stepped back a pace or two. At length one of them, pointing to the burning match, asked in the same tongue that was used by the Walloos, "What is that, O Stranger?"

"Magic fire," I answered, adding by an inspiration, "which I am bringing as a present to the great god Heu-Heu."

This information seemed to mollify them, for, lowering their spears, they turned to speak to another man who at this moment arrived upon the scene. He was a stout, fine-looking man of considerable presence, with a hooked nose and flashing black eyes. Also he wore a priestly cap upon his head and his white robes were broidered.

"Very big fellow, this, Baas," Hans whispered to me, and I nodded, observing as I did so that the other priests bowed as they addressed him.

"Dacha in person," thought I to myself, and sure enough Dacha it was.

He advanced and, looking at the wax match, said:

"Where does the magic fire of which you speak live, Stranger?"

"In this case covered with holy secret writing," I replied, holding before his eyes a box labelled "Wax Vestas, Made in England," and adding solemnly, "Woe be to him that touches it or him that bears it without understanding, for it will surely leap forth and consume that foolish man, O Dacha."

Now Dacha followed the example of his companions and stepped back a little way, remarking, "How do you know my name, and who sends this present of self-conceiving fire to Heu-Heu?"

"Is not the name of Dacha known to the ends of the earth?" I asked—a remark which seemed to please him very much; "yes, as far as his spells can travel, which is the sky and back again. As to who sends the magic fire, it is a great one, a wizard of the best, if not quite so good as Dacha, who is named Zikali, who is named the Opener-of-Roads, who is named the *Thing-that-should-never-have-been-born.*"

"We have heard of him," said Dacha. "His messengers were here in our father's day. And what does Zikali want of us, O Stranger?"

"He wants leaves of a certain tree that grows in Heu-Heu's garden, that is called the Tree of Visions, that he may mix them with his medicines."

Dacha nodded and so did the other priests. Evidently they knew all about the Tree of Visions, as I, or rather Zikali, had named it.

"Then why did he not come for them himself?"

"Because he is old and infirm. Because he is detained by great affairs. Because it was easier for him to send me, who, being a lover of that which is holy, was anxious to do homage to Heu-Heu and to make the acquaintance of the great Dacha."

"I understand," the priest replied, highly gratified, as his face showed. "But how are you named, O Messenger of Zikali?"

"I am named 'Blowing-Wind,' because I pass where I would, none seeing me come or go, and therefore am the best and swiftest of messengers. And this little one, this small but great-souled one with me"—here I pointed to the smirking Hans, who by now was quite alive to the humours of the situation and to its advantages from our point of view—"is named 'Lord-of-the-Fire' and 'Light-in-Darkness'" (this was true enough and worked in very well) "because it is he who is guardian of the magic fire" (also true, for he had half a dozen spare boxes in his pockets that he had stolen at one time or another) "of which, if he is offended, he can make enough to burn up all this island and everyone thereon; yes, more than is hidden in the womb of that mountain."

"Can he, by Heu-Heu!" said Dacha, regarding Hans with great respect.

"Certainly he can. Mighty though I be, I must be careful not to anger him lest myself I should be burnt to cinders."

At this moment a doubt seemed to strike Dacha, for he asked:

"Tell me, O Blowing-Wind and O Lord-of-Fire, how you came to this island? We observed a canoe manned with some of our rebellious subjects who serve that old usurper the Walloo, which is being hunted that they may be killed for the sacrilege in approaching this holy place. Were you perchance in that canoe?"

"We were," I answered boldly. "When we arrived at yonder town I met a lady, a very beautiful lady, named Sabeela, and asked her where dwelt the great Dacha. She said here—more, that she knew you and that you were the most beautiful and noblest of men, as well as the wisest. She said also that with some of her servants, including a stupid fellow called Issicore, of whom she never can be rid wherever she goes, she herself would paddle us to the island on the chance of see-ing your face again." (I may explain to you fellows that this lie was perfectly safe, as I knew Issicore and his people had escaped.) "So she brought us here and landed us that we might look at the ruined city before coming on to see you. But then your people roughly hunted her away, so that we were obliged to walk to your town. That is all."

Now Dacha became agitated. "I pray Heu-Heu," he said, "that those fools may not have caught and killed her with the others."

"I pray so also, since she is too fair to die," I answered, "who would be a lovely wife for any man. But stay, I will tell you what has chanced. Lord-of-the-Fire, make fire."

Hans produced a match and lit it on the seat of his trousers, which was the only part of him that was not damp. He held it in his joined hands and I stared at the flame, muttering. Then he whispered:

"Be quick, Baas, it is burning my fingers!"

"All is well," I said solemnly. "The canoe with Sabeela the Beautiful escaped your people, since other canoes, seven—no, eight of them," I corrected, studying the ashes of the match, also the blister on Hans's finger, "came out from the town and drove yours away just as they were overtaking the Lady Sabeela."

This was a most fortunate stroke, for at that moment a messenger arrived and gave Dacha exactly the same intelligence, which he punc-tuated with many bows.

"Wonderful!" said the priest. "Wonderful! Here we have magi-cians indeed!" and he stared at us with much awe. Then again a doubt struck him.

"Lord," he said, "Heu-Heu is the ruler of the savage Hairy People who live in the woods and are named Heuheuas after him. Now a tale has reached us that one of these people has been mysteriously killed with a noise by some strangers. Had you aught to do with her death, Lord?"

"Yes," I answered. "She annoyed the Lord-of-the-Fire with her attentions, so he slew her, as was right and proper. I cut off the finger of another who wished to shake hands with me when I had told him to go away."

"But how did he slay her, Lord?"

Now I may explain that there was one inhabitant of this place that greeted us with no cordiality at all, namely a large and particularly ferocious dog, that all this while had been growling round us and finally had got hold of Hans's coat, which it held between its teeth, still growling.

"Scheet! Hans, scheet seen dood!" ("Shoot! Hans, shoot him dead!") I whispered, and Hans, who was always quick to catch an idea, put his hand into his pocket where he kept his pistol, and pressing the muzzle against the brute's head, fired through the cloth, with the result that this dog went wherever bad dogs go.

Then there was consternation. Indeed, one of the priests fell down with fear and the others turned tail, all of them except Dacha, who stood his ground.

"A little of the magic fire!" I remarked airily, "and there is plenty more where that came from," at the same time, as though by accident, slapping Hans's pocket, which I saw was smouldering. "And now, noble Dacha, it is setting in wet and we are hungry. Be pleased to give us shelter and food."

"Certainly, Lord, certainly!" he exclaimed, and started off with us, keeping me well between himself and Hans, while the others, who had returned, followed with the dead dog.

Presently, recovering from his fear, he asked me whether the Lady Sabeela had said anything more about him.

"Only one thing," I answered: "that it was a pity that a maiden should be obliged to marry a god when there were such men as you in the world."

Here I stopped and watched the effect of my shot out of the corner of my eye.

His coarse but handsome face grew cunning, and he smacked his lips.

"Yes, Lord, yes," he said hurriedly. "But who knows? Things are not always what they seem, Lord, and I have noted that sometimes the faithful servant tithes the master's offering."

"By Jingo! I've got it!" thought I to myself. "*You*, my friend, are Heu-Heu, or at any rate his business part." But aloud, glancing at the redoubtable Hans, I only remarked something to the effect that Dacha's powers of observation were keen and that, like the Lord-of-the-Fire himself, as he said truly, things were not always what they seemed.

We crossed a bare platform of rock, to the right of which, beyond a space of garden, I observed the mouth of a large cave. At the edge of this platform a strange sight was to be seen, for here, just on the borders of the lake, at a distance of about twenty paces from each other, burned two columns of flame which hitherto had been hidden from us by the lie of the ground and trees, between which columns was a pillar or post of stone.

"The 'eternal fires,'" thought I to myself, and then inquired casually what they were.

"They are flames which have always burned in that place from the beginning; we do not know why," Dacha replied indifferently. "No rain puts them out."

"Ah!" I reflected, "natural gas coming from the volcano, such as I have heard of in Canada."

Then we turned to the right along the outer wall of the garden I have mentioned, and came to some fine houses, that, to my fancy, had a kind of collegiate appearance, all one-storied and built against the rock of the mountain. As a matter of fact, I was right, for these were the dwellings of the priests of Heu-Heu and their numerous female belongings. These priests, I should say, had their privileges, for whereas the people on the mainland for the most part married only one wife, they were polygamous, the ladies being supplied to them through spiritual pressure put upon the unfortunate Walloos, or, if that failed, by the simple and ancient expedient of kidnapping. Once, however, they had arrived upon the island and thus became dedicated to the god, they vanished so far as their kinsfolk were concerned, and never afterwards were they allowed to cross the water or even to attempt any communication with them. In short, those who became alive in Heu-Heu, became also dead to the world.

Hans and I were led to the largest of this group of houses, that abutting immediately on to the garden wall, the inhabitants of which apparently had already been advised of our coming by messenger, since we found them in a bustle of preparation. Thus I saw handsome, white-robed women flitting about and heard hurried orders being given. We were taken to a room where a driftwood fire had been lighted on the hearth because the night was damp and chill, at which we warmed and dried ourselves after we had washed. A while later a priest summoned us to eat and then retired outside the door awaiting our convenience.

"Hans," I said, "all has gone well so far; we are accepted as the friends of Heu-Heu, not as his enemies."

"Yes, Baas, thanks to the cleverness of the Baas about the matches and the rest. But what has the Baas in his mind?"

"This, Hans; that all must continue to go well, for remember what is our duty, namely, to save the lady Sabeela, if we can, as we have sworn to do. Now if we are to bring this about we must keep our eyes open and our wits sharp. Hans, I daresay that they have strange liquors in this place which will be offered to us to make us talk. But while we are here we must drink nothing but water. Do you understand, Hans?"

"Yes, Baas, I understand."

"And do you swear, Hans?"

Hans rubbed his middle reflectively, and replied:

"My stomach is cold, Baas, and I should like a glass of something more warming than water after all this damp and the sight of those stone men. Yet, Baas, I swear. Yes, I swear by your Reverend Father that I will only drink water, or coffee if they make it, which, of course, they don't."

"That is all right, Hans. You know that if you break your oath my Reverend Father will certainly come even with you, and so shall I in this world or the next."

"Yes, Baas. But will the Baas please remember that a gin bottle is not the only bait that the devil sets upon his hook. Different men have different tastes, Baas. Now if some pretty lady were to come and tell the Baas that he was oh! so beautiful and that she loved him, oh! ever so much, someone like that Mameena, for instance, of whom old Zikali is always talking as having been a friend of yours, will the Baas swear by his Reverend Father——"

"Cease from folly and be silent," I said majestically. "Is this the time and place to chatter of pretty women?"

Nevertheless, in myself I appreciated the shrewdness of Hans's repartee, and as a matter of fact an attempt was made to play off that trick on me, though if I am to get to the end of this story, I shall have no time to tell you about it.

Our compact sealed, we went through the door and found the priest waiting outside. He led us down a passage into a fine hall plentifully lit with lamps for now the night had fallen. Here several tables were spread, but we were taken to one at the head of the hall where we were welcomed by Dacha dressed in grand robes, and some other priests; also by women, all of them handsome and beautifully arrayed in their wild fashion, whom I took to be the wives of these worthies. One of them, I noticed, had a singular resemblance to the Lady Sabeela, although she appeared to be her elder by some years.

We sat down at the table in curious, carved chairs, and I found myself between Dacha and this lady, whose name, I discovered, was Dramana. The feast began, and I may say at once that it was a very fine feast, for it appeared that we had arrived upon a day of festival. Indeed, I had not eaten such a meal for years.

Of course, it was barbaric in its way. Thus the food was served in great earthenware dishes, already cut up; there were no knives or forks, the fingers of the eaters taking their place, and the plates consisted of the tough green leaves of some kind of water lily that grew in the lake, which were removed after each course and replaced by fresh ones.

Of its sort, however, it was excellent and included fish of a good flavour, kid cooked with spices, wild fowl, and a kind of pudding made of ground corn and sweetened with honey. Also, there was plenty of the strong native beer, which was handed round in ornamented earthenware cups that were, however, inlaid not with small diamonds and rubies, but with pearls found, I was informed, in the shells of freshwater mussels, and set in the clay when damp.

These pearls were irregular in shape and for the most part not large, but the effect of them thus employed, was very pretty. Still, some attained to a considerable size, since Dramana and other women wore necklaces of them bored and strung upon fibres. Without going into further details, I may say that this feast and its equipment convinced me more than ever that these people had once belonged to some unknown but highly civilized race which was now dying out in its last home and sinking into barbarism before it died.

In pursuance of our agreement Hans, who squatted on a stool behind me, for he would not sit at the table, and I, saying that we were bound by a vow to touch nothing else, drank water only, although I heard him groan each time the beer cups went round. I may add that this happened frequently, and the amount of liquor consumed was considerable, as became evident by the behaviour of the drinkers, many of whom grew more or less intoxicated, with the usual unpleasant results that I need not describe. Also they grew affectionate, for they threw their arms about the women and began to kiss them in a way which I considered improper. I observed, however, that the lady called Dramana drank but little. Also, as she sat between me and an extremely deaf priest who became sleepy in his cups, she was, of course, freed from any such unwelcome attentions.

All these circumstances, and especially the fact that Dacha was much occupied with a handsome female on his left, gave Dramana and myself opportunities of conversation which I think were welcome to her. After a few general remarks, presently she said in a low voice:

"I hear, Lord, that you have seen Sabeela, the daughter of the Walloo, chief of the mainland. Tell me of her, for she is my sister on whom I have not looked for a long while, for we never visit the mainland, and those who dwell there never visit us—unless they are obliged," she added significantly.

"She is beautiful but lives in great terror because she, who desires to be married to a man, must be married to a god," I answered.

"She does well to be afraid, Lord, for by you sits that god," and with a shiver of disgust and the slightest possible motion of her head, she indicated Dacha, who had become quite drunken and at the moment was engaged in embracing the lady on his left, who also seemed to be somewhat the worse for alcoholic wear, or to put it plainly, "half seas over."

"Nay," I answered, "the god I mean is called Heu-Heu, not Dacha."

"Heu-Heu, Lord! You will learn all about Heu-Heu before the night is over. It is Dacha whom she must marry."

"But Dacha is your husband, lady."

"Dacha is the husband of many, Lord," and she glanced at several of the most handsome women present, "for the god is liberal to his high priest. Since I was bound between the eternal fires there have been eight such marriages, though some of the brides have been handed on to others or sacrificed for crimes against the god, or attempting to escape, or for other reasons.

"Lord," she went on, dropping her voice till I could scarcely catch what she said, although my hearing is keen, "be warned by me. Unless you are indeed a god greater than Heu-Heu, and your companion also, whatever you may see or hear, lift neither voice nor hand. If you do, you will be rent to pieces without helping any one and perhaps bring about the death of many, my own among them. Hush! Speak of something else. He is beginning to watch us. Yet, O Lord, help me if you can. Yes, save me and my sister if you can."

I glanced round. Dacha, who had ceased embracing the lady, was looking at us suspiciously, as though he had caught some word. Perhaps Hans thought so as well, for he managed to make a great clatter, either by tumbling off his stool or dropping his drinking cup, I know not which, that drew away Dacha's half-drunken attention from us and prevented him from hearing anything.

"You see to find the Lady Dramana pleasant, O Lord Blowing-Wind," sneered Dacha. "Well, I am not jealous and I would give such guests of the best I have, especially when the god is going to be so good to me. Also the Lady Dramana knows better than to tell secrets and what happens here to those who do. So talk to her as much as you like, little Blowing-Wind, before you blow yourself away," and he leered at me in a manner that made me feel very uncomfortable.

"I was asking the Lady Dramana about the sacred tree of which the great wizard, Zikali, desires some of the leaves for his medicine," I said, pretending not to understand.

"Oh!" he answered, with a change of manner which suggested that his suspicions were in course of being dissipated, "oh, were you? I thought you were asking of other things. Well, there is no secret about that, and she shall show it to you tomorrow, if you like; also anything else you wish, for I and my brethren will be otherwise engaged. Meanwhile, here comes the Cup of Illusions that is brewed from the fruit of the tree of which you must taste though you be a water-drinker, yes, and the yellow dwarf, Lord-of-the-Fire, also, for in it we pledge the god into whose presence we must enter very soon."

I answered hurriedly that I was weary and would not trouble the god by paying my respects to him at present.

"All who come here must pass the god, Lord Blowing-Wind," he answered, glaring at me, and adding: "Either they must pass the god living, or, if they prefer it, they may pass him dead. Did not Zikali tell you that, O Blowing-Wind? Choose, then. Will you wait upon the god living, or will you wait upon him dead?"

Now I thought it was time to assert myself, and looking this ill-conditioned brute in the eyes, I said slowly:

"Who is this that talks to me of death, not knowing perchance that I am a lord of death? Does he seek such a fate as that which befell the hound without your doors? Learn, O Priest of Heu-Heu, that it is dangerous to use ill-omened words to me or to the Lord-of-the-Fire, lest we should answer them with lightnings."

I suppose that these remarks, or something in my eye, impressed him. At any rate, his manner became humble, almost servile indeed, especially as Hans had risen and stood at my side, holding in his extended hand the box of matches, at which all stared suspiciously. Well they might have stared, had they known that his other hand, innocently buried in his pocket, grasped the butt of an excellent Colt revolver. I should have told you, by the way, that as we could not bring them with us to the feast we had left our rifles hidden in our beds, loaded and full clocked, so that they would be sure to go off if any thief began to finger them.

"Pardon, Lord, pardon," said Dacha. "Could I wish to insult one so powerful? If I said aught to offend, why, this beer is strong."

I bowed benignantly, but remembered the old Latin saying to the effect that drink digs out the truth. Then, by way of changing the subject, he pointed to the end of the room. Here appeared two pretty women dressed in exceedingly light attire and with wreaths upon their heads, who bore between them a large bowl of liquor in which floated red flowers. (The whole scene, I should say, much resembled some picture I had seen of an ancient Roman—or perhaps it was Egyptian feast taken from a fresco.) They brought the bowl to Dacha, and with a simultaneous movement of their graceful forms lifted it up, whereon all of the company who were not too drunk rose, bowed towards the bowl and twice cried out together:

"The Cup of Illusions! The Cup of Illusions!"

"Drink," said Dacha to me. "Drink to the glory of Heu-Heu." Then observing that I hesitated, he added: "Nay, I will drink first to show that it is not poisoned," and muttering, "O Spirit of Heu-Heu, descend upon thy priest!" drink he did, a considerable quantity.

Then the women brought the bowl, which reminded me of the loving-cup at a Lord Mayor's feast, and held it to my lips. I took a pull at it, making motions of my throat as though it were a long one, though in reality I only swallowed a sip. Next it was handed to Hans to whom I murmured one Boer Dutch word over my shoulder. It was *"Beetje,"* which means "little," and as I turned my head to watch him, I think he took the advice.

After this the bowl, in which, I should add, the liquor was of a greenish colour and tasted something like Chartreuse, was taken from one to another till all present had drunk of it, the girls who bore it finishing up the little that was left.

This I saw, but after it I did not see much else for a while, for, small as had been my draught, the stuff went to my head and seemed to cloud my brain. Moreover, all kinds of queer visions, some of them not too desirable, sprang up in my mind, and with them a sense of vastness that was peopled by innumerable forms; beautiful forms, grotesque forms, forms of folk that I had known, now long dead, forms of others whom I had never seen, all of whom had this peculiarity, that they seemed to be staring at me with a strange intentness. Also these forms grouped themselves together and began to enact dramas of one kind or another, dramas of war and love and death that had all the vividness of a nightmare.

Presently, however, these illusions passed away and I remained filled with a great calm and a wonderful sense of well-being, also with my powers of observation rendered most acute.

Looking about me, I noted that all who had drunk seemed to be undergoing similar experiences. At first they showed signs of excitement; then they grew very still and sat like statues with their eyes fixed on vacancy, speaking not a word, moving not a muscle.

This state lasted quite a long time, till at length those who had drunk first appeared to awake, for they began to talk to each other in low tones. I noted that every sign of drunkenness had vanished; one and all they looked as sober as a whole Bench of Judges; moreover, their faces had grown solemn and their eyes seemed to be filled with some cold and fateful purpose.

CHAPTER 10

The Sacrifice

After a solemn pause, Dacha rose and said in an icy voice:

"I hear the god calling us. Let us pass into the presence of the god and make offering of the yearly sacrifice."

Then a procession was formed. Dacha and Dramana went first, Hans and I followed next, and after us came all who had been at the feast, to a total of about fifty people.

"Baas," whispered Hans, "after I had drunk that stuff, which was so nice and warming that I wished you had let me have more of it, your Reverend Father came and talked to me."

"And what did he say to you, Hans?"

"He said, Baas, that we were going into very queer company and had better keep our eyes skinned. Also that it would be wise not to interfere in matters that did not concern us."

I reflected to myself that within an hour I had received advice of the same sort from a purely terrestrial source, which was an odd coincidence, unless indeed Hans had overheard or absorbed it subconsciously. To him I only observed, however, that such mandates must be obeyed, and that whatever chanced he would do well to sit quite still, keeping his pistol ready, but only use it in case of absolute necessity to save ourselves from death.

The procession left the hall by a back entrance behind the table at which we had sat, and entered a kind of tunnel that was lit with lamps, though whether this was hollowed in the rock or built of blocks of stone I am not sure. After walking for about fifty paces down this tunnel, suddenly we found ourselves in a great cavern, also dimly lit with lamps, mere spots of light in the surrounding blackness.

Here all the priests, including Dacha, left us; at least, peering about, I could not see any of them. The women alone remained in the cave, where they knelt down singly and at a distance from each other like scattered worshippers in a dimly lit cathedral when no service is in progress.

Dramana, to whose charge we seemed to have been consigned, led us to a stone bench upon which she took her seat with us. I noted that she did not kneel and worship like the others. For a while we remained thus in silence, staring at the blackness in front where no lamps burned. It was an eerie business in such surroundings that I confess began to get upon my nerves. At length I could bear it no longer, and in a whisper asked Dramana whether anything was about to happen, and if so, what.

"The sacrifice is about to happen," she whispered back. "Be silent, for here the ears of the god are everywhere."

I obeyed, thinking it safer, and another ten minutes or so went by in an intolerable stillness.

"When does the play begin, Baas?" muttered Hans in my ear. (Once I had taken him to a theatre in Durban to improve his mind, and he thought that this was another, as indeed it was, if of an unusual sort.)

I kicked him on the shins to keep him quiet, and just then at a distance I heard the sound of chanting. It was a weird and melancholy music that seemed to swing backwards and forwards between two bands of singers, each strophe and antistrophe, if those are the right words, ending in a kind of wail or cry of despair which turned my blood cold. When this had gone on for a little while, I thought that I saw figures moving through the gloom in front of us. So did Hans, for he whispered:

"The Hairy People are here, Baas."

"Can you see them?" I asked in the same low voice.

"I think so, Baas. At any rate, I can smell them."

"Then keep your pistol ready," I answered.

A moment later I saw a lighted torch floating in the air in front of us, though the bearer of it I could not see. The torch was bent downwards, and I heard the sound of kindling taking fire. A little flame sprang up revealing a pile of logs arranged for burning, and beyond it the tall form of Dacha wearing a strange headdress and white, priest-like robes, different from those in which he had been clad at the feast. Between his hands, which he held in front of him, was a white human skull reversed, I mean that its upper part was towards the floor.

"Burn, Dust of Illusion, burn," he cried, "and show us our desires," and out of the skull he emptied a quantity of powder on to the pile of wood.

A dense, penetrating smoke arose which seemed to fill the cave,

115

vast though it was, and blot out everything. It passed away and was followed by a blaze of brilliant flame that lit up all the place and revealed
a terrific spectacle.

Behind the fire, at a distance of ten paces or so, was an awful object, an appalling black figure at least twelve feet in height, a figure of
Heu-Heu as we had seen him depicted in the Cave of the Berg, only
there his likeness was far too flattering. For this was the very image of
the devil as he might have been imagined by a mad monk, and from
his eyes shot a red light.

As I have said before, the figure was like to that of a huge gorilla
and yet no ape but a man, and yet no man but a fiend. There was the
long gray hair growing in tufts about the body. There was the great,
red, bushy beard. There were the enormous limbs and the long arms
and the hands with claws on them where the thumbs should be, and
the webbed fingers. The bull neck on the top of which sat the small
head that somehow resembled an old woman's with a hooked nose;
the huge mouth from which the baboon-like tusks protruded, the
round, massive, able-looking brow, the deepest glaring eyes, now alight
with red fire, the cruel smile—all were there intensified. There, too,
was the shape of a dead man into the breast of which the clawed foot
was driven, and in the left hand the head that had been twisted from
the man's body.

Oh! evidently the painter of the picture in the Berg can have been
no Bushman as once I had supposed, but some priest of Heu-Heu
whom fate or chance had brought thither in past ages, and who had
depicted it to be the object of his private worship. When I saw the
thing I gasped aloud and felt as though I should fall to the ground
through fear, so hellish was it. But Hans gripped my arm and said:

"Baas, be not afraid. It is not alive; it is but a thing of stone and
paint with fire set within."

I stared again; he was right.

*Heu-Heu was but an idol! Heu-Heu did not live except in the hearts of
his worshippers!*

Only out of what Satanic mind had this image sprung?

I sighed with relief as this knowledge came home to me, and began to observe details. There were plenty to be seen. For instance, on
either side of the statue stood a line of the hideous Hairy Folk, men
to the right and women to the left, with white cloths tied about their
middles. In front of this line behind their high priest, Dacha, were the
other priests, Heu-Heu's clergy, and on a raised table behind them just
at the foot of the base of the statue, which I now saw stood upon a

kind of pedestal so as to make it more dominant, lay a dead body, that of one of the Hairy women, as the clear light of the flame revealed.

"Baas," said Hans again, "I believe that is the gorilla-woman I shot in the river. I seem to know her pretty face."

"If so, I hope we shall not join her on that table presently," I answered.

After this suddenly I went mad; everybody went mad. I suppose that the vapour from that accursed powder had got into our brains. Had not Dacha called it the "Dust of Illusions"? Certainly, of illusions there were plenty, most of them bad, like those of a nightmare.

Still, before they possessed me completely, I had the sense to understand what was happening to me and to grip hold of Hans, who I saw was going mad also, and command him to sit quiet. Then came the illusions which really I can't describe to you. You fellows have read of the effects of opium smoking; well, it was that kind of thing, only worse.

I dreamed that Heu-Heu got off his pedestal and came dancing down the hall, also that he bent over me and kissed me on the forehead. In fact, I think it was Dramana who kissed me, for she, too, had gone mad. Everything that I had done bad in my life re-enacted itself in my mind and, all put together, seemed to make me a sinner indeed, because you see the good was entirely omitted. The Hairy Folk began an infernal dance before the statue; the women round us raved and shouted with extraordinary expressions upon their faces; the priests waved their arms and set up yells of adoration as did those of Baal in the Old Testament. In short, literally there was the devil to pay.

Yet strangely enough it was all wildly, deliriously exciting and really I seemed to enjoy it. It shows how wicked we must be at bottom. A sight of hell while you remain on the *terra firma* of our earth is not uninteresting, even though you be temporarily affected by its atmosphere.

Presently the nightmare came to an end, suddenly as it had commenced, and I woke to find my head on Dramana's shoulder, or hers on mine, I forget which, with Hans engaged in kissing my boot under the impression that it was the chaste brow of some black maiden whom he had known about thirty years before. I kicked him on his snub nose, whereon he rose and apologized, remarking that this was the strongest *dacca*—the hemp which the natives smoke with intoxicating effects—that he had ever tasted.

"Yes," I answered, "and now I understand where Zikali's magic comes from. No wonder he wants more of the leaves of that tree and thought it worth while to send us so far to get them."

Then I ceased talking, for something in the atmosphere of the place absorbed my attention. A sudden chill seemed to have fallen upon it and its occupants who, in strange contrast to their recent excesses, now appeared to be possessed by the very spirit of Mrs. Grundy. There they stood, exuding piety at every pore and gazing with rapt countenance at the hideous image of their god. Only to me those countenances had grown very cruel. It was as though they awaited the consummation of some dreadful drama with a kind of cold joy, which, of course, may have been an aftermath of their unholy intoxication. It was the scene at the feast repeated but with a difference. There they had been drunken with liquor and sobered by the potent stuff they had swallowed after it; now they had been made drunken with fumes and were sobered by I knew not what. Their master Satan, perhaps!

The fire still burnt brightly though it gave off no more of these fumes, being fed I suppose with natural fuel, and by the light of it I saw that Dacha was addressing the image with impassioned gestures. What he said I do not know, for my ears were still buzzing and of it I could hear nothing. But presently he turned and pointed to us and then began to beckon.

"What is it he wants us to do?" I asked of Dramana who now was seated at my side, a perfect model of propriety.

"He says that you must come up and make your offering to the god."

"What offering?" I asked, thinking that perhaps it would be of a painful nature.

"The offering of the sacred fire that the Lord of Fire," and she pointed to Hans, "bears about with him."

I was puzzled for a moment till Hans remarked:

"I think she means the matches, Baas."

Then I understood, and bade him produce a new box of Best Wax Vestas and hold it out in his hand. Thus armed we advanced and, passing round the fire, bowed, as the Bible potentate whom the Prophet cured bargained he should be allowed to do in the House of Rimmon, to the beastly effigy of Heu-Heu. Then in obedience to the muttered directions of Dacha, Hans solemnly deposited the box of matches upon the stone table, after which we were allowed to retreat.

Anything more ridiculous than this scene it is impossible to imagine. I suppose that its intense absurdity was caused, or at any rate accentuated by its startling and indeed horrible contrasts. There was the towering and demoniacal idol; there were the rogue priests, their faces alight with a fierce fanaticism; there, looking only half human, were the long lines of savage Hairy Folk; there was the burning fire reflecting itself to the farthest recesses of the cavern and showing the forms of the scattered worshippers.

Finally there was myself, a bronzed and tattered individual, and the dirty, abject-looking Hans holding in his hand that absurd box of matches which finally he deposited in the exact middle of the stone table about six inches from the swollen body of the aboriginal whom he had shot in the river. In those vast surroundings this box looked so lonely and so small that the sight of it moved me to internal convulsions. Shaking with hysterical laughter I returned to my seat as quickly as I could, dragging Hans after me, for I saw that his case was the same, although fortunately it is not the custom of Hottentots to burst into open merriment.

"What will Heu-Heu do with the matches, Baas?" asked Hans. "Surely there must be plenty of fire where he is, Baas."

"Yes, lots," I replied with energy, "but perhaps of another sort."

Then I observed that Dacha was pointing to the right and that the eyes of all present were fixed in that direction.

"The sacrifice comes," murmured Dramana, and as she spoke a woman appeared, a tall woman covered with a white robe or veil, who was led forward by two of the Hairy People. She was brought to the front of the table on which lay the body and the matches, and there stood quite still.

"Who is this?" I asked.

"Last year's bride, with whom the priest has done and passes on into the keeping of the god," answered Dramana with a stony smile.

"Do you mean that they are going to kill the poor thing?" I said, horrified.

"The god is about to take her into his keeping," she replied enigmatically.

At this moment one of the savage attendants snatched away the veil which draped the victim, revealing a very beautiful woman clad in a white kirtle which was cut low upon her breast and reached to her knees. Tall and stately, she stood quite still before us, her black hair streaming down upon her shoulders. Then, as though at some signal, all the women in the audience stood up and screamed:

"Wed her to the god! Wed her to the god and let us drink of the cup that through her unites us to the god!"

Two of the Hairy Folk drew near to the girl, each of whom had something in his hand, though what it was at the moment I could not see, and stood still, as though waiting for a sign. Then followed a pause during which I glanced about me at the faces of the women, made hideous by the unholy passions that raged within them, who stood with outstretched arms pointing at the victim. They looked horrible, and I hated them, all except Dramana, who, I noted with relief, had not cried aloud and did not stretch out her hands like the rest.

What was I about to see? Some dreadful act of voodooism such as negroes practise in Haiti and on the West Coast? Perhaps. If so, I could not bear it. Whatever the risk might be I could not bear it; almost automatically my hand grasped the stock of my revolver.

Dacha seemed as though he were about to say something, a word of doom mayhap. I measured the distance between me and himself with my eyes, calculating where I should aim to put a bullet through his large head and give the god a sacrifice which it did not expect. Indeed, had he spoken such a word, without doubt I should have done it, for as you fellows know I am handy with a pistol, and probably, as a result, never have lived to tell you this story.

As this juncture, however, the victim waved her arms and said in a loud, clear voice:

"I claim the ancient right to make my prayer to the god before I am given to the god."

"Speak on," said Dacha, "and be swift."

She turned and curtseyed to the hideous idol, then wheeled about again and addressed it in form although really she was speaking to the audience.

"O Fiend Heu-Heu," she said in a voice filled with awful scorn and bitterness, "whom my people worship to their ruin, I who was stolen from my people come to thee because I would have none of yonder high-priest and therefore must pay the price in blood. So be it, but ere I come I have something to tell these priests who grow fat in wickedness. Hearken! A spirit is in me, giving me sight. I see this place a sea of water, I see flames bursting through the water, turning thy hideous effigy to dust and burning up thy evil servants, so that not one of them remains. The Prophecy! The Prophecy! Let all who hear me bethink them of the ancient prophecy, for at length its hour is fulfilled!"

Then she stared towards Hans and myself, waving her arms, and I thought was about to address us. If so, she changed her mind and did not.

So far the priests and the congregation had listened in the silence of amazement, or perhaps of fear. Now, however, a howl of furious execration broke from them, and when it died down I heard Dacha shouting:

"Let this blaspheming witch be slain. Let the sacrifice be accomplished!"

The two savages stepped towards her, and now I saw that what they held in their hands were coils of rope with which doubtless she was to be bound. If so, she was too swift for them, for with a great bound she sprang upon the table where lay the body of the Hairy woman and the box of matches. Next instant I saw a knife flashing in her hand; I suppose it had been concealed somewhere in her dress. She lifted it and plunged it to her heart, crying as she did so:

"My blood be on you, Priests of Heu-Heu!"

Then she fell down there upon the table and was still.

In the hush that followed I heard Hans say:

"That was a brave lady, Baas, and doubtless all she said will come true. May I shoot that priest, Baas, or will you?"

"No," I began, but before I could get out another word my voice was overwhelmed by a tumult of shouts, "The god has been robbed of his sacrifice and is hungry. Let the strangers be offered to the god."

These and other like things said the shouts.

Dacha looked towards us, hesitating, and I saw that it was time to act. Rising, I called out:

"Know, O Dacha, that before one hand is laid upon us I will make you as my companion, Lord-of-the-Fire, made the dog without your doors."

Evidently Dacha believed me, for he grew quiet humble. "Have no fear, Lords," he said. "Are you not our honoured guests and the messengers of a Great One? Go in peace and safety."

Then at his command or sign the brightly burning fire was scattered, so that the cave grew almost dark, especially as some of the lights had gone out.

"Follow me swiftly—swiftly," said Dramana, and taking my hand she led me away through the gloom.

Presently we found ourselves in the passage, though for aught I know it was another passage; at any rate, it led to the hall where we had feasted. This was now empty, although in it lights still burned. Crossing it, Dramana conducted us back to the house, where a hasty examination showed us that our rifles were just as we had left them; nothing had been touched. Here, seeing that we were quite alone, for all had gone to the sacrifice, I spoke to her.

"Lady Dramana," I said, "does my heart tell me truly or do I only dream that you desire to depart from out of the shadow of Heu-Heu?"

She glanced about her cautiously, then answered in a low voice:

"Lord, there is nothing that I desire so much—unless perchance it be death," she added with a sigh. "Hearken! Seven years ago I was bound upon the Rock of Offering, where my sister will stand tomorrow, having been chosen by the god and dedicated to him by the mad terror of my people, which means, Lord, that I had been chosen by Dacha and dedicated to Dacha."

"Why, then, do you still live?" I asked, "seeing that she who was chosen last year must be sacrificed this year?"

"Lord, am I not the daughter of the Walloo, the ruler of the people of the Mainland, and might not the title to that rule be acquired through me while I breathe? It is not the best of titles, it is true, because I was born of a lesser wife of my father, the Walloo, whereas my sister Sabeela is born of the great wife. Still, at a pinch, it might serve. That is why I still live."

"What then is Dacha's plan, Lady Dramana?

"It stands thus, Lord. Hitherto for many generations, it is said since the great fire burned upon the island and destroyed the city, there have been two governments in this land: that of the priests of Heu-Heu, who govern the minds of its people, also the wild Wood Folk, and that of the Walloos, who govern their bodies and are kings by ancient right. Now Dacha, who, when he is not lost in drink or other follies, is farseeing and ambitious, purposes to rule both minds and bodies and it may be to bring in new blood from outside our country and once more to build up a great people, such as tradition tells we were in the beginning, when we came here from the north or from the west. He does but wait until he has married my sister, the lawful heiress to the Walloo, my father, who by now must be an old and feeble man, to strike his blow, and in her name to seize the government and power.

"The priests, as you have seen, are but few and cannot do this of their own strength, but they command all the savage folk who are called the Children of Heu-Heu. Now these people are very angry because the other day one of their women was killed upon the river, she who lay on the altar before the god, and this they think was done by the Walloo, not understanding that it was your servant, the yellow man there, who slew her. Or if they understand, they believe that he did so by the order of Issicore who, we hear, is betrothed to my sister Sabeela.

"Therefore they wish to make a great war upon the Walloo under the guidance of the priests of Heu-Heu, whom they call their Father, because his image is like to them. Already their mankind are gathering on the island, rowing themselves hither upon logs or bundles of reeds, and by tomorrow night all will be collected. Then, after what is called the Holy Marriage, when my sister Sabeela has been brought as an offering by the Walloo and bound to the pillar between the Everlasting Fires, led by Dacha they will attack the city on the mainland, which they dare not do alone. It will surrender to them, and Dacha will kill my old father and the lord Issicore who stands next to him, and any of the ancient blood who cling to him, and cause himself to be declared Walloo. After this his purpose is to poison the Forest Folk as he well knows how to do and as I have told you, perhaps to bring new blood into the land which is rich and wide, and found a kingdom."

"A big scheme," I said, not without admiration, for on hearing it, to tell the truth, I began to conceive a certain respect for that villain Dacha, who, at any rate, had ideas and presented a striking contrast to the helpless and superstition-ridden inhabitants of the mainland.

"But, Lady," I went on, "what is to happen to me and to my companion who is named Lord-of-the-Fire?"

"I do not know, Lord, who have had little talk with Dacha since you came, or with any to whom he reveals his secrets. I think, however, that he is afraid of you, believing you to be magicians, or in league with the greatest of magicians, the prophet Zikali, who dwells in the south, with whom the priests of Heu-Heu communicate from time to time. Also it is probable that he holds that you may be able to help him to build up a nation and that therefore he would wish to keep you in his service in this country, only killing you if you try to escape. On the other hand, when the Wood Folk come to understand that it was really you, or one of you, who killed the woman, they may clamour for your lives. Then, if he thinks it wisest to please them, at the great feast which is called the finishing of the Holy Marriage, you may be tied upon the altar as a Sacrifice while the blood is drained from you, to be drunk by the priests with the lips of Heu-Heu. Perhaps that matter will be settled at the Council of the Priests tomorrow, Lord."

"Thank you," I said, "never mind the details."

"Meanwhile," she went on, "for the present you are safe. Indeed I, who by my rank am the Mistress of Households, have been commanded to honour you in every way, and tomorrow, when the priests are engaged in preparations for the Holy Marriage, to show you all that you would see, also to provide you with boughs from the Tree of Illusions which Zikali the prophet desires."

"Thank you," I said again, "we shall be most happy to take a walk with you, even if it rains, as I think from the sounds upon the roof it is doing at present. Meanwhile, I understand that you wish to get out of this place and to save your sister. Well, I may as well tell you at once, Lady Dramana, that my companion, who chooses to assume the shape of a yellow dwarf, and I, who choose to be as I am, *are* in fact great magicians with much more power than we seem to possess. Therefore, it is quite possible that we may be able to help you in all ways, and to do other things more remarkable. Yet we may need your aid, since generally that which is mighty works through that which is small, and what I want to know is whether we can count upon it."

"To the death, Lord," she answered.

"So be it, Dramana, for know that if you fail us certainly you will die."

CHAPTER 11

The Sluice Gate

All that night it poured, not merely in the usual tropical torrent, but positively in waterspouts. Seldom in my life have I heard such rain as that which fell upon the roof of the house where we were, which must have been wonderfully well built, for otherwise it would have given away. When we rose in the morning and went to the door to look out, all the place was swimming and a solid wall of water seemed to stretch from heaven to earth.

"I think there will be a flood after this, Baas," remarked Hans.

"I think so, too," I answered, "and if we were not here I wish that it might be deep enough to drown every human brute upon this island."

"It cannot do that, Baas, because at the worst they would climb up the mountain, though it might get into the cave and give Heu-Heu a washing—which he needs."

"If it got into the cave, it would probably get into the mountain as well," I began—then stopped, for an idea occurred to me.

I had noticed that this cave sloped downwards somewhat steeply, I mean into the base of the mountain and towards its centre. Probably, in its origin it was a vent blown through the rock at some time in the past when the volcano was very active, which, for aught I knew, re-mained unblocked, or only slightly blocked. Suppose now that a great volume of water ran down that cave and vanished into the interior of the mountain, was it not probable that something unusual would happen? The volcano was still alive—this I knew from the smoke that hung above it, also by the stream of red-hot lava that we had seen trickling down its southern face—and fire and water do not agree well together. They make steam, and steam expands. This thought took such a persistent hold on me that I began to wonder whether it did not partake of the nature of an inspiration. However, I said nothing of it to Hans, who, being a savage, did not understand such matters.

A little later food was brought to us by one of the serving priests. With it came a message from Dacha to the effect that he grieved he could not wait on us that day as he had many matters to which he must attend, but that the Lady Dramana would do so shortly and show us all there was to be seen, if the rain permitted.

In due course she arrived—alone, as I had hoped she would—and at once began to talk of the rainfall of the previous night, which she said was such as had never been known in their country. She added that all the priests had been out that morning, dragging the great stone sluice gate into its place so as to keep out the water of the lake, lest the arable land should be flooded and the crops destroyed.

I told her that I was much interested in such matters, and asked questions about this sluice which she could not answer as she knew little of its working. She said, however, that she would show it to me so that I might study the system.

I thanked her and inquired whether the lake had risen much. She answered, Not yet, but that probably it would do so during the day and the following night when it became filled with the water brought down by the flooded river which ran into it from the country to the north. At any rate, this was feared, and it had been thought best to set the sluice in place, a difficult task because of its weight. Indeed, a woman who had gone to help out of curiosity had been caught by a lever—I understood that was what she meant—and killed. She still lay by the sluice, since it was not lawful for the priests of Heu-Heu or their servants to touch a dead body between the Feast of Illusions, which had been held on the previous night, and the Feast of Marriage, which would be held on the night of the morrow, when, she added significantly, they often touched plenty.

"It is a Feast of Blood, then?" I said.

"Yes, Lord, a Feast of Blood, and I pray that it may not be of your blood also."

"Have no fear of that," I answered airily, though in truth I felt much depressed. Then I asked her to tell me exactly what was going to happen as to the delivery of the "Holy Bride."

"This, Lord," she said. "Before midnight, when the moon should be at its fullest, a canoe comes, bringing the bride from the City of the Walloos. Priests receive her and tie her to the pillar that stands on the Rock of Offerings between the Everlasting Fires. Then the canoe goes and waits at a distance. The priests go also and leave the bride alone. I know it all, Lord, for I have been that bride. So she stands until the first ray of the rising sun strikes upon her. Then from the mouth of the cave comes out the high priest dressed in skins to resemble the image of the god, and followed by women and some of the Hairy savage folk shouting in triumph. He looses the bride, and they bear her in the cave, and there, Lord, she vanishes."

"Do you think that she will be brought at all, Dramana?"

"Certainly she will be brought, since if my father, the Walloo, or Issicore, or any refused to send her, they would be killed by their own people, who believe that then disaster would overtake them. Unless you can save her by your arts, Lord, my sister Sabeela must become the wife of Heu-Heu, which means the wife of Dacha."

"I will think the matter over," I said. "But if I make up my mind to help, am I right in understanding that you also desire to escape from this island?"

"Lord, I have told you so already, and I will only add this. Dacha hates me and when I have served his purpose and he has in his hands Sabeela, the true heiress to the chieftainship over our people unless first I tread her road, certainly it will be my lot to stand where that poor woman stood last night, who slew herself to escape worse things. Oh, Lord, save me if you can!"

"I will save you—if I can," I replied, and I meant it—almost as much as I meant to save myself.

Then I impressed upon her that she must obey me in all things without question, and this she swore to do. Also I asked her if she could provide us with a canoe.

"It is impossible," she replied. "Dacha is clever; he has bethought him that you might depart in a canoe. Therefore, every one of them has been moved round to the other side of the island where they are kept under watch of the Savage Folk. That is why he gives you leave to roam about the place, because he knows that you cannot leave it, unless you have wings, for the lake is too wide for any man to swim, and if it were not, the Walloo shore is haunted by crocodiles."

Now, my friends, as you may guess, this was a blow indeed. However, I kept my countenance and said that as this was the case something else must be arranged, only asking casually if there were any crocodiles about this part of the island coast. She answered that there were none, because, as she supposed, the flames of the Everlasting Fires, or some smell from the smoke of the mountain, frightened them away.

Next, as the torrents of rain had ceased, at any rate for a while, I suggested that we should go out, and we did so. Also I did not mind much about the weather, as to protect us from it she had brought with her for our use and her own three of the strangest waterproofs that ever I saw. These consisted of two giant leaves from some kind of water lily that grew on the borders of the lake, sewn together, with a hole at the top of the leaves, where the stalk comes, for the wearer's head to go through, and two openings left for his arms. For the rest no mackintosh ever turned wet so well as did these leaves, the only drawback about them, as I was informed, being that they must be renewed once in every three days.

Arrayed in these queer garments we went out in rain that here we should call fairly heavy, though it was but the merest drizzle compared to what had gone before. This rain I may explain, had great advantages so far as we were concerned, seeing that in it not even the most curious woman put her nose outside her own door. So it came about that we were able to examine the village of the priests of Heu-Heu quite unobserved and at our leisure.

This settlement was small since there were never more than fifty priests in the college, if so it may be called, to whom, of course, must be added their wives and women, on an average, perhaps, of three or four per man.

The odd thing was that there seemed to be no children and no old people. Either offspring did not arrive and folk died young upon the island, or in both cases they were made away with, perhaps as sacrifices to Heu-Heu. I am sorry to say that in the pressure of great dangers I do not remember making any inquiry upon the point, or if I did I cannot recall the answer given. It was only afterwards that I reflected upon this strange circumstance. The fact remains that on the island there were no young and no aged. Another possible explanation, by the way, is that both may have been exported to the mainland.

Here I will add that with the exception of Dramana and a few discarded wives who may have been doomed to sacrifice, the women were fiercer bigots and more cruel votaries of Heu-Heu than were the men themselves. So, indeed, I had observed when I sat among them at the Feast of Illusions in the cave.

For the rest they all lived in dwellings such as that which was given to us, and were waited upon by servants or slaves from the savage race that was called Heuheua. Low as these Heuheua were and disgusting as might be their appearance, like our South African Bushmen, they were clever in their way, and, when trained, could do many things. Also they were faithful to the commands of their god Heu-Heu, or rather to those of his priests, though they hated the Walloos, from whom these priests sprang, and waged continual war against them.

Soon we had left the houses and were among the cultivated lands, all of which Dramana informed us were worked by the Heuheua slaves. These laboured here in gangs for a year at a time, and then were returned to their women in the forests on the mainland, for, except as servants, none of them were allowed upon the island. Those lands were extraordinarily fertile, as was shown by the crops on them, which, although much beaten down by the torrential rain, were now ready for harvest. They were enclosed by a kind of sea wall built of blocks of lava and must at some time have been reclaimed from the muddy shallows of the lake, which accounted for their richness. Everywhere about them ran irrigation channels that were used in the dry sowing season and controlled by the sluice gate that has been mentioned. That is all I have to say about the gardens, except that the existence of this irrigation system is to my mind another proof that these Walloos sprang originally from some highly civilized race. Their fields extended to that extremity of the island which was nearest to the Walloo coast, and I know not how far in the other direction, for I did not go there.

Standing upon this point we saw in the distance a number of moving specks upon the water. I asked Dramana if they were hippopotami, and she answered:

"No, Lord, they are the Hairy Folk who, in obedience to the summons of the god, cross the lake upon bundles of reeds that they may be ready to fight in the coming war against the Walloo. Already there are hundreds of them gathered upon the farther side of the mountain, and by tonight all their able-bodied men will have come, leaving only the females, the aged, and the children hidden away in the depths of the forests. On the third day from now they will paddle back across the lake, led by the priests under the command of Dacha, and attack Walloo."

"A great deal may happen in three days," I said, and dropped the subject.

We walked back towards the village and the cave mouth by the sea wall, upon the top of which ran a path, and thus at last came to the Rock of Offering, upon each side of which burned the two curious columns of flame that, I took it, were fed with natural gas generated in the womb of the volcano. They were not very large fires—at any rate, when I saw them—the flame may have been about eight or ten feet high, no more. But there they burned, and had done so, Dramana said, from the beginning of things. Between them, at a little distance, stood a post of stone with rings also of stone, to which the bride was bound. I noted that from these rings hung new ropes placed there to serve as the bonds of Sabeela during the coming night.

Having seen all there was to see on this Rock of Offering, includ-ing the steps by which the victim was landed, we went on to a long shed with a steep reed roof, which contained the machinery, if so I can call it, that regulated the irrigation sluice. It had a heavy wooden door which Dramana unlocked with an odd-shaped stone key that she produced from a bag she was wearing. This key, she told us, had been given to her by Dacha with strict orders that she was to return it after we had examined the place, should we wish to do so.

As it happened there was a good deal to examine. Near one end of the shed the main irrigation canal, which may have been twelve feet wide, passed beneath it. Here, under the centre of the roof, was a pit of which the water that stood in it prevented us from seeing the depth. On either side of this pit were perpendicular grooves cut in the solid rock, very deep grooves that were exactly filled by a huge slab of dressed stone six or seven inches thick. When this stone, or the upper part of it, was lifted out of the rock floor of the channel, where normally it stood in its niche, forming part of the bed of the channel, it entirely cut off the inflow of water from the lake, and was, moreover, tall enough to stop any possible additional inflow at a time of flood.

Perhaps I can make the thing clear in this way. When Good and I were last in London together we went to Madame Tussaud's and saw the famous guillotine that was used in the French Revolution. The knife of that guillotine, you will remember, was raised between uprights, and when brought into action, let fall again to the bottom of the apparatus, severing the neck of the victim in its course. Now imagine that those uprights were the rock walls of the pit, and that the knife, instead of being but a narrow thing, were a great sheet of steel, or rather stone. Then, when it was drawn to the top of the uprights from the niche at the bottom, it would entirely fill the space to the head of the grooves, and none of the water that normally passed over it could flow between the uprights, or rather walls, because the sheet of stone barred its passage. Now do you understand?

* * * * * * * *

As Good, who was stupid about such matters, looked doubtful, Allan went on:

* * * * * * * *

"Perhaps a better illustration would be that of a portcullis; even you, Good, have seen a portcullis, which, by the way, must mean a door in a groove. Imagine a subterranean or rather subaqueous, portcullis that, when it was desired to shut it, rose in its grooves from below instead of falling from above, and you will have an exact idea of the water door of the priests of Heu-Heu. I'd draw it for you if it wasn't so late."

"I see now," said Good, "and I suppose they wound the thing up with a windlass."

"Why not say with a donkey engine at once, Good? Windlasses had not occurred to the Walloos. No, they acted on a simpler and more ancient plan. They lifted it with a lever. Near the top of this slab of rock, or water door, was drilled a hole. Through this hole passed a bolt of stone, of which the ends went into the cut-out base of the lever, thus forming a kind of hinge. The lever itself was a bar of stone—evidently they would not trust to wood which rots—massive and about twenty feet long, so as to obtain the best possible purchase. When the door was quite down in its niche at the bottom of the bed of the channel, the end of the lever naturally rose high into the air, almost to the top of the pitched roof of the shed, indeed."

****

When it was desired to raise the door so as to regulate the amount of water passing into the irrigation channel beyond, or to cut if off altogether in case of flood, the lever was pulled down by ropes that were tied to its end by the strength of a number of men and that end was passed into, or rather under, one or other of half a dozen hooks of stone hollowed into a face of solid rock. Here, of course, it remained immovable until it was released, again by the united strength of a number of men, and flew back to the roof, letting the portcullis slab drop into its bed or groove at the bottom of the channel, thus admitting the lake water.

On the present occasion, as a great flood was anticipated, this slab was raised to its full extent, and when I saw it, the top of it stood five or six feet above the level of the water, while the end of the handle of the lever was made fast beneath the lowest hook of rock within a foot of the floor.

Hans and I examined this primitive but effective apparatus for preventing inundations very carefully. Supposing, thought I, that any one wanted to release that lever so that the door fell and water rushed in over it, how could it be done? Answer: it could only be done by the application of the united force of a great number of men pressing on the end of the lever till it was pushed clear of the point of the hook, when naturally it would fly upwards and the door would fall. Or, secondly, by breaking the lever in two, when, of course, the same thing

131

would happen. Now two men, that is Hans and myself, could not possibly release this beam of stone from its hook; indeed, I doubt whether ten men could have done it. Nor could two men possibly break that beam of stone. Perhaps, if they had suitable marble saws, such as workers in stone use, and plenty of time, they might cut it in two, although it seemed to be made of a kind of rock that was as hard as iron. But we had no saw. Therefore, so far as we were concerned the task was impossible; that idea must be dismissed.

Still, there is a way out of most difficulties if only it can be hit upon. My own mental resources were exhausted, it is true, but Hans remained, and possibly he might have some suggestion of value to make. He was a curious creature, Hans, and often his concentrated primitive instincts led him more directly to the mark than did all my civilized reasonings.

So speaking without emphasis in Dutch, for I did not wish Dramana to guess my internal excitement, I put the problem to Hans in these words:

"Supposing and you and I, Hans, with none to help, except perhaps this woman, found it necessary to break that bar of stone and cause the water gate to fall, so as to let in the lake flood over it, how could we do it with such means as we have in this place?"

Hans stared about him, twiddling his hat in his usual vacuous fashion, and remarked, "I don't know, Baas."

"Then find out, for I want to learn if your conclusions agree with my own," I answered.

"I think that if they agree with the Baas's, they will agree with nothing at all," said Hans, delivering this shrewd and perfectly accurate shot with such a wooden expression of utter stupidity that I could have kicked him.

Next, without more words, he removed himself from my neighbourhood and began to examine the lever in a casual fashion, especially the hook of rock which held it in its place. Presently he remarked in Arabic, so that Dramana might understand, that he wanted to see how deep the pit was, which we could not do from the floor of the shed, and instantly climbed up the slope of the beam-like lever with all the agility of a monkey, and sat himself, cross-legged, on the top of it, just below the stone hinge that I have described. Here he remained for a while, apparently staring into the darkness of the hole or pit on the farther side of the stone slab, where, of course, it was almost empty, as the door cut off the water from the irrigation channel on the island side.

"That hole is too dark to see into," he said, presently, and swarmed down the shaft again. Then he called my attention to the body of the dead woman who Dramana had told us was struck by the lever and killed while it was being dragged into place, which lay almost out of sight in the shadow by the wall of the shed. We went to look at her. She was a tall woman, handsome, like all these people, and young. Outwardly she showed no signs of injury, for her long white robe was unstained. I suppose that she had been crushed between the lever and the hook, or perhaps struck in the side of the head as it was being swung into place. Whilst we were examining the corpse of this unfortunate, Hans said to me, still speaking in Dutch, "Does the Baas remember that we have two pound tins of the best rifle powder in our bag and that he scolded me because I did not take them out when we left the house of the Walloo, saying that it was foolish to bring them with us as they would be quite useless to us on the island?"

I replied that I had some recollection of the incident, and that, as a matter of fact, they had been heavy to carry. Then Hans proceeded to set a riddle in his irritating and sententious way, asking, "Who does the Baas think knows most about things that are to happen—the Baas or the Baas's Reverend Father in Heaven?"

"My father, I presume, Hans," I replied airily.

"The Baas is right. The Baas's father in the sky knows much more than the Baas, but sometimes I think that Hans knows better than either, at any rate, here on the earth."

I stared at the little wretch, rendered speechless by his irreverent impudence, but he went on unabashed:

"I did not forget to leave that powder behind, Baas; I brought it with me thinking that it might be useful, because with powder you can blow up men and other things. Also, I did not wish it to stay where we might never see it again."

"Well, what about the powder?" I asked.

"Nothing much, Baas. At least, only this. These Walloo do not bore stones very well; they make the holes too big for what has to go through them. That in the water gate is so large that there would be room to put two pound flasks of powder beneath the pin, so that the strain lifts it up to the top of the hole."

"And what would be the use of putting two flasks of powder in such a place?" I inquired carelessly, for at the moment I was thinking about the dead woman.

"None at all, Baas; none at all. Only I thought the Baas asked me how we could loose that stone arm. If two pounds of powder were put into the hole, covered with a little mud, and fired, I think that they would blow out the bit of rock at the top of the hole, or break the pin, or both. Then, as there would be nothing to hold it, the stone door would fall down and the lake would come in and water the fields of the priests of Heu-Heu, if in his wisdom and kindness the Baas thinks they want it at harvest time, and after so much rain."

"You little wretch," I said; "you infernal, clever little wretch! Hang me if I don't think you have got hold of the right end of the stick this time. Only the business will take a lot of thinking out and arrangement."

"Yes, Baas, and we had better do that in the house, which, as the Baas knows, is quite close, only about a hundred paces away. Let us get out of this place, Baas, before the lady begins to smell rats; only, as you go, take a good squint at that hole in the top of the stone door and the rock pin that goes through it."

Then Hans, who all this while had been staring at the body of the woman and apparently talking about her, bowed towards it, remarking in Arabic, "Allah, I mean Heu-Heu, receive her into his bosom," and retreated reverentially.

So we went away, but I, lingering behind, examined the hole and the pin very carefully.

Hans was quite right: there was just room left in the former to accommodate two tin flasks of powder, also, there were not more than three inches of rock on the topside of the hole. Surely two pounds of powder would suffice to blow out this ring of stone and perhaps to shatter the pin as well.

CHAPTER 12

The Plot

We left the shed and, after she had locked its door very carefully and returned the stone key to her pouch, were taken by Dramana to see the famous Tree of Illusions, of which the juice and leaves, if powdered and burnt, could produce such strange dreams and intoxicating effects. It grew in a large walled space that was called Heu-Heu's Garden, though nothing else was planted there. Dramana assured us indeed that this tree had a poisonous effect upon all other vegetation.

Passing the wall by a door of which she also produced some kind of key out of her bag, we found ourselves standing in front of the famous tree, if so it can be called, for its growth was shrub-like and its topmost twigs were not more than twenty feet above the ground. On the other hand, it covered a great area and had a trunk two or three feet thick from which projected a vast number of branches whereof the extremities lay upon the soil, and I think rooted there, after the manner of wild figs, though of this I am not certain.

It was an unholy product of nature, inasmuch as it had no real foliage, only dark green, euphorbia-like and flesh fingers—indeed, I think it must have been some variety of euphorbia. At the extremities of these green fingers appeared purple-coloured blooms with a most evil smell that reminded me of the odour of something dead; also down their sides—for, like the orange, the tree appeared to have the property of flowering and fruiting at the same time—were yellow seed vessels about the size of those of a prickly pear. Except that the trunk was covered with corrugated gray bark and that the finger-like leaves were full of resinous white milk like those of other *euphorbias*, there is nothing more to say about it. I should add, however, that Dramana told us no other specimen existed, either on the mainland or the island, and that to attempt its propagation elsewhere was a capital offence. In short, the Tree of Illusions was a monopoly of the priests.

Hans set to work and cut a large faggot of the leaves, or fingers, which he tied up with a piece of string he had in his pocket, to be conveyed to Zikali, though there seemed to be such a small prospect of their ever reaching him. It was not an agreeable job, for when it was cut the white juice of the tree spurted out, and if it fell upon the flesh, burned like caustic.

I was glad when it came to an end because of the stench of the flowers, but before I left I took the opportunity, when Dramana was not looking, of picking some of the ripest of the fruits and putting them in my pocket, with the idea of planting the seeds should we ever escape from that country. I am sorry to say, however, that I never did so, as the sharp spines that grew upon the fruits wore a hole in the lining of my pocket, which already was thin from use, and they tumbled out unobserved. Evidently the Tree of Illusions did not intend to be reproduced elsewhere; at least, that was Hans's explanation.

On our way back to the house we had to pass round a lava boulder on the lake side of the sluice shed, crossing by a little bridge the water channel that ran beneath it, near to a flight of landing steps that were used by fishermen. I examined this channel which pierced the sea wall and here, outside the sluice gate, was about twenty feet wide. At the side of it, built into the wall, was a slab of stone on which were marks, cut there, no doubt, to indicate the height of the water level and the rate at which it rose. I noticed that the topmost of these marks was already covered, and that during the little while I stood and watched, it vanished altogether, showing that the water was rising rapidly.

Seeing that I was interested, Dramana remarked that the priests said that tradition never told of the water having reached that topmost mark before, even during the greatest rains. She added that she supposed it had done so now owing to the unprecedented wetness of the summer and great tempests farther up the river that fed the lake, of which we were experiencing the last.

"It is fortunate that you have such a strong door to keep out the water," I said.

"Yes, Lord," she answered, "since if it broke all this side of the island would be flooded. If you look you will see that already the lake stands higher than the cultivated lands and even than the mouth of the Cave of Heu-Heu. It is told in tradition that when first, hundreds of years ago, these lands were reclaimed from the mud of the lake and the wall was built to protect them, the priests of Heu-Heu trusted to the rain for their crops. Then came many dry seasons, and they cut a way through the wall and let in water to irrigate them, making the sluice gate that you have seen to keep it out if it rose too high. An old priest of that time said that this was madness and would one day prove their destruction, but they laughed at him and made the sluice. He was wrong also, since thenceforward their crops were doubled, and the gate is so well-fashioned that no floods, however great, have ever passed through or over it; nor can they do so, because the top of the stone gate rises to the height of a child above the level of the water wall which separates the lake from the reclaimed land."

"The lake might come over the crest of the wall," I suggested.

"No, Lord. If you look you will see that the wall is raised far above its level, to a height that no flood could ever reach."

"Then safety depends upon the gate, Dramana?"

"Yes, Lord. If the flood were high enough, which it never has been within the memory of man, the safety of the town would depend upon the gate, and that of the Cave of Heu-Heu also. Before the mountain broke into flame and destroyed the city of our ancestors, the new mouth was made on the level, for formerly, it is said, it was entered from the slope above. Moreover, there is no danger, because if any accident happened and the flood broke through, all could flee up the mountain. Only then the cultivated land would be ruined for a time and there might be scarcity, during which people must obtain corn from the mainland or draw it from that which is stored in pits in the hillside, to be used in case of war or siege."

I thanked her for her explanation of these interesting hydraulic problems, and after another glance at the scale rock, on which the marks had now vanished completely, showing me that the lake was still rising rapidly, we went to the house to rest and eat.

Here Dramana left us, saying that she would return at sundown. I begged her to do so without fail. This I did for her own sake, a fact that I did not explain. Personally, I was indifferent as to whether she came back or not, having learned all she could teach us, but as I was planning catastrophe, I was anxious, should it come, to give her any chance of escape that might offer for ourselves. After all, she had been a good friend to us and was one who hated Dacha and Heu-Heu and loved her sister Sabeela.

Hans led her to the door and in an awkward fashion made much ado in helping her to put on her leaf raincoat, which she had discarded and was carrying. For now suddenly the rain, which had almost ceased while we walked, had begun to fall again in torrents.

When we had eaten and were left alone within closed doors, Hans and I took counsel together.

"What is to be done, Hans?" I asked, wishing to hear his views.

"This, I think, Baas," he answered. "When it draws near to midnight we must go to hide near the steps, there by the Rock of Offerings, not the smaller ones near the sluice gate. Then when the canoe comes and lands the Lady Sabeela to be married, as soon as she has been taken and tied to the post we must swim out to it, get aboard, and go back to Walloo-town."

"But that would not save the Lady Sabeela, Hans."

"No, Baas, I was not troubling my head about the Lady Sabeela who I hope will be happy with Heu-Heu, but it would save *us*, though perhaps we shall have to leave some of our things behind. If Issicore and the rest wish to save Lady Sabeela, they had better cease from being cowards who are afraid of a stone statue and a handful of priests, and do so for themselves."

"Listen, Hans," I said. "We came here to get a bundle of stinking leaves for Zikali and to save the Lady Sabeela who is the victim of folly and wickedness. The first we have got, the second remains to be done. I mean to save that unfortunate woman, or to die in the attempt."

"Yes, Baas. I thought the Baas would say that, since we are all fools in our different ways, and how can any one dig out of his heart the folly that his mother put there before he was born? Therefore, since the Baas is a fool, or in love with Lady Sabeela because she is so pretty—I don't know which—we must make another plan and try to get ourselves killed in carrying it out."

"What plan?" I asked, disregarding his crude satire.

"I don't know, Baas," he said, staring at the roof. "If I had something to drink, I might be able to think of one, as all this wet has filled my head with fog, just as my stomach is full of water. Still, Baas, do I understand the Baas to say that if that stone gate were broken the lake would flow in and flood this place, also the Cave of Heu-Heu, where all the priests and their wives will be gathered worshipping him?"

"Yes, Hans, so I believe, and very quickly. As soon as the water began to run it would tear away the wall on either side of the sluice and enter in a mighty flood; especially now as the rain is again falling heavily."

"Then, Baas, we must let the stone fall, and as we are not strong enough to do it ourselves, we must ask this to help us," and he produced from his bag the two pounds of powder done up in stout flasks of soldered tin as it had left the maker in England. "As I am called Lord-of-the-Fire, the priests of Heu-Heu will think it quite natural," he added with a grin.

"Yes, Hans," I said, nodding, "but the question is—how?"

"I think like this, Baas. We must pack these two tins tight into that hole in the rock door beneath the pin with the help of little stones, and cover them over thickly with mud to give the powder time to work before the tins are blown out of the hole. But first we must bore holes in the tins and make slow matches and put the ends of them into the holes. Only how are we to make these slow matches?"

I looked about me. There on a shelf in the room stood the clay lamps with which it was lighted at night, and by them lay a coil of the wick which these people used, made of fine and dry plaited rushes, many feet of it.

"There's the very stuff!" I said.

We got it down, we soaked it in a mixture of the native oil, mixed with gunpowder that I extracted from a cartridge, and behold! in half an hour we had two splendid slow matches that by experiment I reckoned would take quite five minutes to burn before the fire reached the powder. That was all we could do for the moment.

"Now, Baas," said Hans, when we had finished our preparations and hidden the matches away to dry, "all this is very nice, but supposing that the stone falls and the water runs in and everything goes softly, how are we to get off the island? If we drown the priests of Heu-Heu—though I do not think we shall drown them because they will bolt up the mountain-side like rock rabbits—we drown ourselves also, and travel in their company to the Place of Fires of which your Reverend Father was so fond of talking. It will be very nice to try to drown the priests of Heu-Heu, Baas, but we shall be no better off, nor will the Lady Sabeela if we leave her tied to that post."

"We shall not leave her, Hans, that is if things go as I hope; we shall leave someone else."

Hans saw light and his face brightened.

"Oh, Baas, now I understand! You mean that you will tie to the post the Lady Dramana, who is older and not quite so nice-looking as the Lady Sabeela, which is why you told her she must stay with us all the time after she comes back? That is quite a good plan, especially as it will save us trouble with her afterwards. Only, Baas, it will be necessary to give her a little knock on the head first lest she should make a noise and betray us in her selfishness."

"Hans, you are a brute to think that I mean anything of the sort," I said indignantly.

"Yes, Baas, of course I am a brute who think of you and myself before I do of others. But then *who* will the Baas leave? Surely he does not mean to leave *me* dressed up in a bride's robe?" he added in genuine alarm.

"Hans, you are a fool as well as a brute, for, silly as you may be, how could I get on without you? I do not mean to leave any one living. I mean to leave that dead woman in the gate house."

He stared at me in evident admiration and answered, "The Baas is growing quite clever. For once he has thought of something that I have not thought of first. It is a good plan—if we can carry her there without any one seeing us, and the Lady Sabeela does not betray us by making a noise, laughing and crying both together like stupid women do. But suppose that it all happens, there will be four of us, and how are we to get into that canoe, Baas, if those cowardly Walloos wait so long?"

"Thus, Hans. When the canoe lands the Lady Sabeela and she has been tied to the post, if Dramana speaks truth, it waits for the dawn at a little distance. While it is waiting you must swim out to it, taking your pistol with you, which you will hold above your head with one hand to keep the cartridges dry, but leaving everything else behind. Then you must get into the boat, telling the Walloo and Issicore, or whoever is there, who you are. Later, when all is quiet, the Lady Dramana and I will carry the dead woman to the post and tie her there in place of Sabeela. After this you will bring the canoe to the landing steps—the small landing steps by the big boulder which we saw near to the sluice mouth on the lake wall, those that Dramana told us were used by fishermen, because it is not lawful for them to set foot upon the Rock of Offerings. You remember them?"

"Yes, Baas. You mean the ones at the end of a little pier which Dramana also said was built to keep mud from the lake from drifting into the sluice mouth and blocking it."

"When I see you coming, Hans, I shall fire the slow matches and we will run down to the pier and get into the canoe. I hope that the priests and their women in the cave, which is at a distance, will not hear the powder explode beneath that shed, and that when they come out of the cave they will find the water running in and swamping them. This might give them something else to do besides pursuing us, as doubtless they would otherwise, for I am sure they have canoes hidden away somewhere near by, although Dramana may not know where they are. Now do you understand?"

"Oh, yes, Baas. As I said, the Baas has grown quite clever all of a sudden. I think it must be that Wine of Dreams he drank last night that has woke up his mind. But the Baas has missed one thing. Supposing that I get into the canoe safely, how am I to make those people row in to the landing steps and take you off? Probably they will be afraid, Baas, or say that it is against their custom, or that Heu-Heu will catch them if they do, or something of the sort."

"You will talk to them gently, Hans, and if they will not listen, then you will talk to them with your pistol. Yes, if necessary, you will shoot one or more of them, Hans, after which I think the rest will obey you. But I hope that this will not be necessary, since if Issicore is there, certainly he will desire to win back Sabeela from Heu-Heu. Now we have settled everything, and I am going to sleep for a while, with the slow matches under me to dry them, as I advise you to do also. We had little rest last night, and tonight we shall have none at all, so we may as well take some while we can. But first bring that mat and tie up the twigs from the stinking tree for Zikali, on whom be every kind of curse for sending us on this job."

"Settled everything!" I repeated to myself with inward sarcasm as I lay down and shut my eyes. In truth, nothing at all was ever less settled, since success in such a desperate adventure depended upon a string of hypotheses long enough to reach from where we were to Capetown. Our case was an excellent example of the old proverb:

If ifs and ands made pots and pans, There'd be no work for tinkers' hands.

If the canoe came; *if* it waited off the rock; *if* Hans could swim out to it without being observed and get aboard; *if* he could persuade those fetish-ridden Walloos to come to take us off; *if* we could carry out our little game about the powder undetected; *if* the powder went off all right and broke up the sluice-handle as per our plan; *if* we could free Sabeela from the post; *if* she did not play the fool in some female fashion; *if* blackguards of sorts did not manage to cut our throats during all these operations, and a score of other "ifs," why, then our pots and pans would be satisfactorily manufactured and perhaps the priests of Heu-Heu would be satisfactorily frightened away or drowned. As it was, it looked to me as though, so far from not getting any rest that night, we should slumber more soundly than ever we did before—in the last long sleep of all.

Well, it could not be helped, so I just fell back upon my favourite fatalism, said my prayers and went off to sleep, which, thank God, I can do at any time and under almost any circumstances. Had it not been for that gift I should have been dead long ago.

When I woke up it was dark, and I found Dramana standing over me; indeed, it was her entry that roused me. I looked at my watch and discovered to my surprise that it was past ten o'clock at night.

"Why did you not wake me before?" I said to Hans.

"What was the use, Baas, seeing that there was nothing to be done and it is dull to be idle without a drop to drink?"

That's what he said, but the fact was that he had been fast asleep himself. Well, I was thankful, as thus we got rid of many weary hours of waiting.

Suddenly I made up my mind to tell Dramana everything, and did so. There was something about this woman that made me trust her; also, obviously, she was mad with desire to escape from Dacha, whom she hated and who hated her and had determined to murder her as soon as he had obtained possession of Sabeela.

She listened and stared at me, amazed at the boldness of my plans.

"It may all end well," she said, "though there is the magic of the priests to be feared which may tell them things that their eyes do not see."

"I will risk the magic," I said.

"There is also another thing," she went on. "We cannot get into the place where the stone gate is which you would destroy. As I was bidden, when I went back to the cave, I gave up the bag in which I carried the key and that of Heu-Heu's Garden to Dacha, and he has put it away, I know not where. The door is very strong, Lord, and cannot be broken down, and if I went to ask Dacha for the key again he would guess all, especially as the water is rising more fast than it ever rose before in the memory of man, and priests have been to make sure that the stone gate is fixed so that it cannot be moved—yes, and bound down the handle with ropes."

Now I sat still, not knowing what to say, for I had overlooked this matter of the key. While I did so I heard Hans chuckling idiotically.

"What are you laughing at, you little donkey?" I asked. "Is it a time to laugh when all our plans have come to nothing?"

"No, Baas, or rather, yes, Baas. You see, Baas, I guessed that something of this sort might happen, so, just in case it should, I took the key out of the Lady Dramana's bag and put in a stone of about the same weight in place of it. Here it is," and from his pocket he produced that ponderous and archaic lock-opening instrument.

"That was wise. Only you say, Dramana, that the priests have been to the shed. How did they get in without the key?" I asked.

"Lord, there are two keys. He who is called the Watcher of the Gate has one of his own. According to his oath he carries it about him all day at his girdle and sleeps with it at night. The key I had was that of the high priest, who uses it, and others that he may look into all things when he pleases, though this he does seldom, if ever."

"So far so good, then, Dramana. Have you aught to tell us?"

"Yes, Lord. You will do well to escape from this island tonight, if you can, since at today's council an oracle has gone forth from Heu-Heu that you and your companion are to be sacrificed at the bridal feast tomorrow. It is an offering to the Wood-dwellers, who now know that the woman was killed by you on the river and say that if you are allowed to live they will not fight against the Walloos. I think also that I am to be sacrificed with you."

"Are we indeed?" I said, reflecting to myself that any scruples I might have had as to attempting to drown out these fanatical brutes were now extinct for reasons which quite satisfied my conscience. I did not intend to be sacrificed if I could help it, then or at any future time, and evidently the best way to prevent this would be to give the prospective sacrificers a dose of their own medicine. From that moment I became as ruthless as Hans himself.

Now I understood why we were being treated with so much courtesy and allowed to see everything we wished. It was to lull our suspicions. What did it matter how much we learned, if within a few hours we were to be sent to a land whence we could communicate it to no one else?

I asked more particularly about this oracle, but only got answers from Dramana that I could not understand. It appeared, however, that as she said, it had undoubtedly been issued in reply to prayers from the savage Hairy Folk, who demanded satisfaction for the death of their countrywoman on the river, and threatened rebellion if it were not granted. This explained everything, and really the details did not matter.

Having collected all the information I could, we sat down to supper, during which Dramana told us incidentally that it had been arranged that our arms, which were known "to spit out fire," should be stolen from us while we slept before dawn, so as to make us helpless when we were seized.

So it came to this: if we were to act at all, it must be at once.

I ate as much as I was able, because food gives strength, and Hans did the same. Indeed, I am sure that he would have made an excellent meal even in sight of the noose which his neck was about to occupy. Eat and drink, for tomorrow we die, would have been Hans's favourite motto if he had known it, as perhaps he did. Indeed, we did drink also of some of the native liquor which Dramana had brought with her, since I thought that a moderate amount of alcohol would do us both good, especially Hans, who had the prospect of a cold swim before him. Immediately I had swallowed the stuff I regretted it, since it occurred to me that it might be drugged. However, it was not; Dramana had seen to that.

When we had finished our food we packed up our small belongings in the most convenient way we could. One half of these I gave to Dramana to carry, as she was a strong woman, and, of course, as he had to swim, Hans could be burdened with nothing except his pistol and the bundle of twigs from the Tree of Illusions, which we thought might help both to support and to conceal him in the water.

Then about eleven o'clock we started, throwing over our heads goatskin rugs that had served for coverings on our beds, to make us resemble those animals if that were possible.

CHAPTER 13

The Terrible Night

Leaving the house very softly, we found that the torrential rain had dwindled to a kind of heavy drizzle which thickened the air, while on the surface of the lake and the low-lying cultivated land there hung a heavy mist. This, of course, was very favourable to us, since even if there were watchers about they could not see us unless we stumbled right into them.

As a matter of fact I think that there was none, all the population of the place being collected at the ceremony in the cave. We neither saw nor heard anybody; not even a dog barked, for these animals, of which there were few on the island, were sleeping in the houses out of the wet and cold. Above the mist, however, the great full moon shone in a clear sky which suggested that the weather was mending, as in fact proved to be the case, the tempest of rain, which we learned afterwards had raged for months with some intervals of fine weather, having worn itself out at last. We reached the sluice house, and to our surprise found that the door was unlocked. Supposing that it had been left thus through carelessness by the inspecting priests, we entered softly and closed it behind us. Then I lit a candle, some of which I always carried with me, and held it up that we might look about us. Next moment I stepped back horror-struck, for there on the coping of the water shaft sat a man with a great spear in his hand.

Whilst I wondered what to do, staring at this man, who seemed to be half asleep and even more frightened than I was myself, with the greater quickness of the savage, Hans acted. He sprang at the fellow as a leopard springs. I think he drew his knife, but I am not sure. At any rate, I heard a blow and then the light of the candle shone upon the soles of the man's feet as he vanished backwards into the pit of water. What happened to him there I do not know; so far as we were concerned he vanished for ever.

"How is this? You told us no one would be here," I said to Dramana savagely, for I suspected a trap.

She fell upon her knees, thinking, probably, that I was going to kill her with the man's spear which I had picked up, and answered, "Lord, I do not know. I suppose that the priests grew suspicious and set one of their number to watch. Or it may have been because of the great flood which is rising fast."

Believing her explanations, I told her to rise, and we set to work. Having fastened the door from within, Hans climbed up the lever, and by the light of the candle, which could not betray us, as there were no windows to the shed, fixed the two flasks of powder in the hole in the stone gate immediately beneath the pin of the lever. Then, as we had arranged, he wedged them tight with pebbles that we had brought with us.

This done, I procured a quantity of the sticky clay with which the walls of the shed were plastered, taking it from a spot where the damp had come through and made it moist. This clay we stuck all over the flasks and the stones to a thickness of several inches. Only immediately beneath the pin we left an opening, hoping thereby to concentrate the force of the explosion on it and on the upper rim of the hole that was bored through the sluice gate. The slow matches, which now were dry, we inserted in the holes we had made in the flasks, bringing them out through the clay encased in two long, hollow reeds that we had drawn from the roof of our house where we lodged, hoping thus to keep the damp away from them.

Thus arranged, their ends hung to within six feet of the ground, where they could easily be lighted, even in a hurry.

By now it was a quarter past eleven, and the most terrible and dangerous part of our task must be faced. Lifting the corpse of the dead woman who had been killed, presumably, by a blow from the lever that morning, Hans and I—Dramana would not touch her—bore her out of the shed. Followed by Dramana with all our goods, for we dared not leave them behind, as our retreat might be cut off, we carried her with infinite labour, for she was very heavy, some fifty yards to a spot I had noted during our examination in the morning at the edge of the Rock of Offering, which spot, fortunately, rose to a height of six feet or rather less above the level of the surrounding ground. Here there was a little hollow in the rock face washed out by the action of water; a small, roofless cavity large enough to shelter the three of us and the corpse as well.

In this place we hid, for there, fortunately, the shape of the surrounding rock cut off the glare from the two eternal fires, which in so much wet seemed to be burning dully and with a good deal of smoke, the nearer of them at a distance of not more than a dozen paces from us. The post to which the victim was to be tied was perhaps the length of a cricket pitch away.

In this hiding hole we could scarcely be discovered unless by ill fortune someone walked right on to the top of us or approached from behind. We crouched down and waited. A while later, shortly before midnight, in the great stillness we heard a sound of paddles on the lake. The canoe was coming! A minute afterwards we distinguished the voices of men talking quite close to us.

Lifting my head, I peered very cautiously over the top of the rock. A large canoe was approaching the landing steps, or rather, where these had been, for now, except the topmost, they were under water because of the flood. On the rock itself four priests, clad in white and wearing veils over their faces with eyeholes cut in them, which made them look like monks in old pictures of the Spanish Inquisition, were marching towards these steps. As they reached them, so did the canoe. Next, from its prow was thrust a tall woman, entirely draped in a white cloak that covered both head and body, who from her height might very well be Sabeela.

The priests received her without a word, for all this drama was enacted in utter silence, and half led, half carried her to the stone post between the fires, where, so far as I could see through the mist—that night I blessed the mist, as we do in church in one of the psalms—no, it is the mist that blesses the Lord, but it does not matter—they bound her to the post. Then, still in utter silence, they turned and marched away down the sloping rock to the mouth of the cave, where they vanished. The canoe also paddled backwards a few yards—not far, I judged from the number of strokes taken—and there floated quietly.

So far all had happened as Dramana told us that it must. In a whisper I asked her if the priests would return. She answered no; no one would come on to the rock till sunrise, when Heu-Heu, accompanied by women, would issue from the cave to take his bride. She swore that this was true, since it was the greatest of crimes for any one to look upon the Holy Bride between the time that she was bound to the rock and the appearance of the sun above the horizon.

"Then the sooner we get to business the better," I said, setting my teeth, and without stopping to ask her what she meant by saying that Heu-Heu would come with the women, when, as we knew well, there was no such person.

"Come on, Hans, while the mist still lies thick; it may lift at any moment," I added.

Swiftly, desperately, we clambered on to the rock, dragging the dead woman after us. Staggering round the nearer fire with our awful burden, we arrived with it behind the post—it seemed to take an age. Here by the mercy of Providence the smoky reek from the fire propelled by a slight breath of air, combined with the hanging fog to make us almost invisible. On the farther side of the post stood Sabeela, bound, her head dropping forward as though she were fainting. Hans swore that it was Sabeela because he knew her "by her smell," which was just like him, but I could not be sure, being less gifted in that way. However, I risked it and spoke to her, though doubtfully, for I did not like the look of her. To tell the truth, I rather feared lest she should have acted on her threat that as a last resource she would take the poison which she said she carried hidden in her hair.

"Sabeela, do not start or cry out. Sabeela, it is we, the Lord Watcher-by-Night and he who is named Light-in-Darkness, come to save you," I said, and waited anxiously, wondering whether I should ever hear an answer.

Presently I gave a sigh of relief, for she moved her head slightly and murmured, "I dream! I dream!"

"Nay," I answered, "you do not dream, or if you do, cease from dreaming, lest we should all sleep for ever."

Then I crept round the post and bade her tell me where was the knot by which the rope about her was fastened. She nodded downwards with her head; with her hands she could not point, because they were tied, and muttered in a shaken voice, "At my feet, Lord."

I knelt down and found the knot, since if I cut the rope we should have nothing with which to tie the body to the post. Fortunately, it was not drawn tight because this was thought unnecessary, as no Holy Bride had ever been known to attempt to escape. Therefore, although my hands were cold, I was able to loose it without much difficulty. A minute later Sabeela was free and I had cut the lashings which bound her arms. Next came a more difficult matter, that of setting the dead woman in her place, for, being dead, all her weight came upon the rope. However, Hans and I managed it somehow, having first thrown Sabeela's cloak and veil over her icy form and face.

"Hope Heu-Heu will think her nice!" whispered Hans as we cast an anxious look at our handiwork.

Then, all being done, we retreated as we had come, bending low to keep our bodies in the layer of the mist which now was thinning and hung only about three feet above the ground like an autumn fog on an England marsh. We reached our hole, Hans bundling Sabeela over its edge unceremoniously, so that she fell on to the back of her sister, Dramana, who crouched in it terrified. Never, I think, did two tragically separated relations have a stranger meeting. I was the last of our party, and as I was sliding into the hollow I took a good look round.

This is what I saw. Out of the mouth of the cave emerged two priests. They ran swiftly up the gentle slope of rock till they reached the two columns of burning natural gas or petroleum or whatever it was, one of them halting by each column. Here they wheeled round and through the holes in their masks or veils stared at the victim bound to the post. Apparently what they saw satisfied them, for after one glance they wheeled about and ran back to the cave as swiftly as they had come, but in a methodical manner which showed no surprise or emotion.

"What does this mean, Dramana?" I exclaimed. "You told me that it was against the law for any one to look upon the Holy Bride until the moment of sunrise."

"I don't know, Lord," she answered. "Certainly it is against the law. I suppose that the diviners must have felt that something was wrong and sent out messengers to report. As I have told you, the priests of Heu-Heu are masters of magic, Lord."

"Then they are bad masters, for they have found out nothing," I remarked indifferently.

But in my heart I was more thankful than words can tell that I had persisted in the idea of lashing the dead woman to the post in place of Sabeela. Whilst we were dragging her from the shed, and again when we were lifting her out of the hole on to the rock, Hans had suggested that this was unnecessary, since Dramana had vowed that no man ever looked upon the Holy Bride between her arrival upon the rock and the moment of sunrise, and that all we needed to do was to loose Sabeela.

Fortunately some providence warned me against giving way. Had I done so all would have been discovered and humanly speaking we must have perished. Probably this would have happened even had I not remembered to run back and pick up the pieces of cord that I had cut from Sabeela's wrists and left lying on the rock, since the messengers might have seen them and guessed a trick. As it was, so far we were safe.

"Now, Hans," I said, "the time has come for you to swim to the canoe, which you must do quickly, for the mist seems to be melting beneath the moon and otherwise you may be seen."

"No, Baas, I shall not be seen, for I shall put that bundle from the Tree of Dreams on my head, which will make me look like floating weeds, Baas. But would not the Baas like, perhaps, to go himself? He swims better than I do and does not mind cold so much; also he is clever and the Walloo fools in the boat will listen to him more than they will to me; and if it comes to shooting, he is a better shot. I think, too, that I can look after the Lady Sabeela and the other lady and know how to fire a slow match as well as he can."

"No," I answered, "it is too late to change our plans, though I wish I were going to get into that boat instead of you, for I should feel happier there."

"Very good, Baas. The Baas knows best," he replied resignedly. Then, quite indifferent to conventions, Hans stripped himself, placing his dirty clothes inside the mat in which was wrapped the bundle of twigs from the Tree of Illusions, because, as he said, it would be nice to have dry things to put on when he reached the boat, or the next world, he did not know which.

These preparations made, having fastened the bundle on to his head by the help of the bonds which we had cut off Sabeela's hands, that I tied for him beneath his armpits, he started, shivering, a hideous, shrivelled, yellow object. First, however, he kissed my hand and asked me whether I had any message for my Reverend Father in the Place of Fires, where, he remarked, it would be, at any rate, warmer than it was here. Also he declared that he thought that the Lady Sabeela was not worth all the trouble we were taking about her, especially as she was going to marry someone else. Lastly he said with emphasis that if ever we got out of this country, he intended to get drunk for two whole days at the first town we came to where gin could be brought—a promise, I remember, that he kept very faithfully. Then he sneaked down the side of the rock and holding his revolver and little buckskin cartridge case above his head, glided into the water as silently as does an otter.

By now, as I have said, the mist was varnishing rapidly, perhaps before a draught of air which drew out of the east, as I have noticed it often does in those parts of Africa between midnight and sunrise, even on still nights. On the face of the water it still hung, however, so that through it I could only discover the faint outline of the canoe about a hundred yards away.

Presently, with a beating heart, I observed that something was happening there, since the canoe seemed to turn round and I thought that I heard astonished voices speaking in it, and saw people standing up.

Then there was a splash and once more all became still and silent. Evidently Hans reached the boat safely, though whether he had entered it I could not tell. I could only wonder and hope.

As we could do no good by remaining in our present most dangerous position, I set out to return to the sluice shed where other matters pressed, carrying all our gear as before, but, thank goodness! without the encumbrance of the corpse. Sabeela seemed to be still half dazed, so at present I did not try to question her. Dramana took her left arm and I her right and, supporting her thus, we ran, doubled up, back to the shed and entered it in safety. Leaving the two women here, I went out on to the little pier and crouched at the top of the fishermen's steps, watching and waiting for the coming of Hans with the canoe to take us off, for, as you may remember, the arrangement was that I was not to fire the slow matches until it had arrived.

No canoe appeared. During all the long hours—they seemed an eternity—before the breaking of the dawn did I wait and watch, returning now and again to the shed to make sure that Dramana and Sabeela were safe. On one of these visits I learned that both her father, the Walloo, and Issicore were in the canoe, which made its non-arrival not to be explained, that is, if Hans reached it safely. But if he had not, or perhaps had been killed or met with some other accident in attempting to board it, then the explanation was easy enough, as her crew would not know our plight or that we were waiting to be rescued. Lastly they might have refused to make the attempt—for religious reasons.

The problem was agonizing. Before long there would be light and without doubt we should be discovered and killed, perhaps by torture. On the other hand, if I fired the powder the noise of the explosion would probably be heard, in which case also we should be discovered. Yet there was an argument for doing this, since then, if things went well, the water would rush in and give those priests something to think about that would take their minds off hunting for and capturing us.

I looked about me. The canoe was invisible in the mist. It might be there or it might be gone, only if it were gone and Hans were still alive, I was certain that, as arranged, to advise me he would have fired his pistol, which, to keep the cartridges dry, he had carried above his head in his left hand. Indeed, I thought it probable that, rather than desert me thus, he would have swum back to the island, so that we might see the business through together. The longer I pondered all these and other possibilities, the more confused I grew and the more despairing. Evidently something had happened, but what—what?

The water continued to rise; now all the steps were covered and it was within an inch or two of the surface of the pier on which I must crouch. It was a mighty flood that looked as though presently it would begin to flow over the top of the sea wall, in which case the sluice shed would undoubtedly be inundated and made uninhabitable.

As I think I told you, a few yards to our right, rising above the top of the sea wall to a height of seven or eight feet, was a great rock that had the appearance of a boulder ejected at some time from the crater of the volcano, which rock would be easy to climb and was large enough to accommodate the three of us. Moreover, no flood could reach its top, since to do so it must cover the land beyond to a depth of many feet. Considering it and everything else, suddenly I came to a conclusion, so suddenly indeed and so fixedly that I felt as though it were inspired by some outside influence.

I would bring the women out and make them lie down upon the top of that boulder, trusting to Dramana's dark cloak to hide them from observation even in that brilliant moonlight. Then I would return to the shed and set light to the match, and, after I had done this, join them upon the rock whence we could see all that happened, and watch for the canoe, though of this I had begun to despair.

Abandoning all doubts and hesitations, I set to work to carry out this scheme with cold yet frantic energy. I fetched the two sisters, who, imagining that relief was in sight, came readily enough, made them clamber up the rock and lie down there on their faces, throwing Dramana's large dark cloak over both of them and our belongings. Then I went back to the shed, struck a light, and applied it to the ends of the slow matches, that began to smoulder well and clearly. Rushing from the shed, I locked the heavy door and sped back to the rock, which I climbed.

Five minutes passed, and just as I was beginning to think that the matches had failed in some way, I heard a heavy thud. It was not very loud; indeed, at a distance of even fifty yards I doubted whether any one would have noticed it unless his attention were on the strain. That shed was well built and roofed and smothered sounds. Also this one had nothing of the crack of a rifle about it, but rather resembled that which is caused by something heavy falling to the ground.

After this for a while nothing particular happened. Presently, however, looking down from my rock I saw that the water in the sluice, which, being retained by the stone door in the shed, hitherto had been still, was now running like a mill race, and with a thrill of triumph learned that I had succeeded.

The sluice was down and the flood was rushing over it!

Watching intently, a minute or so later I observed a stone fall from the coping of the channel, for it was full to the brim, then another, and another, till presently the whole work seemed to melt away. Where it had been was now a great and ever-growing gap in the sea wall through which the swollen waters of the lake poured ceaselessly and increasingly. Next instant the shed vanished like a card house, its foundations being washed out, and I perceived that over its site, and beyond it, a veritable river, on the face of which floated portions of its roof, was fast inundating the low-lying lands behind that had been protected by the wall.

I looked at the east; it was lightening, for now the blackness of the sky where it seemed to meet the great lake, had turned to grey. The dawn was at hand.

With a steady roar, through the gap in the sea wall which grew wider every moment, the waters rushed in, remorseless, inexhaustible; the aspect of them was terrifying. Now our rock was a little island surrounded by a sea, and now in the east appeared the first ray from the unrisen sun stabbing the rain-washed sky like a giant spear. It was a wondrous spectacle and, thinking that probably it was the last I should ever witness upon earth, I observed it with great interest.

By this time the women at my side were sobbing with terror, believing that they were going to be drowned. As I was of the same opinion, for I felt our rock trembling beneath us as though it were about to turn over or, washed from its foundations, to sink into some bottomless gulf, and could do nothing to help them, I pretended to take no notice of their terror, but only stared towards the east.

****

It was just then that, emerging out of the mist on the face of the waters within a few yards of us, I saw the canoe. Hear the sound of the paddles I could not, because of the roar of the rushing water. In it at the stern, with his pistol held to the head of the steersman, stood Hans.

I rose up, and he saw me. Then I made signs to him which way he should come, keeping the canoe straight over the crest of the broken wall where the water was shallow. It was a dangerous business, for every moment I thought it would overset or be sucked into the torrent beyond, where the sluice channel had been; but those Walloos were clever with their paddles, and Hans's pistol gave them much encouragement.

Now the prow of the canoe grated against the rock, and Hans, who had scrambled forward, threw me a rope. I held it with one hand and with the other thrust down the shrinking women. He seized them and bundled them into the canoe like sacks of corn. Next I threw in our gear and then sprang wildly myself, for I felt our stone turning. I half fell into the water, but Hans and someone else gripped me and I was dragged in over the gunwale. Another instant and the rock had vanished beneath the yellow, yeasty flood!

The canoe oscillated and began to spin round; happily it was large and strong, with at least a score of rowers, being hollowed from a single, huge tree. Hans shrieked directions and the paddlers paddled as never they had done before. For quite a minute our fate hung doubtful, for the torrent was sucking at us and we did not seem to gain an inch. At last, however, we moved forward a little, towards the Rock of Sacrifice this time, and with sixty seconds were safe and out of the reach of the landward rush of the water.

"Why did you not come before, Hans?" I asked.

"Oh, Baas, because these fools would not move until they saw the first light, and when the Walloo and Issicore wanted to, told them that they would kill them. They said it was against their law, Baas."

"Curse them all for ten generations!" I exclaimed, then was silent, for what was the use of arguing with such a superstition-ridden set?

Superstition is still king of most of the world, though often it calls itself Religion. These Walloos thought themselves very religious indeed.

* * * * * * * *

Thus ended that terrible night.

CHAPTER 14

The End of Heu-Heu

Opposite to the Rock of Offering the canoe came to a standstill quite close to the edge of the rock. I inquired why, and the old Walloo, who sat in the middle of the boat draped in wondrous and imperial garments and a headdress, that, having worked itself to one side in the course of our struggles, made him look as though he were drunk, answered feebly:

"Because it is our law, Lord. Our law bids us wait till the sun appears and the glory of Heu-Heu comes forth to take the Holy Bride."

"Well," I answered, "as the Holy Bride is sitting in this boat with her head upon my knee" (this was true, because Sabeela had insisted upon sticking to me as the only person upon whom she could rely, and so, for the matter of that, had Dramana, for *her* head was on my other knee), "I should recommend the glory of Heu-Heu, whatever that may be, not to come here to look for her. Unless, indeed, it wants a hole as big as my fist blown through it," I added with emphasis, tapping my double-barrelled Express which was by my side, safe in its waterproof case.

"Yet we must wait, Lord," answered the Walloo humbly, "for I see that there is still a Holy Bride tied to the post, and until she is loosed our law says that we may not go away."

"Yes," I exclaimed, "the holiest of all brides, for she is stone dead and all the dead are holy. Well, wait if you like, for I want to see what happens, and I think they can't get at us here."

So we hung upon our oars, or rather paddles, and waited, till presently the rim of the red sun appeared and revealed the strangest of scenes. The water of the lake, swollen by weeks of continuous rain and the recent tempest, flowing in with a steady rush that somehow reminded me of the ordered advance of an infinite army, through the great gap in the lake wall that was broadening minute by minute beneath its devouring bite—is there anything so mighty as water in the world, I wonder—had now flooded most of the cultivated land to a depth of several feet.

As yet, however, it had not reached the houses built against the mountain, in one of which we had been lodged. Nor had it over-flowed the great Rock of Offering, which, you will remember, stood about the height of a man above the level of the plain, being in fact a large slab of consolidated lava that once had flowed from the crater into the lake in a glacier-like stream of limited breadth. It is true that the circumstance that the rock sloped downwards to the cave mouth seemed to contradict that theory, but this I attribute to some subse-quent subsidence at its base, such as often happens in volcanic areas where hidden forces are at work beneath the surface of the earth.

Well, I repeat, the rock was not yet flooded, and so it came about that, at the proper moment, as had happened on this day, perhaps for hundreds of years, Heu-Heu emerged from the cave "to claim his Holy Bride."

* * * * * * * *

"How could he do that?" asked Good triumphantly, thinking, I suppose that he had caught Allan tripping. "You said that Heu-Heu was a statue, so how could he come out of the cave?"

"Does not it occur to you, Good," asked Allan, "that a statue is sometimes carried? However, in this case it was not so, for Heu-Heu himself walked out of that cave, followed by a number of women, with some of the Hairy Folk behind them, and looking at him as he stalked along, hideous and gigantic, I understood two things. The first of these was, how it came about that Sabeela had vowed to me that many had seen Heu-Heu with their eyes, as Issicore also declared he had done himself, 'walking stiffly.' The second, why it was a law that the canoe which brought the Holy Bride should wait until she was removed at dawn; namely in order that those in it might behold Heu-Heu and go back to their land to testify to his bodily existence, even if they were not allowed to give details as to his appearance, because to speak of this would, they believed, bring a 'curse' upon them."

"But there wasn't a Heu-Heu," objected Good again.

"Good," said Allan, "really you are what Hans called me—quite clever. With extraordinary acumen you have arrived at the truth. There wasn't a Heu-Heu. But, Good, if you live long enough," he went on with a gentle sarcasm which showed that he was annoyed, "yes, if you live long enough, you will learn that this world is full of deceptions, and that the Tree of Illusions does not, or rather did not, grow only in Heu-Heu's Garden. As you say, no Heu-Heu existed, but there did exist an excellent copy of him made up with a skill worthy of a high-class pantomime artist; so excellent indeed that from fifty yards or so away, it was impossible to tell the difference between it and the great original as depicted in the cave."

* * * * * * * *

There in all his hairy, grinning horror, "walking stiffly," marched Heu-Heu, eleven or twelve feet high. Or to come to the facts, there marched Dacha on stilts, artistically draped in dyed skins and wearing on the top of or over his head a wickerwork and canvas or cloth mask beautifully painted to resemble the features of his amiable god.

The pious crew of our boat saw him, and bowed their classic heads in reverence to the divinity. Even Issicore bowed, a performance that I observed caused Dramana, yes, and the loving Sabeela herself, to favour him with glances of indignation, not unmixed with contempt. At least this was certainly the case with Dramana, who had lived behind the scenes, but Sabeela may have been moved by other reflections. Perhaps *she* still believed that there was a Heu-Heu, and that Issicore would have done better to show himself less devoted to these religious observances and less willing to surrender her to the god's divine attentions. You may all have noticed that however piously disposed, there is a point at which the majority of women become very practical indeed.

Meanwhile Heu-Heu stalked forward with a gait that might very literally be called stilted, and the bevy of white-robed ladies followed after him apparently singing a bridal song, while behind these, "moping and mowing," came their hairy attendants. By the aid of my glasses, however, I could see that these ladies, at any rate, were not enjoying the entertainment, whatever may have been the case with Dacha inside his paste boards. They stared at the rising water and one of them turned to run but was dragged back into place by her companions, for probably on this solemn occasion flight was a capital offence. So on they came till they reached the post to which we had tied the dead woman, whereon according to custom, the bridesmaids skipped up to release her, while the Hairy Folk ranged themselves behind.

Next moment I saw the first of these bridesmaids suddenly stand still and stare; then she emitted a yell so terrific that it echoed all over the lake like the blast of a train. The others stared also and in their turn began to yell. Then Heu-Heu himself ambled round and apparently had a look, a good look, for by now someone had torn away the veil which I had thrown over the corpse's head. He did not look long, for next moment he was legging, or rather stilting, back to the cave as fast as he could go.

This was too much for me. By my side was my double-barrelled Express rifle loaded with expanding bullets. I drew it from its case, lifted it, and got a bead on to Heu-Heu just above where I guessed the head of the man within to be, for I did not want to kill the brute but only to frighten him. By now the light was good and so was my aim, for a moment later the expanding bullet hit in the appointed spot and cleared away all that top hamper of wicker and baboon skins, or whatever it may have been. Never before was there such a sudden dis-robement of an ecclesiastical dignitary draped in all his trappings.

Everything seemed to come off at once, as did Dacha from his stilts, for he went a most imperial crowner that must have flattened his hooked nose upon that lava rock. There he lay a moment, then, leaving his stilts behind him, he rose and fled after the screaming women and their ape-like attendants back into the cave.

"Now," I remarked oracularly to the old Walloo and the others who were terrified at the report of the rifle, "now, my friends, you see what your god is made of."

The Walloo attempted no reply, apparently he was too astonished—disillusionment is often painful, you know—but one of his company who seemed to be a kind of official timekeeper, said that the sun being up and the Holy Bridal being accomplished, though strangely, it was lawful for them to return home.

"No, you don't," I answered. "I have waited here a long time for you and now you shall wait a little while for me, as I want to see what happens."

The timekeeper, however, a man of routine, if one devoid of curiosity, dipped his paddle into the water as a signal to the other rowers to do likewise, whereon Hans hit him hard over the fingers with the butt of his revolver, and then held its barrel to his head.

This argument convinced him that obedience was best, and he drew in the paddle, as did the others, making polite apologies to Hans.

So we remained where we were and watched.

There was lots to see, for by now the water was beginning to run over the rock. It reached the eternal fires with the result that they ceased to be eternal, for they went out in clouds of smoke and steam. Three minutes later it was pouring in a cataract down the slope into the mouth of the cave. Before I could count a hundred, people began to come out of that cave in the greatest of hurries, as wasps do if you stir up their nest with a stick. Among them I recognised Dacha, who had a very good idea of looking after himself.

He and the first of those who followed, wading through the water, got clear and began to scramble up the mountainside behind. But the rest were not so fortunate, for by now the stream was several feet deep and they could not fight it. For a moment they appeared struggling amid the foam and bubbles. Then they were swept back into the mouth of the cave and gathered to the breast of Heu-Heu for the last time. Next, as though at a signal, all the houses, including that in which we had been lodged, crumbled away together. They just collapsed and vanished.

Everything seemed finished and I wondered whether I would put a bullet into Dacha, who now was standing on a ridge of rock and wringing his hands as he watched the destruction of his temple, his god, his town, his women, and his servants. Concluding that I would not, for something seemed to tell me to leave this wicked rascal to destiny, I was about to give the order to paddle away when Hans called to me to look at the mountain top.

I did so, and observed that from it was rushing a great cloud of steam, such as comes from a railway engine when it is standing still with too much heat in its boiler, but multiplied a millionfold. Moreover, as the engine screams in such circumstances, so did the mountain scream, or rather roar, emitting a volume of sound that was awful to hear.

"What's up now, Hans?" I shouted.

"Don't know, Baas. Think that water and fire are having a talk together inside that mountain, Baas, and saying they hate each other, just like badly married man and woman who quarrel in a small hut, Baas, and can't get out. Hiss, spit, go woman; pop, bang, go man——" Here he paused from his nonsense, staring at the mountain top with all his eyes, then repeated in a slow voice, "Yes, pop, bang, go man! Just *look* at him, Baas!"

At this moment, with an amazing noise like to that of a magnified thunderclap, the volcano seemed to split in two and the crest of it to fly off into space.

"Baas," said Hans, "I am called Lord-of-the-Fire, am I not? Well, I am not Lord of that fire and I think that the farther off we get from it, the safer we shall be. *Allemagter!* Look there," and he pointed to a huge mass of flaming lava which appeared to descend from the clouds and plunge into the lake about a couple of hundred yards away, sending up a fountain of steam and foam, like a torpedo when it bursts.

"Paddle for your lives!" I shouted to the Walloos, who began to get the canoe about in a very great hurry.

As she came round—it seemed to take an age—I saw a strange and in a way a terrible sight. Dacha had left his ledge and was running down into the lake, followed by a stream of molten lava, dancing while he ran, as though with pain, probably because the stream had scorched him. He plunged into the water, and just then a great wave formed, driven outwards doubtless by some subterranean explosion. It rushed towards us, and on its very crest was Dacha.

"I think that priest wants us to give him a row, Baas," said Hans. "He has had enough of his happy island home, and wishes to live on the mainland."

"Does he?" I replied. "Well, there is no room in the canoe," and I drew my pistol.

The wave bore Dacha quite close to us. He reared himself in the water, or more probably was lifted up by the pressure underneath, so that almost he appeared to be standing on the crest of the wave. He saw us, he shouted curses upon us and shook his fists, apparently at Sabeela and Issicore. It was a horrible sight.

Hans, however, was not affected, for by way of reply he pointed first to me, then to Sabeela and lastly to himself, after which, such was his unconquerable vulgarity, he put his thumb to his nose and as schoolboys say "cocked a snook" at the struggling high priest.

The wave became a hollow and Dacha disappeared "to look for Heu-Heu," as Hans remarked. That was the end of this cruel but able man.

"I am glad," said Hans after reflection, "that the Predikant Dacha should have learned who sent him down to Heu-Heu before he went there, which he knew well enough or he would not have been so cross, Baas. Has it occurred to the Baas what clever people we are, all of whose plans have succeeded so nicely? At one time I thought that things were going wrong. It was after I scrambled into this canoe and those fools would not move to fetch you and the women, because they said it was against their law. While I was putting on my clothes, which got here quite dry because I was so careful, Baas, for I had asked them to paddle to fetch you while I was still naked and been told that they would not, I wondered whether I should try to make them do so by shooting one of them. Only I thought that I had better wait a while, Baas, and see what happened, because if I shot one, the others might have become more stupid and obstinate than before, and perhaps have paddled away after they had killed me. So I waited, which the Baas will admit was the best thing to do, and everything came right in the end, having doubtless been arranged by your Reverend Father, watching us in the sky."

"Yes, Hans, but if you had made up your mind otherwise, whom would you have shot?" I asked. "The Walloo?"

"No, Baas, because he is old and stupid as a dead owl. I should have shot Issicore because he tires me so much and I should like to save the Lady Sabeela from being made weary for many years. What is the good of a man, Baas, who, when he thinks his girl is being given over to a devil, sits in a boat and groans and says that ancient laws must not be broken lest a curse should follow? He did that, Baas, when I asked him to order the men to row to the steps."

"I don't know, Hans. It is a matter for them to settle between them, isn't it?"

"Yes, Baas, and when the lady has got her mind again and at last that hour comes, as it always does when there is something to pay, Baas, I shall be sorry for Issicore, for I don't think he will look so pretty when she has done with him. No, I think that when he says 'Kiss! Kiss!' she will answer, 'Smack! Smack!' on both sides of his head, Baas. Look, she has turned her back on him already. Well, Baas, it doesn't matter to me, or to you either, who have the Lady Dramana there to deal with. She isn't turning her back, Baas, she is eating you up with her eyes and saying in her heart that at last she has found a Heu-Heu worth something, even though he be small and withered and ugly, with hair that sticks up. It is what is in a man that matters, Baas, not what he looks like outside, as women often used to say to me when I was young, Baas."

Here with an exclamation that I need not repeat, for none of us really like to have our personal appearance reflected upon by a candid friend, however faithful, I lifted the butt of my rifle, purposing to drop it gently on Hans's toes. At that point, however, my attention was diverted from this rubbish, which was Hans's way of showing his joy at our escape, by another blazing boulder which fell quite near to the canoe, and immediately afterwards by the terrific spectacle of the final dissolution of the volcano.

I don't know exactly what happened, but sheets of wavering flame and clouds of steam ascended high into the heavens. These were accompanied by earth-shaking rumblings and awful explosions that resounded like the loudest thunder, each of them followed by the ejection of showers of blazing stones and the rushing out of torrents of molten lava which ran into the lake, making it hiss and boil. After this came tidal waves that caused our canoe to rock perilously, dense clouds of ashes and a kind of hot rain which darkened the air so much that for a while we could see nothing, no, not for a yard before our noses. Altogether, it was a most terrifying exhibition of the forces of nature which, by some connection of ideas, made me think of the Day of Judgment.

"Heu-Heu avenges himself upon us!" wailed the old Walloo, "because we have robbed him of his Holy Bride."

Here his speech came to an end, for a good reason, since a large hot stone fell upon his head, and, as Hans who was next to him explained through the fog, "squashed him like a beetle."

When from the outcry of his followers Sabeela realized that her father was dead, for he never moved or spoke again, she seemed to wake up in good earnest, just as though she felt that the mantle of authority had fallen upon her.

"Throw that hot coal out of the boat," she said, "lest it burn through the bottom and we sink."

With the help of a paddle Issicore obeyed her, and, the body of the Walloo having been covered up with a cloak, we rowed on desperately. By good fortune about this time a strong wind began to blow from the shore towards the island which kept back or drove away the hot rain and pumice dust, so that we could once more see about us. Now our only danger was from the rocks, such as that which had killed the Walloo, that fell into the water all around, sending up spouts of foam. It was just as though we were under heavy bombardment, but happily no more of them hit the canoe, and as we got farther off the island the risk became less. As we found afterwards, however, some of them were thrown as far as the mainland.

Still, there was one more peril to be passed, for suddenly we ran into a whole fleet of rude canoes, or rather bundles of reed and brushwood, or sometimes logs sharpened at both ends by fire, on each of which one of the Hairy savages sat astride directing it with a double-bladed paddle.

I presume that these people must have been a contingent of the aboriginal Wood-folk who had started for the island in obedience to the summons of Heu-Heu, where, as I have told, a great number of them were already gathered preparatory to attacking the town of Walloo. Or they may have been escaping from the island; really I do not know. One thing was clear; however low they may have been in the scale of humanity, they were sharp enough to connect us with the awful, natural catastrophe that was happening, for squeaking and jabbering like so many great apes, they pointed to that vision of hell, the flaming volcano now sinking to dissolution, and to us.

Then with their horrible yells of *Heu-Heu! Heu-Heu!* they set to work to attack us.

There was only one thing to be done—open fire on them, which Hans and I did with effect, and meanwhile try to escape by our superior speed. I am bound to say that those hideous and miserable creatures showed the greatest courage, for undeterred by the sight of the death of their companions whom our bullets struck, they tried to close upon us with the object, no doubt, of oversetting the canoe and drowning us all.

Hans and I fired as rapidly as possible, but we could deal with only a tithe of them, so that speed and manoeuvring were our principal hope. Sabeela stood up in the boat and cried directions to the paddlers, while Hans and I shot, first with the rifles and then with our revolvers.

Still, one huge gorilla-like fellow, whose hair grew down to his beetling eyebrows, got hold of the gunwale and began to pull the canoe over. We could not shoot him because both rifles and revolvers were empty; nor did our blows make him loosen his grip. The canoe rocked from side to side increasingly, and began to take in water.

Just as I feared that the end had come, for more hairy men were almost on to us, Sabeela saved the situation in a bold and desperate fashion. By her side lay the broad spear of that priest whom Hans had killed in the sluice shed, knocking him backwards into the water pit. She seized it and with amazing strength stabbed the great beast-like creature who had hold of the canoe and was putting all his weight on it to force the gunwale under water. He let go and sank. By skilful steering we avoided the others, and in three minutes were clear of them, since they could not keep pace with us on their rude craft.

"Plenty to do tonight, Baas!" soliloquized Hans, wiping his brow. "Perhaps if a crocodile does not swallow us between here and the shore, or these fools do not sacrifice us to the ghost of Heu-Heu, or we are not killed by lightning, the Baas will let me drink some of that native beer when we get back to the town. All this fire about has made me very thirsty."

* * * * * * * *

Well, we arrived there at last—a generation seemed to have passed since I left that quay, which we found crowded with the entire terror-stricken population of the place. They received the body of the Walloo in respectful silence, but it seemed to me without any particular grief. Indeed, these people appeared to have outworn the acuter human emotions. All such extremes, I suppose, had been smoothed away from their characters by time, and by the degrading action of the vile fetishism under which they lived. In short, they had become mere handsome, human automata who walked about with their ears cocked listening for the voice of the god and catching it in every natural sound. To tell the truth, however interesting may have been their origin, in their decadence they filled me with contempt.

The reappearance of Sabeela astonished them very much but seemed to cause no delight.

"She is the god's wife," I heard one of them say. "It is because she has run away from the god that all these misfortunes have happened." She heard it also and rounded on them with spirit, having by now quite recovered her nerve, or so it seemed, which is more than could be said of Issicore, who, although he should have been wild with joy, remained depressed and almost silent.

"What misfortunes?" she asked. "My father is dead, it is true, killed by a hot stone that fell upon him and I weep for him. Still, he was a very old man who must soon have passed away. For the rest, is it a misfortune that through the courage and power of these strangers I, his daughter and heiress, have been freed from the clutches of Dacha? I tell you that Dacha was the god; Heu-Heu whom you worship was but a painted idol. If you do not believe it, ask the White Lord here, and ask my sister Dramana whom you seem to have forgotten, who in past years was given to him as a Holy Bride. Is it a misfortune that Dacha and his priests have been destroyed, and with him the most of the savage hairy Wood-folk, our enemies? Is it a misfortune that the hateful smoking mountain should have melted away in fire, as it is doing now, and with it the cave of mysteries, out of which came so many oracles of terror, thus fulfilling the prophecy that we should be delivered from our burdens by a white lord from the south?"

At these vigorous words the frightened crowd grew silent and hung their heads. Sabeela looked about her for a little while, then went on:

"Issicore, my betrothed, come forward and tell the people you rejoice that these things have happened. To save me from Heu-Heu, at my prayer you travelled far to ask succour of the great Magician of the South. He has sent the succour and I have been saved. Yet you helped to row the boat which took me to the sacrifice. For that I do not blame you, because you must do so, being of the rank you are, or be cursed under the ancient law. Now I have been saved, though not by you, who, thinking the White Lord dead upon the Holy Isle, consented to my surrender to the god, and the law is at an end with the destruction of Heu-Heu and his priests, slain by the wisdom and might of that White Lord and his companion. Tell them, therefore, how greatly you rejoice that you have not journeyed in vain, and they did not listen in vain to your petition for help; that I stand before them here also free and undefiled, and that henceforth the land is rid of the curse of Heu-Heu. Yes, tell the people these things and give thanks to the noble-hearted strangers who brought them to pass and saved me with Dramana my sister."

Now, tired out as I was, I watched Issicore not without excitement, for I was curious to hear what he had to say. Well, after a pause, he came forward and answered in a hesitating voice, "I do rejoice, Beloved, that you have returned safe, though I hoped when I led the White Lord from the South, that he would have saved you in some fashion other than by working sacrilege and killing the priests of the god with fire and water, men who from the beginning have been known to be divine. You, the Lady Sabeela, declare that Heu-Heu is dead, but how know we that he is dead? He is a spirit, and can a spirit die? Was it a dead god who threw the stone that killed the Walloo, and will he not perhaps throw other stones that will kill us, and especially you, Lady, who have stood upon the Rock of Offerings, wearing the robe of the Holy Bride?"

"Baas," inquired Hans reflectively, in the silence which followed these timorous queries, "do you think that Issicore is really a man, or is he in truth but made of wood and painted to look like one, as Dacha was painted to look like Heu-Heu?"

"I thought that he was a man yonder in the Black Kloof, Hans," I answered, "but then he was long way off Heu-Heu. Now I am not so sure. But perhaps he is only very frightened and will come to himself by and by."

Meanwhile Sabeela was looking her extremely handsome lover up and down; up and down she looked him, and never a word did she say—at least, to him. Presently, however, she spoke to the crowd in a commanding voice, thus:

"Take notice that my father being dead, I am now the Walloo, and one to be obeyed. Go about your tasks fearing nothing, since Heu-Heu is no more and the most of the Hairy Folk are slain. I depart to rest, taking with me these, my guests and deliverers," and she pointed to me and Hans. "Afterwards I will talk with you, and with you also, my lord Issicore. Bear the late Walloo, my father, to the burial place of the Walloos."

Then she turned and, followed by us and the members of her household, went to her home.

Here she bade us farewell for a while, since we were all half dead with fatigue and sorely needed rest. As we parted, she took my hand

and kissed it, thanking me with tears welling from her beautiful eyes for all that I had done, and Dramana did likewise.

"How comes it, Baas," said Hans as we ate food and drank of the native beer before we lay down to sleep, "that those ladies did not kiss my hand, seeing that I too have done something to help them?"

"Because they were too tired, Hans," I answered, "and made one kiss serve for both of us."

"I see, Baas, but I expect that tomorrow they will still be too tired to kiss poor old Hans."

Then he filled the cup out of which he had been drinking with the last of the liquor from the jar and emptied it at a swallow. "There, Baas," he said; "that's only right; you may take all the kisses, so long as I get the beer."

Exhausted as I was I could not help laughing, although to tell the truth, I should have liked another glass myself. Then I tumbled on to the couch and instantly went to sleep.

****

It is a fact that we slept all the rest of that day and all the following night, waking only when the first rays of the sun shone into our room through the window place. At least, I did, for when I opened my eyes, feeling a different creature and blessing Heaven for its gift of sleep to man, Hans was already up and engaged in cleaning the rifles and revolvers.

I looked at the ugly little Hottentot, reflecting how wonderful it was that so much courage, cunning, and fidelity should be packed away within his yellow skin and projecting skull. Had it not been for Hans, without a doubt I should now be dead, and the women also. It was he who had conceived the idea of letting down the sluice gate by exploding gunpowder beneath the pin of the lever. I had racked my brain for expedients, but this, the only one possible, escaped me. How tremendous had been the results of that inspiration—all of them due to Hans.

Although certain ideas had occurred to me, the most that I had hoped to do was to flood the low-lying lands, and perhaps the cave, in order to divert the attention of the priests while we were attempting escape. As it was we had loosed the forces of nature with the most fearful results. The water had run down the vent-holes of the eternal fires and into the bowels of the volcano, there to generate steam in enormous volumes, of which the imprisoned strength had been so great that it had rent the mountain like a rotten rag and destroyed the home of Heu-Heu for ever, and with it all his votaries.

It was a fearful event in which I thought I saw the mind of Providence acting through Hans. Yes, the cunning of the Hottentot had been used by the Powers above to sweep from the earth a vile tyranny and to destroy a blood-soaked idol and its worshippers.

Without a doubt—or so I believe in my simple faith—this had been designed from the beginning. When some escaped follower of Heu-Heu painted the picture in the Bushmen's cave, probably hundreds of years ago, it was already designed. So was Zikali's desire for a certain medicine, or his insatiable thirst for knowledge, or whatever it was that caused him to persuade me to undertake this mission, and so was all the rest of the story.

Again, with what wonderful judgment Hans had acted after his brave swim to the canoe!

Had he tried to force those fetish-ridden cravens to come to our rescue at once, as I directed him to do, the probability was that, fearing to break their silly law, they would have resisted, or perhaps have rowed right away, leaving us to our fate, after knocking him on the head with a paddle. But he had the patience to wait, although, as he told me afterwards, his heart was torn in two with anxiety for my sake. Balancing everything in his artful and experienced mind he had found patience to wait until the conditions of their "law" were fulfilled, when they came willingly enough.

From Hans my thoughts turned to Issicore. How was it that this man's character had changed so completely since he arrived in his native country? His journey to seek aid made alone over hundreds of miles, was a really remarkable performance, showing great courage and determination. Also as a guide, although silent and abstracted, he had never lacked for resource or energy. But from the day that he arrived home, morally he had gone to pieces. It was with the greatest difficulty that he could be persuaded to row us to the island, where at the first sign of danger he had left us to our fate and fled away.

Again, he had meekly helped to conduct Sabeela, whom, when he was at the Black Kloof evidently he loved to desperation, to her doom without lifting a finger to save her from a hideous destiny. Lastly, only a few hours ago, he had made a pusillanimous and contemptible speech, which I could see shocked and disgusted his betrothed, who, for her part, after her rescue and the death of her father, seemed to have gained the courage that he had lost, and more.

It was inexplicable, at any rate to me, and in my bewilderment I referred the problem to Hans.

He listened while I set out the case as it appeared to me, then

167

answered, "The Baas does not keep his eyes open—at any rate, in the daytime, when he thinks everything is safe. If he did, he would understand why Issicore has become soft as a heated bar of iron. What makes men soft, Baas?"

"Love," I suggested.

"Yes. At times love makes some men soft—I mean men like the Baas. And what else, Baas?"

"Drink," I answered savagely, getting it back on Hans.

"Yes, at times drink makes some men soft. Men like me, Baas, who know that now and again it is wise to cease from being wise, lest Heaven should grow jealous of our wisdom and want to share it. But what makes all men soft?"

"I don't know."

"Then once more I must teach the Baas, as his Reverend Father, the Predikant, told me to do when I saw that the Baas had used up all his wits, saying to me before he died, 'Hans, whenever you perceive that my son Allan, who does not always look where he is going, walks into water and gets out of his depth, swim in and pull him out, Hans.'"

"You little liar!" I ejaculated, but taking no notice, Hans went on, "Baas, it is *fear* that makes all men soft. Issicore is bending about like a heated ramrod because within him burns the fire of fear."

"Fear of what, Hans?"

"As I have said, if the Baas had kept his eyes open, he would know. Did not the Baas notice a tall, dark-faced priest before whom the crowd parted, who came up to Issicore when first we landed on the quay here?"

"Yes, I saw such a man. He bowed politely and I thought was greeting Issicore and making him some present."

"And did the Baas see what kind of a present he made him and hear his words of wisdom? The Baas shakes his head. Well, I did. The present he gave to Issicore was a little skull carved out of black ivory or shell, or it may have been of polished lava rock. And the words of welcome were, 'The gift of Heu-Heu to the lord Issicore, that gift which Heu-Heu sends to all who break the law and dare to leave the Land of the Walloos.' Those were the words, for standing near by, I heard them, though I kept them from the Baas, waiting to see what would happen afterwards.

"Then the priest went away, and what Issicore did with the little black skull I do not know. Perhaps he wears it round his neck, as he hasn't got a watch chain, just as the Baas used to wear things that ladies had given him, or their pictures in a little silver brandy flask."

"Well, and what about this skull, Hans? What does it mean?"

"Baas, I made inquiries of an old man in that canoe, to pass the time away, Baas, as Issicore was at the other end and could not hear me. It means *death*, Baas. Does not the Baas remember how we were told at the Black Kloof that those who dared to leave the Land of Heu-Heu were always smitten with some sickness and died? Well, Baas, Issicore got out all right and left the sickness behind him, I expect because the priests did not know that he was going. But he made a mistake, Baas, that of coming back again, being drawn by his love of Sabeela, just as a fish is drawn by the bait on the hook, Baas. And now the hook is fast in his mouth, for the priests knew of his return well enough, Baas, and of course were waiting for him."

"What do you mean, Hans? How can the priests hurt Issicore, especially when they are all dead?"

"Yes, Baas, they are all dead and can harm no one, but Issicore is right when he says that Heu-Heu is not dead, because the devil never dies, Baas. His priests are dead, but Heu-Heu could kill the old Walloo, and so he can kill Issicore. There is a great deal in this fetish business, Baas, that good Christians like you and I do not understand. It won't work on Christians, Baas, which is why Heu-Heu can't kill us, but those who worship the Black One, at last the Black One takes by the throat."

I thought to myself that here Hans, although he did not know it, was enunciating one of the profoundest and most fundamental of truths, since those who bow the knee to Baal are Baal's servants and live under his law, even to the death, and what is Baal but Heu-Heu, or Satan? The fruit is always the same, by whatever name the tree may be called. However, I did not enter upon this argument with Hans, whom it would have bewildered, but only asked him what he meant and what he imagined was going to happen to Issicore. He answered, "I mean just what I have said, Baas; I mean that Issicore is going to die. That old man told me that those who 'receive the Black Skull,' always die within the month, and often more quickly. From the look of him, I should think that Issicore will not last more than a week. Although so handsome, he is really very dull, Baas, so it does not much matter, especially as the Lady Sabeela will get over it quite soon. That is why Issicore has changed, Baas. It is because the fear of death is upon him. In the same way Sabeela has changed because the fear of death and what to her, perhaps, is worse, has passed away."

"Bosh!" I exclaimed, but internally I had my doubts. I knew something of this fetish business, although I believed it to be the greatest of rubbish, I was sure that it is extremely dangerous rubbish. The secret soul of man, especially of savage, or primitive and untaught man, or the sub-conscious self, or whatever you choose to call it, is a terrible entity when brought into action by the hereditary superstitions that are born in his blood. In nine cases out of ten, if the victim of those superstitions is told with the accustomed ceremonies by the oracle of the god or devil from which they flow, that he will die, he does die. Nothing kills him, but he commits a kind of moral suicide. As Hans had said—Fear makes him soft. Then some kind of nervous disease penetrates his system and at the appointed hour withers up his physical life and causes him to pass away.

* * * * * * * *

Such, as it proved, was to be the fate of that Apollo-like person, the unhappy Issicore.

CHAPTER 15

Sabeela's Farewell

Now of this story there is little left to tell, and as it is very late and I see that you are all yawning, my friends (this was not true, for we were deeply interested, especially over the moral or spiritual problem of Issicore), I will cut that little as short as I can. It shall be a mere footnote.

After we had eaten that morning, we went to see Sabeela, whom we found very agitated. This was natural enough, considering all she had gone through, as after mental strain and the passing of great perils, a nervous reaction invariably follows. Also, in a sudden and terrible fashion, she had lost her father, to whom she was attached. But the real cause of her distress was different.

Issicore, it seemed, had been taken very ill. Nobody knew what was the matter with him, but Sabeela was persuaded that he had been poisoned. She begged me to visit him at once and cure him—a request that made me indignant. I explained to her that I was no authority on their native poisons, if he suffered from anything of the sort, and had few medicines with me, the only one of which that dealt with poisons was an antidote to snake bites. However, as she was very insistent, I said that I would go and see what I could do, which would probably be nothing.

So, together with Hans, I was conducted by some of the old headmen, or councillors of the Walloo, such people as in Zululand we should call *Indunas*, to the house of Issicore, a rather fine building of its sort at the other end of the town. We walked by the road that ran along the edge of the lake, which gave us an opportunity to observe the island, or rather what had been the island.

Now it was nothing but a low, dark mass, over which hung dense clouds of steam. When the winds stirred these clouds, I saw that beneath them were red streams of lava that ran into the lake. There were no more eruptions and the volcano appeared to have vanished away. Much dust was still falling. It lay thick upon the roadway and all the trees and other vegetation were covered with it, turning the landscape to a hue of ashen grey. Otherwise no damage had been done on the mainland, except that here and there boulders had fallen and some of the lower-lying fields were inundated by the great flood, which was now abating, although the river still overflowed its banks.

We reached the house of Issicore and were shown into his chamber, where he lay upon a couch of skins, attended by some women who, I understood, were his relatives. When Hans and I entered, these women bowed and went out, leaving us alone with the patient. A glance told me that he was a dying man. His fine eyes were fixed on vacancy; he breathed in gasps; his fingers clasped and unclasped themselves automatically, and from time to time he was taken with violent shiverings. These I thought must be due to some form of fever until I had tested his temperature with the thermometer I had in my little medicine case and found that it was two degrees below normal. On being questioned, he said that he had no pain and suffered only from great weakness and from a whirling of the head, by which I suppose meant giddiness.

I asked him to what he attributed his condition. He answered, "To the curse of Heu-Heu, Lord Macumazahn. Heu-Heu is killing me."

I inquired why, for to argue about the folly of the business was futile, and he replied, "For two reasons, Lord: first, because I left the land without his leave, and secondly, because I rowed you and the yellow man called Light-in-Darkness to the Holy Isle, to visit which unsummoned is the greatest of crimes. For this cause I must die more quickly than otherwise I should have done, but in any case my doom was certain, because I left the land to seek help for Sabeela. Here is the proof of it," and from somewhere about his person he produced the little black Death's Head which Hans had described to me. Then, without allowing me to touch the horrid thing, he hid it away again.

I tried to laugh him out of this idea, but he only smiled sadly and said, "I know that you must have thought me a coward, Lord, because of the way I have borne myself since we reached this town of Walloo, but it was the curse of Heu-Heu working within me that changed my spirit. I pray you to explain this to Sabeela, whom I love, but who I think also believes me a coward, for yesterday I read it in her eyes. Now while I have still strength I would speak to you. First, I thank you and the yellow man, Light-in-Darkness, who by courage or by magic—I know not which—have saved Sabeela from Heu-Heu, and have destroyed his House and his priests and, I am told, his image. Heu-Heu, it is true, lives on since he cannot die, but henceforward here he is without a home or a shape or a worshipper, and therefore his power over the souls and bodies of men is gone, and among the Walloos, in time his worship will die out. Perhaps no more of my people will perish by the curse of Heu-Heu, Lord."

"But why should you die, Issicore?"

"Because the curse fell on me first, Lord, while Heu-Heu reigned over the Walloos, as he has done from the beginning, he who was once their earthly king."

I began to combat this nonsense, but he waved his hand in protest, and went on:

"Lord, my time is short and I would say something to you. Soon I shall be no more and forgotten, even by Sabeela, whose husband I had hoped to become. I pray, therefore, that you will marry Sabeela."

Here I gasped, but held my peace till he had finished.

"Already I have caused her to be informed that such is my last wish. Also I have caused all the elders of the Walloos to be informed, and at a meeting held this morning they decided that this marriage would be right and wise, and have sent a messenger to tell me to die as quickly as I can, in order that it may be arranged at once."

"Great Heavens!" I exclaimed, but again he motioned to me to be silent, and went on:

"Lord, although she is not of your race, Sabeela is very beautiful, very wise also, and with you for her husband she may be able once more to build up the Walloos into a great people, as tradition says they were in the old days before there fell upon them the curse of Heu-Heu, which is now broken. For you, too, are wise and bold, and know many things which we do not know, and the people will serve you as a god and perhaps come to worship you in place of Heu-Heu, so that you found a mighty dynasty. At first this thought may seem strange to you, but soon you will come to see that it is great and good. Moreover, even if you were unwilling, things must come about as I have said."

"Why?" I asked, unable to contain myself any longer.

"Because, Lord, here in this land you must spend the rest of your life, for in it now you are a prisoner, nor with all your courage can you escape, since none will row you down the river, nor can you force a way, for it will be watched. Moreover, when you return to the house of the Walloo you will find that your cartridges have been taken, so that except for a few that you have about you, you are weaponless. Therefore, as here you must live, it is better that you should do so with

Sabeela rather than with any other woman, since she is the fairest and the cleverest of them all. Also by right of blood she is the ruler, and through her you will become Walloo, as I should have done according to our custom."

At this point he closed his eyes and for a while appeared to become senseless. Presently he opened them again and, staring at me, lifted his feeble hands and cried:

"Greeting to the Walloo! Long life and glory to the Walloo!"

Nor was this all, for, to my horror, from the other side of the partition that divided the house I heard the women whom I have mentioned echo the salutation:

"Greeting to the Walloo! Long life and glory to the Walloo!"

Then again Issicore became senseless; at least, nothing I said seemed to reached his understanding. So after waiting for a time Hans and I went away, thinking that all was over. This, however, was not so, since he lived till nightfall and, I was told, recovered his senses for some hours before the end, during which time Sabeela visited him, accompanied by certain of the notables or elders. It was then, as I suppose, that this ill-fated but most unselfish Issicore, the handsomest man whom ever I beheld, to his own satisfaction, if not to mine, settled everything for what he conceived to be the welfare of his country and his lady-love.

* * * * * * * *

"Well, Baas," said Hans when we were outside the house, "I suppose we had better go home. It is *your* home now, isn't it, Baas? No, Baas, it is no use looking at that river, for you see these Walloos are so kind that they have already provided you with a chief's escort."

I looked. It was true enough. In place of the one man who had guided us to the house there were now twenty great fellows armed with spears who saluted me in a most reverential manner and insisted upon sticking close to my heels, I presume in case I should try to take to them. So back we went, the guard of twenty marching in a soldier-like fashion immediately behind, while Hans declaimed at me:

"It is just what I expected, Baas, for of course if a man is very fond of women, in his inside, Baas, they know it and like him—no need to tell them in so many words, Baas—and being kind-hearted, are quite ready to be fond of him. That is what has happened here, Baas. From the moment that the lady Sabeela saw you, she didn't care a pinch of snuff for Issicore, although he was so good-looking and had walked such a long way to help her. No, Baas, she perceived something in you which she couldn't find in two yards and a bit of Issicore, who after all was an empty kind of drum, Baas, and only made a noise when you hit him—a little noise for a small tap, Baas, and a big noise for a bang. Moreover, whatever he was, he is done now, so it is no use wasting time talking about him.

"Well, this won't be such a bad country to live in now that the most of those Heuheua are dead—look! there are some of their bodies lying on the shore—and no doubt the beer can be brewed stronger, and there is tobacco. So it will be all right till we get tired of it, Baas, after which, perhaps, we shall be able to run away. Still, I am glad none of them wish to marry me, Baas, and make me work like a whole team of oxen to drag them out of their mudholes."

Thus he went on pouring out his bosh by the yard, and literally I was so crushed that I couldn't find a word in answer. Truly, it is the unexpected that always happens. During the last few days I had foreseen many dangers and dealt with some. But this was one of which I had never dreamed. What a fate! To be kept a prisoner in a kind of gilded cage and made to labour for my living too, like a performing monkey. Well, I would find a way between the bars or my name wasn't Allan Quatermain. Only what way? At the time I could see none, for those bars seemed to be thick and strong. Moreover, there were those gentlemen with the spears behind.

In due course we arrived at the Walloo's house without incident and went straight to our room where, after investigation in a corner, Hans called out:

"Issicore was quite right, Baas. All the cartridges have gone and the rifles also. Now we have only got our pistols and twenty-four rounds of ammunition between us."

I looked. It was so! Then I stared out of the window-place, and behold! there in the garden were the twenty men already engaged in marking out ground for the erection of a guard-hut.

"They mean to settle there, so as to be nice and handy in case the Baas wants them—or they want the Baas," said Hans significantly, adding, "I believe that wherever he goes the Walloo always has an escort of twenty men!"

* * * * * * * *

Now for the next few days I saw nothing of Sabeela, or of Dramana either, since they were engaged in the ceremonious obsequies, first of the Walloo and next of the unlucky Issicore, to which for some religious reason or other, I was not invited.

Certain headmen or Indunas, however, were always waiting to pounce on me. Whenever I put my nose out-of-doors they appeared, bowing humbly, and proceeded to take the occasion to instruct me in the history and customs of the Walloo people, till I thought that my boyhood had returned and I was once more reading "Sandford and Merton" and acquiring knowledge through the art of conversation. Those old gentlemen bored me stiff. I tried to get rid of them by taking long walks at a great pace, but they responded nobly, being ready to trot by my side till they dropped, talking, talking, talking. Moreover, if I could outwalk those ancient councillors, the guard of twenty who formed a kind of chorus on these expeditions, were excellent hands with their legs, as an Irishman might say, and never turned a hair. Sometimes they turned me, however, if they thought I was going where I should not, since then half of them would dart ahead and politely bar the way.

At length, on the third or fourth day, all the ceremonies were finished and I was summoned into Sabeela's presence.

As Hans said afterwards, it was all very fine. Indeed, I thought it pathetic with its somewhat tawdry conditions of ancient, almost forgotten ceremonial inherited from a highly civilized race that was now sinking into barbarism. There was the Lady Sabeela, very beautiful to see, for she was a lovely woman and grandly dressed in a half-wild fashion, who played the part of a queen and not without dignity, as perhaps her ancestresses had done thousands of years before on some greater stage. Here too were her white-haired attendants or Indunas, the same who bored me out walking, representing the councillors and high officials of forgotten ages.

Yet the Queen was no longer a queen; she was merging into the savage chieftainess, as the councillors were into the chattering mob that surrounds such a person in a thousand *kraals* or towns of Africa. The proceedings, too, were very long, for each of these councillors or elders made a speech in which he repeated all that the others had said before, narrating with variations everything that happened in the land since I had set foot within it, together with fancy accounts of what Hans and I had done upon the island.

From these speeches, however, I learned one thing, namely, that most of the wild Hairy Folk, who were named Heuheua, had perished in the great catastrophe of the blowing up of the mountain, only a few, together with the old men, the children and the females, being left to carry on the race. Therefore, they said, the Walloos were safe from attack, at any rate, for a couple of generations to come, as might be learned from the wailings which arose in the forest at night—that, as a matter of fact, I had heard myself—pathetic and horrible sounds of almost animal grief. This, said these merciless sages, gave the Walloos a great opportunity, for now was the time to hunt down and kill the Wood-folk to the last woman and child—a task which they considered I was eminently fitted to carry out!

When they had all spoken, Sabeela's turn came. She rose from her throne-like chair and addressed us with real eloquence. First of all she pointed out that she was a woman suffering from a double grief—the death of her father and that of the man to whom she had been affianced, losses that made her heart heavy. Then, very touchingly, she thanked Hans and myself for all we had done to save her. But for us, she said, either she would now have been dead or nothing but a degraded slave in the house of Heu-Heu, which we had destroyed together with Heu-Heu himself, with the result that she and the land were free once more. Next she announced in words which evidently had been prepared, that this was no time for her to think of past sorrows or love, who now must look to the future. For a man like myself there was but one fitting reward, and that was the rule over the Walloo people, and with it the gift of her own person.

Therefore, by the wish of her Councillors, she had decreed that we were to be wed on the fourth morning from that of the present day, after which, by right of marriage, I was publicly to be declared the Walloo. Meanwhile, she summoned me to her side (where an empty chair had been set in preparation for this event) that we might exchange the kiss of betrothal.

Now, as may be imagined, I hung back; indeed, never have I felt more firmly fixed to a seat than at that fearsome moment. I did not know what to say, and my tongue seemed glued to the roof of my mouth. So I just sat still with all those old donkeys staring at me, Sabeela watching me out of the corners of her eyes and waiting. The silence grew painful, and in its midst Hans coughed in his husky fashion, then delivered himself thus.

"Get up, Baas," he whispered, "and go through with it. It isn't half as bad as it looks, and indeed, some people would like it very much. It is better to kiss a pretty lady than to have your throat cut, Baas, for that is what I think will happen if you don't, because a woman whom you don't kiss, after she has asked you in public, *always* turns nasty, Baas."

I felt that there was force in this argument, and, to cut a long story short, I went up into that chair and did—well—all that was required. Lord! what a fool I felt while those idiots cheered and Hans below grinned at me like a whole cageful of baboons. However, it was but ceremonial, a mere formality, just touching the brow of the fair Sabeela with my lips and receiving an acknowledgment in kind.

After this we sat a while side by side listening to those old Walloo Councillors chanting a ridiculous song, something about the marriage of a hero to a goddess, which I presume they must have composed for the occasion. Under cover of the noise, which was great, for they had excellent lungs, Sabeela spoke to me in a low voice and without turning her face or looking at me.

"Lord," she said, "try to look less unhappy, lest these people should suspect something and listen to what we are saying. The law is that we should meet no more till the marriage day, but I must see you alone tonight. Have no fear," she added with a rather sarcastic smile, "for, although I must be alone, you can bring your companion with you, since what I have to say concerns you both. Meet me in the passage that runs from this chamber to your own, at midnight when all sleep. It has no window places and its walls are thick, so that there we can be neither seen nor heard. Be careful to bolt the door behind you, as I will that of this chamber. Do you understand?"

Clapping my hands hilariously to show my delight in the musical performance, I whispered back that I did.

"Good. When the singing comes to an end, announce that you have a request to make of me. Ask that tomorrow you may be given a canoe and paddlers to row to the island to learn what has happened there and to discover whether any of the Wood-folk are still alive upon its shores. Say that if so measures must be taken to make an end of them, lest they should escape. Now speak no more."

At length the song was finished, and with it the ceremony. To show that this was over, Sabeela rose from her chair and curtseyed to me, whereon I also rose and returned the compliment with my best bow. Thus, then, we bade a public farewell of each other until the happy marriage morn. Before we parted, however, I asked as a favour in a loud voice that I might be permitted to visit the island, or, at any rate, to row round it, giving the reasons she had suggested. To this she answered, "Let it be as my Lord wishes," and before any one could raise objections, withdrew herself, followed by some serving woman and by Dramana, who I thought did not seem too pleased at the turn events had taken.

****

I pass on to that midnight interview. At the appointed time, or rather a little before it, I went into the passage accompanied by Hans, who was most unwilling to come for reasons which he gave in a Dutch proverb to the effect of our own; that two's company and three's none. Here we stood in the dark and waited. A few minutes later the door at the far end of it opened—it was a very long passage—and walking down it appeared Sabeela, clad in white and bearing in her hand a naked lamp. Somehow in this garb and in these surroundings, thus illumined, she looked more beautiful than I had ever seen her, almost spirit-like indeed. We met, and without any greeting she said to me, "Lord Watcher-by-Night, I find you watching by night according to my prayer. It may have seemed a strange prayer to you, but hearken to its reason. I cannot think that you believe me to desire this marriage, which I know to be hateful to you, seeing that I am of another race to yourself and that you only look upon me as a half-savage woman whom it has been your fortune to save from shame or death. Nay, contradict me not, I beseech you, since at times the truth is good. Because it is so good I will add to it, telling you the reason why I also do not desire this marriage, or rather the greatest reason; namely, that I loved Issicore, who from childhood had been my playmate until he became more than playmate."

"Yes," I interrupted, "and I know that he loved you. Only then why was it that on his deathbed he himself urged on this matter?"

"Because, Lord, Issicore had a noble heart. He thought you the greatest man whom he had ever known, half a god indeed, for he told me so. He held also that you would make me happy and rule this country well, lifting it up again out of its long sleep. Lastly, he knew that if you did not marry me, you and your companion would be murdered. If he judged wrongly in these matters, it must be remembered, moreover, that his mind was blotted with the poison that had been given to him, for myself I am sure that he did not die of fear alone."

"I understand. All honour be to him," I said.

"I thank you. Now, Lord, know that, although I am ignorant I believe that we live again beyond the gate of Death. Perhaps that faith has come down to me from my forefathers when they worshipped other gods besides the devil Heu-Heu; at least, it is mine. My hope is, therefore, that when I have passed that gate, which perhaps will be before so very long, on its farther side I shall once more find Issicore— Issicore as he was before the curse of Heu-Heu fell upon him and he drank the poison of the priests—and for this reason I desire to wed no other man."

"All honour be to you also," I murmured.

"Again, I thank you, Lord. Now let us turn to other matters. Tomorrow after midday a canoe will be ready, and in it you will find your weapons that have been stolen and all that is yours. It will be manned by four rowers; men known to be spies of the priests of Heu-Heu, stationed here upon the mainland to watch the Walloos, who in time would themselves have become priests. Therefore, now that Heu-Heu has fallen they are doomed to die, not at once but after a while, perhaps, as it will seem, by sickness or accident, because if they live, the Walloo Councillors fear lest they should re-establish the rule of Heu-Heu. They know this well, and therefore they desire above all things to escape the land while their life is yet in them."

"Have you seen these men, Sabeela?"

"Nay, but Dramana has seen them. Now, Lord, I will tell you something, if you have not guessed it for yourself, though I do this not without shame. Dramana does not desire our marriage, Lord. You saved Dramana as well as myself, and Dramana, like Issicore, has come to look on you as half a god. Need I say more, save that, of course, for this reason she does desire your escape, since she would rather that you went free and were lost to both of us than that you should bide here and marry me. Have I said enough?"

"Plenty," I answered, knowing that she spoke truth.

"Then what is there to add, save that I trust all will go well, and that by the dawn of the day that follows this, you and the yellow man, your servant, will be safely out of this accursed land. If that comes about, as I believe it will, for after the dusk has fallen and before the moon rises those who guide the canoe will bring it, not to the quay, but into the mouth of the river down which you must paddle by the moonlight; then I pray of you at times in your own country to think of Sabeela, the broken-hearted chieftainess of a doomed people, as day by day, when she rises and lays herself down to sleep, she will think of you who saved her and all of us from ruin. My Lord, farewell, and to you, Light-in-Darkness, also farewell."

Then she took my hand, kissed it, and, without another word, glided away as she had come.

* * * * * * * *

This was the last that ever I saw or heard of Sabeela the Beautiful. I wonder whether she lived long. Somehow I do not think so; that night I seemed to see death in her eyes.

CHAPTER 16

The Race For Life

Now, like a Scotch parson, I have come to "lastly"—that inspiring word at which the sleepiest congregation awakes. The morning following this strange midnight meeting, Hans and I spent in our room, for it appeared to be the ancient Walloo etiquette that, save by special permission, the prospective bridegroom should not go out for several days before the marriage, I suppose because of some primitive idea that his affections might be diverted by the sight of alien beauty.

At midday we ate, or, so far as I was concerned, pretended to eat, for anxiety took away my appetite. A little while afterwards, to my intense relief, the captain of our prison-warders, for that is what they were, appeared and said that he was commanded to conduct us to the canoe which was to paddle us to inspect what remained of the island. I replied that we would graciously consent to go. So taking all our small possessions with us, including a bundle containing our spare clothes and the twigs from the Tree of Illusions, we departed and were escorted to the quay by our guards, of whose faces I was heartily tired. Here we found a small canoe awaiting us, manned by four secret-faced men, strong fellows all of them, who raised their paddles in salute. Apparently the place had been cleared of loiterers, since there was only one other person present, a woman wrapped in a long cloak that hid her face.

As we were about to enter the canoe this woman approached us and lifted her head. She was Dramana.

"Lord," she said, "I have been sent by my sister, the new Walloo, to tell you that you will find the iron tubes which spit out fire and all that belongs to them under a mat in the prow of the canoe. Also she bids me wish you a prosperous journey to the island that aforetime was named Holy, which island she wishes never to see again."

I thanked her and bade her convey my greeting to the Walloo, my

181

bride to be, adding in a loud voice, that I hoped ere long to be able to do this in person when her "veil fell down."

Then I turned to enter the canoe.

"Lord," said Dramana with a convulsive movement of her hands, "I make a prayer to you. It is that you will take me with you to look my last upon that isle where I dwelt so long a slave, which I desire to see once more—now that I am free."

Instinctively I felt that a crisis had arisen which demanded firm and even brutal treatment.

"Nay, Dramana," I answered, "it is always unlucky for an escaped slave to revisit his prison, lest once more its bars should close about that slave."

"Lord," she said, "the loosed prisoner is sometimes dazed by freedom, so that the heart cries again for its captivity. Lord, I am a good slave and a loving. Will you not take me with you?"

"Nay, Dramana," I answered as I sprang into the canoe. "This boat is fully loaded. It would not be for your welfare or for mine. Farewell!"

She gazed at me earnestly with a pitiful countenance that grew wrathful by degrees, as might well happen in the case of a woman scorned: then, muttering something about being "cast off," burst into angry tears and turned away. For my part I motioned to the oarsmen to loose the craft and departed, feeling like a thief and traitor. Yet I was not to blame, for what else could I do? Dramana, it is true, had been a good friend to us, and I liked her. But we had repaid her help by saving her from Heu-Heu, and for the rest, one must draw the line somewhere. If once she had entered that canoe, metaphorically speaking, she would never have got out of it again.

Presently we were out on the open lake where the wavelets danced and the sun shone brightly, and glad I was to be clear of all those painful complications and once more in the company of pure and natural things. We paddled away to the island and made the land, or rather drew near to it, at the spot where the ancient city had stood in which we had found the petrified men and animals. But we did not set foot on it, for everywhere little streams of glowing lava trickled down into the lake and the ruins had vanished beneath a sea of ashes. I do not think that any one will ever again behold those strange relics of a past I know not how remote.

Turning, we paddled on slowly round the island till we came to the place where the Rock of Offering had been, upon which I had experienced so terrible an adventure. It had vanished, and with it the cave mouth, the garden of Heu-Heu, its Tree of Illusions, and all the rich cultivated land. The waters of the lake, turbid and steaming, now beat against the face of a stony hillock which was all that remained of the Holy Isle. The catastrophe was complete; the volcano was but a lump of lava from the dying heart of which its life-blood of flame still palpitated in red and ebbing streams. I wonder whether its smothered fires will ever break out again elsewhere. For aught I know they may have done so already somewhere on the mainland.

By the time that we had completed our journey round the place on which no living creature now was left, though once or twice we saw the bloated body of a Heuheua savage bobbing about in the water, the sun was setting, and it was dark before we were again off the town of the Walloos. While any light remained by which we could be seen, we headed straight for the landing place, that which we had left when we started for the island.

The moment that its last rays faded, however, there was a whispered conference between our four paddlemen, the ex-neophytes of Heu-Heu. Then the direction of the canoe was altered, and instead of making for the main land, we rowed on parallel with it till we came to the mouth of the Black River. It was so dark that I could not discern the exact time at which we left the lake and entered the stream; indeed, I did not know that we were in it until the increased current told me so. This current was now running very strongly after the great flood and bore us along at a good pace. My fear was lest in the gloom we should be dashed against rocks on the banks, or caught by the overhanging branches of trees or strike a snag, but those four men seemed to know every yard of the river and managed to keep us in its centre, probably by following the current where it ran most swiftly.

So we went on, not paddling very fast for fear of accidents, until the moon rose, which, as she was only a few days past her full, gave us considerable light even in that dark place. So soon as her rays reached us our paddlers gave way with a will, and we shot down the flooded stream as a great speed.

"I think we are all right now, Baas," said Hans, "for with so good a start those Walloos could scarcely catch us, even if they try. We are lucky, too, for you have left behind you two ladies who between them would have torn you into pieces, and I have left a place where the fools who live in it wearied me so much that I should soon have died."

He paused for a moment, then added in a horrified voice:

"*Allemagter!* we are not so lucky after all; we have forgotten something."

"What?" I asked anxiously.

183

"Why, Baas, those red and white stones we came to fetch, of which, before Heu-Heu dropped a red-hot rock upon his head, that old *kraansick*" (that is, mad) "Walloo, promised us as many as we wished. Sabeela would have filled the boat with them if we had only asked her, and we should never have had to work any more, but could have sat in fine houses and drunk the best gin from morning to night."

At these words I felt positively sick. It was too true. Amongst other pressing matters, concerning life, death, marriage, and liberty, I had forgotten utterly all about the diamonds and gold. Still when I came to think of it, although perhaps Hans might have done so, in view of the manner of our parting, I did not quite see how I could have asked Sabeela for them. It would have been an anticlimax and might have left a nasty taste in her mouth. How could she continue to look upon a man as—well, something quite out of the ordinary, who called her back to remind her that there was a little pecuniary matter to be settled and a fee to be paid for services rendered? Further, the sight of us bearing sacks of treasure might have excited suspicion; unless, indeed, Sabeela had caused them to be placed in the boat as she did in the case of the guns. Also they would have been heavy and inconvenient to carry, as I explained to Hans. Yet I did feel sick, for once more my hopes of wealth, or, at any rate, of a solid competence for the rest of my days, had vanished into thin air.

"Life is more than gold," I said sententiously to Hans, "and great honour is better than both."

It sounded like something out of the Book of Proverbs, but somehow I had not got it quite right though I reflected that fortunately Hans would not know the difference. However, he knew more than I thought, for he answered, "Yes, Baas, your Reverend Father used to talk like that. Also he said that it was better to live on watercresses with an easy mind, however angry they might make your stomach, than to dwell in a big hut with a couple of cross women, which is what would have happened to you, Baas, if you had stopped at Walloo. Besides, we are quite safe now, even if we haven't got the gold and diamonds, which, as you say, are heavy things, so safe that I think I shall go to sleep, Baas. *Allemagter!* Baas, *what's that?*"

"Only those poor hairy women howling over their dead in the forest," I answered rather carelessly, for their cries, which were very distressing in the silence of the river, still echoed in my ears. Also I was still thinking of the lost diamonds.

"I wish it were, Baas. They might howl till their heads fell off for all I care. But it isn't. It's paddles. *The Walloos are hunting us, Baas*. Listen!"

I did listen, and to my horror heard the regular stroke of paddles striking the water at a distance behind us, a great number of them, fifty I should say. One of the big canoes must be on our track.

"Oh, Baas!" said Hans, "it is your fault again. Without doubt that lady Dramana loves you so much that she can't make up her mind to part with you and has ordered out a big canoe to fetch you back. Unless, indeed," he added with an access of hopefulness, "it is the Lady Sabeela sending a farewell gift of jewels after us, having remembered that we should like some to make us think of her afterwards."

"It is those confounded Walloos sending a gift of spears," I answered gloomily, adding, "Get the rifles ready, Hans, for I'm not going to be taken alive."

Whatever the cause, it was clear that we were being pursued, and in my heart I did wonder whether Dramana had anything to do with it. No doubt I had treated her rudely because I could not help it, also Dramana had been badly trained among those rascally priests. But I hoped, and still hope, that she was innocent of this treachery. The truth of the matter I never learned.

Our crew of escaping priestly spies had also heard the paddles, for I saw the frightened look they gave to each other and the fierce energy with which they bent themselves to their work. Good heavens! how they paddled, who knew that their lives hung upon the issue. For hour after hour away we flew down that flooded, rushing river, while behind us, drawing nearer minute by minute, sounded the beat of those insistent paddles. Our canoe was swift, but how could we hope to escape from one driven by fifty men when we had but four?

It was just as we passed the place where we had slept on our inward journey—for now we had left the forest behind and were between the cliffs, travelling quite twice as fast as we had done up stream—that I caught sight of the pursuing boat, perhaps half a mile behind us, and saw that it was one of the largest of the Walloo fleet. After this, owing to the position of the moon, that in this narrow place left the surface of the water quite dark, I saw it no more for several hours. But I heard it drawing nearer, ever nearer, like some sure and deadly bloodhound following on the spoor of a fleeing slave.

Our men began to tire. Hans and I took the paddles of two of them to give the pair a rest and time to eat; then for a spell the paddles of the other two, while they did likewise. This, however, caused us to lose way, since we were not experts at the game, though here after the flood the river rushed so fast that our lack of skill made little difference.

At length the daylight came and gathered till at last the glimmer of it reached us in our cleft, and by that faint, uncertain light I saw the pursuing canoe not a hundred yards behind. In its way it was a very weird and impressive spectacle. There were the precipitous, towering cliffs, between or rather above which appeared a line of blue sky. There was the darksome, flood-filled, foaming river, and there on its surface was our tiny boat propelled by four weary and perspiring men, while behind came the great war canoe whose presence could just be detected in a dim outline and by the white of the water where its oarsmen smote it into froth.

"They are coming up fast, Baas, and we still have a long way to go. Soon they will catch us, Baas," said Hans.

"Then we must try to stop them for a while," I answered grimly. "Give me the Express rifle, Hans, and do you take the Winchester."

Then, lying down in the canoe and resting the rifles on its stern, we waited our opportunity. Presently we came to a place where at some time there had been a cliff-slide, for here the debris of it narrowed the river, turning it, now that it was so full, into something like a torrent. At this spot, also, because of the enlargement of the cleft, more light reached us, so that we could see our pursuers, who were about fifty yards away, not clearly indeed, but well enough for our purpose.

"Aim low and pump it into them, Hans," I said, and next instant discharged both barrels of the Express at the foremost rowers.

Hans followed suit, but, as the Winchester held five cartridges, went on firing after I had ceased.

The result was instantaneous. Some men sank down, some paddles fell into the water—I could not tell how many—and a great cry arose from the smitten or their companions. He who steered or captained the canoe from the prow apparently was among the hit. She veered round and for a while was broadside on to the current, exposing her bottom and threatening to turn over. Into this, having loaded, I sent two expanding bullets, hoping to spring a leak in her, though I was not certain if I should succeed, as the wood of these canoes is thick. I think I did, however, since even when she had got on her course again she came more slowly, and I thought that once I saw a man bailing.

On we went, making the most of the advantage that this check gave to us. But by now our men were very tired and their hands were raw from blisters, so that only the terror of death forced them to continue paddling. Indeed, at the last our progress grew very slow, and in fact was due more to the current than to our own efforts. Therefore the following canoe, which as was customary in Walloo boats of that size, probably carried spare paddle men, once more gained upon us.

Hereabouts the river wound between its cliffs so that we only got sight of it from time to time. Whenever we did so I took the Winchester and fired, no doubt inflicting some damage and checking its advance.

At length the winding ceased and we reached the last stretch, a clear run of a mile or so before the river ended in the swamp that I have described.

By this time pursuers and pursued, both of us, were going but slowly, drifting rather than paddling, since all were exhausted. Whenever I could get a sight I fired away, but still with a sullen determination and in utter silence our assailants came up, till now they were scarcely twenty paces from us, and some of them threw spears, one of which stuck in the bottom of our canoe, just missing my foot. At this spot the cliffs drew so near together at the top that I ceased shooting, as I could not see to aim, and, having no cartridges to waste, decided to keep those that remained for the emergency of the last attack.

Now we were in the ultimate reach of the river, and now at last we grounded upon the first mudbank of the swamp. Those who remained unhurt of the following Walloos made a final effort to overtake us; by the strong light that flowed from the open land beyond us I could see their glaring eyeballs and their tongues hanging from their jaws with exhaustion. I yelled an order.

"Seize everything we have and run for it!" I cried, grabbing at my rifle and such other articles as were within reach, including the remaining cartridges.

The others did likewise—I do not think that anything was left in that canoe except the paddles. Then I leapt on to the shore and ran to the right, following the edge of the swamp, the rest coming after me. Fifty yards or more away I sank down upon a little ridge from sheer exhaustion and because my cramped legs would no longer carry me, and watched to see what would happen. Indeed, I was so worn out that I felt I would rather die where I was than try to flee farther.

We grouped ourselves together, awaiting the crisis, for I thought that surely we should be attacked. But we were not. At the mudbank the pursuing Walloos ceased from their efforts. For a little while they sat dejectedly in their craft till they had recovered breath.

Then for the first time those mute hunting-hounds gave tongue, for they shouted maledictions on us, and especially on our four paddlers, the neophytes of Heu-Heu, telling these that although to follow them farther was not lawful, they would die, as Issicore died who left the land. One of our men, stung into repartee, retaliated in words to the effect that some of them had died in attempting to keep us in the land, as they would find if they counted their oarsmen.

To this obvious truth the pursuers made no answer, nor did they inform us who sent them on the chase. Securing our small canoe, they laid in it certain dead men who had fallen beneath the bullets of Hans and myself, and departed slowly up stream, towing it after them. This was the last that I saw of their handsome, fanatical faces and of their confounded country in which I went so near to death, or to becoming a prisoner for life, that might have been worse.

"Baas," said Hans, lighting his pipe, "that was a great journey and one which it will be nice to think about, now that it is over, though I wish that we had killed more of those Walloo men-stealers."

"I don't, Hans; I hated being obliged to shoot them," I answered; "nor do I wish to think any more of that race for our lives, unless it comes back in a nightmare when I can't help doing so."

"Don't you, Baas? I find such thoughts pleasant when the danger is past and we who might have been dead are alive, and the others who were alive are dead and telling the tale to Heu-Heu."

"Each to his taste; yours isn't mine," I muttered.

Hans puffed at his pipe for a while, and went on, "It's funny, Baas, that those *carles* did not get out of their canoe and come to kill us with their spears. I suppose they were afraid of the rifles."

"No, Hans," I answered, "they are brave men who would not have stopped because of the bullets. They were afraid of more than these: they feared the Curse which says that those who leave their land will die and go to hell. Heu-Heu has done us a good turn there, Hans."

"Yes, Baas, no doubt he has become a Christian in the Place of Fires and is repaying good for evil, turning the other cheek, Baas. I felt like that myself when I thought those Walloos were going to catch us, but now I feel quite different. Baas, you remember how your Reverend Father used to say that if you love Heaven, Heaven looks after you and pulls you out of every kind of mudhole. That's why I'm sitting here smoking, Baas, instead of making meat for crocodiles. If it wasn't for our forgetting about those jewels, it has looked after us very well, but there are so many up there that perhaps Heaven forgot them also."

"No, Hans," I said, "Heaven remembered that if we had tried to carry bags of stones out of that boat, as well as Zikali's medicine and the rest, the Walloos would have caught us before we got away. They were quite close, Hans."

"Yes, Baas, I see, and that was very nice of Heaven. And now, Baas, I think we had better be moving. Those Walloos might forget about the curse for a little while and come back to look for us. Heaven is a queer thing, Baas. Sometimes it changes its face all of a sudden and grows angry—just like the lady Dramana did when you said that you wouldn't take her with you in the canoe yesterday."

* * * * * * * *

Allan paused to help himself to a little weak whisky and water, then said in his jerky fashion, "Well, that's the end of the story, of which I am glad, whatever you may be, for my throat is dry with talking. We got back to the wagon all right after sundry difficulties and a tiring march across the desert, and it was time we did so, for when we arrived we had only three rifle cartridges left between us. You see we were obliged to fire such a lot at the Heuheua, when they attacked us on the lake, and afterwards at those Walloos to prevent them from catching us that night. However, there were more in the wagon, and I shot four elephants with them going home. They had very large tusks, which afterwards I sold for about enough to cover the expenses of the journey."

"Did old Zikali make you pay for those oxen?" I asked.

"No, he did not, because I told him that if he tried it on I would not give him his bundle of *mouti* that we cut from the Tree of Illusions and carried safely all that way. So as he was very keen on the medicine, he made me a present of the oxen. Also I found my own there grown fat and strong again. It was a curious thing, but the old scoundrel seemed to know most of what had happened to us before ever I told him a word. Perhaps he learned it all from one of those acolytes of Heu-Heu who fled with us because they feared that they would be murdered if they stayed in their own land. I forgot to tell you that these men—most uncommunicative persons—melted away upon our homeward journey. Suddenly they were missing. I presume that they departed to set up as witch doctors on their own account. If so, very possibly one or more of them may have come into touch with Zikali, the head of the craft in that part of Africa, and before I reached the Black Kloof.

"The first thing he asked me was: 'Why did you not bring any gold and diamonds away with you? Had you done so, you might have become rich who now remain poor, Macumazahn.'

"'Because I forgot to ask for them,' I said.

"'Yes, I know you forgot to ask for them. You were thinking so much of the pain of saying goodbye to that beautiful lady whose name I have not learned that you forgot to ask for them. It is just like you, Macumazahn. *Oho! Oho!* it is just like you.'

"Then he stared at his fire for a while, in front, of which, as usual, he was sitting, and added: 'Yet somehow I think that diamonds will make you rich one day, when there is no woman left to say good-bye to, Macumazahn.'

"It was a good shot of his, for, as you fellows know, that came about at King Solomon's mines, didn't it? when there was 'no woman left to say good-bye to.'"

Here Good turned his head away, and Allen went on hurriedly, I think because he remembered Foulata, and saw that his thoughtless remark had given pain.

"Zikali was very interested in all our story and made me stop at the Black Kloof for some days to tell him every detail.

"'*I* knew that Heu-Heu was an idol,' he said, 'though I wanted you to find it out for yourself, and therefore told you nothing about it, just as I knew that handsome man, Issicore, would die. But I didn't tell him anything about that either, because, if I had, you see he might have died before he had shown you the way to his country, and then I shouldn't have got my *mouti*, which is necessary to me, for without it how should I paint more pictures on my fire? Well, you brought me a good bundle of leaves which will last my time, and as the Tree of Illusions is burned and there is no other left in the world, there will be no more of it. I am glad that it is burned, for I do not wish that any wizard should arise in the land who will be as great as was Zikali, Opener-of-Roads. While that tree grew the high priest of Heu-Heu was almost as great, but now he is dead and his tree is burned, and I, Zikali, reign alone. That is what I desired, Macumazahn, and that is why I sent you to Heuheua Land.'

"'You cunning old villain!' I exclaimed.

"'Yes, Macumazahn, I am cunning just as you are simple, and my heart is black like my skin, just as yours is white like your skin. That is why I am great, Macumazahn, and wield power over thousands and accomplish my desires, whereas you are small and have no power and will die with all your desires unaccomplished. Yet, in the end, who knows, who knows? Perhaps in the land beyond it may be otherwise. Heu-Heu was great also and where is Heu-Heu today?'

"'There never was a Heu-Heu,' I said.

"'No, Macumazahn, there never was a Heu-Heu, but there were priests of Heu-Heu. Is it not so with many of the gods men set up?

They are not and never were, but their priests *are* and shake the spear of power and pierce the hearts of men with terrors. What, then, does it matter about the gods whom no man sees, when the priest is there shaking the spear of power and piercing the hearts of their worshippers? The god is the priest or the priest is the god—have it which way you like, Macumazahn.'

"'Not always, Zikali.' Then, as I did not wish to enter into argument with him on such a subject, I asked, 'Who carved the statue of Heu-Heu in the Cave of Illusions? The Walloos did not know.'

"'Nor do I, Macumazahn,' he answered. 'The world is very old and there have been peoples in it of whom we have heard nothing, or so my Spirit tells me. Without doubt one of those peoples carved it thousands of years ago, an invading people, the last of their race, who had been driven out elsewhere and coming south, those who were left of them, hid themselves away from their enemies in this secret place amid a horde of savages so hideous that it was reported to be haunted by demons. There, in a cave in the midst of a lake where they could not be come at, they carved an image of their god, or perhaps of the god of the savages, whom it seems that it resembled.

"'Mayhap the savages took their name from Heu-Heu, or mayhap Heu-Heu took his name from them. Who can tell? At any rate, when men seek a god, Macumazahn, they make one like themselves, only larger, uglier, and more evil, at least in this land, for what they do elsewhere I know not. Also, often they say that this god was once their king, since at the bottom all worship their ancestors who gave them life, if they worship anything at all, and often, too, because they gave them life, they think that they must have been devils. Great ancestors were the first gods, Macumazahn, and if they had not been evil they would never have been great. Look at Chaka, the Lion of the Zulus. He is called great because he was so wicked and cruel, and so it was and is with others if they succeed, though, if they fail, men speak otherwise of them.'

"'That is not a pretty faith, Zikali,' I said.

"'No, Macumazahn, but then little in the world is pretty, except the world itself. The Heuheua are not pretty, or rather were not, for I think that you killed most of them when you blew up the mountain, which is a good thing. Heu-Heu was not pretty, nor were his priests. Only the Walloos, and especially their women, remain pretty because of the old blood that runs in them, the high old blood that Heu-Heu sucked from their veins.'

"'Well, Heu-Heu has gone, Zikali, and now what will become of the Walloos?'

"'I cannot say, Macumazahn, but I expect they will follow Heu-Heu, who has taken hold of their souls and will drag them after him. If so, it does not matter, since they are but the rotting stump of a tree that once was tall and fair. The dust of Time hides many such stumps, Macumazahn. But what of that? Other fine trees are growing which also will become stumps in their season, and so on for ever.'

* * * * * * * *

"Thus Zikali held forth, though of what he said I forget much. I daresay that he spoke truth, but I remember that his melancholy and pessimistic talk depressed me, and that I cut it as short as I could. Also it did not really explain anything, since he could not tell me who the Walloos or the Hairy Folk were, or why they worshipped Heu-Heu, or what was their beginning, or what would be their end.

"All these things remained and remain lost in mystery, since I have never heard anything more of them, and if any subsequent travellers have visited the district where they live, which is not probable, they did not succeed in ascending the river, or if they did, they never descended it again. So if you want to know more of the story, you must go and find it out for yourselves. Only, as I think I said, I won't go with you."

* * * * * * * *

"Well," said Captain Good, "it is a wonderful yarn. Hang me, if I could have told it better myself!"

"No, Good," answered Allan, as he lit a hand candle, "I am quite sure that you could not, because, you see, facts are one thing and what you call 'yarns' are another. Good-night to you all, good-night."

Then he went off to bed.

The Treasure
of the Lake

Preface by Allan Quatermain

I cannot remember that anywhere in this book I have stated what it was that first gave me the idea of attempting to visit Mone, the Holy Lake, and the Dabanda who live upon, or, to be precise, at some distance from its shores. Therefore I will do so now.

There is a certain monastery in Natal where I have been made welcome from time to time, among whose brethren was a very learned monk, now "gone down", as the Zulus say, who, although our faiths were different, honoured me with his confidence upon many matters, and I think I may add with his friendship. Brother Ambrose, as he was called in religion—what his real name may have been I do not know—a Swede by birth, would have been an archaeologist, also an anthropologist pure and simple, had he not chanced to be a saint. As it was he managed to combine much knowledge of these sciences with his noted and singular holiness. For example, he was the greatest authority upon Bushmen's paintings that I have ever met, and knew more of the history, religions, customs, and habits of the inhabitants of Southern, Eastern, and South-central Africa—well, than I did myself. Thus it came about, our tastes being so similar on these and other subjects, that when we could not meet and talk, often we corresponded.

One of his learned letters, which I still preserve, was written to me many years ago from Mozambique, whither he had gone upon a journey connected with the missionary enterprises of his order. From it, for the sake of accuracy, I will quote some passages.

Brother Ambrose says:

> In this island I have come into touch with a man, a rescued slave whom it was my privilege to baptize and to attend through his last illness, during which he made many confidences to me. Peter, as he was called because he was received into the Church

upon the feast day of that saint, was a man of unusual appearance. His general cast of countenance and physique were Arab, and his native language was a somewhat archaic dialect of Arabic. His eyes, however, were large and round, almost owl-like, indeed—by the way, he had a singular faculty of seeing in the dark—and his handsome features were remarkable for a melancholy, which I think must have been inherited and not due to his experiences of life.

He told me that he belonged to a small tribe dwelling in the neighbourhood of mountains called Ruga, far beyond a great lake—I am not sure what lake—which mountains I gathered are not far distant from some branch of the Congo River in the remote interior. The home of his tribe, if I understood him aright, was a large hollow of land enclosed by cliffs. In the centre of this hollow lies a big sheet of water surrounded by forest which, he said, is considered holy. When I asked him why it was holy, he replied because on an island in this water dwelt a priestess who is a Shadow of God, or of the gods, a beautiful woman with many magical powers, who utters oracles and bestows blessings on her worshippers (which, being interpreted, means, I take it, a fetish or rather the head servant of a fetish credited with the power of making rain and of averting misfortunes). About this person he told me many legends too absurd to record, amongst others that she and her husband, who is the chief of the tribe—for she has a husband—are sacrificed at a certain age, when her place is taken by another 'Shadow', who is reputed to be her daughter.

One other thing he told me which I am sure will interest you very much; indeed, although I am very busy, I write this letter chiefly in order to pass on the superstition, or legend, or whatever it may be, before I forget exactly what he said. You and I have often discussed the mysteries of the African forms of taboo. Well, Peter described a variety of it that was quite new to me. He declared that to his tribe all wild game are taboo and may not be killed or eaten by any member of the tribe, who, it seems, are largely vegetarians, but supplement this diet with the flesh of goats and cattle, of which they possess many herds. Nor is this all, for he assured me further that his people exercised great power over these untamed beasts, living with them on the same terms of familiarity as we do with dogs and horses and other domestic animals. Thus he asserted positively that they can send them away to or call them back from any given spot, and make them do their bidding in various other fashions, even to the extent of being able to cause them to attack anyone they choose.

I tried to extract from him what he believed to be the reason for this alleged remarkable authority over the wild fauna of his country, but all I could make out was that the priests taught some form of the old Pythagorean doctrine of metempsychosis (as you know, not uncommon in Africa, especially when tyrannical chiefs are concerned); I mean that the souls of men, particularly of those who had led evil lives, are reborn in the bodies of beasts, which beasts are therefore, in a sense, their kin, and on this account feared and venerated.

It was extremely curious to hear these pre-Christian delusions from the mouth of a modern African native, and I wonder very much if his story has any faint foundation in fact. Probably not, but, my dear friend, if ever you get the chance in the course of your explorations, do try to find out. You know that, like you, I hold that scattered here and there through the vast expanse of Africa are the remains of peoples who still preserve fragments of ancient systems and religions, such as the Babylonian star-worship or that of the gods of old Egypt.

Then the letter goes on to tell of the decease of Peter, before Brother Ambrose could further pursue his inquiries about a carving that he had discovered somewhere on the East Coast, which he thought must have been executed by Bushmen in the remote past; although there is, or was, no other evidence that they ever lived so far north.

This incident of the strange story told to Father Ambrose by the dying native, Peter, remained fixed in my mind, and in the end was the real cause of the journey described in the following pages.

I should like to take this opportunity to say that on re-reading this record, which is an expanded version of a diary I kept at the time, I am not sure that I have succeeded in conveying an adequate sense of the eeriness that pervaded the Dabanda people and their country. No wonder that added to the various humiliations which I suffered in their land, this unearthly atmosphere, whereof dwellers in the fetish-ridden districts of Africa have often had experience, at last got upon my nerves to such an extent that if I had stopped there much longer I believe I should have gone crazy.

Another thing that I wish to state is that on weighing the evidence, whatever reasons old Kumpana and others may have given, I am now convinced that Hans was right and that the real cause which led them to procure the return of Kaneke to Mone-land, was that they might execute him in punishment for his crime of sacrilege in earlier life. On this I believe they were determined both from vindictiveness and because, under their iron law, while he lived it was impossible for the mysterious "Treasure of the Lake" to take another man to husband, as for their own secret reasons they desired that she should do.

Lastly, it might be asked why I do not more accurately indicate the exact geographic position of Mone-land and its holy hidden lake. I will face ridicule—especially as I shall never live to feel its shafts—and make a confession. Before I left his country, as Arkle had done in his letter, Kumpana assured me with much quiet emphasis that if I revealed its exact locality and explained how it could be reached by any other white man, the results to them, also to myself and Hans in this or later lives, would be most unpleasant. I did not and do not believe him; still, in view of my experience of the uncanny powers of the Dabanda priests, I thought it wise—well, to keep on the safe side and on this point to remain a little indefinite.

Allan Quatermain

CHAPTER 1

Kaneke's Tale

Now when I grow old it becomes every day more clear to me, Allan Quatermain, that each of us is a mystery living in the midst of mysteries, bringing these with us when we are born and taking them away with us when we die; doubtless into a land of other and yet deeper mysteries. At first, while we are quite young, everything seems very clear and simple. There is a male individual called Father and a female called Mother who, between them, have made us a present to the world, or of the world to us, whichever way you like to put it, apparently by arrangement with the kingdom of heaven; at least that is what we are taught. There are the sun, the moon, and the stars above us and the solid earth beneath, there are lessons and dinner and a time to get up and a time to go to bed—in short there are a multitude of things, all quite obvious and commonplace, which may be summed up in three words, the established order, in which, by the decree of Papa and Mamma and the heavens above, we live and move and have our being.

Then the years go by, the terrible, remorseless years that bear us as steadily from the cradle to the grave as a creeping glacier bears a stone. With every one of them, after the first fifteen or so when we become adult, or in some instances earlier if we chance to be what is called "rather unusual", a little piece of the curtain is rolled up or a little hole is widened in the veil, and beneath that curtain, or through that enlarging hole, we see the mysteries moving in the dusk beyond. So swiftly do they come and go, and so dark is the background, that we never discern them clearly. There, if time is given to us to fix them in our minds, they appear; for a moment they are seen, then they are gone, to be succeeded by others even yet more wondrous, or perhaps more awful.

But why go on talking of what is endless and unfathomable? Amidst this wondrous multitude of enigmas we poor, purblind, slow-witted creatures must make our choice of those we wish to study. Long ago

I made mine, one local and terrestrial, namely the land with which I have been connected all my life—Africa—and the other universal and spiritual, namely human nature. What! some may ask, do you call human nature spiritual? The very words belie you. What is there spiritual about that which is human?

My friend, I answer, in my opinion, my most humble and fallible opinion, almost everything. More and more do I become convinced that we are nearly all spirit, notwithstanding our gross apparent bodies with their deeds and longings. You have seen those coloured globes that pedlars sell—I mean the floating things tinted to this hue or that, that are the delight of children. The children buy these balls and toss them into the air, where they travel one way or the other, blown by winds we cannot see, till in the end they burst and of each there remains nothing but a little shrivelled skin, a shred of substance, which they are told is made from the gum of a tree. Well, to my fancy that expanded skin or shred is a good symbol of the human body, so large and obvious to the sight, yet driven here and there by the breath of circumstance and in the end destroyed. But what was within it which escapes at last and is no more seen? To my mind the gas with which the globe was filled represents the spirit of man, imprisoned for a while; then to all appearance lost.

I dare say that the example is faulty; still, I use it because it conveys something of my idea. So, good or bad, I let it stand and pass on to an easier theme, or at any rate one easier to handle, namely that of the mysteries of the great continent of Africa.

Now all the world is wonderful, but surely among its countries there is none more so than Africa; no, not even China the unchanging, or India the ancient. For this reason, I think: those great lands have always been more or less known to their own inhabitants, whereas Africa, as a whole, from the beginning was and still remains unknown.

To this day great sections of its denizens are quite ignorant of other sections, as much so as was mighty Egypt of the millions of the neighbouring peoples in the time when a voyage to the Land of Punt, which I take to have been the country that we now know as Uganda, was looked upon as a marvellous adventure. Again, there is the instance of Solomon, or rather Hiram and his gold traffic with Ophir, the dim and undefined, that doubtless was the district lying at the back of Sofala. But why multiply such examples, of which there are many? And if this is true of Africa, the Libya of the early world, as a country, is it not still more true of its inhabitants, divided as these are into countless races, peoples, and tribes, each of them with its own gods or ancestral spirits, language, customs, traditions, and mental outlook established in the passage of innumerable ages?

So far as my small experience goes, for though many might think it large it is still small, these are my opinions which I venture to state as an opening to what I have always considered a very curious history, in which it was my fortune to play some small and humble part. For let it be understood at once that I was by no means the chief actor in this business. Indeed, I was never more than an agent, a kind of connecting wire between the parties concerned, an insignificant bridge over which their feet travelled to certain ends that I presume to have been appointed by Fate. Still, I saw much of the play and now, when the curtain has been long rung down, by help of the diary I kept at the time and have preserved, I will try to record such memories of it as remain to me—well, because rightly or wrongly I think that they are worth recording.

Years ago, accompanied by my servant Hans, the old and faithful Hottentot with whom I have experienced so many adventures, I made a great journey to what I may almost call Central Africa, starting in from the East Coast. It was a hazardous adventure into which I had been led by tales that had reached me of the enormous herds of elephants to be found in what I suppose must now be the north of the Belgian Congo. Or perhaps it is still No Man's Land as it was in those days—really, I do not know. Nor is this wonderful, seeing that with a single exception I believe that I was the first white man to set foot in that particular district which lies beyond the Lado Mountains north of Jissa and of the Denbo River.

To be truthful, however, it was not only the elephants that took me to these parts, guessing, as I did, that if I found them it might be of little avail, since probably ivory in bulk would prove impossible to carry. No, it was rather the desire to look upon new things, to discover the Unknown which is so strong a part of my nature, that at times it half reconciles me to the prospect of death which I, who believe that we do not go out, believe also must be a land or a state full of all that is strange and wonderful.

I had heard from natives in the neighbourhood of the great lake Victoria Nyanza that there was a marvellous country between two rivers known as M'bomu and Balo, where dwelt strange tribes who were said to dress like Arabs and to talk a sort of Arabic; also that somewhere in this country was a holy lake, a big sheet of water that none was allowed to approach. Further, that in this lake, which was called Mone (pronounced like groan), a word of unknown meaning, was an island *where dwelt the gods*, or the spirits, for the term used was capable of either interpretation.

Now, when I heard of this Holy Lake called Mone, *where dwelt the gods*, at once my mind went back to the letter of which I have spoken in the preface of this book, that long years before I had received from my late friend, Brother Ambrose, telling me what he had learned from a slave whom he had christened.

Could it be the same, I wondered, as that of which the slave had told Brother Ambrose? Instantly, and with much suppressed excitement, I set to work to make further inquiries, and was informed that a certain Kaneke, a stranger who had been a slave and was now the chief or captain of an Arab settlement some fifty miles away from where I met these natives, could give me information about the lake, inasmuch as he was reported to be born of the people who dwelt upon its borders.

Then and there I changed my plans, as indeed was convenient to me because of the suddenly developed hostility of a chief through whose territory I had intended to pass, and in order to seek out this Kaneke, took a road running in another direction to that which I had designed to travel. Little did I guess at the time that Kaneke was seeking me out and that the natives who told me the legend of the lake were, in fact, his emissaries sent to tempt me to visit him, or that it was he who had incited the chief against me in order to block my path.

Well, in due course I reached Kaneke-town, as it was called, without accident, for although between me and it dwelt a very dangerous tribe whom at first I had purposed to avoid, all at once their chief and headman became friendly and helped me in every way upon my journey. Kaneke, a remarkable person whom I will describe later, received me well, giving me a place to camp outside his village and all the food that we required. Also he proved extraordinarily communicative, telling me directly that he belonged to a tribe called Dabanda, which had its home in the wild parts whereof I have spoken. He added that he was the "high-born" son of a great doctor or medicine-man, a calling which all his family had followed for generations. In some curious way, of which I did not at first learn the details, while undergoing his novitiate as a doctor or magician, this man had been seized by a rival tribe, the Abanda, and ultimately sold as a slave to an Arab trader, one Hassan, who brought him down to the neighbourhood of the great lake.

Here also, according to his own story, it seemed that one night this Kaneke succeeded in murdering Hassan.

"I crept on him in the night. I got him by the throat. I choked the life out of him," he said, twitching his big hands, "and as he died I whispered in his ear of all the cruel things he had done to me. He made signs to me, praying for mercy, but I went on till I had killed him, whispering to him all the while. When he was dead I took his body and threw it out into the bush, having first stripped him. There a lion found it and bore it away, for in the morning it was gone. Then, Macumazahn" (that is the native name by which I, Allan Quatermain, am known in Africa, and which had come with me to these parts), "I played a great game, such as you might have done, O Watcher-by-Night. I returned to the tent of Hassan and sat there thinking.

"I heard the lion, or lions come, for I think there was more than one of them, as I was sure that they would come who had called them by a charm, and guessed that they had eaten or carried away Hassan the evil. When all was quiet I dressed myself in the robes of Hassan. I found his gun, which on the journey he had taught me to use, that I might shoot the slaves who could travel no farther for him; his pistol also, and saw that they were loaded. Then I sat myself upon his stool and waited for the light.

"At the dawn one of his women crept into the tent to visit him. I seized her. She stared at me, saying: 'You are not my master. You are not Hassan.'

"I answered, 'I am your master. I am Hassan, whose face the spirits have changed in the night.'

"She opened her mouth to cry out. I said:

"'Woman, if you try to scream, I will kill you. If you are quiet I will take you. Look on me. I am young. Hassan was old. I am a finer man, you will be happier with me. Choose now. Will you die, or live?'

"'I will live,' she said, she who was no fool.

"'Then I am Hassan, am I not?' I asked.

"'Yes,' she said, 'you are Hassan and my lord. I am sure of it now.'

"For I tell you, that woman had wit, Macumazahn, and I was sorry when, two years afterwards, she died.

"'Good,' I said. 'Now, when the servants of Hassan come you will swear that I am he and no other, remembering that if you do not swear you die.'

"'I will swear,' she answered.

"Presently the headman of Hassan came, a big fat fellow who was half an Arab, to bring him his morning drink. I took it and drank. The light of the rising sun struck into the tent. He saw and started back.

"'You are not Hassan,' he said. 'You are the slave Kaneke, whom we bought.'

"'I am Hassan,' I answered. 'Ask my wife here, whom you know, if I am not Hassan. Also, if I am not, where is Hassan?'

"'Yes, he is Hassan, my husband,' broke in the woman.

"'This is witchcraft!' he cried, and ran away.

"'Now he is gone to fetch the others,' I said to the woman. 'Fasten back the sides of the tent that I may see, and give me the guns.'

"She obeyed, though then she sat exposed, and I took the double-barrelled gun and held it ready.

"Presently, they all came, five or six Arabs, or half Arabs, and a score or so of black soldiers. Even the slaves came, dragging their yokes, fifty or more of them of whom perhaps thirty were men, all known to me, for had we not shared the yoke? There they stood huddled together behind the Arabs, staring.

"'Take a knife,' I whispered to the woman; 'slip out, get among the slaves and cut the thongs of the yokes.'

"She nodded—have I not told you that girl had wits, Macumazahn?—and slipped away.

"Cried the fat one, the captain:

"'This fellow, whom we all know for Kaneke, the slave whom we bought, says that he is Hassan our lord. Yes, there he sits in Hassan's robes and says that he is Hassan. Dog, where is Hassan?'

"'Inside this garment,' I answered. 'Listen. I made a bargain with Hassan, I who am a wizard. I forgave him his sins against me, and in return he gave me his soul while his body flew away to Paradise.'

"'The liar!' shouted the captain. 'Kill him!' and he brandished a spear.

"'Admit that I am Hassan or I will send you to where you will learn that I am no liar,' I said quietly.

"In answer he lifted the spear to stab me. Then I shot him dead.

"'Now am I Hassan?' I asked, while the rest stared at him.

"One or two who were frightened said 'Yes'. Others stood silent, and a big fellow began to put a cap upon his gun. I shot him with the other barrel, then, rising, roared in a great voice:

"'On to them, slaves, if you would be free!' for by now I saw that the woman had cut many of the thongs.

"Those men were brave, they came of good stock. They heard, and leapt on to the Arabs with a shout, knocking them down with the yokes and throttling them with their hands. Soon it was over. Most of them were killed, but two or three crawled before me crying that I was certainly Hassan.

"'Very well,' I said. 'Take away these'—here I pointed to the dead

204

men—'and throw them into yonder ravine, and bid the women prepare food while I make prayer according to my custom.'

"Then I took Hassan's beautiful prayer-rug, spread it and made obeisance in the proper fashion, muttering with my lips as I had often watched him do; after which everything went smoothly. That is all the story, Macumazahn."

When he had finished this tale, which, true or false, of its sort was remarkable even in equatorial Africa, where such things happen, or happened, by the score without anybody hearing of them, I sat awhile considering Kaneke. To tell the truth he was worth study. A giant of a man in size, he was not a negro by any means, for his features had a somewhat Semitic cast and he was yellow-hued rather than black. Moreover, he had hair, not wool, wavy hair that he wore rather long. His eyes were so prominent, round, and lustrous that they gave an owl-like cast to his countenance, his features well cut, although the lips were somewhat coarse and the nose was hooked like a hawk's beak, while his hands and feet were thin and shapely, and in curious contrast to his great athletic frame and swelling muscles. His age might have been anything between thirty-five and forty, and he carried his years well, moving with the swing and vigour of youth.

It was his face, however, that commanded my attention as a student of character. It was extraordinarily strong and yet dreamy, almost mystical, indeed, when in repose, the face of a thinker, or even of a priest. Contemplating him I could almost believe the strange tale he had told me, which in the case of most natives I should have set down as an outrageous lie. For here, without doubt, was a man who could conceive a plot of the sort and execute it without hesitation. Yet he was one to whom I took a dislike from the moment I set eyes upon him. Instinctively, however attractive he might be in some ways, I felt that at bottom he was dangerous and not to be trusted. Still, he interested me very much, as did his story, especially that part of it in which he said that he called the lions "by a charm".

"What happened afterwards, Kaneke?" I asked at last.

"Oh, very little, Macumazahn. I became Hassan, though they called me 'the Changeling'; that is all. I did not travel on towards the coast because I thought it safer to stop where I was, not daring to go either forward or back. So I gathered people about me and founded the town in which you are. Once some Arabs came to kill me, but I killed them, and after that I was no more molested, because, you see, I was looked upon as a ghost-man, one who had a great *juju*, one not to be touched; and all were afraid of me."

"You mean you became a witch-doctor again, Kaneke."

"Yes, Macumazahn. Or, rather, I was that already, a diviner and a master of spells, like my fathers before me. So here I set up as a sort of wise man as well as a warrior, and soon gained a great repute, which caused all the people round about to send to me to give them medicines and charms, or to make rain. Thus, and with the help of trade, I became rich and powerful as I am today."

"Then you are a happy man, Kaneke."

He rolled his big round eyes and looked at me earnestly, asking:

"Is any man happy, Macumazahn, or at least any man who thinks? The beasts are happy; can man be happy like the beasts who never look to tomorrow or to the hour of death?"

"Now that you mention it, Kaneke, I do not suppose that any man is happy, except sometimes for an hour when he forgets himself in drink, or love, or war."

"Or when he talks with the heavens," added Kaneke, which I thought a strange remark. "Yes, then and in sleep he is sometimes happy till he wakes to the sorrow of the day."

He paused a little and went on:

"If this be so with all men, how much more is it so with those who have known the yoke and who must grow old far from their homes, as I do? For such there is no joy, for even their dreams are haunted. In these they see the village where they were born and the distant mountains and the face of their mother, and hear the voices of their playmates and of those they loved, that now are still."

I sighed as the truth of his words came home to me.

"If you feel thus," I answered presently, "why do you not return to your home?"

"I will tell you, Macumazahn. There are many reasons, among them these. Here I rule over people who would not wish to go with me and who, if I forced them, would run away, or perhaps poison me. Indeed, they would not let me go because I am necessary to them, protecting them from their enemies and from wild beasts, and giving them rain, as I can do. Again, the road is long and dangerous, and maybe I should not live to come to its end. Also, if I did, what should I find? I was my father's eldest son, born of his chief wife, and to me he told the secrets of his wisdom that have come down to us through the generations. But I have been absent for years and mayhap another has taken my place. My people would not welcome me, Macumazahn. They might kill me, especially if they who know all, have learned that I have betrayed my own goddess by bending the knee to the Prophet, even though I never bent my heart. Still, it is true that I wish to risk all and return, even if it be to die."

Now I grew deeply interested, for always I have loved to discover the mysteries of these strange African faiths.

"Your own goddess?" I asked. "What goddess?"

All this time we were seated in the shade of a flat-topped, thick-leaved tree of the banyan species, the Tree of Council it was called, that grew upon a little knoll at a distance from Kaneke's town. He rose and walked all round this place, as though to make sure that no one was near us. Then he stared up into its branches, where he discovered a monkey sitting. I knew that it was there, but he did not seem to have noticed it. At this monkey he began to shout out something, as though he were giving it orders, till at last the little beast ran along the boughs of the tree, dropped to the ground and bolted for the bush in the distance.

"Why do you hunt it away?" I asked.

"A monkey can hear and is very like a man. Perhaps a monkey can tell tales, Macumazahn."

I laughed, for of course I understood that this was an African way of indicating that the matter to be discussed was most solemn and private. By driving away that monkey Kaneke was swearing me to the strictest secrecy—or so I thought.

He came back and moved his stool, I noted, into such a position that the light of the westering sun striking through the lower boughs of the tree flickered on my face and left his in shadow. I lit my pipe leisurely, so that for some time there was silence between us. The fact is I was determined that he should be the first to speak. It is a good rule with any native when a subject of importance is concerned.

"You asked me of my goddess, Macumazahn."

"Did I, Kaneke?" I replied, puffing at my pipe to make it burn. "Oh yes, I remember. Well, who is she and where does she live? On earth or in heaven—which is the home of goddesses?"

"Yesterday, Macumazahn, you—or perhaps it was that little yellow man, your servant Hans—asked me if I had ever heard of a lake called Mone which lies in the hidden land where dwell my people, the Dabanda, beyond the Ruga-Ruga Mountains."

"I dare say. I remember having heard of this lake, which interested me because of legends connected with it, though I forget what they were. What about it?"

"Only that it is there my goddess dwells, Macumazahn."

"Indeed. Then I suppose that she is a water-spirit."

"I cannot say, Macumazahn. I only know that she dwells with her women on the island in the lake, and at night, when it is very dark, sometimes she and her companions are heard upon the water, or passing through the forests, singing and laughing.

"Did you ever see her, Kaneke?"

He hesitated like one who seeks time to make up a plausible story, or so I thought, then answered:

"Yes. Once when I was young. I had been sent to look for some goats of ours that had strayed, and following them into the forest which slopes down to the lake, I lost myself there. Night came on and I lay down to sleep under a tree, or rather to watch for the dawn, so that with the light I might escape from that darksome, haunted place, of which I was afraid."

"Well, and what happened?"

"So much that I cannot remember all, Macumazahn. Spirits went by me; I heard them in the tree-tops and above; I heard them pass through the forest, laughing; I felt them gather about me and knew that they were mocking me. At length all those Wood-Dwellers went away, leaving me as terrified as though a lion had come and eaten out of my bowl. The moon rose and her light pierced down through the boughs, a shaft of it here, a shaft of it there, with breadths of blackness between. I shut my eyes, trying to sleep, then hearing sounds, I opened them again. I looked up. There in the heart of one of the pools of light stood a woman, a fair-skinned woman like to one of your people, Macumazahn. She seemed to be young and slender, also beautiful, as I perceived when she turned her head and the moon shone upon her face and showed her soft, dark eyes, which were like those of a buck. For the rest she was clad in grey garments that glimmered like a spider's web filled with dew at dawn. There was a cap upon her head and from beneath it her black hair flowed down upon her shoulders. Oh, she was beautiful—so beautiful . . ." and he paused.

"That what, Kaneke?" I asked curiously.

"Lord, that I committed a great crime, the greatest in the whole world, the crime of sacrilege against her who is called the Shadow."

"Shadow! Whose shadow?"

"The Shadow of the *Engoi*, the goddess who dwells in heaven and is shone upon by the star we worship above all other stars." (This, I found afterwards, was the planet Venus.) "Or perhaps she dwells in the star and is shone upon by the moon—I do not know. At least, she who lives upon the island in the lake is the shadow of the *Engoi* upon earth, and that is why she is called *Engoi* and Shadow."

"Very interesting," I said, though I understood little of what he said, except that it was a piece of African occultism to which as yet I had not the key. "But what crime did you commit?"

"Lord, I was young and my blood was hot and the beauty of this wanderer in the forest made me mad. Lord, I threw my arms about her and embraced her. Or, rather, I tried to embrace her, but before my lips touched hers all my strength left me, my arms fell down and I became as a man of stone, though I could still see and hear. . . ."

"What did you see and hear, Kaneke?" I asked, for again he paused in his story.

"I saw her lovely face grow terrible and I heard her say, 'Do you know who I am, O man Kaneke, who are not afraid to do me violence in my holy, secret grove where none may set his foot?' Lord, I tried to lie, but I could not who must answer, 'I know that you are the *Engoi*; I know that your name is Shadow. I pray you to pardon me, O Shadow.'

"'For what you have done there is no pardon. Still, your life is spared, if only for a while. Get you gone and let the Council of the *Engoi* deal with you as it will.'"

"And what happened then?"

"Then, Lord, she departed, vanishing away, and I too departed, flying through the forest terribly afraid and pursued by voices that proclaimed my crime and threatened vengeance. Next day the Council seized me and passed judgment on me, driving me from the land so that I fell into the hands of our enemies, the Abanda, who dwell upon the slopes of the mountains, and in the end was sold as a slave."

"And how did this Council know what you had done, Kaneke?"

"What is known to the Shadow is known to her Council, and what is known to her Council is known to the Shadow, Lord."

Now I considered Kaneke and his story, and came to the conclusion, a perfectly correct one, as I think, that he was lying to me. What his exact offence against this priestess may have been I don't know and never learned in detail, though I believe that it was much worse than what he described. All that was certain is that he had committed some sacrilegious crime of such a character that, notwithstanding his rank, he was forced to fly out of his country in order to save his life, and to become an exile, which he remained.

Leaving that subject without further comment, I asked him who were these Abanda who delivered him into slavery.

"Lord," he replied, "they are a branch of a people from whom we separated ages ago and who live on the plains beyond the mountains. They hate us and are jealous of us because the *Engoi* gives us rain and fruitful season, whereas often they suffer from drought and scarcity. Therefore they wish to take the land and Lake Mone, so that the *Engoi* may once more be their goddess also. More, they are a mighty people, whereas we are very few, for from generation to generation our numbers dwindle."

"Then why do they not invade and defeat you, Kaneke?"

"Because they dare not, Lord; because if they set foot within the land of Mone a curse will fall upon them, seeing that it and we who dwell there are protected by the Stars of Heaven. Yet always they hope that the day will come when they can defy the curse and conquer us, who hold them back by wisdom and not by spears. And now, Macumazahn, I must go to make my prayer before the people to that prophet in whom I do not believe. Yet come to me again when the evening star has risen, for I have more to say to you, Macumazahn."

I got up, then said:

"One more question before I go, Kaneke. Is this *Engoi* of whom you speak, who lives in a lake, a woman or—something more?"

"Lord, how can I answer? Certainly she is a woman, for she is born and dies, leaving behind her a daughter to take her place. Also she is something more, or so we are taught."

"What do you mean?"

"I mean that the same flesh or Shadow dwells in every *Engoi*, although the flesh which holds it changes from generation to generation. There is a legend that she is an angel who sinned and fell from heaven."

"What is the legend and how did she sin?"

A cunning look came over the face of Kaneke as he answered:

"The priests' tale runs, Lord, that an *Engoi* of long ago loved a white man and that when he was forbidden to her, she killed him to take him to heaven with her. Therefore she must return to the world again and again till she finds that white man" (here he glanced at me) "and makes amends to him for her crime. She is looking for him now, and the Stars declare that the time is at hand when she will find him again."

"Do they really?" I remarked. "Well, I hope she won't be disappointed," I added, reflecting to myself that Kaneke was a first-class imaginative liar, for though the idea of the sinful spirit returning to inhabit mortal flesh is as old as the world, his adaptation of it was ingenious.

What, I wondered, as I walked away, did that specious but false-hearted ruffian Kaneke want to get out of me? Whatever his object, certainly the man could not be trusted. According to his own account he was a fugitive outcast who had committed murder, one also who for his personal advantage pretended to profess a faith in which he admitted that he had no belief, showing thereby that he was of a traitorous and contemptible character. So sure was I of this, that but for one thing I would have put an end to my acquaintance with him then and there. He knew the way to Lake Mone and declared that it was his country. And I—well, I burned to find out the truth about this holy lake and the mysterious priestess who dwelt in the midst of its waters, she, without doubt, of whom Brother Ambrose had written to me so many years ago.

CHAPTER 2
Allan's Business Instincts

I went to my camp, which was situated upon the outskirts of Kaneke's village in a deserted garden where bananas, oranges, papaws, and other semi-tropical products fought for existence in a neglected confusion, working out the problem of the survival of the fittest. Here I found Hans the Hottentot, who had been my servant and in his own way friend from my youth up, as he was that of my father before me. He was seated in front of the palm-leaf shelter watching a pot upon the fire made of mealie-cobs from which the corn had been stripped, looking very hot and cross.

"So you have come at last, Baas," he said volubly. "An hour ago that coast cook-boy, Aru, went off, leaving me to watch this stew which he said must be kept upon the simmer, neither boiling nor going cold, or it would be spoiled. He swore that he was going to pray to Allah, for he is a Prophet-worshipper, Baas. But I know what his prophet is like, for I found him kissing her last night; great fat girl with a mouth as wide as that plate and a bold eye that frightens me, Baas, who have always been timid of women."

"Have you?" I said. "Then I wish you would be timid of other things too, gin-bottles, for instance."

"Ah, Baas, a gin-bottle, I mean one that is full, is better than a woman, for of a gin-bottle you know the worst. You swallow the gin, you get drunk and it is very sad, and next morning your head aches and you think of all the sins you ever did. Yes, Baas, and if the gin was at all bad, their number is endless, and their colour so black that you feel that they can never be forgiven, however hard your reverend father, the Predikant, may pray for you up there. But, Baas, as the morning goes on, especially if you have the sense to drink a pint of milk and the luck to get it, and the sun shines, you grow better. Your sins roll away, you feel, or at least I do, that the prayers of your reverend father may have prevailed there in the Place of Fires, and that the slip is overlooked because Life's road is so full of greasy mud, Baas, that few can travel it without sometimes sitting down to think. Now with women, as the Baas knows better perhaps than anyone, the matter is not so simple. You can't wash her away with a pint of milk and a little sunshine, Baas. She is always waiting round the corner; yes, even if she is dead—in your mind you know, Baas."

"Be silent, Hans," I said, "and give me my supper."

"Yes, Baas; that is what I am trying to do, Baas, but something has gone wrong after all, for the stuff is sticking to the pot and I can't get it out even with this iron spoon. I think that if the Baas would not mind taking the pot and helping himself, it would be much easier," and he thrust that blackened article towards me.

"Hans," I said, "if this place were not Mahommedan where there is no liquor, I should think that you had been drinking."

"Baas, if you believe that Prophet-worshippers do not drink, your head is even softer than I imagined. It is true that they have no gin here, at least at present, because they have finished the last lot and cannot get any more till the traders come. But they make a kind of wine of their own out of palm trees which answers quite well if you can swallow enough of it without being sick, which I am sorry to say I can't, Baas, and therefore this afternoon I have only had two pannikins full. If the Baas would like to try some—"

Here I lifted the first thing that came to hand—it was a three-legged stool—and hurled it at Hans, who slipped cleverly round the corner of the hut, probably because he was expecting its advent.

A while later, after I had tackled the stew—which had stuck to the pot—with unsatisfactory results, and lit my pipe, he returned to clear up, in such a chastened frame of mind that I gathered the palm-wine—well, let that be.

"What has the Baas been doing all the afternoon in this dull place?" he asked humbly, watching me with a furtive eye, for there was another stool within reach, also the pot. "Talking to that giant rain-maker, who looks like an owl in sunlight—I mean Kaneke—or perhaps to one of his wives; she who is so pretty," he added, by an after-thought.

"Yes," I said, "I have—to Kaneke, I mean, not to the wife, whom I do not know; indeed, I never heard that he had any wives."

Then I added suddenly, for now that he had recovered from the palm-wine I wished to surprise the truth out of his keen mind:

"What do you think of Kaneke, Hans?"

Hans twiddled his dirty hat and fixed his little yellow eyes upon the evening sky, then he took the pot and, finding a remaining leg of fowl, ate it reflectively, after which he produced his corn-cob pipe and asked me for some tobacco. This, by the way, I was glad to see, for when Hans could smoke I knew that he was quite sober.

These preliminaries finished, he remarked.

"As to what was it that the Baas wished me to instruct him? Oh, I remember. About that big village headman, Kaneke. Well, Baas, I have made inquiries concerning him from his wife, who says she is jealous of him and therefore in a mood to speak the truth. First of all he is a great liar, Baas, though that is nothing for all these people are liars—not like me and you, Baas, who often speak the truth, or at least I do."

"Stop fooling, and answer my question," I said.

"Yes, Baas. Well, I said that he was a liar, did I not? For instance, I dare say he has told the Baas a fine tale about how he came to settle here, by killing the head of the slave-gang, after which all the other slavers acknowledged him as their chief. The truth is that he and the other slaves murdered the lot of them because he said he was a good Mahommedan and could not bear to see them drinking gin against the law, which for my part I think was clever of him. They surprised them in their sleep, Baas, and dragged them to the top of that cliff over the stream, where they threw them one by one into the water, except two who had beaten Kaneke. These he flogged to death, which I dare say they deserved. After this the people here, who hated the slavers because they robbed them, made Kaneke their chief because he was such a holy man who could not bear to see followers of the Prophet drink gin, also because they were afraid lest he should throw them over the cliff too. That is why he must be so strict about his prayers, because, you see, he must keep his fame for holiness and show that he is as good as he wishes others to be."

Hans stopped to re-light his pipe with an ember, and I asked him impatiently if he had any more to say.

"Yes, Baas, lots. This Kaneke is not one man, he is two. The first Kaneke is a tyrant, one full of plots who would like to rule the world, a lover of liquor too, which he drinks in secret; fierce, cunning, cruel. The second Kaneke is one who dreams, who hears voices and sees things in the sky, who follows after visions, a true witch-doctor, a man who would seek what is afar, but who, living in this soft place, is like a lion in a cage. His mother must have made a mistake, and instead of bearing twins, got two spirits into one body where they must fight together till he dies."

"I dare say. Many men have two spirits in one body. Is that all, Hans?"

"Yes—that is, no, Baas. You know this Kaneke brought you here, don't you, Baas, and that all those troubles which we met with, so that we could not go the road we wanted because that tribe sent to say they would kill us if we did, were made by him so that you might come to his village."

"I know nothing of the sort."

"Well, it was so, Baas. The jealous woman told me all about it."

"Why? What for? There is no big game here that I can shoot, and I am not rich to give him presents. Indeed, he has asked for nothing and feeds us without payment."

"I am not sure, Baas, but I think that he wishes you to go somewhere with him; that the lion wants to come out of the cage and to kill for himself, instead of living on dead meat of which he is tired. Has he spoken to you about that holy lake of which we have heard, Baas? If not, I think he will."

"Yes, Hans. It seems that it is in his country where he was born and that he had an adventure there in his youth, because of which his people drove him away."

"Just so, Baas, and presently you will find that he desires to go back to his country and have more adventures or to pay off old scores, or both. Do you wish to go with him, Baas?"

"Do you, Hans?"

"I think not, Baas. This Kaneke is a spook man, and I am afraid of spooks who always make me feel cold down the back."

Here Hans stared at the sky again, then added:

"And yet, Baas, I'd rather go to the lake or anywhere than stop in this place where there is nothing to do and the palm-wine makes one sick, especially as after all, a good Christian like Hans has nothing to fear from spooks, whom he can tell to go to hell, as your reverend father did, Baas. Lastly, as your reverend father used to say, too, when he stood in the box in a nightshirt, it doesn't matter what I wish to do, or what you wish to do, since we shall go where we must, yes, where it pleases the Great One in the sky to send us, Baas, even if He uses Kaneke to drag us there by the hair of the head. And now, Baas, I must wash up those things before it gets dark, after which I have to meet that jealous wife of Kaneke's yonder in a quiet place, and learn a little more from her, for as you know, Baas, Hans is always a seeker after wisdom."

"Mind that you don't find folly," I remarked sententiously. Then remembering my promise and noting that the evening star was showing brightly in the quiet sky, I rose and went through the gate of the town, for my camp was outside the fence of prickly pears which was planted round the palisade, thinking as I walked that in his ridiculous way Hans had spoken a great truth. It was useless to bother about plans, seeing that we should go where it was fated that we should go, and nowhere else. Doubtless man has free will, but the path of circumstance upon which he is called to exercise it is but narrow.

At the gate I found a white-robed man waiting to guide me to Kaneke's abode, "to keep off the dogs and see that I did not step upon a thorn", as he said.

So I was conducted through the village, a tidy place in its way, to the north end, where outside the fence was that cliff with a stream, now nearly dry, running at the bottom of it over which Hans said Kaneke had thrown the slave-traders.

Round Kaneke's house, that was square, thatched, and built of whitewashed clay, was a strong palisade through which the only entrance was by a double gate, for evidently this chief was one who took no risks. At the inner gate my guide bowed and left me. As he departed it was opened by Kaneke himself, who, I noted, made it fast behind me with a bar and some kind of primitive lock. Then he bowed before me in almost reverential fashion, saying:

"Enter, my lord Macumazahn, White Lord whose fame has travelled far. Yes, whose fame has reached me even in this dead place where no news comes."

Now I looked at him, thinking to myself for the second time, "I do wonder what it is you want to get out of me, my friend." Then I said:

"Has it indeed? That is very strange, seeing that I am no great one, no Queen's man who wears ribbons and bright stars, nor even rich, but only a humble hunter who shoots and trades for his living."

"It is not at all strange, O Macumazahn. Do you not know that every man of account has two values?—one his public value in the market-place, which may be much or little; and the other his private value, which is written in all minds that have judgment. Nor is it strange that I should be acquainted with this second and higher value of yours that stands apart from wealth, or honours cried by heralds. Have I not told you that I am one of the fraternity of witch-doctors, and do you not know that throughout Africa such doctors communicate with one another by curious and secret ways? I say that before ever you set foot upon our shores I knew that you were coming in a ship, also much concerning you. Amongst others a certain Zikali who dwells in the land of the Zulus, a chief of our brotherhood, sent me a message."

"Oh, did he?" I said. "Well, Zikali's ways are dark and strange, so I can almost believe it. But, friend Kaneke, is it wise to talk thus openly here? Doubtless you have women in your house, and women's ears are long."

"Women," he answered. "Do you suppose that I keep such trash about me in my private place? Not so. Here my servants are men who are sworn to me, and even these leave me at sundown, save for the guard without my gates."

"So you are a hermit, Kaneke."

"At night I am a hermit, for then I commune with heaven. In the day I am as other men are, better than some and worse than others."

Now I bethought me of Hans' definition of this strange fellow whom he described as having two natures and not for the first time marvelled at the little Hottentot's acumen and deductive powers.

Kaneke led me across the courtyard of beaten polished earth to the *stoep* or veranda of his house, which was more or less square in shape, consisting apparently of two rooms that had doors and windows after the Arab fashion, or rather window-places closed with mats, for there was no glass. On this *stoep* were two chairs, large string-seated chairs of ebony with high backs, such as are sometimes still to be found upon the East Coast. The view from the place was fine, for beneath at the foot of a precipice lay the river bed, and beyond it stretched a great plain. When I was seated Kaneke went into the house where a lamp was burning, and returned with a bottle of brandy, two glasses, curious old glasses, by the way, and an earthen vessel of water. At his invitation I helped myself, moderately enough; then he did the same—not quite so moderately.

"I thought that you were a Mahommedan," I said, with an affectation of mild surprise.

"Then, Macumazahn, you have a bad memory. Did I not tell you a few hours ago that I am nothing of the sort. In the daytime out yonder I worship the Prophet. Here at night, when I am alone, I worship, not the Moslem crescent, but yonder star," and he pointed to Venus now shining brightly in the sky, lifted his glass, bowed as though to her, and drank.

"You play a risky game," I said.

"Not very," he said, shrugging his shoulders. "There are few zealots in this place, and I think no one who from time to time will not drink a tot. Moreover, am I not a witch-doctor, and although such arts are forbidden, have they not all consulted me and are they not afraid of me?"

"I dare say, Kaneke, but the question is, are you not also afraid of them?"

"Yes, Macumazahn, at times I am," he answered frankly, "for even a 'heaven-herd'" (he meant a rain-maker) "has a stomach, and some of these Great Lake people understand poisons very well, especially the women. You see, Macumazahn, I am a slave who has become a master, and they do not forget it."

"What do you want with me?" I asked suddenly.

"Your help, Lord. Although I am rich here, I wish to get out of this place and to return to my own country."

"Well, what is there to prevent you from doing so?"

"Much, Lord, without an excuse, as I told you before sundown. Indeed, it is impossible. If I tried to go I should be murdered as a traitor and a renegade. That is the tree of Truth; ask me not to count the leaves upon it and tell you why or how they grow."

"Good. I see your tree and that it is large. But what do you want with me, Kaneke?"

"Lord, have I not told you that your repute has reached me and the rest? Now I add something which you will not believe, but yet is another tree of Truth. I am not all a cheat, Lord. Visions come to me, as they did to my fathers; moreover, I have looked upon the face of *Engoi*, and he who has seen the *Engoi* partakes of her wisdom. Lord, in a vision, I have been warned to seek your help."

"Is that why you blocked my road by raising that Lake tribe against me, and otherwise, Kaneke, so that I was forced to come to your town?"

"Yes, Lord, though I do not know who betrayed me to you. Some of the women, perhaps, or that little yellow man of yours, who hears in his sleep like a mere-cat—yes, even when he seems to be drunk—and is quick as a snake at pairing-time. Because of the vision, I did bring you here."

"What do you want me to do?" I repeated, growing impatient. "I am tired of talk. Out with it that I may hear and judge, Kaneke."

He rose from his seat, and, stepping to the edge of the veranda, stared at the evening star as though he sought an omen. Then he returned and answered:

"You are a wanderer, athirst for knowledge, a seeker for new things, Lord Macumazahn. You have heard of the holy hidden lake called Mone, on which no white man has looked, and desire to solve its mysteries, and what I have told you of it has whetted your appetite. Without a guide you can never reach that lake. I, who am of the people of its guardians, alone can guide you. Will you take me with you on your journey?"

"Hold hard, my friend," I said. "You are putting the tail of the ox before the horns. I may wish to find that place, or I may not, but it seems that you must find it, I don't know why, and that you cannot do so without me."

"It is so," he answered with something like a groan. "I will open the doors of my heart to you. I must seek that lake, for those upon whom the Shadow has fallen must follow the Shadow even though its shape be changed; and it has come to me in a dream, thrice repeated, that if I try to do so without your help, Lord, I shall be killed. Therefore, I pray you, give me that help."

Now my business instincts awoke, for though some do not think so, I am really a very sharp business man, even hard at times, I fear.

"Look here, friend Kaneke," I said, "I came to this country because I have heard that beyond it is a land full of elephants and other game, and you know I am a hunter by trade. I did not come to search for a mysterious lake, though I should be glad enough to see one if it lay in my path. So the point is this: if I were to consent to undertake a journey which according to your own account is most dangerous and difficult, I should require to be paid for it. Yes, to be largely paid," and I looked at him as fiercely as I suppose a usurer does at a minor who requires a loan.

"I understand. Indeed, it is natural. Listen, Lord, I have a hundred sovereigns in English gold that I have saved up coin by coin. When we get to the lake they shall be yours."

I sprang from my chair.

"A hundred sovereigns! When we get to the lake, which probably we shall never do! Man, I see that you wish to insult me. Good night, indeed good-bye, for tomorrow I leave this place," and I lifted my foot to step off the veranda.

"Lord," he said, catching at my coat, "be not offended with your slave. Everything I have is yours."

"That's better," I said. "What have you?"

"Lord, I deal in ivory, of which I have a good store buried."

"How much?"

"Lord, I think about a hundred bull-tusks, which I proposed to send away at next new moon. If you would accept some of them—"

"Some?" I said. "You mean all of them, with the one hundred pounds for immediate expenses."

He rolled his eyes and sighed, then answered:

"Well, if it must be so, so be it. Tomorrow you shall see the ivory."

Next he went into the house and returned presently with a canvas bag, of which he opened the mouth to show me that it was full of gold.

"Take this on account, Lord," he said.

Again my business instincts came to my help. Remembering that if I touched a single coin I should be striking a bargain, whatever the ivory might prove to be worth, I waved the bag away.

"When I have seen the tusks, we will talk," I said; "not before. And now good night."

Next morning a messenger arrived, again inviting me to Kaneke's house.

I went, accompanied this time by Hans to whom I had explained the situation, whereon that worthy gave me some excellent advice.

"Be stiff, Baas," he said; "be very stiff, and get everything you can. It is unfortunate that you do not sell women like these Arabs, for this Kaneke has a nice lot of young girls whom he would give you for the asking, were you not too good a Christian. Listen, Baas, I have learned that you can't ask too much, for yonder Kaneke must get out of this place, and soon, if he wants to go on living. I am sure of it, and without your help he is afraid to move."

"Cease your foolish talk," I answered, though in my heart I had come to the same conclusion.

On reaching the house, as before the gate was opened by Kaneke, who looked rather doubtfully at Hans, but said nothing. Within, for the most part arranged against the fence, was the ivory. My eyes gleamed at the sight of it, for it was a splendid lot though in some cases rather black with age as if it had been hidden away for a long time, and among it were three or four tusks as large as any that I ever shot. Hans, who was a fine judge of ivory, went over it piece by piece, which took a long time. I made a calculation of its value and from market rates then prevailing, allowing twenty-five per cent for transport and other costs, I reckoned that it was worth at least £700, and Hans, I found, put it somewhat higher.

Then we bargained for a long time, and in the end came to the following agreement, which I reduced to writing: I undertook to accompany Kaneke to his own country of the Dabanda tribe, unless, indeed, sickness or disaster of any sort made this impossible, after which I was to be at liberty to return or to go where I would. He, on his part, was to pay me the ivory as a fee, also to deliver it free to my agent at Zanzibar, a man whom I trusted, who was to sell it to the best advantage and to remit the proceeds to my bank at Durban.

Further, the bag which proved to contain one hundred and three sovereigns was handed over to me. At this I rejoiced at the time, though afterwards I regretted it, for what is the use of dragging about gold in wild places where it has no value? Kaneke undertook also to guide me to his country, to arrange that I should be welcome there and generally to protect me in every way in his power.

Such, roughly, was our contract which I concluded with secret exultation while that ivory was before my eyes. I signed it in my large, bold handwriting; Kaneke signed it in crabbed Arabic characters of which he had acquired some knowledge; and Hans signed it as a witness with a mark, or rather a blot, for in making it he split the pen. Thus all was finished and I went away exultant, as I have said, promising to return in the afternoon to make arrangements about the despatch of the ivory and as to our journey.

"Hans," I said, for there was no one else to talk to, "I did that business very well, did I not? Take a lesson from me and learn always to strike when the iron is hot. Tomorrow Kaneke might have changed his mind and offered much less."

"Yes, Baas, very well indeed, though sometimes if the iron is too hot the sparks blind one, Baas. Only I think that tomorrow Kaneke would have offered you double, for I know that he has much more ivory buried. If you had taken a lesson from me, you would have waited, Baas. Did I not tell you that he must get out of this place and would pay all he had for your help?"

"At any rate, Hans," I replied, somewhat staggered, "the pay is good, as much as I could ask."

"That depends upon what price the Baas puts upon his life," said Hans reflectively. "For my part I do not see that all the tusks of all the elephants in the world are of any use when one is dead, for they won't even make a coffin, Baas."

"What do you mean?" I asked angrily.

"Oh, nothing, Baas, except that I believe that we shall both be dead long before this business is finished. Also have you thought, Baas, that probably this ivory will never get to the coast at all? Because you see Kaneke, who, I think, is also good at business, will arrange for it to be stolen on the road and returned to him later, just as you or I would have done, Baas, had we been in his place. However, the Baas has the hundred sovereigns which no doubt will be very useful to eat when we are starving in some wilderness, or as a bribe to Kaneke's fetish, whatever it may be. Or—"

Here, unable to bear any more, I turned upon Hans with intent to do him personal injury, whereon he bolted, grinning, leaving me to wait upon myself at dinner. It was not a cheerful meal, for, as I reflected, the little wretch was probably right. To secure very doubtful advantages I had to let myself in for unknown difficulties and dangers, in company with a native of whom I knew little or nothing, except that he was an odd fish, and whose servant I had practically become in consideration for value received. For even if I never saw that ivory again, or its proceeds, there were the hundred sovereigns weighing down my pocket—and my conscience—like a lump of lead.

Most heartily did I wish that I had never touched the business. I thought of sending back the gold to Kaneke by Hans, but for various reasons dismissed the idea. Of these the chief was that probably it would never reach him, not because Hans was dishonest where money was concerned, but for the reason that it would go against what he called his conscience, to return anything to a person of the sort from whom it had been extracted. He might bury it; he might even give it to that jealous wife from whom he acquired so much backstairs information; but Kaneke, I was sure, would never see its colour unless I took it myself, which I was too proud to do.

Then suddenly my mood changed, transformed, perhaps, by some semi-spiritual influence, or as is more likely, by that of a good meal, for it is a humiliating fact that our outlook upon life and its affairs depends largely upon our stomach. What a rabbit of a man was I that I should be scared from a great project by the idle chatter and prognostications of Hans, uttered probably to exercise his mischievous mind at my expense. If I were, and on that account turned my face towards the coast again, Hans, who loved adventure even more than I do, would be the first to reproach me, not openly, but by means of the casual arrows of his barbed wit. Moreover, it was useless to run away from anything, for as he himself had said but yesterday, we must go where Fate drives us. Well, Fate had driven me to pocket Kaneke's sovereigns and a kind of note of hand in ivory, so there was an end of the matter. I would start for the home of the Dabanda people, and for the unvisited shores of the Lake Mone, and if I never got there, what did it matter? All our journeyings must end some day, be it next month, or next year, or a decade hence.

I sent for Hans, who came looking pious and aggrieved, perhaps the most aggravating of his many moods.

"Hans," I said, "I have made up my mind to go with Kaneke to the Dabanda country, and if you try to prevent me any more, I shall be angry with you and send you down to the coast with the ivory."

"Yes, Baas," he answered in a meek voice. "The Baas could scarcely do less, could he, after taking that fellow's money, which no doubt he made by selling girls; that is, unless he wished to be called a thief.

Moreover, I never tried to stop the Baas. Why should I when I shall be glad to go anywhere out of this place, where, to tell the truth, that jealous little wife of Kaneke who tells me so much, is beginning to think me too handsome and to roll her eyes and to press her hand upon her middle whenever she sees me, which makes me feel ill, Baas."

"You mean you make her feel ill, you little humbug," I suggested.

"No, Baas. I wish it were so, for then I could think better of her. For the rest, Baas, if I pointed out the dangers of this journey, it was not for my own self, but only because the Baas's reverend father left him in my charge and therefore I must do my best to guide him when I see him going astray."

At this I jumped up and Hans went on in a hurry.

"The Baas will not send me away to the coast with the ivory as he threatened to do, will he? He knows that in one way I am weak and perhaps if I was separated from him, grief might cause me to drink too much of that palm-wine and make myself ill." Then, reading in my face that I had no such intention, Hans took my hand, kissed it, and departed.

At the corner of the cook-house he turned and said:

"The Baas has made his will, has he not? So I need only remind him that if he wishes to write any good-bye-we-shall-meet-in-heaven letters, he had better do so at once, so that they can be sent down to the coast with the ivory."

CHAPTER 3

The Trial of Kaneke

I will pass over all the details concerning the dispatch of the ivory on its long road to Zanzibar and our other preparations for departure. Suffice it to say that the stuff went off all right on the shoulders of porters, together with a lot more, for Hans guessed well when he said that Kaneke had plenty of other tusks hidden away, although he declared that these belonged to someone else. What is more, here I will state that, strange as it may seem, in due course the ivory reached Zanzibar in safety and was delivered to my agent, who sold it according to instructions and, minus his commission, remitted the proceeds, which were more than I had expected, to my bank in Durban. So in this matter Kaneke dealt honestly.

What happened to the remainder of the ivory, which I presume to have been his, I do not know, nor can it have interested him, as he never returned to receive its price. Nor do I know what other goods went with that caravan which was led by Arabs, for I was careful not to inquire.

Notwithstanding the insinuations of Hans, I saw no girl slaves, and imagine them to have been apocryphal. Indeed, I believe that what Kaneke really dealt in was guns and powder. Once a year a caravan came up from Zanzibar laden with these and other goods, such as cloth, calico, and beads, returning with the ivory that Kaneke had collected in the interval. The money which he made on these transactions was large and kept in an English bank at Zanzibar, as I learned in after years. I wonder what became of it.

Well, the string of porters, headed by Arabs mounted upon donkeys, departed and were no more seen. We, too, prepared to depart. Here I should explain that my following was limited. I had with me two gun-bearers, skilled hunters both of them, who had been strongly recommended to me in Zanzibar and who, having learned my repute as a professional big-game shot, which had followed me from the

South, were very glad to enter my service. One of these men was, it appeared, an Abyssinian by birth with a name so unpronounce-able that I christened him Tom, though the natives called him "Little Holes", because his face was marked with small-pox.

The other was born of a Somali woman and an Arab, or perhaps a European father. To tell the truth he was remarkably British in his appearance with a round, open face and almost straight, reddish hair, although of course—except in certain lights—his skin was dark. His name, he informed me proudly, speaking in excellent English, for he had been educated at one of the first Mission schools and served as gun-bearer to several English sportsmen, was Jeremiah Jackson. Who his father might have been he had no idea, and as his mother died before he was five, she had never told him.

This man I called Jerry, because of the natural association of the name with that of Tom, for who has not heard of Tom and Jerry, the typical "gay dogs" of the Georgian days of whom my father used to tell me? Both of them were of about the same age, somewhere between thirty and forty. Both were Christians of a sort, for Tom belonged to the Abyssinian section of that faith, and both were brave and compe-tent men. Of the two Tom had the more dash, but perhaps owing to a European strain of blood Jerry was the cooler and the more dogged. Soon I became very friendly with them, but Hans looked upon them suspiciously, at any rate at first, I think because he was jealous.

These gun-bearers were well paid, according to the rate of that day; still, as they had come with me to hunt elephants and not to make long journeys of exploration, I thought it right to explain to them my change of plans and to give them the opportunity of returning to the coast with the ivory if they wished.

Tom said at once that he would go on with me to the end of the journey, whatever it might be, for he was a born adventurer with that touch of a mystic in him which I have observed to be not uncommon among such Abyssinians as I have met. Jerry, more cautious, began to talk about his wife, from whom it appeared he was separated, and his little daughter who was at a Mission school, which caused Hans, who was present, to make some sarcastic remark about "family men", who, he said, should stop at home and nurse the babies. This caused Jerry to fire up and say that he would come too and that Hans would see which of them wished to nurse babies before all was done.

When the matter was settled I thanked them both and told them that Kaneke had given me a hundred pounds in gold, a sum that, in view of the dangers of the trip, I proposed to divide into three parts, one for each of them and one for Hans. Now they thanked me warmly, only Jerry remarked that he thought it probable he would never live to earn his third, for which he was sorry as it would have been an endowment for his little daughter.

"You are mistaken," I said. "I propose to give you this money now, trusting to the honour of you both to stick to me to the end, so that if there is anyone in whom you put sufficient faith, among those who are going to the coast with the ivory,"—for this was before the caravan had started—"you can send it to your friends in his charge." They were much astonished and, I could see, touched, swearing, both of them, Tom who was a Protestant by God, and Jerry by the Virgin Mary, that they would never desert me, but would see the business through to the end, whatever it might be. When they had finished their protestations I turned to Hans, who all this while had stood by twirling his hat with a superior smile upon his ugly little face, and asked him if he did not thank me for his share.

"No, Baas. I am not going to take the money, so why should I thank you for nothing? I am not a hired man like these two hunters. I am the Baas's guardian appointed to look after him by his reverend father, and when I want anything of the Baas, I take it as a guardian has a right to do."

Then as he marched off I called after him in Dutch, which the others did not understand:

"You are a jealous, ill-conditioned little beggar, and I shall keep your share for myself." This I did until eventually he drew it a long while afterwards. I should add that besides Tom and Jerry I had about twenty native bearers, who agreed, though very doubtfully, to go on with me and carry the loads.

As the date fixed for our departure drew near, I observed that Kaneke grew more and more nervous, though exactly of what he was afraid I could not understand. He summoned a meeting of the headmen of his village, at which I was present, and explained that he proposed to accompany me upon an elephant-shooting trip whence we should return in due course. This intimation was very ill received, although he had added that they could elect one of their number to act as father of the village during his absence. They said that the time was coming when they expected him to pray for rain, and if he were not there to do so they would get none.

Here I should explain that the religion of these people was a strange mixture between that of Mahomet and the superstitions of the East Coast savages. Indeed a man called Gaika, a truculent, fierce-eyed fellow, not quite an Arab, for he had a dash of negroid blood, leapt up and denounced him venomously, ostensibly because of this proposed journey.

Kaneke, to my astonishment, remained very meek and calm, saying that he would think the matter over and speak with them again, after which the meeting broke up.

"What is at the back of all this?" I asked of Hans, who had been present with me, when we were in our camp again.

"The Baas is very blind," he said. "Does he not see that this Gaika wishes to kill Kaneke and take his place?"

I pointed out that if it were so he ought to be glad to get rid of him out of the town.

"Not so," answered Hans, "for they think he is really going to gather men from other tribes where his name as a witch-doctor is great, with whom he will return and put them all to death. Baas," he added in a whisper, "they have a plan to kill Kaneke, whom they both hate and fear, but they are not quite ready with their plan, which is why they do not want him to go away."

"How do you know all this—through that woman?" I asked.

Hans nodded.

"Some of it, Baas. The rest I picked up here and there when I seemed to be asleep, or when I am asking that old fellow who is called a Mullah to teach me the religion of Mahomet, which he thinks I am going to adopt. Yet, Baas, I sit in that mosque-hut of his listening to his nonsense and telling him that my soul is growing oh! so happy, and all the while I keep my ears open and pick up lots of things. For they think me very wise, Baas, and tell me plenty which they would not trust to you."

I looked at Hans with disgust, mixed with admiration, reflecting that without doubt he had got the hang of the business. But I said no more, for that place was a nest of spies.

That afternoon I had sent our porters on to a certain spot about three miles away, together with the loads. This I did because I was afraid lest they should be corrupted and the goods stolen. So now only Hans, Tom, and Jerry remained with me in the town.

Next morning Hans brought me my coffee as usual and said in a casual fashion:

"Baas, there is trouble. Kaneke was seized while he was asleep last night. They broke into his house and tied him with ropes. It seems that yesterday afternoon he had a quarrel with one of them and killed him with a blow of his fist, or with a stone that he held in his hand, for he is strong as an ox."

I whistled and asked what was going to happen.

"They are going to try him for murder this morning, Baas, according to their law, and they have sent to ask if you will be present at the trial. What shall I say, Baas?"

At first I was inclined to answer that I would have nothing to do with the business, but on reflection I remembered that if I did so it would be set down to fear; also that I had taken Kaneke's ivory and gold and that it would be mean to desert him in his trouble. So I sent an answer to say I would attend the trial with my servants.

At the appointed hour we went accordingly, armed, all four of us, and at the gate of the town were informed that the trial was to take place at the Tree of Council, which, it will be remembered, stood outside the village. So thither we marched and on arrival found all the population of the place, numbering perhaps three or four hundred people, assembled around the tree but outside of its shadow. In that shadow sat about a dozen white-robed men, elders, I suppose, whom I took to be the judges, some of them on the ground and some on stools.

As we advanced through the crowd towards them they stared doubtfully at our rifles, but in the end I was given a seat on the right of the Court, if so it may be called, but at a little distance, while my three retainers stood behind me. We were not spoken to, nor did we speak. Presently the crowd parted, leaving an open lane up which marched Kaneke with his hands bound behind his back, guarded by six men armed with spears. I noted that all looked upon him coldly as he went by. To judge by their faces he had not a friend among them.

Finally he was placed in such a position that he had the judges, who sat with their backs to the trunk of the tree, in front of him, with myself on his right, and the audience on his left. There he stood quietly, a fine and striking figure notwithstanding his bonds, taller by a head than any of that company. Somehow he reminded me of Samson bound and being led in to be mocked by the Philistines, so much so that I wondered where Delilah might be. Then I remembered Hans' tale of the jealous wife and thought that I knew—which I didn't. He rolled his big eyes about him, taking in everything. Presently they fell upon me, to whom he bowed. Of his judges he took no notice at all, or, for the matter of that, of the people either.

The "Mullah man", as Hans called the priest, opened the proceedings with some kind of prayer and many genuflexions. Then Gaika, who appeared to act as Attorney General and Chief Justice rolled into one, set out the case at considerable length and with much venom. He narrated that Kaneke was a slave belonging to some strange people, who by murder many years before, and cunning, had acquired authority over them. Then he proceeded to detail all his crimes as a ruler which, if he could be believed, were black indeed. Among them were cruelty, oppression, theft, robbery of women, and I know not what besides.

These were followed by a string of offences of another class: necromancy which was against the law of the Prophet, bewitchments, raising of spirits, breaches of the law of Ramadan, betrayal of the Faith by one who was its secret enemy, worship of strange gods or devils, drinking of spirituous liquors, plottings with their enemies against the people, midnight sacrifice of lambs and infants to the stars, and so forth. Lastly came the immediate charge, that of the murder of an elder on the previous day. For all of these crimes Gaika declared the slave and usurper Kaneke to be worthy of death.

Having settled his hash in this fashion, he sat down and called upon the prisoner to plead.

Kaneke answered in a resonant voice that struck me, and I think all present, as powerful and impressive.

"To what purpose is it that I should plead," he said, "seeing that my chief judge and enemy has already declared me guilty of more crimes than anyone could commit if he lived for a hundred years? Still, letting the rest be, I will say that I am guilty of one thing, namely of killing a man yesterday in a quarrel, in order to prevent him from stabbing me, though it is true that I did not mean to kill him, but only to fell him to the ground; so that it was Allah who killed him, not I. Now I will tell you, O people, why I am put upon my trial here before you, I who have lifted you up from nothingness into a state of wealth and power.

"It is that yonder Gaika may take my place as your headman. Good. He is welcome to my place. Know that I weary of ruling over you and protecting you. What more need I say? It is enough. For a long while you have plotted to kill me. Now let me go my way, and go you yours."

"It is not enough," shouted Gaika. "You, O Kaneke, say that you would accompany the white hunter, Macumazahn yonder, to shoot elephants. It is a lie. You go to raise against us the tribes to the north who have a quarrel with us from our father's time, saying that these seized their young people and sold them as slaves. We know that it is your plan and it is for that reason that for years we have never allowed you to leave our town. Nor shall you leave it now. Nay, you shall stay here for ever while your spirit dwells in hell, where wizards go."

He ceased, and from the audience rose a murmur of applause.

Whatever his good qualities might be—if he had any—evidently Kaneke was not popular among his flock. As the prisoner made no answer, Gaika went on, addressing the other judges thus:

"My brothers, you have heard. To call witnesses is needless, since some of you saw this Kaneke murder our brother yesterday. Is he guilty of this and other crimes?"

"He is guilty," they answered, speaking all together.

"Then what should be his punishment?"

"Death," they answered, again speaking all together, while the audience echoed the word "Death".

"Kaneke," shouted Gaika in triumph, "you are doomed to die. Not one among these hundreds asks for mercy on you; no, not even the women. Nor have you any children to plead for you, since doubtless, being a magician, you slew them unborn lest they should grow up to kill you. Yet according to the law it is not lawful that you should be despatched at once. Therefore we send you back to your own house under guard, that there you may pray to Allah and His Prophet for forgiveness of your sins. Tomorrow at the dawn you shall be brought back here and beaten to death with clubs, that we may not shed your blood. Have you heard and do you understand?"

Then at length Kaneke spoke again. Showing no fear, he spoke quietly, almost indifferently, yet in so clear a voice that none could miss a word, saying in the midst of a deep silence:

"O Gaika, son of a dog, and all the rest of you, sons and daughters of dogs, I hear and I understand. So tomorrow you would beat me to death with clubs. It may happen or it may not, but if I know I shall not tell you. Still, listen to the last wisdom that you shall hear from my lips. You are right when you say that I am a magician. It is so, and as such I have foreknowledge of the future. I call down a curse on you all. Let Allah defend you if he can, and will, and Mahomet make prayer for you. This is the curse: a great sickness shall fall on you; I think it will begin tonight. I think that some who are already sick are seated yonder," and he nodded towards the crowd, "although they know it not. Yes, they began to be sick a minute ago, when the words of cursing left my lips" (here there was a sensation among the audience, every one of them staring at his neighbour). "Most of you will die of this sickness because after I am gone there will be none to doctor you. The rest will flee away. They will scatter like goats without a herd. They will be taken by those whose sons and daughters you used to steal, and become slaves and die as slaves."

Then he turned towards me and added, "Farewell, Lord Macumazahn. If it is fated that in flesh I cannot guide you on your journey to the place whither you would go, yet fear not, for my spirit will guide you and when you are come there safely, then give a message from me to one of whom I have spoken to you, which message shall be delivered to you, perhaps in the night hours when you are asleep. I do not ask you to lift your gun and shoot this rogue," and he nodded towards Gaika, "because you are but one and would be overwhelmed with your servants. Nay, I only ask you to hearken to the message when it comes and to do what it bids you."

Not knowing what to say I made no answer to this peculiar appeal, although Hans, to judge by his mumblings and fidgets, appeared to wish me to say something. As I still declined, with his usual impertinence he took it upon himself to act as my spokesmen, saying in his debased Arabic:

"The great lord, my master, bids me inform you, Kaneke, that he is sorry you are going to be killed. He tells me to say also that, if you are killed and become a spook, he begs that you will keep away from him, as spooks, especially of those who are magicians and have been put to death for their evil deeds, are not nice company for anyone."

When I heard this, indignation took away my breath, but before I could speak a word Gaika addressed me fiercely, crying out:

"White Wanderer, we believe that you are in league with this evildoer and plot mischief against us. Get out of our town at once, lest you share his fate."

Now this unprovoked assault made me furious, and I answered in the first words that came to my tongue:

"Who are you that tell lies and dare to talk to me of Fate? Let my fate be, fellow, and have a care for your own, which perhaps is nearer than you think."

Little did I guess when I spoke thus, at hazard as it seemed, that very soon doom would overtake this ruffian, and by my hand. Are we sometimes filled with the spirit of prophecy, I wonder? Or do we, perhaps, know everything on our inmost souls whence now and again bursts a rush of buried truth?

After this the company broke up in confusion. Kaneke was hustled away by his guards; men who waved their spears in a threatening fashion advanced upon us and were so insolent that at last I looked round and lifted the rifle I carried—I remember that it was one of the first Winchester repeaters of a sort that carried five cartridges. Thereon they fell back and we were allowed to regain our huts in peace.

I did not stop there long. Nearly all our gear had been sent forward with the bearers; indeed, no more of it remained than the four of us could carry ourselves, although the arrangement was that some of Kaneke's men should do us this service on the morrow. As this was now out of the question we loaded ourselves, also a donkey that I possessed, with blankets, guns, cooking-pots, ammunition, and I know not what besides, and started, I riding on the donkey and looking, as I have since reflected, like the White Knight in Alice in Wonderland.

Then, keeping clear of the town, we trekked for the place where our bearers were encamped, reaching it unmolested about an hour later. This spot, chosen by myself, was on the lowest slope of a steep hill covered with thorn trees, through which ran a little stream from a spring higher up the slope. The first thing I did was to cut down a number of these thorns and drag them together into a fence, making what is called a *boma* in that part of Africa, behind which we could protect ourselves if necessary. By the time that this was done and my tent was pitched, it was late in the afternoon. Feeling tired, more, I think, from anxiety than exertion, I lay down and after musing for a while upon the fate of the unfortunate Kaneke and wishing, much as I disliked the man, that I could save him from a doom I believed to be unjust, which seemed impossible, I fell asleep, as I can do at any time. In my sleep a curious dream came to me, which after all was not wonderful, seeing how my mind was occupied.

I dreamed that Kaneke spoke to me, though I could not see him, but distinctly I heard, or seemed to hear, his voice saying:

"Follow the woman. Do what the woman tells you, and you will save me."

Twice I heard this, and then I do not know how long afterwards, I woke up, or rather was awakened by Hans setting some food upon the camp table near the tent. On going out I saw that it was night, for the full moon was just rising and already giving so clear a light in a cloudless sky, that I could see to eat without the aid of a lamp.

"Hans," I said presently, "what did Kaneke mean when he talked of a great sickness that was about to smite the town?"

"The Baas observes little," answered Hans. "Did he notice nothing among the people of that caravan which took away the ivory?"

"Yes, I noticed that they were a dirty lot and smelt so much that I kept clear of them."

"If the Baas had come a little closer, he would have seen that two or three of them had pimples coming all over their faces."

"Small-pox?" I suggested.

"Yes, Baas, small-pox, for I have seen it before. Also, they had been mixing with the people of the town who have not had small-pox for many years, for Kaneke kept it away by his charms, or stopped it when it broke out. Baas, this time he did not keep it away, and quite a number of the townspeople, as I heard this morning, are feeling bad, with sore throats and headaches, Baas. Kaneke knew all this as well as I do and that is why he talked about a pestilence. It is easy to prophesy when one knows, Baas."

"Is it easy to send dreams, Hans?" I asked; then before he could answer I told him of the words I had seemed to hear in my sleep.

For a moment I caught sight of a look of astonishment upon Hans' wrinkled and impassive countenance. Then he answered in an unconcerned fashion:

"I dare say, Baas, if one knows how. Or perhaps Kaneke sent no dream. Perhaps the Baas heard me and the woman talking together, for she is here and waiting to see the Baas after he has eaten."

CHAPTER 4

White-Mouse

"A woman!" I said, springing up. "What woman?"

"Kaneke's jealous wife who likes me so much, she whom they call White-Mouse because she is so quick and silent, I suppose. She has a plan to save that bull of a man, just as the dream said, or you overheard."

"Then she must be fond of him after all, Hans."

"I suppose so, Baas. Or perhaps she thinks she will get him back again now, because some other woman, of whom she is jealous, has got small-pox, of which she hopes that she will die, or become very ugly. At least that is her tale, Baas."

"I will see her at once," I said.

"Best eat your supper first, Baas; it is always wise to keep women waiting a while, for that makes them think more of you."

Knowing that Hans always had a reason for what he said, even when he seemed to be talking the most arrant nonsense, I took his advice.

When I had finished my food he led me to a patch of bush that grew round a pool at the foot of the slope about two hundred yards from the camp. We entered and presently from beneath a tree a little woman glided out so silently that she might have been a ghost, and stood still with the moonlight falling on her white robes. She threw back a hood that covered her head, revealing her face, which was refined and in its way very pretty; also so fair for an Arab that I thought she must have European blood in her. She looked at me a little while, searching my face with her dark, appealing eyes, then suddenly threw herself on her knees, took my hand, and kissed it.

"That will do," I said, lifting her up. "What do you want with me?"

"Lord," she said in Arabic, speaking in a low, impassioned voice, "I am that slave of Kaneke whom here they call White-Mouse, though elsewhere I have another name. Although he has treated me badly, for he who loves a Shadow cares for no woman, his spell is still upon me. Therefore I would pray you to save him if you can."

"Me!"

"Yes, Lord, you." Then as I said nothing she went on quickly, "I know that you white men do not work without pay, and I have nothing to give you, except myself. I will be a good servant to you and Kaneke will not mind. He has told me to go where I will."

"Don't be frightened, Baas," whispered Hans into my ear in Dutch. "When she says you—she must mean me."

I hit him in the middle with the point of my elbow, which stopped his breath. Then I said:

"Set out your plan, White-Mouse, if you have one. But please understand that I do not want you as a servant."

"Then you can drive me away, Lord, for if you do my will, your slave I shall be till death. Only one thing do I ask, that you do not give me to that little yellow monkey, or to either of your hunters."

"How well she acts!" grunted the unconquered Hans behind me.

"The plan, the plan," I said.

"Lord, it is this: there is a path up the cliff on the crest of which is the house of Kaneke, wherein he lies bound awaiting death at the rising of the morrow's sun. It is known to few; indeed only to Kaneke and myself. I will lead you with your two hunters and this yellow one up that path and into Kaneke's house. There, if it be needful, you can deal with those who guard him—there are but three of them, for the rest watch without the fence—and get him away down the cliff."

"This is nonsense," I said. "I examined that cliff when I visited Kaneke. There is no fence upon its edge because it overhangs in such a fashion that without long ropes, such as we have not got, made fast above, it cannot be climbed or descended."

"It seems to do so, Lord, but beneath its overhanging crest there is a hole, which hole leads into a tunnel. This tunnel ends beneath the pavement of Kaneke's house just in front of where he sits to watch the stars. Do you understand, Lord?"

I nodded, for I knew that she meant the *stoep* where Kaneke and I had drunk brandy and water together.

"The pavement is solid," I said. "How does one pass through it?"

"A block of the hard floor, which is made of lime and other things so that it is like stone, can be moved from beneath. I have its secret, Lord. That is all. Will you come with me now? The beginning of the gorge is not very far from this place which, as you know, by any other road is a long way from the town. Therefore we need not start yet because I do not wish to reach the house until two hours after midnight, when all men are asleep, except those who watch the sick in the town, where a pestilence has broken out, as Kaneke foretold, and these will take little heed if they hear a noise."

"No, I won't," I answered firmly. "This is a mad business. Why should I give my life and those of my servants to try to save Kaneke, whom I have only known for a week or two and who may be all that his enemies say?"

She considered the point, then answered:

"Because he alone can guide you to that hidden place whither you wish to go."

"I don't wish to go anywhere in particular," I replied testily; "unless it is back to Zanzibar."

Again she considered, and said:

"Because you have taken Kaneke's ivory and gold, Lord."

At this I winced a little and then replied:

"I took the ivory and gold in payment for services to be rendered to Kaneke, if he could accompany me upon a certain journey, and he paid, asking nothing in return if he could not do so. Through no fault of mine he is unable to come, and therefore the bargain is at an end."

"That is well said, Lord, in the white man's merchant-fashion. Now I have another reason to which I think any man will listen. You should help Kaneke because I, your slave, who am a woman young and fair, pray you to do so."

"Ah! she is clever; she knows the Baas," I heard Hans mutter reflectively, words that hardened my heart and caused me to reply:

"Not for the sake of any woman in Africa, nor of all of them put together, would I do what you ask, White-Mouse. Do you take me for a madman?"

She laughed a little in a dreary fashion and answered:

"Indeed I do not, who see that it is I who am mad. Hearken, Lord: like others I have heard tales of Macumazahn. I have heard that he is generous and great-hearted; one who never goes back upon his word, a staff to lean on in the hour of trouble, a man who does not refuse the prayer of those in distress; brave too, and a lover of adventure if a good cause may be served, a great one whom it pleases to pretend to be small. All these things I have heard from that yellow man, and others; yes, and from Kaneke himself, and watching from afar, although you never knew I did so, I have judged these stories to be true. Now I see that I am mistaken. This lord Macumazahn is as are other white traders, neither better nor worse. So it is finished. Unaided I am not able to save Kaneke, as by my spirit I have sworn that I would. Therefore I pray your pardon, Lord, who have put you to trouble, and here before your eyes will end all, that I may go to make report of this business to those I serve far away."

While I stared at her, wondering what she meant, also how much truth there was in all this mysterious tale, suddenly she drew a knife from her girdle, and tearing open her robe, lifted it above her bared breast. I sprang and seized her wrist.

"You must love this man very much!" I exclaimed, more, I think, to myself than to her.

"You are mistaken, Lord," she answered, with her strange little laugh. "I do not love him; indeed I think I hate him who have never found one whom I could love—as yet. Still, for a while he is my master, also I have sworn to hold him safe by certain oaths that may not be broken and—I keep my word, as I must do or perish everlastingly."

For a little while there was silence between us. Never can I forget the strangeness of that scene. The patch of bush by the edge of the pool, the little open space where the bright moonlight fell, and standing full in that moonlight which shone upon the whiteness of her rounded breast, this small, elfin-faced woman with the dark eyes and curling hair, a knife in her raised right hand.

Then myself, much perplexed and agitated, rather a ridiculous figure, as I suspect, clasping her wrist to prevent that knife from falling; and in the background upon the edge of the shadow, sardonic, his face alight with the age-old wisdom of the wild man who had eaten of the tree of Knowledge, interested and yet indifferent, hideous and yet lovable—the Hottentot, Hans. And the look upon that beautiful woman's face, for in its way it was beautiful, or at any rate most attractive, the inscrutable look, suggestive of secrets, of mysteries even—oh! I say I shall never forget it all.

As we stood thus facing each other like people in a scene of a play, a thought came to me, this thought—if that woman was prepared to die because she had failed in an effort to save from death the man whom she declared she hated (why was she prepared to die and why did she hate him? I wondered), ought I not to try to save her even at some personal risk to myself? Also if I could, ought I not to help Kaneke, whose goods I had taken? Certainly it was impossible to allow her to immolate herself in this fashion before my eyes. I might take away her knife, but if I did she could find a second; also there were many other roads to self-destruction by which she might travel.

"Give me that dagger," I said, "and let us talk."

She unclasped her hand and it fell to the ground. I set my foot upon it and loosed her.

"Listen," I went on. "I am minded to do what you wish if I can."

"Yes, Lord, already I have read that in your face," she replied, smiling faintly.

"But, White-Mouse," I continued, "I am not the only one concerned. I cannot undertake this business alone. Others must risk their lives as well. Hans here, for instance, and I suppose the two hunters. I cannot lay any commands upon them in such a matter and I do not know if they will come of their own will."

She turned and looked at the Hottentot, a question in her eyes. Hans fidgeted under her gaze, then he spat upon the ground and said:

"If the Baas goes I think that the Baas will be a fool. Still, where the Baas goes, there I must go also, not to pull Kaneke out of a trap, but because I promised the Baas's reverend father that I would do so. As for those other men I cannot say. I think they will answer, 'No, thank you', but if they reply, 'Oh yes', then I believe that we should be better without them, because they are so stupid and think so much about their souls that they would be sure to grow frightened at the wrong time, or to make a noise and bring us all to trouble. In a hole such as White-Mouse talks of, two men are better than four. Also it would be wiser to send Tom and Jerry on with the porters, for should we drag Kaneke out of this hole, those Arabs will try to follow and drag him back, and the farther off we are with the stores the safer we shall be. Porters go slowly, so we can catch them up, Baas."

"You hear," I said to the woman. "What is your word?"

"This yellow one, whom I thought but a vain fool, is wise—for once, Lord. What has to be done I cannot do alone, for there must be some to deal with the guards and hold the mouth of the hole while I cut Kaneke's bonds. Yet for this business two will serve as well as four; indeed better, for they can get back into the tunnel more quickly. Therefore I say do as the yellow man says. Order your hunters to march on with the porters and the stores as long before the break of day as the men will move. If you escape with Kaneke, you can run upon their spoor and join them much faster than will the Arabs who must go round. Then if the Arabs overtake you, they will be tired and you can beat them off with your guns."

"And what will you do?" I asked curiously, for I noticed that she left herself out of the plan.

"Oh! I do not know," she answered, with another of her strange smiles. "Lord, have I not said that I am your slave? Doubtless in this fashion or in that I shall follow my master as a slave should, or perhaps I shall go before him."

Now I remembered that she had spoken of Kaneke as her "master", and presumed that she alluded to him, although in the hyperbole of her people she spoke of herself as my slave. However, I did not pursue the subject, which at the time interested me little, who had more important matters to consider. Indeed, I set myself to extract details from her which I need not enumerate, and to examine her scheme of rescue.

When I had learned all I could, bidding the woman, White-Mouse, to remain hidden, I went back to the camp with Hans and sent for Tom and Jerry. In as careless a fashion as I could, I told them that with Hans I must return towards the town to speak with a man who had promised to meet me secretly upon a matter of importance. Then I ordered them to rouse the porters two hours before dawn and to march on with them towards a certain hill which we had all visited together upon a little shooting-expedition I had made while we were at Kaneke's town, to kill duiker buck and *pauw*, as we called bustards, for a change of food.

Although I could see that they were troubled, Tom and Jerry said that they would obey my instructions and, that there should be no mistake, fetched the headman of the porters, that I might repeat them to him, which I did. This done, they went away to sleep, Tom saying, as he bade me good night, that he would have preferred to accompany me back to the town where he thought I might come into danger. I thanked him, remarking that I was quite safe. So we parted; I wondering whether I should ever see them again and what they would do if I returned no more. Travel back to the coast, probably, and become rich according to their ideas by selling the guns and goods.

Then I lay down to rest for a while, making Hans do likewise.

At the appointed time I woke from my doze, as I can always do, and left the tent to find Hans awaiting me without and checking such things as we must carry. These were few—a water-bottle filled with cold tea, a small flask of spirits, a strip or two of biltong or dried meat in case we should need food, and a few yards of thin cord. For arms I took a Winchester repeater and a pocketful of cartridges, also a revolver and a sharp butcher's knife in a sheath. Hans had no rifle, but carried two revolvers and a knife, also a couple of candles and a box of matches.

Having made sure that we had collected everything and packed our other belongings to be cared for by Tom and Jerry as arranged, we slipped away to the patch of bush by the pool, taking with us extra food, for we remembered that White-Mouse must be hungry. We did not find her at once, whereon Hans explained to me that having made fools of us, doubtless she had run away. While he was still talking I saw her leaning against the trunk of a tree. Or rather I saw her eyes, which at first I took for those of some animal, for she was no longer a white figure, but a black, having covered her white robe with a thin dark garment she had brought with her in a bundle. I offered her the food, but she shook her head, saying:

"Nay, I eat no more"—words which frightened me a little.

Indeed, altogether there was something fateful and alarming about this woman. She glanced at the moon, then whispered:

"Lord, it is time to depart. Be pleased to follow me and do not smoke, or make fire, or talk too loud."

So off she went, gliding ahead like a shadow, while we marched after, I with a doubting heart. Our road ran along the bank of a little stream, of which the spring I have spoken of seemed to be the source, that wended its way through thin bush to the mouth of the gorge, which here sloped up to the high lands. Doubtless it was this stream, once a primeval torrent, that in the course of thousands of years dug out this cleft in the bosom of the earth. As we went Hans murmured his reflections into my ear.

"This is a strange journey, Baas, made at night, when we ought to be asleep. I wonder that the Baas should have undertaken it. I think, although he does not know it, he would never have done so had not White-Mouse been so pretty. Perhaps the Baas has noted that when a woman asks for anything of a man, generally he finds it impossible to give it her if she be old and ugly, and quite possible if she is young and very pretty."

"Rubbish!" I answered. "I gave way because, if I had not, White-Mouse would have killed herself, and for no other reason."

"Yes, but if she had been a hideous old grandmother, with a black face wrinkled like that of the Baas, he would not have cared whether she killed herself or not. For who wants a slave with a skin like the hide of a buck that has lain for three months in the sun and rain?"

"As I have told you, I want no slave, Hans," I answered indignantly.

"Ah! so the Baas says now, but sometimes he changes his mind. Thus a little while ago the Baas swore that never, never would he go up the hole to try to save Kaneke. And yet we are taking this long walk with lions about and God knows what at the end of it, to do what the Baas said could not be done. Why, then, did he change his mind, unless it is because that woman is such a pretty mouse with big eyes and a queer smile and not an ugly old yellow-toothed rat? Also, is he sure that all this story of hers is true? For my part I don't believe it, and even doubt whether she is Kaneke's wife as she pretended to me."

At this moment we began to enter the gorge, and our guide turned and laid her finger on her lips in token that we must be silent. Of this I was very glad, for really Hans' jeers were intolerable.

Very soon we descended into the cleft itself, which proved to be a huge donga with sheer sides quite two hundred feet high where it was deepest. The bottom along which the shrunken river ran was strewn with boulders washed from the cliffs above, that made progress slow and difficult. Especially was this so as we scrambled down the deeps, where often little of the moonlight reached us, and sometimes even the sky was hidden by tropical shrubs and tall palms and grasses which grew along the edge of the torrent bed.

Fortunately the journey was not very long, for after about half an hour of this break-back work White-Mouse halted.

"Here is the place," she whispered. "Listen. You can hear the dogs in the town above."

It was true; I could, and the sound of those brutes howling at the moon, as they do at night in Africa, was eerie enough in our depressing circumstances.

"This is the place," she repeated, then after studying the sky a while, added: "Presently will be the time. Meanwhile let us rest, for we shall need all our strength."

Motioning to Hans to remain where he was, she led me to a flat stone out of his hearing, on which I sat down, while she crouched on the ground at my feet, native fashion, a little black ball in the shadow with the faint light gleaming upon a white patch that I knew to be her face.

"Lord," she said, "you go upon a dangerous business, yet I say to you, fear nothing for yourself or the yellow man."

"Why? I fear much."

"Lord, those who have to do with Kaneke's people, as I have from a child, catch something of their wisdom and mind; also I too have been taught to read the stars he worships."

"So our friend is an astrologer," thought I to myself. That is new to me in Africa, but aloud I said:

"Well, what wisdom have you caught or read in the stars?"

"Only that you are both safe, Lord, now and on the journey you will make with Kaneke; yes, and for many years after."

"I am glad to hear it," I remarked somewhat sarcastically, though in my heart I was cheered, as even the most instructed and civilized of us are when anyone speaks words of good omen. Also in that darksome place at the dead of night, on the edge of a desperate adventure, a little comfort went a long way, for when the bread is dry some butter is better than none at all, as Hans used to observe.

"Lord, a word more and I cease to trouble you. Do you believe in blessings, Lord?"

"Oh yes, White-Mouse, though I don't see any about me just now."

"You are wrong, Lord; I see them. They are thick upon your head, they shall be with you through life, and afterwards thousands shall love you. Among them is that blessing which I lay upon you."

"You are very kind, I am sure, White-Mouse. But as you say you hate this Kaneke I don't understand why you should bless me for what I am trying to do."

"No, Lord, and perhaps while you live you never will. Yet I would have you know one thing. I am not Kaneke's jealous wife as I made yonder yellow one believe, or his wife at all, or any man's, any more than my name is White-Mouse. Lord, you go to seek a wonderful one whom I serve, and I think that you will find her far away. Perhaps I shall be there in her company, and in helping her you will again help me. Now it is time to be at our work."

Then she took my hand and kissed it. I remember that her kiss felt like a butterfly alighting on my flesh, and that her breath was wonderfully sweet. Next she beckoned to Hans, who, devoured by curiosity, was glowering at us from a distance, and led the pair of us a little way up the cliff which sloped at its bottom because of debris washed up by the torrent in ancient days, or perhaps fallen from above. We came to some bushes, in the midst of which lay a large boulder. Here she halted and spoke to us in a whisper, saying:

"On the farther side of that stone is the mouth of the cleft. If you look you will see that the crest of the cliff overhangs its topmost part by many feet, so that it is impossible for it to be ascended or descended, even with any rope the Arabs have, because the height is too great. As I have told you, this tunnel, or waterway, runs to the top for the most part underground, though here and there it is open to the sky. After it reaches that sheer face of the cliff which the stone lip overhangs, the passage pierces the solid rock and is very steep. Here two lamps are hid which I will light with the little fire sticks that your servant has given to me. One lamp must be left as a guide in the descent when you return; the other I, who go first, will carry to show you where to set your feet. Do you understand, Lord?"

"Yes, but what I want to know is, what happens when we reach the top of the tunnel?"

"Lord, as I have said, at its head the hole is closed with a moving block that seems to be part of the floor of the courtyard of Kaneke's house. I have its secret and can cause it to open, which I will do after I have hidden the lamp. Then we must creep into the courtyard. Kaneke, as I believe, is on the *stoep* of the house with his hands tied behind him, and bound with a rope round his middle to a post that supports the roof of the *stoep*. It may be, however, that he is in one of the rooms of the house, in which case our task will be difficult—"

"Very difficult," I interrupted with a groan.

"My hope is," she went on, taking no heed of my words, "that those who guard him will be asleep, or perhaps drunk, for doubtless they will have found the white man's drink that Kaneke keeps in the house, which they love, all of them, although it is forbidden by their law. Or Kaneke himself may have told them where it is and begged them to get him some of it. If so, I shall cut his bonds so that he may come to the mouth of the hole and climb into it and thus escape."

"And if they are awake and sober—as they ought to be?" I said.

"Then, Lord, you and the yellow man must play your part; it is not for me to tell you what it is," she answered dryly. "There will not be many of these men set to keep one who is bound, and the most of the guard watch outside the fence, thinking that if any rescue is attempted, it will be from the town. Now I have told you all, so let us start."

Well, start we did; White-Mouse, going first, went round the boulder and pulled aside some loose stones, revealing an orifice, into which we crept after her, Hans nipping in before me. For some way we crawled in the dark up a slope of rock. Then, as she had said would be the case, light reached us from the sky because here the cleft was open. Indeed, there were two or three of these alternating lengths of darkness and light.

After ten minutes or so of this climbing White-Mouse halted and whispered:

"Now the real tunnel begins. Rest a while, for it is steep."

I obeyed with gratitude. Presently there was the sound of a match being struck. She had found the lamp, an earthenware affair filled with palm-oil such as the Arabs used in those days, and lit it. After the darkness its light seemed dazzling. By it I saw a round hole running upwards almost perpendicularly; it was the tunnel which she had told us pierced the lip of solid cliff that overhung the gorge. To all appearance it had been made by man, though a long while ago.

243

Perhaps it was a mine-shaft, hollowed by primeval metal-workers; after all, these are common in Africa, where I have seen many of them in Matabele Land.

At any rate, on its walls I noted gleaming specks that I took to be ore of some sort, but of course this guess may be quite wrong. Up this shaft ran a kind of ladder with little landing-places at intervals, made by niches cut in the rock to give foot-and hand-holds. There was a rope also that must have been fastened to something above, which, I may add, looked to me rather rotten, as though it had been there a long while. My heart sank as I contemplated it and the niches, and most heartily did I wish myself anywhere else than in that beastly hole. However, it was no use showing fear; there was nothing to be done except go through with the business, so I held my tongue, though I heard Hans praying, or cursing, or both, in front of me.

"Forward now. Have no fear," whispered our guide. "Set your hands and feet in the niches as I do; they will not break away, and the rope is stronger than it looks."

Then she slung or strapped to her back the second lamp, which I forgot to say she had lit also and placed in a kind of basket so made that it could be used in this fashion without setting fire to its bearer, thus giving us light whereby to climb, and sprang at the face of the rock. Up she went with an extraordinary nimbleness, which caused me to reflect in an inconsequent fashion that she was well named Mouse, a creature that can run up a wall.

We followed as best we could, clasping the rotten-looking rope, which seemed to be made of twisted buffalo-hide, with our right hands and the niches in which we must afterwards set our feet with our left. I think that rope was the greatest terror of this horrible journey; though, as we were destined to prove, White-Mouse was right when she said that it was stronger than it looked—very strong, in truth, though this we did not know at the time.

No, not the greatest, for even worse than the rope, that is when we had ascended a long way, was the lamp which we had left burning at the bottom of the hole, because the spark of light it gave showed what a terrible distance there was to fall if one made a mistake. I only looked at it once, or at most twice; it frightened me too much. Another minor trouble in my case was my Winchester repeater that was slung upon my back, of which the strap cut my shoulder and the lock rubbed my spine. Much did I regret that I had not followed the example of Hans and left it behind.

We reached the first landing-place and rested. After eyeing me with some anxiety, for doubtless my face showed trepidation, Hans, I imagine to divert my mind, took the chance to deliver a little homily.

"The Baas," he said, wiping the sweat from his face with the back of his hand, "is very fond of helping people in trouble, a bad habit of which I hope the Baas will break himself in future. For see what happens to those who are such fools. Not even to help my own father would I come into this hole again, especially as I don't know who he was. However, Baas," he added more cheerfully—for secretly agreeing with Hans, I made no reply—"if this is an old mine-shaft as I suppose, think how much worse it must have been for the miners to climb up it with a hundred-pound bag of ore on their backs, than it is for us; especially as they weren't Christians, like you and me, Baas, and didn't know that they would go to heaven if they tumbled off, like we do. When one is fording a bad river safely, Baas, as we are, it is always nice to remember that lots of other people have been drowned in it."

Will it be believed that even then and there that little beast Hans made me laugh, or at any rate smile, especially as I knew that his cynicism was assumed and therefore could bring no ill luck on us? For really Hans had the warmest of hearts.

Presently, off we went again for another spell of niches and apparently rotten rope, and in due course came safely to the second landing-place. Here White-Mouse bade us wait a little.

Saying that she would return presently, she went up a third flight of niches at great speed, and reaching yet another landing-place, did something—we could not see what.

Then she returned, and her descent was strange to see. Taking the rope in both hands (afterwards we discovered that it was made fast to a point or hook of stone on the third landing-place in such fashion that it hung well clear of the face of the rock below), she came down it hand over—or rather under—hand, sometimes setting her foot into one of the niches, but more often swinging quite clear. She was wonderful to look on; her slight figure illumined by the lantern on her back and surrounded by darkness, appeared more like a spirit floating in mid-air than that of a woman. Presently she stood beside us.

"Lord," she said, when she had rested a minute, "I have been to see whether the catch of the stone which covers the mouth of the hole is in order. It works well and I have loosed it. Now at a push this stone, that like the rest of the courtyard is faced with lime plaster, will swing upwards, for it is hung upon a bar of iron, and remain on edge, leaving a space large enough for any man to climb into the courtyard by the little ladder that is set upon the landing-place. Be careful, however, not to touch the stone when you have passed the opening into the court-yard, for if so much as a finger is laid upon it, it will swing to again and make itself fast, cutting off retreat."

"Cannot it be opened from above?" I asked anxiously.

"Yes, Lord, if one knows how, which it is impossible to explain to you except in the courtyard itself, as perhaps I shall have no time or chance to do. Still, do not be afraid, for I will fix it with a wedge so that it cannot shut unless the wedge is pulled away. Nay, ask no more questions, for I have not time to answer them," she went on impa-tiently, as I opened my mouth to speak. "Have I not told you that all will be well? Follow me with a bold heart."

Then, as though to prevent the possibility of further conversation, she went to the edge of the resting-place and began to climb, Hans and I scrambling after her as before. Of this ascent I remember little, for my mind was so fixed upon what was to happen when we reached the top that, dreadful as it was, it made small impression on me. Also by now I was growing more or less used to this steeplejack work, and since I had seen the woman hanging on to it, gained confidence in the rope. The end of it was that we reached the third landing-place in safety, being now, as I reckoned, quite two hundred feet above the spot where the actual tunnel sprang from the cleft which sometimes went underground and sometimes was open to the sky.

CHAPTER 5

The Rescue

When we had recovered breath White-Mouse unfastened the lantern from her back and showed us a stout wooden ladder with broad rungs almost resembling steps, which ran from the edge of the resting-place to what looked like a solid roof, but really was the bottom of the movable stone.

"Examine it well," she said, "and note that this resting-place is not beneath the stone, but to the right of it. Therefore I can leave the lamp burning here that it may be ready for use in the descent; for if the basket is set in front of the flame the light will not show in the courtyard above."

This she proceeded to do, and it was then that I noted how the hide rope was fastened to a hook-shaped point of rock at the edge of the platform, also—which I did not like—that it was somewhat frayed by this edge, although originally that length of it had been bound round with grass and a piece of cloth.

Now we were in semi-darkness and my spirits sank proportionately.

"What are we to do, White-Mouse?" I asked.

"This, Lord. I will go up the ladder and push open the stone, as I told you. Then I will climb into the courtyard and creep to the *stoep* where I am sure Kaneke lies bound, hoping that there I may be able to cut his cords without awakening those who guard him, who, I trust, will be asleep, or drunk, or both. You and Hans will follow me through the hole and stand or kneel on either side of it with your weapons ready. If there is trouble you will use those weapons, Lord, and kill any who strive to prevent the escape of Kaneke."

Now my patience was exhausted, and I asked her:

"Why should I do this thing? Why should I take the lives of men with whom I have no quarrel in order to rescue Kaneke, and very probably lose my own in the attempt?"

"First, because that is what you came here to do, Lord," she answered quietly. "Secondly, because it is necessary that Kaneke should be saved in order that he may guide you, which he alone can do, to a place where you will save others, and thus serve a certain holy one against whom he has sinned in the past."

Now I remembered the story that this Kaneke had told me about a mysterious woman who lived on an island in a lake whom he had affronted, and answered:

"Oh yes, I have heard of her and believe nothing of the tale."

"Doubtless you are right not to believe the tale as Kaneke told it to you, Lord. Learn that once he tried to work bitter wrong to that holy one, being bewitched by her beauty; yes, to do sacrilege to our goddess." (I remembered that "our" afterwards, though at the time I made no comment.) "Being merciful, she spared him, but because of his crime misfortune overtook him, and for years he must dwell afar. Now the hour has come when for certain reasons he is bidden to return and expiate his evil deeds, and not here must his fate find him, Lord—"

"Baas," broke in Hans, "it is no use talking to this White-Mouse, who stuffs our brains with spiders' webs and talks nonsense. She wants us to save Kaneke for her own ends or those of others of whom she is the voice, and we have said that we will try. Now either we must keep our word or break it and climb down this hole again, if we can—which would be much better. Indeed, Baas, I think we should start—"

Here White-Mouse looked at Hans with remarkable effect, for he stopped suddenly and began to fan himself with his hat.

"Which advice does the Lord Macumazahn desire to take?" she asked of me in a cold and quiet voice.

"Go on," I said, nodding towards the ladder, "we follow you."

Next instant she was running up it with Hans at her heels, for as before, he slipped in before me. I may add that it was quite dark on that ladder, which was very unpleasant.

Soon something above me swung back. I felt a breath of fresh air on my face, and looking upwards, saw a star shining in the sky, for at that moment a cloud had passed over the moon, which star gave me comfort, though I did not know why it should.

I reached the top of the ladder and saw that White-Mouse had vanished and that Hans was scrambling into the courtyard. Then he gave me his hand and dragged me after him. The place was quite quiet and because of the cloud I could only see the house as a dark mass and trace the outlines of the *stoep*, which I remembered very well. Presently I heard a faint stir upon this *stoep* and got my rifle ready; Hans, on the other side of the mouth of the pit, already had his revolver in his hand.

A while went by, perhaps a minute—it seemed an hour—and looking upwards, to my dismay, I perceived the edge of the moon appearing beyond the curtain of cloud. Swiftly she emerged and flooded the place with light, as an African moon can do. Now I saw all. Coming down the steps of the *stoep*, very slowly as though he were cramped by his bonds, was the great form of Kaneke leaning on the shoulder of the frail girl, as a man might upon a stick. Pieces of rope still hung to his arms and legs, and she had a bared knife in her hand. In the shadow of the *stoep* I made out the dim figures of men, two I saw, but in fact there were three, who appeared to be asleep.

As he reached the courtyard Kaneke stumbled and fell on to his hands and knees with a crash, but recovering himself, plunged towards us. The men on the *stoep* sat up—then it was that I counted three. White-Mouse flung off her dark cloak and stood there in shining white, looking like a ghost in the moonlight; indeed, I believe her object was to personate a ghost. If so it was successful as far as two of the men were concerned, for they howled aloud with terror, crying out something about *Afreets*. The third, however, who was bolder or perhaps guessed the truth, rushed at her. I saw the knife flash and down he went, yelling in fear and pain. The others vanished, I think into the house, for I heard them shouting there. Kaneke reached us. The woman flitted after him, saying:

"Into the pit! Into the pit! Help him, Lord!"

We did so and he scrambled down the ladder.

At this moment a terrific hubbub arose. The guard outside the fence were rushing through the gate, a number of them, I do not know how many.

Hans snatched the rifle from my hand and pushed me to the edge of the hole—I noticed that the gallant fellow did not wish to go first this time! I clambered down the ladder with great rapidity, calling to Hans to follow, which he did so fast that he trod upon my fingers.

"Where's White-Mouse?" I said.

"I don't know, Baas. Talking with those fellows up there, I think."

"Out of the way!" I cried. "She can't be left. They will kill her!"

I climbed past him up the ladder again until I could look over the edge of the hole.

This is what I saw and heard: White-Mouse, the knife in her hand, was haranguing the oncoming Arabs so fiercely that they shrank together before her, invoking curses on them as I imagine, which frightened them very much, and pointing now at one and now at another with the knife. As she called down her maledictions she retreated slowly backwards towards the mouth of the pit, whence she must have rushed to meet the men as they burst through the gateway, I presume in order to give us time to get down the ladder. Suddenly the crowd of them seemed to recover courage. One shouted:

"It is White-Mouse, not a ghost!" Another invoked Allah; a third called out: "Kill the foreign sorceress who has brought the spotted sickness on us and snatched away the star-worshipper."

They came forward—doubtfully lifting their spears, for they did not seem to have any firearms.

"Give me my rifle," I called to Hans, for in my hurry I forgot that I had a pistol in my pocket, my purpose being to get on the top step of the ladder, and thence open fire on them, so as to hold them back till White-Mouse could join us.

"Yes, Baas," called Hans from below as he began to climb the ladder again with the rifle in his hand, a slow job, because it cumbered him. I bent down as far as I could to grasp it, thus lowering my head, although I still managed to watch what was going on in the courtyard.

Just as my fingers touched the barrel of the Winchester, White-Mouse hurled her knife at the first of her attackers. Then she turned, followed by the whole crowd of them, and ran for the pit. One caught hold of her, but she slipped from his grasp and, although another gripped her garment, reached the stone which stood up edgeways some three feet above the level of the pavement of the courtyard.

In a flash I divined her purpose. It was not escape she sought, indeed, now that was impossible, but to let fall the block of rock or cement, and thus make pursuit of us also impossible. Horror filled me and my blood seemed to freeze, for I understood that this meant that she would be left in the hands of her enemies.

It was too late to do anything; indeed, as the thought passed my mind she hurled her weight against the stone (if she had ever wedged it open, as she said she would, which I doubt, she must have knocked away the prop with her foot). I saw it begin to swing downwards, and ducked instinctively, which was fortunate for me, for otherwise it would have struck my head and killed me. As it was it crushed in the top of the soft hat I was wearing. Down it came with a clang, leaving us in the dark.

"Hans," I cried, "bring that lantern and help me to try to push up this stone!"

He obeyed, although it took a long while, for he had to go back to the resting-place to fetch it. Then, standing side by side upon the ladder, we pushed at the stone, but it would not stir a hair's breadth. We saw something that looked like a bolt, and worked away at it, but utterly without result. We did not know the trick of the thing, if there was one. Then I bethought me of Kaneke who all this while was on the landing-place beneath, and sent Hans to ask him how to raise the stone. Presently he returned and reported that Kaneke said that if once it had been slammed down in this fashion, it could only be opened from above with much labour, if, indeed, this could be done at all.

I ran down the ladder in a fury and found Kaneke seated on the landing-place, a man bemused.

I reviled him, saying that he must come and move the stone, of which doubtless he knew the secret, so as to enable us to try to rescue the woman who had saved him. He listened with a kind of dull patience, then answered:

"Lord, you ask what cannot be done. Believe me I would help White-Mouse if I could, if indeed she needs help, but the catches that loose this mass of rock are very delicate and doubtless were destroyed by its violent closing. Moreover by this time of a certainty she is killed, if death can touch her, and even were it possible to lift it, you would be killed also, for those sons of Satan will wait there hoping that this may happen."

Still I was not satisfied, and made the man come up the ladder with me, which he did very stiffly, threatening to shoot him if he did not. This, to tell the truth, at that moment I would have done without compunction, so enraged and horrified was I at what had happened which, perhaps unjustly, I half attributed to him.

Well, he came and explained certain things to me about the catches whereof I forget the details, after which we pushed with all our might, till the stave of the ladder on which we stood began to crack, in fact; but nothing happened. Evidently in some way the block was jammed on its upper side, or perhaps the pin or hinges upon which it was balanced had broken. I do not know and it matters nothing.

All was finished. We were helpless. And that poor woman—oh, that poor woman!—what of her?

I returned to the landing-place and sat down to rest, almost weeping. Hans, I observed, was in much the same state, without a gibe or an impertinence left in him.

"Baas," he said, "if we had got out of the hole too, it would have been no better; worse, indeed, for we should have been killed as well as

White-Mouse, even if we had managed to shoot some of those Prophet-worshipping dogs before they spotted us. Alas, Baas, I think that White-Mouse meant to get herself killed from the first. Perhaps she had had enough of that man," and he nodded towards Kaneke, who sat brooding and taking no heed, "or perhaps her job was done and she knew it. Or perhaps she can't be killed, as this Kaneke seems to think."

Listening to him, I reflected that he must be right, for now I re-membered that White-Mouse had spoken several times of the escape of Hans, Kaneke, and myself, and never of her own, though when she did so I had not quite caught her drift. The woman meant to die, or knew that she would die, it did not matter which, seeing that the end was the same. Or she meant something else that was dark to me.

Presently, Hans spoke again:

"Baas," he said, "this place is a good grave, but I do not want to be buried in it, and oil in these Arab lamps does not last for ever; they are not like those of the widow, which the old prophet kept burning for years and years to cook meal on, as your reverend father used to tell us. Don't you think we had better be moving, Baas?"

"I suppose so," I answered, "but what about Kaneke? He seems in a bad way."

"Oh, Baas, let him come or let him stay behind. I don't care which. Now I will strap the basket with the lantern on to my back as White-Mouse did, and go first, and you must follow me, and Kaneke can come when he likes, or stop here and repent of his sins."

He paused, then added (he was speaking in Dutch all this time):

"No, Baas, I have changed my mind. Kaneke had better go first. He is very heavy, also stiff, and if he came last and fell on to our heads, where should we be, Baas? It is better that we should fall on Kaneke rather than that Kaneke should fall on us."

Being puzzled what to do, I turned to speak to the man. Hans, who was fixing the basket on his back, had set down the lamp which was to be placed in such a position that its light fell full upon Kaneke. By it I saw that his face had changed. While I was questioning him about the bolts of the stone, it had been that of a man bemused, of one who awakes from a drunken sleep, or has been drugged, or is in the last stage of terror and exhaustion. Now it was very much alive and grown almost spiritual, like to the face of one who is rapt in prayer. The large round eyes were turned upwards as though they saw a vision, the lips were moving as if in speech, yet no word came from them, and from time to time they ceased to move, as though the ears listened for an answer.

252

I stared at him, then said politely in Arabic:

"Might I ask what you are doing, friend Kaneke?"

He started and a kind of veil seemed to fall over his face; I mean that it changed again and became normal.

"Lord," he answered, "I was returning thanks for my escape."

"You take time by the nose, for you haven't escaped yet," I replied, adding rather bitterly, "and were you returning thanks for the great deed of another who has not escaped, of the woman who is called White-Mouse?"

"How do you know that she has not escaped?"

"Because you yourself said that she must be dead—if she could die, which of course she can."

"Yes, I said some such words, but now I think that she has been speaking to me, although it may have been her spirit that was speaking."

"Look here!" I said, exasperated. "Who and what is, or was, White-Mouse? Your wife, or your daughter?"

"No, Lord, neither," he answered, with a little shiver.

"Then who? Tell me the truth or I have done with you."

"Lord, she is a messenger from my own country who came a while ago to command me to return thither. It is because of her that these Arabs hate me so much, for they think she is my familiar through whom I work magic and bring evil upon them."

"And is she, Kaneke?"

"Baas," broke in Hans, "have you finished chatting, for the oil in that lamp burns low and I have only two candles. Those niches will not be nice in the dark, Baas."

"True," I said.

Then I bid Kaneke go first, suggesting that he knew the road, with Hans following him and I coming last.

"My legs are stiff, Lord," he said, "but my arms are recovered. I go."

He went; he went with the most amazing swiftness. In a few seconds he was over the edge of the pit and descending rapidly, hand over hand, as it seemed to me only occasionally touching the niches with his feet. Not that I had much time to judge of this, for presently he was out of sight and only by the jerking of the hide rope could we tell that he was there at all.

"Will it break, Baas?" asked Hans doubtfully. "That brute Kaneke weighs a lot."

"I don't know and I don't much care," I answered. "White-Mouse said we should get through safely, and I am beginning to believe in White-Mouse. So say your prayers and start."

He obeyed, and I followed.

I will omit the details of that horrible descent. Hans and I reached the second platform and rested. Unfortunately in starting again I looked down, and far, far below saw the lamp we had left burning at the bottom, which gave me such an idea of precipitous death that I grew dizzy. My strength left me and I almost fell, especially as just then my foot slipped in one of the niches, leaving all my weight upon my arms. I think I should have fallen, had not a voice, doubtless that of my subconscious self at work, seemed to say to me:

"Remember, if you fall, you will kill Hans as well as yourself."

Then my brain cleared, I recovered control of my faculties, and slipping down the rope a little way I found the next niche with my left foot. Doubtless this return was even more fearsome than the ascent, perhaps owing to physical weariness, or perhaps because the object of the effort was achieved and there was now nothing left to hope for except personal safety, the thought of which is always the father of fear. I am not sure; all I know is that my spine crept and my brain sickened much more than had been the case on the upward adventure.

At length, thank God, the worst of it was over and we reached the sloping passage or gulley, or whatever it may have been, that in places was open to the sky. By help of the lamps that now were almost spent, we scrambled down this declivity with comparative ease, and so came out of the mouth of the hole into the little clump of bush that concealed it.

I sat down trembling like a jelly; the perspiration pouring off me, for the heat of that place had been awful. Hans, who although so tough, was in little better case than myself, found the water-bottle full of cold tea which, to save weight, we had left hidden with everything else we could spare, including our jackets, and passed it to me. I drank, and the insipid stuff tasted like nectar; then gave it to Hans, although I could gladly have swallowed the whole bottleful.

When he had taken a pull I stopped him, remembering Kaneke, who must also be athirst. But where was Kaneke? We could not see him anywhere. Hans opined that he had bolted into some hiding-place of his own, and being too weary to argue or even to speculate upon the matter, I accepted the explanation.

After this we finished the cold tea and topped it up with a nip of brandy apiece, carefully measured in a little cup. The flask itself, to which the cup was screwed, I did not dare to give to Hans, knowing that temptation would overcome him and he would empty it to the last drop.

Much refreshed and more thankful than I can say at having escaped the perils of that darksome climb, I put the extinguished lamps into poor White-Mouse's basket, thinking that they might come in useful afterwards (or perhaps I wished to keep them as a souvenir, I don't remember which). Then by common consent we started for the bottom of the great gulley, proposing to trek up it back towards the camp. On reaching the stream we stopped to drink water—for our thirst was still unsatisfied—and to wash the sweat from our faces, also to cool our feet bruised by those endless niches of the shaft.

Whilst I was thus engaged, hearing a sound, I peeped round a stone and perceived the lost Kaneke kneeling upon the rock like a man at prayer, and groaning. My first thought was that he must be hurt, perhaps in the course of his remarkably rapid descent, and my second that he was grieving over the death of White-Mouse, or mayhap because of his separation from his wives whom he would see no more. Afterwards, however, I reflected that the latter was improbable, seeing that he was so ready to leave them. Indeed, I doubted whether he had really any wives, or children either. Certainly I never saw any about the house in which he dwelt like a hermit; there was nothing to show that these ever existed. If they did, I was sure that Hans would have discovered them.

However, this might be, not wishing to spy upon the man's private sorrows, I coughed, whereon he rose and came round the rock.

"So you are here before us," I said.

"Yes, Lord," he answered, "and waiting for you. The descent of the shaft is easy to those who know the road."

"Indeed. We found it difficult, also dangerous. However, like the woman called White-Mouse"—here he winced and bowed his head—"that is done with. Might I ask what your plans are now, Kaneke?"

"What they have always been, Lord. To guide you to my people, the Dabanda, who live in the land of the Holy Lake. Only, Lord, I think that we had better leave this place as quickly as we can, seeing it is certain that, thinking we have escaped, the Arabs, my enemies, will follow to your camp to attack you there."

"I agree," I answered. "Let us go at once."

So off we went on our long tramp up the darksome gorge, I, to tell the truth, full of indignation and in the worst of tempers. At length I could control myself no longer.

"Kaneke," I said, for he was walking at my side, Hans being a little ahead engaged in picking our way through the gloom and watching for possible attacks—"Kaneke, it seems that I and my servant are suffering many things on your behalf. This night we have run great risks to save you from death, as has another who is gone, and now you tell me that because of you we are to be attacked by those who hate you. I think it would be better if I repaid to you what I have received, together with whatever money the ivory you gave me may bring, and you went your way, leaving me to go mine."

"It cannot be," he answered vehemently. "Lord, although you do not know it, we are bound together until all is accomplished as may be fated. Yes, it is decreed in the stars, and destiny binds us together. You think that I am ungrateful, but it is not so; my heart is full of thankfulness towards you and I am your slave. Ask me no more, I pray you, for if I told you all you would not believe me."

"Already you have told me a good deal that I do not believe," I replied sharply, "so perhaps you had better keep your stories and promises to yourself. At any rate, I cannot desert you at present, for if I did, I suppose those Arab blackguards would cut your throat."

"Yes, Lord, and yours too. Together we shall best them, as you will see, but separated they will kill us both, and your servants and porters also."

After this we went on in silence and in the end, without molestation except from a lion, emerged from the gorge and came to the knoll where I had camped. We struck this beast in the open bushy country just outside the mouth of the gorge, or rather it struck us and followed us very persistently, which made me think that it must have been in great want of food. Occasionally it growled, but for the most part slunk along not more than thirty or forty paces to our right, taking cover in the high grass or behind bushes. Also twice it went ahead to clumps of thorn trees as though to waylay us. I think I could have shot it then, but Hans begged me not to fire for fear of letting our whereabouts be known to Arabs who might be searching for us. So instead we made detours and avoided those clumps of trees.

This seemed to irritate the lion, which for the third time crept forward and, as I saw clearly by the light of the sinking moon, crouched down on our path about fifty paces in front of us in such a spot that, owing to the nature of the land, it was difficult to circumvent it without going a long way round.

Now I thought that I must accept the challenge of this savage or starving animal, but Hans, who was most anxious that I should not shoot, remarked sarcastically that since the "owl-man", as he called Kaneke, was such a wonderful wizard, perhaps he would exert his powers and send it away.

Kaneke, who had been marching moodily along as fast as his legs, still stiff from the bonds, would allow, paying little or no attention to the matter of the lion, heard him and seemed to wake up.

"Yes," he said, "if you are afraid of the beast I can do that. Bide here, I pray you, Lord, till I call you."

Then, quite unarmed, without so much as a stick in his hand indeed, he walked forward quietly to where the lion, a large one with a somewhat scrubby mane, lay upon a rock between the bank of the stream and a little cliff. I watched him amazed, holding my rifle ready and feeling sure that unless I could shoot it first, which was improbable because he was in my line of fire, there would soon be an end of Kaneke. This, however, did not happen, for the man trudged on and presently was so close to the lion that his body hid it from my sight.

After this I heard a growl which degenerated into a yelp like to that of a beast in pain. The next thing I saw was Kaneke standing on the rock where the lion had been, outlined very clearly against the sky, and beckoning to us to come forward. So we went, not without doubt, and found Kaneke seated on the rock with his face towards us as though to rest his legs, and as it seemed once more lost in reverie.

"The lion has gone," he said shortly, "or rather the lions, for there were two of them, and will return no more to trouble you. Let us walk on, I will go first."

"He is a very good wizard, Baas," said Hans reflectively in Dutch, as we followed. "Or perhaps," he added, "that lion is one of his familiars which he calls and sends away as he likes."

"Bosh!" I grunted. "The brute bolted, that is all."

"Yes, Baas. Still, I think that if you or I had gone forward without a gun it would have bolted us, for as you know, when a lion follows a man like that, its belly has been empty for days. This Kaneke's other name must be Daniel, Baas, who used to like to sleep with lions."

I did not argue with Hans; indeed, I was too tired to talk, but stumped along till presently we came to the site of the camp which we had left early on that eventful night—days ago it seemed to be. Here I found that my orders had been obeyed and that Tom and Jerry had gone forward with the porters, as I judged from various indications, such as the state of the cooking-fire, not much more than an hour before. Therefore there was nothing to do but follow their trail, which was broad and easy, even in the low moonlight.

On we marched accordingly, always uphill, which made our weary progress slow. At length came the dawn, a hot, still dawn, and after it the sunrise. By its bright light we saw two things: our porters camping at the appointed spot about half a mile away among some rocks just above a pool of water that remained in a dry river-bed; and behind us, perhaps two miles off, tracking our spoor up the slope that we had travelled, a party of white-robed Arabs, twenty of them or more.

"Now we are in for it," I said. "Come on, Hans, there is no time to spare."

CHAPTER 6

Kaneke's Friends

I know of no greater pick-me-up for a tired man than the sight of a body of enemies running on his spoor with the clear and definite object of putting an end to his mortal existence. On this occasion, for instance, suddenly I felt quite fresh again and covered that half-mile which lay between us and the camp in almost record time. So did the other two, for the three of us arrived there nearly neck and neck.

As we scrambled into the place I observed with joy that Tom and Jerry had taken in the situation, for already the porters were engaged in piling stones into a wall, or in hacking down thorn trees and dragging their prickly boughs together so as to form a *boma*. More, those excellent men had breakfast cooking for us upon a fire, and coffee ready.

Having given such orders as were necessary, though in truth there was little to be done, I fell upon that breakfast and devoured it, for we were starving. Hot coffee and food are great stimulants, and in ten minutes I felt a new man. Then the four of us, namely, Tom, Jerry, Hans, and I, took counsel together, for at the moment I could not see Kaneke who, having bolted some meat, had gone, as I presumed, to help with the *boma*-building. It was needful, for the position seemed fairly desperate.

By now the Arabs, who advanced slowly, were about half a mile away, and with the aid of my glasses I saw that there were more of them than I had thought, forty or fifty indeed, of whom quite half carried guns of one sort or another. I surveyed the position and found that it was good for defence. The camp was on the slope of a little *koppie*, round-topped and thickly strewn with boulders. To our right at the foot of the *koppie* was the long, broad pool I have mentioned.

Behind lay the river-bed half encircling the *koppie*, or rather a swamp through which the river ran when it was full, which swamp was so deep with sticky mud that advance over it would be difficult, if not impossible. To our left, however, was a dry *vlei* overgrown with tall grass and thorn trees, through which wended the native path that we had been following. In front the *veld* over which we had advanced, was open, but gave no cover, for here the grass had been burned leaving the soil bare. Therefore the Arabs could only advance upon us from this direction, or possibly through the thick grass and trees to our left.

But here came the rub. With a dozen decent shots I should have feared nothing. We, however, had but four upon whom we could rely, and Kaneke, who was an unknown quantity. If these Arabs meant business our case was hopeless, for of course no reliance could be placed on the porters, or at any rate upon most of them, who moreover had no guns. In short there was nothing to be done except trust in Providence and fight our hardest.

We got out the guns, Winchester repeaters all of them, of which I had six with me, and opened a couple of boxes of ammunition. The heavy game rifles we loaded and kept in reserve, also a couple of shot-guns charged with *loopers*, as we called slugs, for these are very effective in meeting a rush. Then I told Hans to find Kaneke, that I might explain matters and give him a rifle. He went and returned presently saying that Kaneke was not working at the walls or cutting down thorns.

"Baas," he added, "I think that skunk has run away or turned into a snake and slid into the reeds."

"Nonsense," I answered. "Where could he run to? I will look for him myself; those Arabs won't be here yet awhile."

So off I went and climbed to the top of the *koppie* to get a better view. Presently I thought I heard a sound beneath me, and looking over the edge of the boulder, saw Kaneke standing in a little bay of rock, waving his arms in a most peculiar fashion and talking in a low voice as though he were carrying on a conversation with some unseen person.

"Hi!" I said, exasperated. "Perhaps you are not aware that those friends of yours will be here presently and that you had better come to help to keep them off. Might I ask what you are doing?"

"That will be seen later, Lord," he answered quietly. Then, with a final wave of the hand and a nod of the head, such as a man gives in assent, he turned and climbed up to where I was.

Not one word did he say until we reached the others, nor did I question him. Indeed, I thought it useless as I had made up my mind that the fellow was mad. Still; as he was an able-bodied man who said that he could shoot, I gave him one of the rifles and a supply of cartridges, and hoped for the best.

By now the Arabs had come within four hundred yards, whereon a new trouble developed, for the porters grew frightened and threatened to bolt. I sent Hans to tell them that I would shoot the first man who stirred, and when, notwithstanding this, one of them did begin to run, I fired a shot which purposely missed him by a few inches and flattened on a rock in front of his face. This frightened him so much that he fell down and lay still, which caused me to fear that I had made a mistake and hit him through the head. The effect upon the others was marked, for they squatted on the ground and began to pray to whatever gods or idols they worshipped, or to talk about their mothers, nor did any of them attempt to stir again.

At the sound of this shot the Arabs halted, thinking that it had been fired at them, and began to consult together. After they had talked for some time one man came forward waving a flag of truce made of a white turban cloth tied to a spear. In reply I shook a pocket handkerchief which was far from white, whereon he walked forward to within twenty yards of the *boma*. Here I shouted to him to stop, suspecting that he wished to spy upon us, and went out to meet him with Hans, who would not allow me to go alone.

"What do you and your people want?" I said, in a loud voice to the man, whom I recognized as one of the judges who had tried Kaneke.

"White Master," he answered, "we want the wizard Kaneke, whom you have stolen away from us, and whom we have doomed to die. Give him to us, dead or alive, and we will let you and your people go in peace, for against you we have no other quarrel. If you do not, we will kill you, every one."

"That remains to be seen," I answered boldly. "As for the rest, hand over to me the woman called White-Mouse and I will talk with you."

"I cannot," he answered.

"Why not? Have you killed her?"

"By Allah, no!" he exclaimed earnestly. "We have not killed that witch, though it is true we wished to do so. Somehow in the confusion she slipped from our hands, and we cannot find her. We think that she has turned into an owl and flown to Satan, her master."

"Do you? Well, I think that you lie. Now tell me why you wish to kill Kaneke after he has run away from you, leaving you to walk your own road?"

"Because," answered the Arab in a fury, "he has left his curse upon us, which can only be loosed with his blood. Did you not hear him swear to bring a plague upon us, and has not the spotted sickness broken out in the town so that already many are ill and doubtless will die? Also has he not murdered our brother and bewitched us in many other ways, and will he not utterly destroy us by bringing our enemies upon us, as two moons ago he swore that he would do unless we let him go?"

"So you were keeping him a prisoner?"

"Of course, White Man. He has been a prisoner ever since he came among us, though at times it is true that he has been seen outside the town, and now we know how he came there."

"Why did you keep him a prisoner?"

"That in protecting himself he might protect us also by his magic, for we knew that if he should escape he would bring destruction upon us. And now, will you give him up to us, or will you not?"

There was a certain insolence about the way in which the man asked this question that put my back up at once, and I answered on the impulse of the moment:

"I will not. First, I will see all of you in hell. What business have you and your fellow half-breed Arabs to threaten to attack me, a subject of the Queen of England, because I give shelter to a fugitive whom you wish to murder? And what have you done with the woman called White-Mouse who, you say, has changed into an owl? Produce her, lest I hold you all to account for her life. Oh, you think that I am weak because I have but few men with me here. Yet I tell you that before the sun has set, I, Macumazahn, will teach you a lesson, if, indeed, any of you live to learn it."

The man stared at me, frightened by my bold talk. Then, without a word, he turned and ran back towards his people, zigzagging as he went, doubtless because he feared that I would shoot him. I too, turned, and strolled unconcernedly up the slope to the *boma*, just to show them that I was not afraid.

"Baas," said Hans, as we went, "as usual you are wrong. Why do you not surrender that big-eyed wizard who is putting us to so much trouble?"

"Because, Hans, I should be ashamed of myself if I did, and what is more, you would be ashamed of me."

"Yes, Baas, that is quite true. I should never think the same of you again. But, Baas, when a man's throat's going to be cut, he doesn't remember what he would think afterwards if it wasn't cut. Well, we are all going to be killed, for what we can do against those men I can't see, and when we meet your reverend father presently in the Place of Fires, I shall tell him that I did my best to keep you from coming there so soon. And now Baas, I will bet you that monkey-skin tobacco pouch of mine of which you are so jealous, against a bottle of gin, to be paid when we get back to the coast, that before the day is over I put a bullet through that Arab villain who talked to you so insolently."

We reached the *boma*, where I told Tom and Jerry, also Kaneke, the gist of what had passed. The dashing Tom seemed not displeased at the prospect of a fight, while Jerry the phlegmatic, shook his head and shrugged his shoulders, after which they both retired behind a rock for a few moments, as Hans informed me, to say their prayers and confess their sins to each other. Kaneke listened and made but one remark.

"You are behaving well to me, Lord Macumazahn, and now I will behave well to you."

"Thank you," I answered. "I shall remind you of that if we meet on the other side of the sun, or in that star you worship. Now please go to your post, shoot as straight as you can, and don't waste cartridges."

Then, when the hunters had returned from their religious exercises, we took our places, each in a little shelter of rocks, so arranged that we could fire over the fence of the *boma*. I was in the middle, with Hans and Kaneke on either side of me, while Tom and Jerry were at the ends of the line. There we crouched, expecting a frontal attack, but this did not develop. After a long talk the Arabs fired a few shots from a distance of about four hundred yards, which either fell short or went I know not where. Then suddenly they began to run over the open land where, as I have said, the *veld* was burned, towards the tall grass with thorn trees growing in it that lay upon our left, evidently with the design of outflanking us.

At the head of their scattered band was a tall man in whom, by the aid of my glasses, I recognized the venomous and evil-tempered Gaika, who had acted as chief-justice at Kaneke's trial, a person who had threatened me and of whom I had conceived an intense dislike. Hans, whose sight was as keen as a vulture's, recognized him also, for he said:

"There goes that hyena Gaika."

"Give me my express," I said, laying down the Winchester, and he handed it to me cocked.

"Let no man fire!" I cried as I took it, and lifted the flap-sight that was marked five hundred yards. Then I stood up, set my left elbow upon a stone, and waited my chance.

It came a few moments later, when Gaika must cross a little ridge of ground where he was outlined against the sky. The shot was a long one for an express, but I knew my rifle and determined to risk it. I got on to him, aiming at his middle, and swung the barrel the merest fraction in front to allow time for the bullet to travel. Then, drawing a long breath to steady myself, I pressed the trigger, of which the pull was very light.

The rifle rang out and I waited anxiously, for, although the best of shots need not have been ashamed to do so, I feared to miss, knowing that if this happened it would be taken as an omen. Well, I did not miss, for two seconds later I saw Gaika plunge to the ground, roll over and over and lie still.

"Oh!" said my people simultaneously, looking at me with admiration and pride. But I was not proud, except a little perhaps at my marksmanship, for I was sorry to have to shoot this disagreeable and to us most dangerous man, so much so that I did not fire the other barrel of the express.

For a moment his nearest companions stopped and stared at Gaika; then they fled on towards the high grass and reeds, leaving him on the ground, which showed me that he must be dead. I hoped that they were merely taking cover and that the sudden end of Gaika would have caused them to change their minds about attacking us, which was why I shot him. This, however, was not the case, for a while later fire was opened on us from a score of places in these reeds. Here and there in the centre of clumps of them and behind the trunks of thorns the Arabs had hidden themselves, singly or in pairs, and the trouble was that we could not see one of them. This made it quite useless to attempt to return their fire because our bullets would only have been wasted, and I had no ammunition to throw away in such a fashion. So there we must lie, doing nothing.

It was true that for the present we were not in any great danger, because we could take shelter behind stones upon which the missiles of the Arabs flattened themselves, if they hit at all, for the shooting being erratic, most of them sang over us harmlessly. The sound of these bullets, which sometimes I think were only pebbles coated with lead, or fragments of iron, terrified our bearers, however, especially after one of them had been slightly wounded by a lead splinter, or a fragment of rock. The wretched men began to jabber and now and again to cry out with fear, nor could all my orders and threats keep them quiet.

At length, after this bombardment had continued for nearly two hours, there came a climax. Suddenly, as though at a word of command, the bearers rose and rushed down the slope like a bunch of startled buck. They ran to the bank of the pool which I have mentioned, following it eastwards towards Kaneke's town, till they came to the bed of the river of which the pool formed a part in the wet season, where they vanished.

Of course we could have shot some of them as they went, as Hans, who was feeling spiteful, wanted to do, but this I would not allow, for what was the use of trying to stop a pack of cowards who, as likely as not, would attack us from behind if a rush came, hoped thus to propitiate the Arabs? What happened to those men I do not know, for they vanished completely, nor did I ever hear of them again. Perhaps some of them escaped back to the coast, but being without arms or food, this I think more than doubtful. The poor wretches must have wandered till they starved or were killed by wild beasts, unless indeed they were captured and enslaved.

Now our position was very serious. Here we were, five men and one donkey; for I think I have said that I possessed this beast, a particularly intelligent creature called Donna after a half-breed Portuguese woman the rest of whose name I forget, who had sold it to me with two others that died on the road. Beneath us, completely hidden, were forty or fifty determined enemies who probably were waiting for nightfall to creep up the *koppie* and cut our throats. What could we do?

Hans, whose imagination was fertile, suggested various expedients. His first was that we should try to fire the reeds and long grass in which the Arabs had taken cover, which was quite impracticable, because first we had to get there without being shot; also they were still too green to burn and the wind was blowing the wrong way. His next idea was that we should follow the example of the porters and bolt. This, I pointed out, was foolish, for we should only be run down and killed. Even if we waited till dark, almost certainly the end would be disaster; moreover we should be obliged to leave most of our gear and ammunition behind. Then he made a third proposal in a mixture of Dutch and English, which was but an old one in a new form, namely, that we should try to buy off the Arabs by surrendering Kaneke.

"I have already told you that I will do nothing of the sort. I promised White-Mouse to try to save this man, and there's an end."

"Yes, Baas, I know you did. Oh, what bad luck it is that White-Mouse was so pretty. If only her face had been like a squashed pumpkin, or if she had been dirty, with creatures in her hair, we shouldn't be looking at our last sun, Baas. Well, no doubt soon we shall be talking over the business with her in the Place of Fires, where I am sure she has gone, whatever that liar of a messenger may have said. Now I have finished who can think of nothing more, except to pray to your reverend father, who doubtless can help us if he chooses, which perhaps he doesn't, because he is so anxious to see me again."

Having delivered himself thus, Hans squatted a little more closely beneath his stone, over which a bullet had just passed with a most vicious whiz, and lit a pipe.

Next I tried the two hunters, only to find that they were quite barren of ideas, for they shook their heads and went on murmuring prayers. There remained Kaneke, at whom I glanced in despair. There he sat silent, with a face like a brickbat so impassive was it, giving me the idea of a man who is listening intently for something. For what? I wondered.

"Kaneke," I said, "by you, or on your behalf by another whom I think is dead, we have been led into a deep hole. Here we are who can be counted on the fingers of one hand, under fire from those who hate you, but against whom we have no quarrel, except on your account. The porters have fled away and our enemies, whom we cannot shoot because they are invisible in the reeds and grass of that pan, only await darkness to attack and make an end of us. Now if you have any word of comfort, speak, for it is needed, remembering that if we die, you die also."

"Comfort!" he answered in his dreamy fashion. "Oh yes, it is at hand. I am waiting for it now, my Lord Macumazahn," and he went on listening like one who has been interrupted in a serious matter by some babbler of trivialities.

This was too much for me; my patience gave way, and I addressed Kaneke in language which I will not record, saying amongst other forcible things that I was sorry I had not followed Hans' advice and abandoned him or surrendered him to the Arabs.

"You could not do that, my Lord Macumazahn," he answered mildly, "seeing that you had promised White-Mouse to save me. No one could break his word to White-Mouse, could he?"

"White-Mouse!" I ejaculated. "Where is she? Poor woman, she is dead, and for you, as the rest of us soon will be. And now you talk to me about my promises to her. How do you know what I promised her, you anathema'd bag of mysteries?"

"I do know, Lord," he replied, still more vaguely and gently. Then suddenly he added, "Hark! I hear the comfort coming," and lifted his hand in an impressive manner, only to drop it again in haste, because a passing bullet had scraped the skin off his finger.

Something caught my ear and I listened. From far away came a sound which reminded me of that made by a pack of wild dogs hunting a buck at night, a kind of surging, barbarous music.

"What is it?" I asked.

Kaneke, who was sucking the scraped finger, removed it from his mouth and replied that it was "the comfort", and that if I would look perhaps I should see.

So I did look through a crack between two stones towards the direction from which the sound seemed to come, namely eastward beyond the dry swamp where the *veld* was formed of great waves of land spotted with a sparse growth of thorn trees, swelling undulations like to those of the deep ocean, only on a larger scale. Presently, coming over the crest of one of these waves, now seen and now lost among the thorns, appeared a vast number of men, savage-looking fellows who wore feathers in their hair and very little else, and carried broad, long-handled spears.

"Who the deuce are these?" I asked, but Kaneke made no answer.

There he sat behind his stone, pointing towards the reeds in which the Arabs were hidden with his bleeding finger and muttering to himself.

Hans who, wild with curiosity, had thrust his sticky face against mine in order to share the view through the chink, whispered into my ear: "Don't disturb him, Baas. These are his friends and he is telling them where those Arabs are."

"How can he tell people half a mile away anything, you idiot?" I asked.

"Oh, quite easily, Baas. You see, he is a magician, and magicians talk with their minds. It is their way of sending telegrams, as you do in Natal, Baas. Well, things look better now. As your reverend father used to say, if only you wait long enough the devil always helps you at last."

"Rot!" I ejaculated, though I agreed that things did look better, that is, unless these black scoundrels intended to attack us and not the Arabs. Then I set myself to watch events with the greatest interest.

The horde of savages, advancing at a great pace—there must have been two or three hundred of them—made for the dry pan like bees for their hive. Whether Kaneke instructed them or not, evidently their intelligence department was excellent, for they knew exactly what they had to do. Reaching the edge of it, they halted for a while and ceased their weird song, I suppose to get their breath and to form up. Then at some signal the song began again and they plunged into those reeds like dogs after an otter.

Up to this moment the Arabs hidden there did not seem to be aware of their approach, I suppose because their attention was too firmly fixed upon us, for they kept on firing at the *koppie* in a desultory fashion. Now of a sudden this firing ceased, and from the thicket below arose yells of fear, surprise, and anger. Next at its further end, that which lay towards Kaneke's town, appeared the Arabs running for all they were worth, and presently, after them, their savage attackers.

Heavens, what a race was that! Never have I seen men go faster than did those Arabs across the plain with the wild pursuers at their heels. Some were caught and killed, but when at last they vanished out of sight, most of them were still well ahead. Hans wanted to shoot at them, but I would not allow it, for what was the use of trying to kill the poor wretches while others were fighting our battle? So it came about that the only shot we fired that day, I mean in earnest, was that which I had aimed at Gaika, which was strange when I had prepared for a desperate battle against overwhelming odds.

All having vanished behind the irregularities of the ground, except a few who had been caught and speared, in the silence which followed the war-song and the shoutings, I turned to Kaneke and asked for explanations. He replied quite pleasantly and briefly, that these black men were some of his "friends" whom the Arabs had always feared he would bring upon them, which was why they kept him prisoner and wished to kill him.

"I had no intention of doing anything of the sort, Lord," he added, "until it became necessary in order to save our lives. Then, of course I asked them for help, whereon they came at once and did what was wanted, as you have seen."

"And pray how did you ask them, Kaneke?"

"Oh, Lord, by messengers as one always asks people at a distance, though they were so long coming I feared lest the messengers might not have reached them."

"He lies, Baas," said Hans, in Dutch. "It is no good trying to pump the truth out of his heart, for you will only tire yourself bringing up more lies."

As I agreed, I dropped the subject and inquired of Kaneke whether his friends were coming back again. He said he thought so and before very long, as he had told them not to attack the town in which dwelt many innocent women and children.

"But, Lord," he went on, with unusual emphasis, "when they do return I think it will be well that you should not go to speak to them. To tell the truth, they are savage people, and being very naked, might take a fancy to your clothes, also to your guns and ammunition. I will

just go down to give them a word of thanks and bring back some porters to take the place of those who have run away, whom, by the way,
I hope they have not met. Foreseeing something of the sort, I asked
them to bring a number of suitable men."

"Did you?" I gasped. "You are indeed a provident person. And now
may I ask you whether you intend to return to your town, or what
you mean to do?"

"Certainly I do not intend to return, Lord, in order to care for
people who have been so ungrateful. Also, that spotted sickness is most
unpleasant to see. No, Lord, I intend to accompany you to the country
of the Lake Mone."

"The Lake Mone!" I said. "I have had enough of that lake, or rather
of the journey to it, and I have made up my mind not to go there."

He looked at me, and under the assumed mildness of that look I
read intense determination as he answered:

"I think you will go to the Lake Mone, Lord Macumazahn."

"And I think I will not, Kaneke."

"Indeed. In that case, Lord, I must talk to my friends when they
return, and make certain arrangements with them."

We stared at each other for what seemed quite a long time, though
I dare say it was only a few seconds. I don't know what Kaneke read
of my mind, but what I read of his was a full intention that I should
accompany him to the Lake Mone, or be left to the tender mercies of
his "friends", at present engaged in Arab-hunting who, it seemed, had
so great a passion for European guns and garments.

Now there are times when it is well to give way, and the knowledge of those times, to my mind, often marks the difference between
a wise man and a fool. As we all know, wisdom and folly are contigu-
ous states, and the line dividing them is very thin and crooked, which
makes it difficult not to blunder across its borders, I mean from the
land of wisdom into that of folly, for the other step is rarely taken, save
by one inspired by the best of angels.

In this instance, although I do not pretend to any exceptional
sagacity, I felt strongly that it would be well to stick on my own side
of the line and not defy the Fates as represented by that queer person Kaneke, and his black "friends" whom he seemed to have summoned from nowhere in particular. After all, I was in a tight place.
To travel back without porters, even if I escaped the "friends" and
the Arabs who now had a quarrel against me, was almost impossible,
and the same might be said of a journey in any other direction. It
seemed, therefore, that it would be best to continue to suffer those

ills I knew of, namely the fellowship of Kaneke on an expedition into the unknown.

"Very well," I remarked casually, after a swift weighing of these matters and a still swifter remembrance of the prophecy of White-Mouse that I should come safely through the business. (Why this should have struck me at that moment I could not say.)—"Very well, it does not much matter to me whether I turn east or west. So let us go to Lake Mone, if there be such a place, though I wonder what will be the end of that journey."

"So do I," replied Kaneke dryly.

CHAPTER 7

The Journey

Now, for sundry reasons, I am going to follow the example of a lady of my acquaintance who makes it a rule to read two three-volume novels a week, and skip, by which I mean that I will compress the tale of our journey to the land of the mysterious Lake Mone into the smallest possible compass. If set out in full the details of such a trek as this through country that at the time was practically unknown to white men—it took between two and three months—would suffice to fill a volume. It might be an interesting volume in its way, to a few who care for descriptions of African races and scenery, but to the many I fear that its chapters would present a certain sameness. So I shall leave them untold and practise the art of précis-writing until I come to the heart of the story.

After the conversation of which I have spoken, we cooked and ate food, which all of us needed badly. Then, being very tired and worn with many emotions, Hans and I went to sleep in the shade of some rocks, leaving Tom and Jerry to keep watch. About three o'clock in the afternoon one of them woke us up, or rather woke me up, for Hans, who could do with very little sleep, was already astir and engaged in overhauling the rifles. They told me that the black men were returning. I asked where Kaneke was, and learned that he had gone to meet them. Then I took my glasses and from a point of vantage kept watch upon what happened.

The savages, impressive-looking fellows in their plume-crowned nakedness, came streaming across the *veld*, some of them carrying in their hands objects which I believe to have been the heads of Arabs, though of this I cannot be sure because they were so far away. They were no longer singing or in haste but walked quietly, with the contented air of men filled with a sense of duty done. Appeared Kaneke marching towards them, whereon they halted and saluted by raising their spears, thus showing me that in their opinion he was a man of great position and dignity. They formed a ring round Kaneke, from the centre of which he seemed to address them. When this ring opened out again, which it did after a while, I observed that a fire had been lit, how, or fed with what fuel, I do not know, and that on it the savages were laying the objects which I took to be the heads of Arabs.

"Kaneke is their great devil, and they are sacrificing to him, Baas," whispered Hans.

"At any rate, on this occasion he has been a useful devil," I answered, "or, rather, his worshippers have been useful."

A while later, when the rite, or sacrifice, or whatever it may have been, was completed, the savages started forward again, leaving the fire still burning on the *veld*, and marched almost to the foot of the *koppie*, which caused me some alarm, as I thought they might be coming to the camp. This was not so, however, for when they were within a few hundred yards, of a sudden they broke into a chant, not the same which they had used when advancing, but one which had in it a kind of note of farewell, and departing at a run past the outer edge of the dry *vlei* from which they had driven the Arabs, soon were lost to sight. Yes, their song grew fainter and fainter, till at length it was swallowed up in silence and the singers vanished into the vast depths of distance whence they came.

Where did they come from and who were they? I know not, for on this matter Kaneke preserved a silence so impenetrable that at length the mystery of their appearance and disappearance began, to my mind, to take the character of an episode in a dream. Or, rather, it would have done so had it not been for the circumstance that they did not all go. On the contrary, about twenty were left, who stood before Kaneke with folded arms and bent heads, their spears thrust into the ground in front of them, blade upwards, by means of the iron spikes that were fixed to the handles. Also at the feet of each man was a bundle wrapped round with a mat.

"Hullo!" I said. "What do those men want? Do they mean mischief?"

"Oh no, Baas," answered Hans. "The Baas will remember that Kaneke promised us some more porters, and these are the men. Doubtless he is a great wizard, and for aught I know, may have made them and all the rest out of mud; like Adam and Eve, Baas. Still, I am beginning to think better of Kaneke, who is not just a humbug, as I thought, but one who can do things."

Meanwhile at some sign the men picked up the bundles and slung

them over their shoulders, drew their spears from the ground and followed Kaneke towards the camp, where we waited for them with our
rifles ready in case of accidents.

"Baas," said Hans, as they approached, "I do not think that these
men are the brothers of those who attacked the Arabs just now; I think
that they are different."

I studied them and came to the same conclusion. To begin with, so
far as I could judge who had only seen our wild rescuers from a distance, these were lighter in colour, brown rather than black, indeed, also
they were taller and their hair was much less woolly, only curling up at
the ends which hung down upon their shoulders. For the rest, they were
magnificently built, with large brown eyes not unlike those of Kaneke,
and well-cut features with nothing negroid about them. Nor, in truth,
were they of Arab type who seemed rather to belong to some race that
was new to me, and yet of very ancient and unmixed blood.

Could they, I wondered, belong to the same people as Kaneke
himself? No; although so like him, it seemed impossible, for how
would they have got here?

Very quietly and solemnly the men approached to where I was
sitting on a stone, walking in as good a double line as the nature of
the ground would allow, as though they had been accustomed to dis-
cipline, and laying their right hands upon their hearts, bowed to me
in a courtly fashion that was almost European; so courtly, indeed, that
I felt bound to stand up, take off my hat, and return the bow. To Hans
they did not bow, but only regarded him with a mild curiosity, or to
the hunters either, for these they seemed to recognize were servants.

The sight of the donkey, Donna, however, appeared to astonish
them, and when at that moment she broke into her loudest bray, intimating that she wished to be fed, they looked downright frightened,
thinking, I suppose, that she was some strange wild beast.

Kaneke spoke a word or two to them in a tongue I did not know,
whereon they smiled as though in apology. Then he said:

"Lord Macumazahn, you, and still more your servant Hans, have
mistrusted me, thinking either that I was mad or leading you into
some trap. Nor do I wonder at this, seeing that much has happened
since yesterday which you must find it hard to understand. Still, Lord,
as you will admit, all has gone well. Those whom I summoned to aid
us have done their work and departed, to be seen of you no more; the
Arabs over whom I ruled and who went near to murdering me, and
would have murdered you because you refused to deliver me to them,
as Hans wished that you should do, have learned their lesson and will

not trouble you again. These men"—and he pointed to his companions—"you will find brave and trustworthy, nor will they be a burden to you in any way; nay, rather they will bear your burdens. Only, I pray you, do not question them as to who they are or whence they come, for they are under a vow of silence. Have I your promise?"

"Oh, certainly," I answered, adding with inward doubt, "and that of Hans and the hunters also. And now as I understand nothing of all this business, which I do not consider has gone as well as you say, seeing that White-Mouse, the woman who saved your life, although, as she told me, she was not your wife—"

"That is true, as I have said already," interrupted Kaneke, bowing his head in a way that struck me as almost reverential.

"—Seeing that White-Mouse," I repeated, "doubtless is dead at the hands of those Arabs of yours who hated you, which blackens everything, perhaps you will be so good as to tell me, Kaneke, what is to happen next."

"Our journey, Lord," he replied, with a stare of surprise. "What else? Moreover, Lord, be sure that about this journey you need not trouble any more. Henceforward, until we reach the land of my people I will take command and arrange for everything. All that you need do is to follow where I lead and amuse yourself, resting or stopping to shoot when you will, and giving me your orders as to every matter of the sort, which shall be obeyed. This you can do without fear seeing that, as White-Mouse told you, all shall go well with you."

Now once more I was tempted to question him as to the source of his information about what passed between me and White-Mouse, but refrained, remarking only that he was very good at guessing.

"Yes, Lord," he replied. "I have always had a gift that way, as you may have noticed when I guessed that those savages would come to help us, and bring with them men to take the place of the porters who have fled. Well, I notice that you do not contradict my guess and again I assure you that White-Mouse spoke true words."

Now for a minute I was indignant at Kaneke's impudence. It seemed outrageous that he, or any native African, should presume to put me, Allan Quatermain, under his orders, to go where he liked and to do what he chose. Indeed, I was about to refuse such a position with the greatest emphasis when suddenly it occurred to me that there was another side to the question.

Although I had never travelled there, I had heard from friends how people touring in the East place themselves in charge of a dragoman, a splendid but obsequious individual who dry-nurses them day and night, arranges, commands, feeds, masters difficulties, wrangles with extortioners or obstructionists, and finally gently leads his employers whither they would go and back again. It is true I had heard, too, that these skilled and professional persons are rather apt to melt away in times of real danger or trouble, leaving their masters to do the fighting, also that their bills are invariably large. For every system has its drawbacks and these are chances which must be faced.

Still, this idea of being dragomanned, personally conducted like a Cook's tourist, through untrodden parts of Africa, had charms. It would be such a thorough change—at any rate to me. Then and there I determined to accept the offer, reflecting that if the worst came to the worst, I could always take command again. It was obvious that I must accompany Kaneke or run the risk of strange things happening to me at his hands and those of his followers whom he had collected out of nowhere. Therefore the responsibilities of the expedition might as well be his as mine.

So I answered mildly:

"Agreed, Kaneke. You shall lead and I will follow. I place myself and my servants in your hands, trusting to you to guide us safely and to protect us against every danger. Though," I added in a sterner voice, "I warn you that at the first sign of treachery I will shoot you dead. And now tell me, when are we to start?"

"At moonrise, I think, Lord, for then it will be cooler. Meanwhile you and your servants can sleep who need rest after so many labours. Fear nothing; I and my men will watch."

"Baas," said Hans as we went away to act upon this advice, "I never thought you and I, who are getting old, would live to find a new mammy, and such a one with eye and beak of an owl who, like an owl, loves to stare at the stars and to fly at night. However, if the Baas does not mind, I don't."

I made no answer, though I thought to myself that Kaneke's great sleepy eyes were really not unlike those of an owl, that mysterious bird which in the native mind is always connected with omens and magic. Yes, in calling him an owl Hans showed his usual aptitude, especially as he believed that he was the destroyer of that strange and beautiful woman, White-Mouse.

Well, we rested, and ate on waking, and at moonrise departed upon our journey, heading nor'-west. Everything was prepared, even the loads were apportioned among the new porters. Indeed, there was nothing left for us to do except roll up the little tent and tie it, together with my personal belongings, on to the back of Donna, whom Hans fed and

Tom and Jerry led alternately. We met with no adventures. The lion or lions, on whom, according to Hans, Kaneke had thrown a charm, did not trouble us; we saw nothing of the Arabs or the savages whom that strange person called his "friends". In short, we just walked forward where Kaneke guided as safely as though we had been upon an English road, till we came to the place where he said we were to halt.

Such was our first march which in the weeks that followed was typical of scores of others. Nothing happened to us upon that prolonged trek; at least, nothing out of the way. It was as though a charm had been laid upon us, protecting us from all evils and difficulties. A great deal of the country through which we passed was practically uninhabited. I suppose that the slave-traders had desolated it in bygone years, for often we saw ruined villages with no one in them. When they were inhabited, however, Kaneke would go in advance and speak to their headman. What he said to them I do not know, but in the issue we always found the people friendly and ready to supply us with such provisions as they had, generally without payment.

One thing I noted: that they looked on me with awe. At first I put this down to the fact that most of them had never before seen a real white man, but by degrees I came to the conclusion that there was more behind, namely that for some reason or another I was regarded as a most powerful fetish, or even as a kind of god. Thus they would abase themselves upon their faces before me and even make offerings to me of whatever they had, generally grain or fruits.

While they confined themselves to these I took no notice, but when at one village the chief, who could talk a little Arabic, having mixed with slave-traders in his youth, brought a white cock and proceeded to cut its throat and sprinkle my feet with the blood, I thought it time to draw the line. Snatching the dead bird from his hand, I threw it away and asked him why he had done this thing. At first he was too terrified to answer, imagining that his offering was rejected because I was angry with him.

Presently, however, he fell upon his knees and mumbled something to the effect that he was only doing me honour, as the "messenger", or "my messenger", had commended him. For the life of me I could not understand what he meant, unless he alluded to Kaneke. While I was trying to find out, that worthy arrived and gave the chief one look which caused him to rise and run away.

Then I cross-examined Kaneke without result, for he only shrugged his shoulders and said that all these people were very simple and wished to do honour to a white man. Hans took a different view.

"How is it, Baas," he asked, "that they are always prepared to receive us at these places and waiting with gifts? None of those men of the Owl's" (he often called Kaneke the "Owl") "go forward to warn them, for I count them continually, especially at night and in the morning, to find if one is missing. Nor when we are travelling through bush can they see us coming from far away. How, then, do they know?"

"I can't tell you."

"Then I will tell the Baas. The owl-man sends his spirit ahead to give them notice." He paused, then added, "Or perhaps—" Here he stopped, saying that he had left his pipe on the ground, or something of the sort, and departed.

So this mystery remained unsolved, like others.

In every way our good luck was so phenomenal that with the superstition of a hunter, which infects all of our trade, I began to fear that we must have some awful time ahead of us. When we came to rivers they were invariably fordable. When we wanted meat, there was always game at hand that could be shot without trouble by Tom and Jerry—Kaneke, I observed, would never fire at any beast even when I offered to lend him my rifle. The weather was most propitious, or if a bad storm came up we were under shelter. No one fell sick of fever or any other complaint; no one met with an accident. No lion troubled us, no snake bit us, and so forth. At last this unnatural state of affairs began to get upon our nerves, especially upon those of Tom and Jerry, who came to me one evening almost weeping, and declared that we were bewitched and going to our deaths.

"Nonsense," I answered, "you ought to be glad that we have so much good luck."

"Sugar is good," replied Tom, who loved sweet things, "but one cannot live on nothing but sugar; it makes one sick, and I have had bad dreams at night."

"I never expect to see my little daughter again, but if it is the will of Heaven that cannot be helped," remarked the more phlegmatic Jerry, adding, "Master, we do not like this Kaneke whom Hans calls the Owl, and we wish that you would take command, as we do not know where he is leading us."

"Nor do I, so I should be of no use as a guide. But be at ease, for I am making a map of the road for our return journey."

"When we return we shall need no map," said Tom in a hollow voice. "We have heard from Hans that the lady or the witch called White-Mouse promised safety and good fortune to him, and to you, Lord, but it seems that about us she said nothing—"

"Look here," I broke in, exasperated, "if you two men are so frightened for no cause that I can see, except that everything goes well with us, you had better follow the example of the porters at our first camp, and run away. I will give you your rifles and as many cartridges as you want, also the donkey Donna to carry them. I can see no reason why you should not get back to the coast safely, especially as you have money in your pockets."

Tom shook his head, remarking that he thought it probable that they would be murdered before they had completed the first day's journey. Then Jerry, the phlegmatic, showed his real quality, or perhaps the English blood, which I am sure ran in his veins, manifested itself.

"Listen, Little Holes," he said to Tom. "If we go on like this, our master Macumazahn will learn to despise us, and we shall be the laughing stock of the yellow man Hans, and perhaps of Kaneke and his people also. We undertook this journey; let us play the man and go through with it to the end. We can only die once, and because we are Christians, should we also be cowards? You have none to mourn for you, and I have but one daughter, who has seen little of me and who will be well looked after if I return no more. Therefore I say let us put aside our fears, which after all are built on water, and cease to trouble the master with them."

"That is well said," replied Tom, alias Little Holes, "and if it were not for the accursed wizard, one of those who is spoken against in the Holy Book, I should be quite happy. But while he is our guide, he who with his people, as I have seen at night, makes incantations to the stars—"

Here Tom chanced to look up and to perceive Kaneke standing at a distance, apparently out of hearing, with his large eyes fixed upon us. The effect was wonderful. "Be careful. Here is the wizard himself," he whispered to Jerry, whereon they both turned and went away.

Kaneke came up to me.

"Those hunters are afraid of something, Lord," he said quietly. "For days past I have read it in their faces. What is it that they fear?"

"You," I answered bluntly—"you and the future."

"All men should hold the future in awe, Lord, so there they are wise. But why should they dread me?"

"Because they think you are a wizard, Kaneke."

He smiled in his slow fashion, and answered:

"As others have done and do. If a man has more foresight or sees deeper into hearts, or turns from women, or worships that which most men do not worship, or is different from the rest in other ways, then he is always called a wizard, as I am. Lord, what your servants need is that which will change their minds so that they cease to think about themselves. I have come to tell you that tomorrow we enter into forest lands, which at this season are haunted by vast herds of elephants that travel from different quarters and meet here for the purposes of which we men know nothing. It might please you and those brave hunters of yours to see this meeting and to shoot one or two of those elephants, for among them are their kings, mighty bulls."

"I should like to see such a sight," I answered, "but there is little use in shooting the beasts when one cannot carry the ivory."

"It might be buried till you return, Lord; at any rate it will give the hunters occupation for a while."

"Very well," I answered indifferently, for to tell the truth I did not believe in Kaneke's tale of vast herds of elephants that held a kind of parliament in a particular forest.

Next night we camped on the outskirts of this forest of which Kaneke had spoken. It was a very strange place, different from any other that I have seen. In it grew great and solemn trees of a species that was new to me; huge, clean-boiled trees with leafy tops that met together and shut out the sun, so that where they were thickest there was twilight even at midday, nor could any undergrowth live beneath them. But the trees did not grow everywhere, for here and there were wide open spaces in which, for some unknown reason, they refused to flourish. These spaces, that sometimes were as much as a mile across, were covered with scanty bush and grasses.

All that night we heard elephants trumpeting around us, and when morning came found that a great herd of them must have passed within a quarter of a mile of our camp. The sight of their spoor excited the professional instincts of Tom and Jerry, who, forgetting their gloom, prayed me to follow the herd. I objected, for the reason I have given, namely that if we killed any of them it would be difficult to deal with the ivory. Kaneke, however, hearing our talk, declared that the porters needed rest and that he would be very glad if it could be given to them for a day or two, while we amused ourselves with hunting.

Then I gave way, being anxious to learn if there was any truth in Kaneke's story about the meeting-place of elephants that was supposed to exist in this forest. Also I was desirous that the two hunters should find something to do which would take their thoughts into a more cheerful channel. Personally, too, I felt that I should be glad of a change from this continuous marching unmarked by any incident.

So, after we had eaten and made our preparations, the four of us, that is Tom, Jerry, Hans, and I, started—Kaneke would not come—carrying large-bore rifles, a good supply of cartridges and some food and water. All the rest of that day we followed the spoor of the elephants, that had not stopped to feed in the glades I have described, as I had hoped that they would do, but appeared to be pushing forward at a great rate towards some definite objective. With one halt we marched on steadily in the shadow of those huge trees, noticing that the elephant-spoor seemed to follow a kind of road which wound in and out between their trunks or struck in a straight line across the stretches of thin bushes and grass.

More than once I wished to return, as did Hans who, like myself saw no use in this adventure. Always, however, Tom and Jerry prayed to be allowed to proceed, so on we went. Towards sunset we lost the spoor in a thick patch of forest. Pushing on to find it again while there was still light, we came suddenly to one of the open spaces that I have mentioned which seemed to be much larger than any other we had seen, also more bare of vegetation. It must have covered at least a thousand acres of ground, and perfectly flat; indeed, I thought that at some faraway epoch it had formed the bottom of a lake.

Near the centre of this oasis in the forest was a mound which, if I may judge from pictures I have seen of them, resembled one of those great tumuli that in certain parts of Europe the wild tribes of thousands of years ago reared over the bones of their chieftains. Or, as I afterwards discovered, more probably it was the natural foundation of some lake-town where a tribe dwelt for safety when all this place was under water. At any rate there it stood, a low, round eminence covered with a scanty growth of flowering bushes and small trees.

Thinking that from this mound we might be able to see the elephants, or at least which way they had gone, we marched thither, I reflecting that at the worst it would be a better place for camping than the gloomy and depressing forest. Having climbed its sloping side, we found that on the top it was flat except for a large depression in the centre, where perhaps once had stood the huts of its primeval inhabitants. What was of more interest to us, however, than the past history of the place, was that at the bottom of this depression lay a pool of water supplied by some spring, or by rain that had fallen recently.

Seeing this water, which we needed who had drunk all our own, I determined that we would pass the night on the mound, although the most careful search from its top failed to show any sign of the elephants we had been spooring.

"Yes, Baas," said Hans, when I gave my orders, "but, all the same, I don't like this place, Baas, and should prefer to get back to the forest after we have drunk and filled our bottles."

I inquired why.

"I don't know, Baas. Perhaps the spooks of those who once lived here are all about, though we can't see them. Or—but tell me, Bass, why did that Owl-man, Kaneke, send us after those elephants?"

"To give Tom and Jerry something to think about, Hans."

He grinned and answered:

"Kaneke does not care whether those fellows have anything to think about or not. I should believe that he did it to give us the slip, only I am sure that he does not want to go on alone. So, Baas, it must be to teach us some lesson and show us how powerful he is, so powerful that he makes the Baas do what he wants, which no one has done before."

I reflected that Hans was right. I had not desired to come upon this absurd hunt, yet somehow Kaneke had pushed me into it.

"I don't believe there are any elephants," went on Hans with conviction. "The spoor? Oh, a magician like Kaneke can make spoor, Baas. Or if there seem to be elephants, then I believe that they are really ghosts that put on that shape. Let us go back to the forest, Baas—if the Owl-man will give you leave."

Now I felt that the time had come for me to put my foot down, and I did so with firmness.

"Stop talking nonsense, Hans," I said. "I don't know what's the matter with all you fellows. Is your brain going soft as a rotten coconut, like those of Tom and Jerry? We will sleep here tonight and return tomorrow to the camp."

"Oh, the Baas thinks he is going to sleep tonight. Yes, he thinks he is going to sleep," sniggered Hans. "Well, we shall see," and he bolted, still sniggering, before my wrath could descend upon him.

The sun set and presently the big moon came up. We ate of the food we had with us; as we had nothing to cook it was needless to light a fire, nor indeed did I wish to do so, for in such a spot a fire was a dangerous advertisement. So, as it seemed foolish to set a watch in the middle of that open space, where there being no buck there would be no lions—for lions do not hunt elephants—we just lay down and went to sleep, as tired men should do. I remember thinking, as I dropped off, how extraordinarily quiet the place was. No beast called, no nightbird cried, nothing stirred on that dead and windless calm. Indeed, the silence was so oppressive that for once I should have welcomed the familiar ping! of a mosquito, but here there were none.

So off I went and at some time unknown, to judge by the moon it was towards the middle of the night, was awakened by a sense of oppression. I dreamed that a great vampire bat was hanging over me and sucking my toe. Now I was lying on my face, as I often do when camping out to avoid the risk of moon blindness, just at the edge of that hole where, as I have told, water had collected, in such a position that I could look down into the pool. This water was very still and clear and thus formed a perfect mirror.

As it happened there was something remarkable for it to reflect, namely the head, trunk, and tusks of one of the hugest elephants I ever saw—not Jana himself could have been much bigger! As my mirror showed, he was standing over me; yes, I lay between his fore-legs, while he was engaged in sniffing at the back of my head with the tip of his trunk which, however, never actually touched me.

Talk of a nightmare, or of a night-elephant for the matter of that, never did I know of one to touch it. Of course I thought it was a dream of a particularly vivid order arising from undigested biltong, or something of the sort. But that did not make it any better, for although I had wakened the vision did not go away, as every decent nightmare does. Moreover, if it were a dream, what was the hideous stabbing pain in my leg? (Afterwards this was explained: Hans was trying to arouse me without calling the elephant's attention to himself by driving into my thigh the point of a "wait-a-bit" thorn which he used to pin up his trousers.) Also was it possible that in a dream an elephant could blow so hard upon the back of one's neck that it sent dust and bits of dry grass up one's nostrils, inducing a terrible desire to sneeze?

While I was pondering the question in a perfect agony and staring at the alarming picture in the water, the gigantic beast ceased its investigation of my person and stepping over me with calculated gentleness, went to where Tom and Jerry were lying at a little distance. Whether these worthies were awake or asleep I do not know, for what happened terrified them so much that it produced aphasia on this and some other points, so that they could never tell me. The beast sniffed, first at Tom and then at Jerry; one sniff each was all it vouchsafed to them. Then with its trunk it seized, first Tom and next Jerry, and with an easy motion flung them one after the other into the pool of water. This done, avoiding Hans as though it disliked his odour, it walked away over the crest of the cup or depression in the mound, and vanished.

Instantly I sat up, boxed the ears of Hans, who was still stabbing at me idiotically with his wait-a-bit thorn and giving me great pain, for speak to him I dared not, and slipped down the slope to the lip of the pool to save Tom and Jerry from drowning, if indeed they were not already dead. As it happened, my attentions were needless, for the pool was quite shallow and this pair, whom the elephant had not hurt at all, were seated on its bottom and indulging in suppressed hysterics, their heads appearing above the surface of the water.

A more ridiculous sight than they presented, even in the terror of that occurrence, cannot be imagined. In all my life I never saw its like. Think of two men of whom nothing was visible except the heads, seated in the water and gibbering at each other in a dumb paroxysm of fear.

I whispered to them to come out, also that if they made a noise I would kill them both, whereupon somewhat reassured at my appearance, they crawled to the bank of the pool, which proved that none of their bones were broken, and emerged wreathed in water-cresses. Then leaving them to recover as best they could, followed by Hans and carrying my heavy rifle, I crept to the edge of the depression and peeped over.

There, as the bright moonlight showed me, not twenty yards away stood the enormous bull upon a little promontory or platform which projected from the side of the mound, reminding one of a rostrum erected for the convenience of the speaker at an open-air meeting. Yes, there it stood as though it were carved in stone.

CHAPTER 8

The Elephant Dance

Never shall I forget that amazing scene, bitten as it is into the tablets of my mind by the acids of fear and wonder. Imagine it! The wide plain or lake bottom surrounded upon all sides by the black ring of the forest and plunged in a silence so complete that it seemed almost audible. Then there, just beneath us, the gigantic and ancient elephant—for it was ancient, as I could see by various signs, standing motionless and in an attitude which gave a strange impression of melancholy, such melancholy as might possess an aged man who, revisiting the home of his youth, finds it a desolation.

"Baas," whispered Hans, "if you shift a little more to the left you might get him behind the ear and shoot him dead."

"I don't want to shoot him," I replied, "and if you fire I will break your neck."

Hans, I know, thought I made this answer because my nerve was shaken and I feared lest I should bungle the job. But as a matter of fact, it was nothing of the sort. For some unexplained reason I would as soon have committed a murder as shoot that elephant, which had just spared my life when I lay at its mercy.

Low as we spoke, I suppose that the bull must have heard us. At any rate it turned its head and looked in our direction, which caused me to fear lest I should be obliged to fire after all. It was not so, however, for having apparently satisfied itself that we were harmless, once more it fell into contemplation, which must have lasted for another two minutes.

Then suddenly it lifted its trunk and emitted a call or cry louder and more piercing than that of any trumpet. Thrice it repeated this call, and for the third time as its echoes died the silence of the night was broken by a terrifying response. From every part of the surrounding ring of forest rose the sound of elephants trumpeting in unison, hundreds of elephants, or so it seemed.

"*Allemagter!* Baas," whispered Hans in a shaky voice, "that old spook beast is sending for his friends to kill us. Let us run, Baas."

"Where to, seeing that they are all round us?" I asked faintly, adding: "If he wanted to kill us he could do so for himself. Lie still. It is our only chance; and tell those hunters behind to stop praying so loudly and to unload their rifles, lest they should be tempted to fire."

Hans crept away to the edge of the pool, where the dripping Tom and Jerry were putting up audible petitions in the extremity of their terror. Then watching, I saw the most marvellous sight in my hunting experience. As though they were the trained beasts of India or of the ancient kings, marching in endless lines and ordered ranks, appeared three vast herds of elephants. From the forest in front of us, from that to our right and that to our left, and from aught I know from behind also, though these I could not see, they came out into the moonlit open space, and marched towards the mound with their regulated tread, which shook the earth.

Perhaps I saw double. Perhaps my nerves were so shaken that I could not estimate numbers, but I should be prepared to swear that there were at least a thousand of them, and afterwards the others declared that there were many more. In each troop the bulls marched first, the moonlight shining on their white tusks. Then came the cows with calves running at their side, and last of all the half-grown beasts, sorted seemingly according to their size.

So Kaneke had not lied. This was the meeting of the elephants which he had prophesied we should see. Only how in Heaven's name did he know anything about it? For a few moments I began to think that he was really what Hans and the hunters believed him to be— some kind of magician who perhaps had sent us hither that we might be torn to pieces or trampled to death.

Then I forgot all about Kaneke in the immediate interest of that wild and wondrous spectacle. The herds arrived. They arranged themselves in a semicircle, deep, curved lines of them, in front to the mound upon which stood the ancient bull. For a while they were still, then as though at a signal, they knelt down. Yes, even the calves knelt, with their trunks stretched out straight upon the ground in front of them.

"They do homage to their king, Baas," whispered Hans, and so in truth it seemed to be.

The giant bull trumpeted once, as though in acknowledgment of the salute. The herds rose, and there followed a marvellous performance that might have been taken for a dream. The bulls massed themselves together in squadrons, as it were, and charged past the mound from right to left, trumpeting as they charged. After them came the regiments of the cows, and lastly those of the partly grown beasts, all trumpeting; even the little calves set up piercing squeals. They re-formed, but not as they were before. For now the bulls faced the cows and the rest. Then began a kind of dance, so swift and intricate that I could not follow it, a kind of unearthly quadrille it seemed to be, in which the males sought out the females, or it may have been the other way about, and they caressed each other with their trunks. Perhaps it was some kind of ceremony of betrothal, I do not know.

It ceased as suddenly as it had begun. The herds massed themselves as at first, then wheeled and marched off in their three divisions back to the forest whence they came. Soon all were gone except the old king-bull, who still stood silent just beneath us, majesty and loneliness personified.

"Do you think he is going to stop here always, Baas?" whispered Hans. "Because if so, really it might be best to shoot him now that the others have gone away."

"Be silent," I answered; "he may understand you."

Yes, my nerves were so upset by what I had seen that I was fool enough to talk thus.

"Yes, Baas," assented Hans in his hoarse whisper, "I forgot that; he may, so I didn't really mean what I seemed to say about shooting him. It was only a joke. Also it might bring the others back."

At that moment, to my horror, the king-bull turned and walked straight up to us. I couldn't have shot him if I had wished, because as I had made the others do, I had unloaded my rifle to keep myself out of temptation. Also I did not wish; I was too much afraid. He stood still, contemplating us, a giant of a creature with a mild and meditative eye. Then he lifted his trunk and I muttered a prayer, thinking that all was over. But no, he only placed the tip of it against the middle of Hans, who somehow had got to his knees, and let off one fearful scream accompanied by such a blast of air that it blew Hans backwards down the slope on to the recumbent forms of Tom and Jerry.

This done, the bull turned again, walked down the mound and out across the plain, a picture of stately solitude till at last he vanished in the dark shadow of the forest.

When he was lost to sight I went down to the pool and drank, for the perspiration induced by terror seemed to have dried me up. Then I looked at my three retainers, who were huddled in a heap on the edge of the pool.

"I am dead," muttered Hans, who was lying on the other two.

"That Satan of an elephant has blown out my inside. It has gone; there is nothing left but my backbone."

"No wonder, as you cursed him and wanted Macumazahn to shoot him," muttered Tom. "For did not that *afreet* of a beast cast us into the pool for nothing at all?"

"Whether you have a stomach or not, be pleased to cease sitting on my face, yellow man, or I will make my teeth meet in you," gurgled Jerry.

Thus they went on, and so ridiculous were the aspect and the talk of the three of them, that at last I burst out laughing, which relieved my nerves and did me good. Then I lit my pipe, hoping that those elephants would not see the light or smell the tobacco down in that hole, and not caring much if they did, for I seemed to desire a smoke more than anything on earth.

"Let us talk," I said to the others. "What are we to do?"

"Get out of this, master, and at once," said Tom. "That beast is not an elephant, it is an evil spirit in the shape of one. Yes, I who am a Christian and have renounced all superstitions, say that it is an evil spirit."

"Little Holes is quite right," broke in Jerry. "If it had been an elephant, it would have killed us, but being an evil spirit it threw us into the water."

"Fool!" grunted Hans, rubbing his middle, "do you make an evil spirit better than an elephant? In truth, as the Baas knows, the bull is neither; it is a chief or a king who once lived in this place as a man, and now had turned into an elephant, and all those other beasts whom you did not see, being so much afraid, were once his people, but now also are elephants. That is quite clear to the Baas, and to me who am a better Christian than either of you. Still, I agree with you that the sooner we see the last of this haunted place, the better it will be."

Thus they wrangled on till they were tired. When they had finished I said:

"Here we stop till dawn breaks. Do you three climb to the top of this hole and keep watch. I am tired and am going to sleep. Wake me if you see the elephants coming back."

So I lay down and slept, or at any rate dozed, which, as I have said—thank Heaven!—I can do at any time after any experience. I am a fatalist, one who does not trouble as to what is to happen in the future, because I know it must happen and that worry is therefore useless. If the elephants were going to kill me, I could not help it; meanwhile I would get some rest.

So I slept, and dreamed that I saw this place standing in the middle of a lake and full of people. They were tall, dark men and women, the latter decently dressed in garments that were dyed with various colours. The mound was covered with huts that were thatched with reeds, and wooden jetties, to which canoes were tied, ran out into the surrounding shallow water. On the broad surface of the lake were other canoes, each containing one or two men who were engaged in fishing, while round this lake lay the dense forest, as it did today. In my dream the hollow in which now was the pool by which I lay, was thatched over, the roof being supported by carved posts of black wood. They were very curious carvings, but when I woke up I could not remember their details.

There was a meeting going on in this large public gathering place, and a man who wore a cloak and cap made of feathers, the chief, I take it, had risen from a chair fashioned of four tusks of ivory with a seat of twisted rushes, and was addressing the assembly, apparently upon some important subject, for his audience of old men seemed to be much impressed. He beat his breast and put some question to them. Then, while they debated in low tones as to their answer, I woke up to find that it was light.

Of course this dream was all nonsense born of imaginings as to what might have been the previous history of that place, and I paid no attention to it. Still, it fitted in well enough with the surroundings, so well that had I been mystically minded, I might have been inclined to believe that it did really portray some incident of past history that had happened when this mound was an island in a lake inhabited by a primeval people who dwelt there in order to be safe from the attacks of enemies.

Hans, like myself, had been asleep, but the hunters, who were far too frightened to think of shutting their eyes, reported that they had neither seen nor heard any elephants.

"Then let's go off home, before they come back," I said cheerfully.

So I took a drink of water, ate a handful of watercress, which I have always found a very sustaining herb, and away we started; glad enough to see the last of that haunted mount, as Hans called it. While we were on the plain we felt quite merry, at least Hans and I did, although it was strange to look at that lonesome lake bottom and think of the scene that had been enacted within a few hours, so strange, indeed, that I was almost tempted to believe we had been the victims of a vision of the night, induced by Kaneke's tale as to the great herds of elephants which came together in this district.

When we entered the forest, however, our mood changed, for

about this place with its endless giant trees that shut out the light of the sun, there was an air of gloom which was most depressing. On we marched into the depths, following our own trail backwards, for I had been careful to mark the trunk of a tree here and there, Red Indian fashion, so that we might make no mistake upon our return. To lose oneself in that forest would indeed be a dreadful fate. When we had tramped for a good while and reached the spot where we had missed the spoor on the previous day, I observed that Hans was growing anxious, for he kept glancing over his shoulder.

"What is the matter?" I asked.

"If the Baas will look back the Baas will see; that is, unless I have become drunk upon water and stream grasses," he replied in a weak voice.

I did look back and I did see. There, about a hundred yards behind, standing between two tree-trunks, exactly on our spoor, was our friend the king-elephant!

I halted, for I confess that for a moment my knees grew weak.

"Perhaps it is only a shadow—or a fancy," I said.

"Oh no, Baas. It's him right enough. I have felt him in the small of my back for the last half-mile, but did not dare to look. Still, if the Baas has any doubts, perhaps he would like to go and see."

At this moment, Tom and Jerry, who were well ahead, came tearing up to announce that they had caught sight of elephants to their right and left, and that we must go back.

"Oh yes," said Hans, "you are both very brave men, as you have always told me, so please go back," and he pointed with his finger at the apparition behind us, that seemed to have come nearer as we were talking, although, if so, it was once more standing still.

They saw it, and really I thought that one or both of them would collapse in a fit, for they were horribly frightened, as indeed I was myself. However, I pulled myself together and spoke to them severely, ending with an order to advance.

"Oh yes," repeated Hans who, in this extremity seemed to be moved to a kind of grim humour.

"Advance, you brave hunters, for that is your trade, isn't it? and please protect me, the poor little yellow man. No, don't look at those trees, because we are not lizards or woodpeckers and nothing else could run up them. And if we could, what would be the use, seeing that those spook elephants would only wait till we came down again. Advance, brave hunters, who told me only the other night that all elephants will run away from a man."

So we went on till at last I cut his drivel short.

"Come on," I said, "and keep together, for there is nothing else to be done. Remember that if anyone fires unless we are actually charged, probably it will mean the death of all of us. Now follow me."

They obeyed; indeed they followed uncommonly close, so close that when I halted for a moment, the barrel of the rifle of one of them, which I observed was at full cock, poked me in the back.

Soon I became aware that we were absolutely surrounded by elephants. That is to say, the great bull was behind, while unnumbered other beasts were on our right and left, though in front I could detect none. It was as though they were seeing us off the premises and politely leaving a road by which we might depart as quickly as possible. They saw us, there was no doubt of that, for occasionally one of them would stretch out its trunk and sniff as we passed within twenty or thirty yards of it. Moreover there was another thing. All these elephants were standing at intervals head on to our trail, forcing us as it were to keep to a straight and narrow road.

But each of them, when we had passed it, fell in behind the big bull and marched after it. Of this there could be no question, for when we were crossing one of the open glades that I have described, I looked back and saw an enormous number of them, hundreds there seemed to be, stretching along in a solemn and purposeful procession. Yet to right and left there were more ahead. It was as though all the elephants in Central Africa were gathered in that forest!

Well, it is useless to continue the description, because to do so would only be to say the same thing over and over again. For hours this went on, till we got near the camp, indeed, towards which we were travelling much faster than when we left it. Here the forest thinned and the glades were more frequent. I counted them one by one until I knew that we were close to the last of them and about a mile from the *boma*, or perhaps a little more. Just then one of the hunters looked back and gasped out:

"Lord, the elephants are beginning to run."

I verified the statement. It was true. The king-bull was breaking into a dignified trot, and all his subjects were following his example. Needless to say, we began to run too.

Oh, that last mile! Seldom have I done such time since I was a boy in the long-distance race at school, and fast as I went, the others kept pace with me, or went faster. We streaked across that glade and after us thundered the elephants, the ground shaking beneath their ponderous footfall. They were gaining, they were quite close, I could hear their deep breathing just behind. There ahead was the camp, and there, standing on a great ant-hill just in front of it, conspicuous in his white robe, was Kaneke watching the chase.

Suddenly the elephants seemed to catch sight of him, or perhaps they saw the smoke from the fire. At any rate they stopped dead, turned, and without a sound melted away into the depths of the forest, the king-bull going last as though he were loth to leave us.

I staggered on to the camp, dishevelled, breathless, ridiculous in my humiliation, as I was well aware. For was I not supposed throughout much of Africa to be one of the greatest elephant-hunters of my day?—and here I appeared running away from elephants with never a shot fired. It is true that the audience was small, a mysterious person called Kaneke, a very spider of a man that seemed to have got me into his web, and a score of porters, probably his tribesmen. But that made the matter no better; indeed, if there had been no one at all to see my disgrace, I should have felt almost equally shamed. I was furious, especially with Kaneke, whom I suspected, I dare say unjustly, of being at the bottom of the business. Also I had lost my hat, and what is an Englishman without his hat?

Kaneke descended from his ant-heap to meet me, all smiles and bows.

"I trust that your hunting has been good, Lord, for you seem to have found plenty of elephants," he said.

"You are laughing at me," I replied. "As you know, I have not been hunting; I have been hunted. Well, perhaps one day you will be hunted and I shall laugh at you."

Then I waved him aside and went into my tent to recover breath and composure.

Throwing myself down on the little folding canvas stretcher-bed which, whenever it was possible, I carried with me upon my various expeditions, I watched the arrival of the others who, after the elephants turned, had come on more slowly. Tom and Jerry were almost speechless with rage. They shook their fists at Kaneke; indeed, if their rifles had been at hand, which was not the case for these were dropped in their last desperate race for life (they were recovered afterwards, unhurt, together with my hat), I think it very likely that they would have shot him, or tried to do so.

"You have made us cowards before our master's eyes," gasped one of them, I forget which. Then they passed on out of my range of vision.

Lastly Hans arrived (he had not dropped his rifle), who squatted on the ground and began to fan himself with his hat.

"Why is everybody so angry with me, Hans?" said Kaneke.

"I don't know," answered Hans, "but perhaps if you gave me a drop out of that bottle which you keep under your blanket I might be able to remember—I mean the one the Baas gave you when you had the toothache."

Kaneke went into the shelter made of boughs where he slept, and returning with a flask of square-face gin, poured a stiff tot of it in to a pannikin, which he gave to Hans, who gulped it down.

"Now I am beginning to remember," said Hans, licking the edge of the empty tin. "They are angry with you, Kaneke, because they think that you have played a great trick upon them who being a wizard, have clothed a lot of spooks that serve you in the shapes of elephants and caused them to hunt us that you might laugh."

"Yet I have done nothing of the sort, Hans," answered Kaneke indignantly. "Am I a god that I can make elephants?"

"Oh no, Kaneke, certainly whatever you may be you are not a god. Nor indeed do I believe anything of this story, like those silly hunters. Yet for your own sake I hope that the next time you send us out hunting, nothing of this sort will happen, because, Kaneke, we can still shoot, and those hunters might be tempted to learn whether a wizard's skin can turn bullets. And now, as your toothache has gone, I will take that gin and give it back to the Baas, because he has not much of it, and even a wizard cannot make good gin."

Then Hans rose and snatched the bottle out of Kaneke's hand. I must add that to his credit he returned it to me undiminished, which—in Hans—was an act of great virtue.

Such was the end of that elephant-hunt, by means of which I had hoped to relieve the tedium of that strangely uneventful journey and to restore the moral tone of Tom and Jerry, also, to a lesser degree, that of Hans and myself. Certainly the first end was achieved, for whatever may be thought of our experiences at the meeting-place of elephants, and afterwards, they were not tedious. But of the second as much could not be said. Indeed, it left the hunters thoroughly frightened, the more so because they did not know exactly of what they were afraid.

All the circumstances of the business were unnatural. None of us had seen elephants behave as did those great herds, and the very mercy that the beasts showed to us was beyond experience.

Why did not the old king-bull either run away or kill us there upon the ground? Why did it and the rest of them hunt us back to the camp in that fashion, yet without doing us any actual harm? No wonder that these uneducated men saw magic at work and were scared.

Thrusting such nonsense from my mind, for nonsense I knew it to be, I could not help remembering the odd coincidence that on this prolonged adventure of our expedition, nothing seemed to materialize. So far it had the inconsequence of a dream. Thus, at the beginning of it, when we expected a desperate fight for our lives, there was no fight, at least on our part. Only one shot was fired, that with which I killed the Arab Gaika, who, be it noted, was Kaneke's particular foe, whose death he ardently desired. In the same way when we went out with much preparation to slay elephants and found them in enormous numbers no shot was fired and the beasts chased us ignominiously back to our camp. Further, there were more incidents of the same kind which I need not particularize.

I was sick of the whole job and longed to escape. Indeed, that night I went to Kaneke and told him so, pointing out that the hunters were off their balance and that as I could not send them back alone I thought it would be well if he parted company with me and my men, as I proposed to retrace my steps towards the coast. Kaneke was much disturbed and argued with me, very politely at first, pointing out the many dangers of such a course. As I would not give way, he changed his tone, and told me flatly that what I proposed would mean the death of all four of us.

"At whose hands? Yours, Kaneke?" I asked.

"Certainly not, Lord," he answered. "However cruelly you break your bargain with me, and this after taking my pay," (here he was alluding to the cash and ivory which, like a fool, I had accepted), "I should not be base enough to lift a hand against one who saved my life at what he believed to be the risk of his own, although in truth no risk was run."

"What do you mean? How do you know that, Kaneke?"

"I mean what I say, and I do know it, Lord. Even in that pit which you thought so dangerous you were quite safe, as you were when the Arabs attacked you and the elephants chased you, and as you will be to the end of this adventure, if only you keep your promises. For was this not vowed to you at the beginning?"

"Yes, Kaneke, by an unhappy woman whom I see no more."

"Those who are not seen may still be present, Lord, or their strength may remain behind them. But if you turn back before your mission is ended, it will depart. Those tribes who have welcomed you upon your outward journey will one and all fight against you on your return, until in this way or in that you are brought to your deaths. Never again will you look upon the sea, Lord."

"That's pleasant!" I exclaimed, controlling my temper as best I could. "Listen. You talk of my mission. Be so good as to tell me what it is. The only mission that I have, or had, was to visit a certain lake called Mone, if it exists, in order to satisfy my curiosity and love of seeing new things. Well, I have changed my mind; I no longer desire to travel to the Lake Mone."

"Yet I think you must go there, Lord, as I must, for that which is stronger than we are draws us both. In this world, Lord, we do not serve ourselves, we serve something else; I cannot tell what it is. Everything we do or seem to do, good and bad together, is done to carry out the purpose of what we cannot see. Like that beast Donna of yours, we travel our road, sometimes willingly, sometimes to satisfy our appetites, sometimes driven forward with strokes. Each of us has his powers, which are given to him, not that he may gain what he desires, but that he may fulfil an invisible purpose. Thus you have yours and I have mine. I know that your servants and others hold me to be a magician, and now and again you are tempted to believe them. Well, perhaps in a certain way I am something of a magician, that is to say, strength works through me, though whence that strength comes I cannot say."

"All this does not leave me much wiser, Kaneke."

"How can we who have no wisdom at all ever grow wiser, Lord? To do so, first we must be wise, and that will not happen to us until we are dead. All our lives we toil that we may grow wise—in death, when we may learn that wisdom is nothingness, or nothingness wisdom."

"Oh, have done!" I said in a rage. "Your talk goes round and round, and ends nowhere. You are fooling me with words, but I suppose that what you mean is, that we must go on with you."

"Yes, Lord, I mean that, amongst other things, unless indeed you wish to stop altogether and go to seek wisdom in the stars, or wherever she may dwell. Safety and good fortune have been promised to you and to the yellow man your servant, knowledge also such as you love. These lie in front of you, but behind lies that which all men shun, or so I read what is written."

"Where do you read it, Kaneke?"

"Yonder," he answered, pointing to the sky that was thick with stars, though the moon had not yet risen.

I stared at this solemn-faced, big-eyed man. Of all that he said I believed nothing, holding that if not merely a clever cheat, like others of his kind, he was a self-deluder. Yet of one thing I was sure, that if I tried to cross his will and deserted him, his prophecies would certainly be fulfilled, so far as we were concerned. Evidently this Kaneke was one who had authority among natives. It would be easy for him to pass a word back over the road that we had travelled, or in any direction that we might go, which word would mean what he foretold for us, four men only who must be at the mercy of a mob of savages, namely— death. On the other hand, if we went forward, his vanity would see to it that what he had asserted should come true, namely that we should be safe. Not till afterwards did I remember that only Hans and I were included in that assertion. Nothing was said about the two hunters.

On the whole, after this talk I hated Kaneke more than ever. Something told me that however plausible and smooth-tongued he might be, at heart the man was deceitful, one, too, whose ends were not good.

CHAPTER 9

Explanations

Next morning early I laid all this matter before Tom and Jerry, telling them that I had made up my mind to go forward with Kaneke and that Hans would accompany me, as I considered on the whole that this would be the safer course. If, however, they wished to return, I would give them rifles with a fair share of our ammunition, also the donkey Donna to take the place of porters. In fact, only in more detail, I repeated the offer which I made before we went out to hunt, or rather to be hunted by, elephants, explaining that I did so because after that experience they might have changed their mind about its acceptance.

They consulted together, then Tom the Abyssinian, who was always the spokesman, said:

"Master, after what we went through on the mound in the midst of the plain and in the forest with those elephants, which we believe to have been creatures bewitched, it is true that we are much more frightened even than we were before. So frightened are we that were it not for one matter, we would now do what we said we would not do, and attempt to work our way towards the coast, even though we must go alone."

"What matter?" I asked.

"This, Macumazahn. We are men disgraced; not only did we show fear and run when on duty, we did worse, we threw away our guns that we might run more quickly, and therefore, although they have been found and brought back by Kaneke's people, I say that we are men disgraced."

"Oh!" I said, trying to soothe their pride. "Hans and I ran also. Who would not have run with all those elephants thundering after him? It was the only thing to do."

"Yes, Macumazahn, you ran also, and it was the only thing to do. But, Lord, neither you nor Hans threw away your rifle against the hunter's law—"

"No, we should never do that," I said, trying to interrupt, but he went on rapidly:

"—So ashamed are we, Macumazahn, that I tell you, were it not that we are Christians, both of us, we should have hung ourselves or otherwise have put an end to our lives. But being Christians, this we cannot do, for then we should go to answer for that crime to a greater Master than you are. For this reason, Macumazahn, seeing that we may not wipe out our shame as savages would do, we propose to redeem our honour in another fashion. We hold that if we go forward with Kaneke we shall die, for we believe ourselves to be men bewitched, yes, men doomed by that wizard, whatever may be the fate of you, master, and of Hans. If so, thus let it be, for we are determined that if we must die, we will do so in some great fashion which will cause you to forget that we are men who broke the hunter's law and threw away our guns, with which it was our duty to defend you, and to remember us only as two faithful servants who knew how to give their lives to save that of their master."

I was so astonished at this solemn speech that I began to wonder whether Tom, in order to console himself for the slur upon his honour, the breach of the "hunter's law", as he called it, had got at my scanty stock of spirits.

"What do you say?" I asked, looking hard at Jerry.

"Oh, Macumazahn," answered that phlegmatic person, "I say that Little Holes is quite right. We two who have always had a good name—as the writings about us told you—when trouble came have shown ourselves to be not watch-dogs, but jackals. Yes, we are fellows who in the hour of danger have thrown away our rifles, which we should have kept to the last to protect the white lord who paid us. Therefore we will not go back, although we believe that we walk to our deaths, being under a curse. No, we will go on hoping that before the end you may learn that we are not really jackals but stout watch-dogs; yes, if God is good to us, that we are more, that we are bull-buffaloes, that we are lions."

"Stuff and rubbish!" I exclaimed. "You make trees of grass stalks. I never thought you jackals, who know you to be great-hearted. I dare say if I had remembered to do so when those elephants were at my heels, I should have thrown away my own rifle that I might run the faster. Still, I think that on the whole you are wiser to come on than to try to return alone, for reasons that I have told you. If there are dangers in front of us there are worse behind, because, although he is no wizard, as you think, Kaneke is better as a friend than as an enemy. So

I pray you to cease from dreams and quakings born of superstitions at which Christians should mock, and to go on with bold hearts." Then, as I thought we had talked enough, I shook them both by the hand, to show that I was not angry with them, and sent them away.

Afterwards very diplomatically I began to tell Hans something of this conversation, hoping to learn from him of what these hunters really were afraid.

"Oh, Baas," he broke in, "it is no use to speak to me about what passed between you and those fellows with half your tongue and your head turned aside"—by which he meant telling only a part of the truth—"because I was on the other side of that bush and heard every word."

"You are a dirty little spy," I said indignantly.

"Yes, Baas, that's it, because if one wants to know the truth, one must sometimes be a spy. Well, there's nothing to be said. No doubt Little Holes and Jerry are quite right; they are bewitched, or at least the Owl-man while he is flitting about at night has read their deaths written in the stars, which they know. But they know also that, as they have got to die, it doesn't matter whether they go with us or by themselves. So, if coming on will make them depart to the place of Fires happy and singing instead of sad and ashamed, thinking themselves lions instead of jackals, as they said—why, Baas, let them come on and don't trouble your head any more about them. For my part, however much I love them, I am quite content that it should be they who have to die, and not you and me. So cheer up, Baas, and take things as they happen."

"Get out, you heartless little beast," I said, and Hans got out. But all the while I knew that he was not really heartless, and, what is more, he knew that I knew it. Hans in his own way was, on the outside, just a rather cynical and half-savage philosopher, but within, a very warm-natured person.

The end of it all was that we marched on as before, and, as before, nothing particular happened. Kaneke, our guide, for I had not the faintest idea where we were going, led us through every variety of African country. We forded rivers, or if they were too deep and wide, were conveyed across them by friendly natives on rafts or in canoes, for when Kaneke had spoken to their chiefs, all the natives became most helpful. On one occasion, it is true, as there were no natives, or such as there were had no boats or rafts, we were obliged to swim, which I did with trembling, being afraid of crocodiles. However, the crocodiles, if there were any, politely left us alone, so that as usual we came over safely.

After passing the last of these rivers our path ran through a dense forest for two days. On the afternoon of the second day the forest grew thinner and at length changed to a plain, or rather barren land that was covered with small timber, bush-*veld* in short. This place was intensely hot, filled with game of every kind and, as we soon discovered from numerous bites, infested with tsetse-fly which lived upon the game. As tsetse, except for the irritation of their bites, are harmless to man and we had no horses or cattle, they did not alarm us, for up to that time I shared the belief that donkeys were immune as men and buck to their poison. This, however, proved not to be the case, at any rate in the case of Donna that I was riding a good deal because the heat made walking a most laborious business.

One day I noticed that she seemed suddenly to have grown weak and stumbled so frequently that at length I dismounted. Relieved of my weight she came on well enough without being led, for the intelligent and affectionate beast would follow me or Hans, who fed her, like a dog. When we camped that night she would not eat and was seized with a fit of staggering.

At once I guessed what must be the matter. Probably she had been infected a long while before and the added doses of the poison in this fly-haunted plain had brought matters to a crisis, helped by a shower of rain, which often develops the illness. There was nothing to be done, for this venom has no known antidote. So we lay down and went to sleep as usual. In the middle of the night I was awakened by feeling something pushing at me. At first I was frightened, thinking it must be a lion or some other beast, until I discovered that poor Donna had managed to thrust her way through the thorn fence we had built and even into my tent, of which the flaps were open because of the heat, and by prodding at me with her nose, was calling attention to her state and asking my assistance.

Of course I could do nothing except lead her out of the tent and offer her water, which she would not drink. I tried to go away, but whenever I moved she made piteous efforts to follow me, for the poor thing was growing weaker every minute, till at last she tumbled down. I sat myself at her side and presently she rolled over, laying her head, whether by accident or design, upon my knee and died.

I have told of her end in some detail, because with the single exception, that of a dog named Stump which once I owned when I was young, it was the most touching and piteous that I have known where an animal is concerned. Surely if there is any other life for us men, there must be one also for creatures which are capable of so much affection; at least I do not think I should care for a heaven where these were not.

When it was all over I went back to my tent and slept as best I could, to be awakened at the first dawn by a sound of lamentation. Rising, I peeped over the fence to discover its origin and in the faint light saw—what do you think?—Hans, whom it pleased to seem so callous and hard-hearted, seated on the ground blubbering—there is no other word for it—and kissing poor Donna's nose. Then I went back to bed, where in due course he brought me my coffee, as was his custom at sunrise.

"Baas," he said in a cheerful voice, "there is good news this morning. Those tsetse-flies have finished off Donna."

"Why is that good news?" I asked.

"Oh, Baas, because the Owl-man, Kaneke, says there are mountains ahead of us which she could not have climbed. He told me only the other day that we should have to shoot her there, or leave her to be eaten by lions, which would have been a pity. Also she was growing weak and really was of very little use, so I am glad that she is dead, as now I shall be saved the trouble of feeding her."

"Yes, Hans," I answered, "I saw how glad you were when I looked over the fence just as the light began to glint upon the spears of Kaneke's porters."

At this Hans put down the coffee in a hurry and departed, apparently much ashamed of himself, because, as he said after I had told him the story, he did not like being spied upon when his stomach was upset and made him behave like a fool. I should add that the hunters were depressed at this incident, not that they cared particularly for Donna, but because they said that now our luck had changed and that death was "a hungry lion", who, having tasted beast's flesh, would long for that of men.

They were right. Our luck had changed. The decease of poor Donna marked the end of our peaceful progress.

A few days later we came to mountains which for a long time past we had seen in the distance, bold hills upon which at nightfall a wonderful and mysterious blue light seemed to gather—the Ruga Mountains, I believe they were called. It was quite true that here we should have been obliged to leave Donna, dead or alive, for their ascent proved to be a most precipitous business. Indeed, had not Kaneke known the path, never could we have climbed them, because of certain precipices that rose in tiers of terraces and must be circumvented, since to scramble up the faces of them was impossible.

However he did know it, though to call it a path is a misnomer, because there was nothing to show that it was used by man. For three or four days we crept along the base of those great bare cliffs, always at length finding some crack by which their flanks could be turned. So it went on, an exhausting business, and as we mounted higher, very cold at night, for although there was no snow, the air grew thin and piercing.

At length we reached the summit of the mountains, which I found to be table-topped, a very common African formation. (What caused it? I wonder. Were the crests shorn off by ice in some remote era of the world's history, say, a few hundred million years ago?) As it was nightfall I could see no more, especially as a sort of blinding Scotch mist, the fog called the "table-cloth" which so often hangs about these flat-topped mountains, came up and obscured everything.

Next morning before the dawn Hans woke me up saying that Kaneke wished to speak with me. I went grumbling in all the clothes I had, with a blanket on the top of them and an old otter-skin *kaross*, that I used above the thin cork mattress of my portable bedstead, thrown over that, for the cold was bitter, or seemed so, after those hot tsetse-haunted lowlands. I found Kaneke seated on a stone near to the edge of the tableland. He rose and greeted me in his ceremonious fashion, saying:

"Lord, you should not have slept so long, for after midnight the mist melted or was blown away, and the stars were more beautiful and brighter than I have seen them since last I stood upon this place a long while ago. Indeed, so clear were they that in them I read many things which hitherto had been hidden from me."

"Did you?" I exclaimed. "I hope that among them you read that we shall soon escape from this cold which is gnawing my bones."

"Yes, Lord, I can promise you that before long you will be hot enough. Hearken," he went on with a change of tone, "the time has come when I must tell you something of my country and of what lies before us. Look! The sun rises in the east. The sight is fine, is it not?"

I nodded. It was very fine. The rays of the morning light revealed a vast plain lying some thousands of feet beneath us, and far away, set apparently in the centre of this plain, other mountains shaped like a flattened ring. Or perhaps it was a single mountain; at that distance I could not be sure.

"See," went on Kaneke, pointing to this mass, "yonder within that wall of cliff is the home of my people, the Dabanda, and there too is the holy lake, Mone. From here the place looks small, but it is not small. For a whole day a swift-footed man might run and not cross it from side to side."

"What is it?" I asked. "A valley?"

"I think not, Lord. I think that it is the cup of one or more of those great mountains that once vomited out fire; a huge basin with steep walls that cannot be climbed, and slopes within that run down to the forest at its base, which forest surrounds the Holy Lake."

"How large is this lake, Kaneke?"

"I do not know. Perhaps if a man could walk on water it would take him two hours to reach the island in its centre; one hour to cross that island and another two hours to come to the farther shore."

"That is a big piece of water, Kaneke, which means that the whole space within the lip of the rock must be large. Are your people who dwell in it also large?"

"Nay, Lord. Perhaps they can count five hundred men of an age to bear arms; not more. Still, they are strong because they are holy, and for another reason."

"What other reason?"

He dropped his voice as he answered:

"Did I not tell you the story of the goddess who dwells in my country, she whose title is *Engoi* the Divine, and whose name is Shadow?"

"You told me a story of which I remember something, as I remember also that I did not believe a word of it."

"There you are both right and wrong, Lord Macumazahn, because some of that story was lies with which I filled your ears for my own purposes, and some was true. For instance, what I said about the *Engoi* waiting for a white man was a lie. It was a bait in my trap. Lord, it was necessary that you should come with me; why, I do not quite know, but so I was commanded."

"Who commanded you?"

"That is my secret, Lord."

Now I bethought me of the deceased White-Mouse, and did not pursue the matter, but asked:

"What do you mean by telling me that this lie was a bait?"

"What I say, Lord. I have learned through your servant, the yellow man, who told it not to me but to another, that you worship all that is beautiful, especially beautiful women, who when they see you, so you announce, fall in love with you at once. Now you will understand, Lord, why I baited my trap with this story of one who was very lovely and waited for a white man, namely because I knew that you would believe yourself to be that man and come with me upon that journey, being sure that she who is named Shadow would reward you by kissing your feet and redeeming you from your sins towards the other beautiful women, whom the yellow man says you throw aside one after another as soon as you are tired of them."

Now when I heard this preposterous and most shameless yarn, it is true that, cold as it was, I nearly burst with heat and rage. If that mischievous and romancing little Hans had been there, which he was not, I declare that it would have gone ill with him; indeed, so angry was I with Kaneke for repeating his calumnies, that I nearly made a physical attack upon him. On second thoughts, however, I refrained—first, because he was a much larger and stronger man than myself, and, secondly, because I wished to get at the kernel of this mystery, for I felt that, divested of the trappings invented by Kaneke, there remained something most unusual to be elucidated. So I put the brake upon my temper and answered:

"I thought that in your way you were a wise man, Kaneke, but now I see that after all you are but a fool, who otherwise would have known that Hans is an even bigger liar than you announce yourself to be, and that the last thing I wish is to run after beautiful women, or any woman, which always ends like our adventures with the elephants, in the hunter being hunted. But let that be. Was any of your story true?"

"Yes, Lord, much. We have a goddess who is called Shadow, and who, as we believe and not we alone, controls the gifts of heaven, sending rain or withholding it, causing women to bear children or making them barren, and doing many such things that bring happiness or misery to men, though this goddess I have never seen, except once, as I told you."

"A goddess! Do you mean that she is immortal?"

"No, Lord, but I mean that her power is immortal, or at least that it goes on from generation to generation. The goddess, as I think, when her office is fulfilled, dies or perhaps is killed."

"What office?"

"Lord, the Chief of my tribe, the Dabanda, is her head-priest. When the goddess is of ripe age he is married to her, and in due time becomes the father of a daughter, of which she is the mother. Perhaps he is also the father of male children, but if so they are never heard of, so I suppose that they are killed. When this daughter, the *Engoi*-to-be, grows up, her mother, the *Engoi*-that-was, vanishes away."

"Vanishes! How does she vanish?"

"I do not know, Lord. Some say that she who is called Shadow is drawn up to heaven, some that she who is also called the Lake-dweller,

303

or Treasure of the Lake, swims out into the lake and is lost beneath its waters, and some that the virgins who attend her, poison her with the scent of certain flowers that bloom upon the island. At least she departs, and her daughter, the new *Engoi*, reigns in her place and, like her mothers before her, is married to her high-priest, the Chief of the Dabanda."

"What!" I asked, horrified. "Do you mean to say that this chief marries his own daughter?"

"Oh no, Lord. The chief never outlives the Shadow. He knows when she is going to fade, and he fades at the same time, or earlier."

"How does he 'fade', as you call it?"

"That is a matter for him to choose, Lord. Generally, if he seeks honour, in fighting our enemies the Abanda, among whom he will rush alone until he is cut down. Or sometimes he chooses other roads to darkness. At least he must walk one of them, because if he does not he is seized and burnt alive; as the end is the same it does not matter how it is reached."

"My word," I exclaimed, "it is strange that this goddess finds it easy to get a husband!"

"It is not at all strange, Lord," answered Kaneke haughtily, "seeing that to wed the *Engoi* is the greatest honour that can befall any man in the world. Moreover, he knows that when his life here is over he will dwell with her for ever in joy in heaven. Yes, they will be twin stars shining to all eternity. Therefore before the Chief marries the Shadow, he names some child he loves to be the husband of the Shadow which shall appear.

"Thus it came about, Lord, that when I was but little, I was named by the Chief, the half-brother of my mother, to wed the *Engoi*-to-be. But I committed the great crime. I entered the sacred forest, hoping to look upon the *Engoi*, of whose beauty I had heard, not her whom I should wed, for as yet she did not live, but one who went before her. It was for this crime that misfortunes fell upon me, as I have told you, and I was driven from the land to atone my sins. Now I have been called back again to become the husband of the new *Engoi*, for such is my glorious destiny."

"Oh," I said, "now at last I get the hang of the thing. Well, every man to his taste, but after what you have told me, I am glad that no one nominated me to marry an *Engoi* or Shadow, or whatever you call her."

"Strange are the varying ways of men! That which you, White Lord, think of small account, we hold to be the greatest honour which can befall one born of woman. It is true that death lies beyond the honour, but what of this, seeing that soon or late death must come? It is true also that he who is named and consecrated the spouse of the *Engoi* of days to come, must look upon no other woman."

Here I could not help remarking:

"But surely, Kaneke, you told me a story of a woman who helped you to become chief of the Arabs in your town yonder, saying that you grieved much when she died; also I think you spoke to me of your wives who dwelt without your fence."

"Very likely, Lord, for have I not told you many things? Also, did I say that the child that brought the woman to her death was mine, or show you the wives who dwelt without my fence? Learn that I had not, nor even had a wife, which is one of the reasons why those Arabs held me a magician. What does a man want with wives who is sealed as the husband of the *Engoi*, yes of the Shadow herself, if only for a year, or even for an hour?"

"Nothing. Of course, nothing," I answered with enthusiasm. Then a thought struck me, and I added, "But supposing that when at last he sees this *Engoi*, he does not like her, or that she does not like him, having met some other man whom she prefers?"

"Lord Macumazahn, you speak in ignorance, therefore I forgive you what might otherwise be considered insult, or even blasphemy. It is not possible that her appointed husband should not like the *Engoi*. Even were she hideous he would adore her, seeing the soul within. How much more, then, will he do so, since she is always the loveliest woman on the earth, filled with light like a star and crowned with wisdom from above."

"Indeed! In that case there is nothing more to be said. Only then, Kaneke, why do her adoring people drown or otherwise make away with such divine beauty and wisdom as soon as her daughter begins to grow up?"

"As regards your second question," went on Kaneke, taking no notice of an interruption which doubtless he considered irreverent and trivial, "still less is it possible that the *Engoi* should prefer any other man to him to whom she is vowed, for the reason that she never sees one."

"Oh," I said, "now I understand. That accounts for everything, including your banishment from your home. A woman who never sees any man except the one she must marry is of course easily pleased, even if she is called a goddess."

"Lord Macumazahn," replied Kaneke, much offended, "I see that you wish to make a mock of me and my faith."

"As you did of that of the Mahommedans," I suggested mildly.

"I see also," he went on, "that you think I tell you lies."

"As you have just admitted you did in the past."

He waved his hand, as though to thrust this trifle aside, and went on;

"Yet you will learn that as to the Lady Shadow, Treasure of the Lake, and her husband, who is called 'Shield of the Shadow', I speak the truth. Indeed, you should have learnt it already, for have I not told you that amongst other powers, he who is affianced to her whose title is *Engoi*, yes, even before he has married her, has command over wild beasts and men. What of the lion that I turned aside on that night when you climbed the pit? What of those whom I called to rescue you when the Arabs came up against you? What of the elephants which hunted you when you went out to hunt them, and ceased when they saw me?"

"What indeed?" I echoed. "Perhaps when you have time you will answer your own questions. Meanwhile I will put one more to you. Why have you plotted and planned and so brought it about that I should be your companion upon this very mysterious business?"

"Because it was conveyed to me that I must do so, Lord Macumazahn, for reasons that as yet are not made clear to me. Doubtless you are appointed to be of service to the *Engoi* and therefore to me. Also I know that there will be a great war between my people, the Dabanda, and the Abanda, who dwell in their thousands upon the farther side of yonder mountain and who desire—as they have always done—that their chief should wed the Shadow and thus bring rain and prosperity upon them, and in this war you, who are a great general or so I have heard, and who are so skilled with a rifle as I have seen, may be of use to me."

"I see," I said. "As I was when I rescued you from your house and afterwards when I shot that fellow Gaika. Well, perhaps I may and perhaps I mayn't, since no one knows to whom he will be of use. Meanwhile I thank you for telling me many things, some of which may be true. And now I will go to breakfast, so good-bye for the present," and I departed, aware that if I had disliked Kaneke before, now I positively detested him.

To me the man seemed to be a mixture of a liar, a braggart, a self-seeker, and a mystic, a most unpleasant compound, or so I thought. Yet I had taken his money and was bound to serve him, or at any rate to serve this wonderful *Engoi*, whose personal name was Shadow, if such a woman existed. Possibly she might be better than Kaneke; at any rate I hoped so.

CHAPTER 10

The Wanderer

By evening that day we had reached the plain at the foot of the mountain and advanced some little way into its desolation. I use this word advisedly, for when once we had got away from the foothills where there was water, we entered most unpromising country upon which it was evident rain fell but seldom.

The vegetation here was almost entirely of the cactus order, grey or green prickly growths that stored up moisture within themselves. Some of these were enormous, thick and tall as moderate-sized trees, and, as I should judge, of great antiquity, their form suggesting huge candelabra (for they had no proper leaves) or straight fingers pointing up to heaven from flat bases, shaped like to the palm of the hand. Others again were round green lumps, ranging from the size of a football down to that of a pin-cushion, all of them, big or little, being covered with sharp spikes, which made progress among them difficult and, indeed, dangerous, for the prick of some of the species is poisonous. These cacti, I should add, or a large proportion of them, bore the most beautiful but unnatural-looking flowers of every size and brilliant hue.

Another feature of this strange semi-desert area was the outcrop here and there of columns of stone that from a distance looked like obelisks, monoliths sometimes, but generally formed of round, water-worn rocks resting one upon another. How they came here I cannot imagine; it is a matter for geologists, but I noticed that they seemed to be composed of hard rock left, perhaps, when millions of years ago the lava from the great extinct volcanic area towards which we were heading, was washed away by floods.

Through this curious country we travelled for three days, coming on the second day to a small oasis where there was a spring of water, which I was glad to see for our bottles were empty and we had begun to thirst. I must add that we went at a great rate. Two or three of the porters, relieved of their loads, which the others added to their own, marched ahead, quite five hundred yards ahead, which, as Hans remarked, showed that they knew the way and were scouts sent out to guard against surprise. Kaneke followed, in the midst of the remaining porters, who acted as his bodyguard. Then came Hans and I, the two hunters bringing up the rear.

"Now I begin to believe, Baas," said Hans to me, "that something of all that story which Kaneke has told is true, for though they will never say so, it is evident that these men who know the road so well belong to his people, also that they are afraid of being attacked. Otherwise they would not go so fast through this wilderness of thorns, or look so frightened."

"How do you know what tale Kaneke told me? Were you listening behind a stone?" I asked, but got no answer, for at that moment Hans pricked, or pretended to prick, his foot upon a cactus, and dropped behind to dig out the thorn.

I pass on to the evening of the third day. We were at length getting clear of the cactus scrub and reaching the foot of the westernmost slope of the huge and massive mountain, which Kaneke had told me was the shell of an extinct volcano within whose crater dwelt his people, the Dabanda. There was but an hour to sunset, and though much distressed by the heat and the lack of water, we were marching at a great rate to reach a point where Kaneke said we should find a spring. This he was anxious to do before dark, for now the nights were almost moonless. Presently as we trudged forward, begrimed with dust and gasping from the still heat, Hans, who was at my side, poked me in the ribs, exclaiming in Dutch:

"Kek!" (that is, "Look!")

I did look in the direction to which he pointed, and saw so strange a sight that at first I thought I must be suffering from delusions. There, running towards us down the slope of a low ridge of the mountain mass where it merged into the plain, appeared a man, a very exhausted man, who came or rather staggered forward in short rushes, halting after every few paces as though to get his breath. This much I could see with my eyes, but when I took my glasses, which I always carry with me, I saw more, namely that this man was white! Yes, there could be no mistake, for his garments, which seemed to have been torn from his shoulders, showed the white skin beneath. Moreover his beard and hair were red, or even golden, and his height and breadth were greater than are those of most natives.

Next moment I saw something else also, for on that ridge of ground which he had crossed, appeared a number of black spearsmen, who evidently were hunting him. Dropping the glasses into my pocket, I sang out to Tom and Jerry to give me my Winchester, which one of them carried as well as his own, the heavy rifles and ammunition being in charge of the bearers. In a minute it was in my hands, with a bagful of cartridges.

"Now follow me," I said, and the four of us ran forward, passing through the bearers.

By this time the exhausted white man was within about fifty paces of us, while his pursuers, not more than six yards or so behind, were beginning to throw spears at him as though they were determined to kill him before he could reach us. As it chanced it was some of them who were killed, for at my word we opened fire, and being decent shots, all four of us, down they went. The man arrived, unhurt, and sank to the ground, gasping out:

"My God! you are white! Give me a rifle."

I didn't, because I hadn't one at hand, nor, indeed, was he in a fit state to handle a gun. Also, next minute there began a general engagement on a small scale.

More spearsmen—tall, shapely fellows—appeared over the ridge, thirty of forty of them perhaps. Our bearers threw down their loads and came into action with great vigour, uttering a war-cry of *"Engoi!—Engoi!"* We fired away with the repeating rifles.

It was all over in a few minutes, for a good many of the attackers were down and the rest had bolted back across the ridge, while our losses were nil, except for one man who had received a spear-cut in the shoulder. They had gone, pursued by the porters who, from peaceful bearers of baggage suddenly were turned into perfect tigers, furious fighting-men who, weary as they were, rushed into battle like the best of Zulu veterans. The transformation was so marked and instantaneous that it astonished me, as it did Hans, who said:

"Look at those fellows, Baas. They are fighting, not strangers, but old enemies whom they have hated from their mothers' breasts. And look at Kaneke. He bristles with rage like a porcupine." (This was quite true; the man's hair and beard seemed to be standing on end and his eyes, usually so sleepy, flashed fire.)

"Did you see him tackle that tall one whom you missed," (this was a lie. I never shot at the man), "the warrior who threw a knife at you—snatching the spear from his hand and driving it through him? I think they must be Abandas whom, as we have heard, the Dabandas hate."

"I dare say," I answered, "but if so they are uncommonly like Kaneke's crowd; of the same blood perhaps."

Then I bethought me of the white man, whom I had forgotten in the excitement of the scrap, and went to look for him. I found him seated on the ground, having just emptied a water-bottle that Jerry had given him.

"There is something in horoscopes, after all," he panted out, for he had not yet recovered his breath.

"Horoscopes! What the devil do you mean?" I asked, thinking that he must be crazy.

"What I say," he answered. "My father was cracked on astrology and cast mine when I was born. I remember that it foretold that I should meet a white man in a desert and that he would save me from being killed by savages."

"Did it indeed? To change the subject, might I ask your name?"

"John Taurus Arkle," he murmured. "Taurus from the constellation under which I was born, or so I understand," he added with a little smile and in the voice of one whose mind wandered; then shut his eyes and began to faint.

Faint he did; so thoroughly that he had to be revived from my scanty store of spirits. While he was recovering I took stock of the man, who evidently was off his head from exhaustion. That he was an Englishman of good birth was clear from that unfailing guide, his voice and manner of speaking. Also he was well named John Taurus, i.e. John Bull, though perhaps if the constellation Leo had been in the ascendant or whatever it is called when he was born, that of Lion would have suited him even better.

To tell the truth his physical qualities partook of both a *taurine* and a *leonine* character. The wide breast, the strong limbs and the massive brow were distinctly bull-like, while the yellow beard and hair which, having been neglected, hung down on to his shoulders like a mane, also the eyes which, when the sun shone on them, gleamed with a sort of golden hue, as do those of lions, did suggest something *leonine*.

In short, although not handsome, he was a most striking person, like to no one else I had ever seen; aged, as I guessed, anything between thirty and thirty-five years. Much did I wonder how he came to be in this strange place where, as I believe from what Kaneke had told me, at that time I was the first white man to set foot.

The gin did its work, and in due course John Taurus Arkle—a strange name enough—regained his wits. While he was still unconscious Kaneke, looking both disturbed and fierce, the spear with which he had killed its owner still in his hand, came up and stared at him.

"It's all right," I said; "only a swoon. He will recover presently."

"Is it so, Lord?" he answered, staring at Arkle with evident disapproval and, I thought, dislike. "I hoped that he was dead."

"And why, pray?" I inquired shortly.

"Because this white man will bring trouble on us, as I always feared."

"As you feared! What do you mean?"

"Oh, only that the stars told me something about him; as I read them, that we should find his body."

Stars, I thought to myself; more stars. But aloud I said:

"Well, you read them wrongly—if at all, for he is alive, and please understand that I mean to keep him so. But what is this talk of trouble?"

"Talk," said Kaneke, pointing with the spear to certain silent forms that lay around. "Is there not already trouble here? Moreover I learned something from one of those Abanda fellows before he died, namely that this white man had forced his way over the mountain crest into my country of the Dabanda; that he had been driven out into that of the Abanda; that he was forced to fly before them who wished to kill him, as they do all strangers; that he fled, and being very strong and swift of foot, outran them, till at last, when he was being hunted down like a tired buck by wild dogs, he met us, and that happened which was decreed."

"Yes," I repeated after him, "that happened which was decreed, whether in your stars or elsewhere. But I want to know what is to happen next. It appears that neither the Dabanda nor the Abanda like this white lord, who henceforth must be our companion."

"Why must he be our companion, Macumazahn? See, he is senseless. One tap on the head and he so will remain for ever, who, if he comes on with us among peoples whom he has offended—I know not how—may cost us our lives."

In an absent-minded fashion I took the revolver from my belt and began to examine it as though to see whether it were loaded.

"Look here, Kaneke," I said, "let us come to an understanding. You have just been suggesting to me that to suit some purpose of your own I should murder, or allow you to murder, one of my own countrymen who has been attacked by your people and other savages, and escaped. Perhaps you do not understand what that means to a white man, so I am going to tell you."

Here suddenly I lifted the revolver and held it within a few inches of his eyes. Then I said in a quiet voice:

"Look here, my friend, in your country when you take an oath that may not be broken, by whom do you swear?"

"By the *Engoi*, Lord," he answered in a startled voice. "To break an oath sworn by the *Engoi* is death, and more than death."

"Good. Now swear to me by the *Engoi* that you will not harm this white lord or cause him to be harmed."

"And if I refuse?" he asked sullenly.

"If you refuse, Kaneke, then I will give you time to change your mind, while I count fifty between my teeth. If, after I have counted fifty, you still refuse, or are silent, then I will send a bullet through your head, because, friend Kaneke, it is time to settle which of us two is master."

"If you kill me, my people will kill you, Macumazahn."

"Oh no, they won't, Kaneke. Have you forgotten that a certain lady called White-Mouse, in whom I put much faith, promised me that I should come quite safe out of this journey. Don't trouble yourself about that matter, for I will settle with your people after you are dead. Now I am going to begin to count."

So I counted, pausing at ten and at twenty. At thirty I saw Kaneke's fingers tighten on the handle of the spear with which he had killed the Abanda man.

"Be pleased to drop that spear," I said, "or I shall stop counting."

He opened his hand and it fell to the ground.

Then I counted on to forty, and pausing once more, remarked that time was short, but that perhaps he was right to have done with it and to take his chance of what awaited him in or beyond the stars he worshipped, seeing that this world was full of sorrows.

I counted on to forty-five, at which number I aligned the pistol very carefully on a spot just above Kaneke's nose.

"Forty-six, forty-seven, forty-eight," I said, and began to press upon the trigger.

Then came the collapse, for Kaneke threw himself down and in truly Eastern fashion began to kiss the ground before my feet. As he did so I fired, the bullet of course passing over his head.

"Dear me!" I exclaimed, "how fortunate that you made up your mind. This pistol is much lighter triggered than I thought or perhaps the heat has affected the spring. Well, do you swear?"

"Yes, Lord," he said hoarsely. "I swear by the *Engoi* that I will not harm yonder white man, or cause him to be harmed. That was the oath you asked, but I know that in it lies one that is wider, namely that henceforth, instead of your serving me, I must serve you, who have conquered me."

"That's it. You have put it very well," I replied cheerfully. "And now—a gift for a gift. I am quite ready to renounce my new-won lordship over you, and taking this white wanderer with me if he will come, to leave you to go your own ways, while I and my servants go mine, you promising not to follow or molest me in any manner. Is that your wish?"

"No, Lord," he answered sullenly. "You must accompany me to the Lake Mone."

"Very good, Kaneke, so be it. Tell me how matters stand and I will give you my orders. But remember that if you disobey one of them or try to trick me, or to injure this white lord, I who have only counted forty-eight, shall count forty-nine and fifty. It is agreed?"

"It is agreed, Lord," he replied humbly. "Hearken. Yonder," and he pointed to some rocks upon a slope not more than a few hundred yards away, where grew trees of a different and more vigorous character from any about us—"yonder, I say, is the spring we seek. Lord, we must reach it at once, for our water is done, the white man has drank the last, and very soon it will be quite dark and impossible to travel."

"Good," I said. "Go on with your men and prepare the camp. I will follow with the wanderer as soon as he can walk. Afterwards we can talk."

He looked at me doubtfully, wondering, I was sure, whether I had it in my mind to give him the slip. If so, probably he concluded that without water and with a sick man it would not be possible for me to do so. At least he went to collect his people, and presently I saw them march with the loads up to the rocks where grew the green trees. To make certain of his movements I sent Hans with them, telling him to return at once and report if there was a spring and if so whether Kaneke was preparing to camp.

To tell the truth I was by no means certain as to his intentions. Possibly he meant to melt away in the darkness, leaving us in the wilderness to our fate. This would not have troubled me very much had it not been for the fact that nearly all the ammunition and food, also some of my rifles, were among the loads. Otherwise, indeed, I should have been glad to see the last of Kaneke, for I was filled with doubts of him and of the business into which he was dragging me. However, I must take my chance; amongst so many risks what was one more?

When he had gone I went to where the stranger lay behind some stones, and to my joy found that he was coming out of his swoon, for he had sat up and was staring about him.

"Who are you and where am I? Oh, wasn't there a fight? Give me water."

313

"Keep quiet a little, Mr. Arkle," I said. "I hope to have some water presently." (I had given Hans a bottle to fill.) "There has been a fight. By God's mercy we managed to save you. You shall tell me about your adventures afterwards."

He nodded, fixing his attractive eyes, which reminded me of those of a retriever, on my face. Then, doubtless unaware that he was speaking out loud, he said something rather rude, namely:

"Queer-looking little chap; hair like that of a half-clipped poodle; skin like an old parchment, but tough as nails; and straight. Yes, I am sure, straight. John Taurus, you are in luck. Well, it's time."

Of course I took no notice, but went to speak to Tom and Jerry, who were standing close by bewildered and whispering, asking them how many cartridges they had fired in the scrap, and answering their questions as best I could, till presently in the waning light I caught sight of Hans returning.

"It is all right, Baas," he said. "There's a good spring yonder, as the Owl-man said, and he is camping by it. Here's water."

I took the bottle and handed it to Arkle, who seized it eagerly. Then suddenly a thought struck him and he held it out to me, saying in his pleasant, cultivated voice:

"You too look thirsty, sir. Drink first," words that showed me that I had to deal with a gentleman.

To tell the truth I was dry, perished with thirst, indeed. But not to be outdone I made him take the first pull. Then I drank and gave some to Tom and Jerry. Between us those two quarts did not go far; still, a pint apiece was something.

"Can you walk a little?" I asked Arkle.

"Rather," he said. "I'm a new man, and thank God those scoundrels didn't get my boots. But where are we going?"

"To the camp yonder first. Afterwards to the Lake Mone if we can."

A flash of joy passed across his face.

"That will suit me very well," he said. Then it fell, and he added: "You are very good to me, and it is my duty to warn you that the journey is dangerous, and if we get there, that the place and people are—well, not canny. Indeed, you would be wise to turn back, for I think that death is very fond of Lake Mone."

"I guessed as much," I said. "Have you been there, Mr. Arkle?"

He nodded.

"Then take my advice and say nothing of your experiences to those with whom we are going to camp, for I suppose you talk Arabic. I will explain why afterwards."

He nodded again, then asked:

"What is your name, sir?"

I told him.

"Allan Quatermain," he said. "Seems familiar to me somehow. Oh, I remember, a man I knew—Lord Ragnall—told me about you. Indeed, he gave me a letter of introduction in case I went south. But that's gone with the rest. Odd to have met you in this fashion, but so is everything in this place. Now, Mr. Quatermain, if I may put my hand on your shoulder, for my head still swims a bit, I am ready to walk."

"Right," I answered, "but again I beg you not to be ready to talk, at any rate in any language but our own, for except Hans, who can be trusted on all important matters"—and I pointed to the Hottentot—"none of these people understand English."

"I see," he said, and we started, Arkle, who limped badly, towering above me, for he was a very big man, and leaning on me as though I were a stick.

We reached the camp without difficulty just as darkness fell. While the hunters pitched my tent which, although low, was large enough to cover two men, Arkle lay down by the stream and drank until I begged him to stop. Then he poured water over his head, and thrust his arms into it to the shoulders, as though to take up moisture like a dry sponge, after which he asked for food. Fortunately, we had still plenty to eat—of a kind, hard cakes made of crushed corn that we had obtained from the last natives we had met, and sliced biltong, that is buck's flesh dried in the sun. These he devoured ravenously, as though they were delicious, which showed me that he was almost starved. Then he lay down in the tent and fell at once into a profound sleep.

For a while I sat listening to his breathing, which sounded quite loud in the intense stillness of the place, and staring at the stars that in the clear sky shone with wonderful brilliance. By their light I saw Kaneke glide past me and, taking his stand upon a flat stone at a little distance, make strange motions with his arms, which he held up above his head.

"The Owl-Man is talking to his star, Baas; that bright one up there," whispered Hans at my side, pointing to the planet Venus. "He does that every night, Baas, and it tells him what to do next day."

"I am glad to hear it," I answered, "for I am sure I do not know what we are to do."

"Oh, just go on, Baas," said Hans. "If you only go on long enough you always come out the other side," a remark which I thought contained a deal of true philosophy, though it left the question of what one would find on the other side quite unsolved.

315

After this, having arranged that Hans and the two hunters were to keep watch alternately, which was unnecessary where Hans was concerned, seeing that he always slept with one eye open, I lay down in the tent, and having said a short prayer, as I am not ashamed to confess I have always done since boyhood, or at any rate nearly always, fell instantly into a profound slumber.

While it was still dark—although, as I could tell by the stars and the smell of the air, the night drew towards morning, I was awakened by Arkle creeping into the tent.

"Been to get a bathe in that spring," he said, when he found that I was awake. "Needed it when one hasn't washed for a week. I feel all right again now."

I remarked that I was glad to hear it, and that he seemed to have had a squeak for his life.

"Yes," he added thoughtfully, "it was a very close thing. Lucky that I am a good runner. I won the three-mile race two years in succession at the Oxford and Cambridge sports. Look here, Mr. Quatermain, you must be wondering who I am and how I came here. I will tell you while it's quiet, if you care to listen.

"The Arkles, though that isn't the name of the firm, for some generations have been in a big way of business in Manchester and London; colonial merchants they call themselves. They deal all over the world, with West Africa among other places. My father, who has been dead some years, struck out a line of his own, however. He was a dreamy kind of a man, a crank his relatives called him, who studied all sorts of odd subjects, astrology among them, as I think I told you. Also he refused to have anything to do with trade, and insisted upon becoming a doctor, or rather a surgeon. He met with great success in his profession, for notwithstanding his fads, he was a wonderful operator. Being well-off he took little private practice, but worked almost entirely at hospitals for nothing.

"When I left college, by his wish I became a doctor too, but shortly after I qualified at Bart's my father, whose only child I was, died. Also my cousin, the only son of my uncle, Sir Thomas Arkle the baronet, was killed in an accident, and my uncle begged me to enter the business. In the end I did so, very unwillingly, to please my relations. To cut the story short, I did not care for business, and when there was so much property entailed upon me with the baronetcy, I could not see why it was necessary that I should remain in an office. On the other hand my uncle did not wish me to return to practice.

"So we compromised; I agreed to travel for some years in the interests of the firm, specially in West Africa, where they wanted to develop their trade, and incidentally in my own interest, because I wanted as a physician to observe man in his primitive state and to study his indigenous diseases. When the tour was finished I was to return and put up for Parliament and in due course inherit the Arkle fortunes, which are large, and advance the Arkle dignity, which is nothing in particular, by the judicious purchase of a peerage, for that is what it came to. That, more or less, was the arrangement."

"Quite so," I said, "or as much of it as you choose to tell me, though perhaps there is a good deal more behind which, quite properly, you prefer to keep to yourself."

"Perfectly true, Mr. Quatermain. By the way, as I am telling you about myself, would you mind telling me who and what you are?"

"Not in the least. I was born in England of a good family, and received a decent education from my father, who was a scholar, a gentleman, and something of a saint. For the rest I am nobody and nothing in particular, only a hunter with some skill at his trade, an observer, like you, of mankind in the rough, and one cursed with a curiosity and a desire to learn new things which, in the end, will no doubt put a stop to all my foolishness."

"Oh no, it won't," he answered cheerfully, "that is, not until the time appointed. I'll cast your horoscope for you, if you like—my father taught me the trick—and tell you when it will happen."

"No, you won't," I answered firmly.

At this moment Hans arrived with the coffee and informed me that Kaneke was anxious that we should march at sunrise, as here we were in danger.

Then followed anxious consultations. Arkle had a coat, or rather a Norfolk jacket, but no shirt; and one of my spares, a flannel garment that had cost me fifteen shillings at Durban and had never been used, must be provided for him. Luckily it was over-size, so he managed to drag it on to his great frame. Then a hat must be found, and so forth. Lastly it was necessary to provide him with one of the spare Winchester rifles and some cartridges.

Even before we were ready Kaneke arrived, not a little agitated, as I could see, and prayed us to hasten.

"Where to, Kaneke?" I asked.

"Up the side of the mountain and over its lip, Lord, that we may take shelter among my people the Dabanda. For be sure that after what happened yesterday, the Abanda will kill us if they can. If this white wanderer whom your servants call Red-Bull cannot march, he must be left behind."

Here Arkle, who it seemed understood and could speak Arabic perfectly, looked Kaneke up and down and replied that this was unnecessary, as he believed that he could get along.

So, having swallowed some food, presently off we went, guided by Kaneke up the steep mountain side.

"Did you call that man, Kaneke?" Arkle inquired when that worthy was out of earshot.

"Yes," I answered; "but why do you ask?"

"Oh, only because of late I have heard a good deal of a person named Kaneke from a native I know. But perhaps there are two Kanekes. The one he spoke of was a young fellow who committed a great crime."

Then rather abruptly he changed the subject, leaving me wondering.

CHAPTER 11

Arkle's Story

At first Arkle walked rather lamely, being troubled with stiffness and his sore heel, but soon these wore off for the time, and in the fresh air of the morning his vigour returned to him. Certainly he was a splendid-looking man, I reflected, as I marched at his side, a perfect specimen of the finest stamp of the Anglo-Saxon race.

While we went he continued his story.

"You were quite right in supposing that there were other reasons which induced me to come to Africa besides those I mentioned. I will tell them to you, if you care to hear them, for I may as well put my cards on the table. If not, please say so, for I do not wish to bore anybody with my affairs."

I replied that nothing would please me better, for to tell the truth my curiosity was much excited.

"Here goes, then," he said, "though I expect that the tale won't raise your opinion of me and my intelligence. As I have said, I am what is called a man with prospects or rather I was, for these seem far enough off today, and as such, having plenty of money to spend, I was exposed to many temptations. Mr. Quatermain, I cannot pretend that these were always resisted. I will pass over my follies, of which I am ashamed, with the remark that they were such as are common to impetuous young men.

"In short, I lived fast, so fast that my uncle and connections—my mother, by the way, died when I was young—being nonconformist of that puritanical stamp which often combines piety with a continual thirst for worldly advancement, were quite properly scandalized, and remonstrated. They said that I must change my mode of life, and as a first step, get married. This my uncle desired above all things, for there was no other heir, and as he often used to remark in a solemn voice, life is uncertain.

"At length I gave way and became engaged to a lady very well born indeed and very handsome, but without means, which, as I would have plenty, did not matter. To be honest, I did not greatly care for this lady, nor did she care for me, being, as I discovered afterwards, in love with somebody else. In fact the marriage would have been one of mutual convenience, nothing more. Now I am going to make you laugh.

"Although no one knew it and I scarcely expect you to believe it, I, a man who, as I have said, could and did plunge into dissipations, have another side to my nature. At times, Mr. Quatermain, I am a dreamer and what is called a mystic. I suppose I inherited it from my father, at any rate there it is."

"There is nothing wonderful in that," I remarked; "the old story of the flesh and the spirit, nothing more."

"Perhaps. At least I put faith in queer and unprovable things, for instance in what are called 'soul affinities', and even in the theory that we have lived before. Would you believe that the great lump of British flesh and blood which you see before you developed a 'soul affinity', if that is the right term, with someone I had never met?"

I looked at him doubtfully, reflecting that the hardships through which he had passed had probably touched his brain. He read my mind, for he went on:

"Sounds as though I were a bit cracked, doesn't it? So I thought myself, and should still think, were it not for the fact that I have found this affinity in Africa."

"Where?" I asked lightly. "At Lake Mone?"

"Yes," he replied, "at Lake Mone, where I always expected that I should find her."

I gasped, and felt as though I should like to sit down, which, owing to our hurry, was impossible. Evidently the poor man was rather mad.

"As I have begun it I had better go on with my story, taking things as they happened," he continued in a matter-of-fact voice. "I tell you that in the midst of my wild and rather unedifying career I began to be haunted by visions which came upon me at night."

"Dreams?" I suggested.

"No, always when I was awake and looking at the stars, and generally when I was in the open air. The first, I remember, developed in Trafalgar Square at three in the morning after I had been to a dance."

"The wine is not always very good at those dances, I have been told, or if it is, sometimes one drinks too much of it," I suggested again.

"Quite true, but as it happened this one was given by a relative of mine who is a strict teetotaller and never allows anything spirituous in her house. I had to go to meet my fiancée; it was a terrible affair. When it was over I went for a walk and came to Trafalgar Square, which at that hour was very quiet and lonely. There I stood staring at the Nelson Column, or rather at the stars above it, for it was frosty and they were beautiful that night. Then the thing came. I saw a desolate sheet of water lit up by the moon, an eerie kind of a place. Presently a form, that of a woman draped in white, appeared gliding over the water towards me, floating, not walking. It reached the shore and advanced to where I stood, and I saw that this woman was young and very beautiful, with large, tender eyes.

"She stopped opposite to me, considering me, and a change came over her face as though after long search she had found that which she sought. Looking at her, I too seemed to have found that which I sought. She held out her arms, she spoke to me; distinctly I heard her words, not with my ears but through some inner sense. What is more, I understood one or two of them, though they were in Arabic.

"I have always had a taste for studying out-of-the-way subjects, and it happened that in my medical reading I had become interested in the works of some of the old Arabian physicians, and in order to understand them had found it necessary to master something of the language in which they were written. This was some years before, and I had forgotten most of what I had learned, but not everything. So it came about that I caught the meaning of a sentence here and there—such as these:

"'At last, O long sought. At last upon the earth.' ... 'Not in dreams.' ... 'Follow, follow.' ... 'Far away you will find and remember.' ... 'Yes, there the gates will be opened, the gates of the past and the future.'

"At this point the vision, or whatever you like to call it, came to a prosaic end, for a policeman arrived, eyed me suspiciously, and said:

"'Move on, young gentleman. This ain't no place for the likes of you on a cold night. Go home and sleep it off.'

"I remember that I burst out laughing; the contrast was so ridiculous. Then because my heart was full of a strange joy, such as is described by the old mystics who think that they have been in communication with things Divine, I presented that policeman with half a sovereign, wished him good night, walked away quietly to my rooms in St. James's Place, and went to bed a changed man."

"What do you mean by a *changed man*?" I asked.

"Oh, only that I seemed different in every way. It was as though something had been torn, or a veil had been lifted from my eyes, so that now I saw all sorts of new things; at least the old things took on new aspects. From that moment, for example, I hated the dissipations which had attracted me. I acquired different and higher objectives; I came to know, what doubtless is true, that here in the world we are but wanderers lost in a fog which shuts off glorious prospects, divine realities, so that we can see little except dank weeds hanging from the rocks by which we feel our way, and pebbles shining in the wet beneath our feet. We make crowns of the weeds and fight for the bright pebbles, but the weeds wither, and the pebbles when they are dry prove to be but common slate. The dream woman that I had seen in Trafalgar Square showed me all this, and a great deal more. I was changed! I who had been a greedy caterpillar, devouring all that I could find, in that half-hour in Trafalgar Square became a chrysalis, and then was transformed into a butterfly."

"Most interesting!" I exclaimed, and with sincerity, for notwithstanding Arkle's fine words and metaphors which I found rather difficult to follow, this story did interest me very much. I didn't believe in the Trafalgar Square vision, but, as an American would say, I did hitch on to that transformation which, in our degree, most of us have experienced at one time or another, however impermanent its results may have proved. In some private Trafalgar Square of their own, nearly all have met the Ideal, or the Divine, and in its unearthly light have seen things high and strange; have seen also how petty and how foul are the objects of their temporal desire.

Half an hour later it is probable that they will have forgotten the former, and be hunting the latter even more fiercely than before. Still, they have had the vision, and those to whom such visions came may always hope. They have learned that there are gates in the gross wall that is built about their souls. . . .

"Most interesting," I repeated, "but how about the lady to whom you were engaged? Did you tell her what you had seen and heard in Trafalgar Square?"

"No, I didn't, at least not all of it. The only difference was that whereas I had merely disliked her before, afterwards I detested her, that is, as a prospective matrimonial partner. However, I may add at once that this engagement affair cleared itself up in a most satisfactory fashion. The lady's aversion to me was even more real than mine to her. Also she was rude enough to believe and to tell me she believed that I was mad."

"That was pretty straight, though if you talked to her—well, as you are doing now, not altogether surprising," I said.

"Quite straight, but I respected her for it. Lastly, as I have said, there was a gentleman in the case. Now can you guess what happened?"

"Of course. You broke it off, that's all."

"Not a bit. We didn't dare, for the row in both families would have been too terrific. No, my hated rival was impecunious like my beloved betrothed, whereas I had a good lump of cash at call, which my father had left me. So I lent him £5000—it's more polite to call it lent—and they bolted to Florida to start orange-farming. I need not say that I proclaimed myself broken-hearted and everyone sympathized with me to my face and laughed at me behind my back, almost as heartily as I laughed myself behind their backs. Meanwhile, I studied Arabic like anything, which amused me, as I am rather quick at languages, and took long midnight walks to develop my spiritual side."

"I say," I said doubtfully, "you are not making fun of me, are you, Mr. Arkle?"

"Certainly not. At least I think I am not, for those Abanda have killed my sense of humour. But you shall judge by the sequel. To cut it short, I did seem to come more and more in touch with that lady of the lake. Yes, in those starlit midnight hours she appeared to talk to me more and more as my Arabic improved, and to tell me all sorts of curious things about the past, the very distant past, I gathered, in which we had been intimately connected and taken part in various adventures, some of them tragic and all in their way striking and even beautiful. I will skip these, for what is the use of repeating a lot of old love-affairs that apparently took place in remote ages, only saying that in the last of them at some indefinite date she brought about my death and her own, that we might go to heaven together or rather to a certain star, a crime for which, according to the visions, she is most anxious to make amends. That is why, still according to the visions, she must live in the distant spot where it happened, for as I understand, the experiment did not succeed—I mean that we never got to that star."

"Look here," I said, "all this sounds rather like a nightmare, doesn't it?"

Yet as the words passed my lips, I remembered Kaneke's yarn about his goddess in the lake who was supposed to have descended from heaven and fallen in love with a man. Surely he said that she had killed this man to take him back to heaven with her, which was not allowed. Therefore she waited in the lake until he appeared again, after which I did not gather what was to happen. The legend was of a sort that is not unknown in Central and West Africa, but really it was odd to hear another version of it from Arkle's lips.

"Very much like a nightmare," he assented cheerfully. "Being a doctor I came to the same conclusion, as did some of the most eminent of my profession whom I consulted. One of them asked me if I had spotted the locale of these strange happenings. I replied, yes, somewhere near some mountains in the central parts of Africa that were called Ruga, where, as I believed, no white man had ever been, though I had found them marked on an old map. 'Well,' he replied, with a twinkle in his eye, 'if I were you I should go and look for the lady there. At the worst you will get some good big-game shooting, and I have noticed that people with hallucinations never come to any harm.'

"I thought this an excellent idea, and shortly afterwards I began to work upon my uncle to send me out to Africa to advance the trade interests of the firm. In the end he and the other partners agreed; you see they sympathized with me very much on my matrimonial fiasco and thought that a change would do me good.

"'In such a case,' said my uncle, who has a gift for platitude, 'new countries, new customs, and new faces are most helpful.' I sighed and shook my head, but said that I hoped so."

"How long have you been here?" I asked.

"Oh, I landed on the West Coast about three years ago. It took me a long while to find those confounded Ruga Mountains, and I met with many adventures on the way. However, at last I fetched up all right with about half a dozen coast servants, good men all of them, for the rest of the crowd had bolted at one time or another. And now I come to the interesting part of the story, if you care to hear it."

"Of course I do. Who wouldn't?" I answered. "Go on."

"Well, I had heard of Lake Mone, the holy lake as it is called; right away from the Congo and beyond it, indeed, rumours of this place had reached me. I have told you that I am not bad at languages, and during my first year in Africa, while I was attending to the business of the firm, I also studied local tongues and customs on every possible occasion. Thus I would get servants who could not talk a word of English, and learn from them. Then I began to work my way up country and at every tribe I came to, or rather at every village, I always made a friend of the chief witch-doctor, for the African witchdoctors know everything that is passing for hundreds of miles around them. Indeed often they seem to know more than this, how or why I can't tell."

"That's quite true," I said, thinking of Zikali, "Opener of Roads", the great wizard of Zululand of whom I have told some tales.

"Now," went on Arkle, "I must explain that I was not certain for what I was searching. The visions which I had experienced in England had shown me the desolate lake and a beautiful woman who spoke about the past and our relations together in that past. But beyond saying, or conveying, that it was in Central Africa she had never mentioned the name of the lake, or told me how to get there, and from the moment that I sailed from Liverpool the visions, or whatever they may have been, ceased. In short I was left without any guidance whatsoever.

"It was here that the witch-doctors came in. I explained my case to several of them, and when their mouths were opened by gifts, also by a belief that although my skin was white I was one of their fraternity, they became communicative. They had heard something of a sacred lake that was inhabited by a great fetish, they believed this fetish was a woman; they would inquire. That was the burden of their song. What is more, they did inquire, once or twice by means of drum messages which, as you know, the natives can send over hundreds of miles, but generally in fashions that were dark to me. Also answers came, from which in the end I learned that the lake where the great rain-doctoress dwelt was named Mone, that her title was the *Engoi*, and that she was known among the people round her as Shadow, or The Shadow.

"Following these clues, such as they were, though of course all the while I understood that this *Engoi*, or Shadow, might be quite different from her of whom I had dreamed, I worked my way slowly eastwards and southwards, till at last I came to certain mountains which I was told bordered the country where the *Engoi* lived. Indeed, from the crest of them I was shown this great volcano, or whatever it may be, that we are climbing now, which was declared to be her home. Also, I was informed that between it and me dwelt a fierce and numerous tribe called the Abanda, whose habit it was to kill anyone who set foot within their borders.

"It was here that the last six men who had clung to me struck. They were good fellows, faithful and brave; I never had to do with better. Still, they came in a body and explained that although they feared no man, they did fear wizards and ghosts. The country of the Abanda, and more especially that of the Dabanda beyond it was, they had sure information, full of both, and the stranger who entered there never came out alive, 'even his spirit remained captive after he was dead'. For these reasons they would not go one step farther.

"I saw that it was quite useless to argue, and therefore I made a bargain. The village where this talk took place was inhabited by some very friendly and peaceful agriculturists in country that the Abanda never visited. This was my bargain: that those men should rest here for one year awaiting my return. If at the end of that time I did not appear again or send them further orders, they were to be at liberty to divide my goods and go wherever they liked. These goods, I should explain, are, or were, of some value, trade-stuff of all kinds for presents or barter, rifles, ammunition, clothes, etcetera."

"How did six men manage to carry all these things?" I asked.

"They didn't. After most of my people deserted, by the help of the witch-doctors and chiefs I arranged for their transport from town to town or from tribe to tribe, letting the bearers go back and procuring others when I moved forward. So if I appear no more those six coast men, old soldiers most of them, will be rich, that is if they can get the stuff away."

"Unless they are more honest than most of their kind, I expect that they have done that already," I said, smiling.

"Possibly. I don't know, and to tell the truth I do not much care, because it is improbable that we shall ever meet again. I realized this when I made up my mind to continue the journey to Lake Mone alone."

"Do you mean to say that you tried to do that, Mr. Arkle?"

"Yes, and what is more, I succeeded. No, that isn't true; I did not go quite alone. At the last moment, when I was about to start, a sharp-eyed, wrinkled old fellow turned up, where from no one seemed to know, who said that he was one of the people who lived in the Land of the Holy Lake, whither he wished to return. He said that his name was Kumpana, and that he wanted no reward except my companionship upon the journey. That was all I could get out of him. Of course this sounded fishy enough, but as I was going on anyhow, it did not matter, although my hunters and the chief of the tribe—which, by the way was called Ruga-Ruga, I suppose after the mountains—implored me not to trust myself to such a guide. You see, I knew I should arrive and therefore I wasn't anxious."

"Now I understand what faith is," I said.

"Yes, faith is everything. We are taught that in the Bible, you remember. Well, I started; by the state of the moon it must be a month ago. I took a gun and as much ammunition as I could carry, also a pistol, a hunting-knife, and a few other necessaries, including an extra pair of boots, while the mysterious old fellow, Kumpana, carried the food. I say that he was old, for he looked so, but I should add that he was one of the finest walkers and the best guide that I ever knew.

"In three days, travelling down hill, we came to the country of the Abanda, or rather to its outskirts. They are a numerous people who live on a great plain upon the other side of this mountain, also on its western slope, in a number of unfortified villages, with one central town, which is much bigger than the rest. Their land, consisting chiefly of decomposed lava, is extremely fertile when there is rain, but just now it is suffering from a severe drought which, Kumpana said, though how he knew it I can't tell you, has endured for three years, so that they are almost starving, and consequently in a state of great excitement.

"This drought, he said also, they attribute to the magic of the Dabanda who live over the rim of the mountain, that is in the great crater of the extinct volcano or group of volcanoes. Therefore—if they dared—they would attack these Dabanda and destroy them, in order to occupy their country and become the subjects of their goddess the *Engoi*. But for some strange reason, which Kumpana could not or would not explain, they do not dare."

"I have heard something of that tale—with differences," I said. "Did you meet any of these Abanda?"

"No, not at that time, thanks to Kumpana. But you know what they are like, for yesterday you saw some of them. In point of fact they almost exactly resemble those bearers of yours, who from the look of them might be either Abanda or Dabanda, for the two people are doubtless of one blood and even speak the same dialect of Arabic."

"How did you avoid them?" I asked, making no comment on this statement.

"By lying hidden during the day and travelling at night. As there was no moon visible we must journey by starlight, and even that failed sometimes when mist or cloud came up. But it seemed to make no difference to old Kumpana, who must know the country like a book. On he went up the steep mountain paths, seeing and climbing like a cat in the dark, and leading me by a string tied to his wrist, for we were afraid to speak except in the lowest whisper. Once or twice we passed quite close to villages, so close that we could see the people gathered round the fires. Here our danger was from the dogs, which smelt us and rushed out barking, but fortunately their masters took no notice, thinking, I suppose, that they smelt jackals or hyenas.

"On the third morning we came to the lip of the crater and had no more to fear from the Abanda. Now another danger arose, for the pass, which was nothing but a cleft in the rock, only large enough in places for one man to squeeze through at a time, was occupied by Dabanda watchmen, who of course challenged us, and were much astonished at my appearance, for I think they had never seen a white man. Kumpana they seemed to know (indeed, I believe that they were waiting for him there), for they talked with him in a friendly and deferential fashion, though I was not allowed to hear what they said.

The end of it was that we were detained here for a day and a night while messengers were sent to a body of priests who are called 'The Council of the *Engoi*'.

"At dawn of the following day, that is twenty-four hours after our arrival, these messengers returned, saying that we were to proceed to the chief town upon the edge of the forest that surrounds the lake. So off we went, escorted by some of the Dabandas, through a lovely country, rich beyond imagining, for there had been plenty of rain here. It reminded me of some of the lands that border on the Rhine, and lower down, of those about Naples, and lower still of the South Sea Islands. That is until I came to the deep belt of forest which surrounds the Holy Lake where no man may set his foot."

"Did you see that lake?" I asked.

"Later I saw it and once or twice on the journey I caught a glimpse of it, a black and gloomy sheet of water with an island in its midst. In the evening we came to a large village where the huts or houses, some of them round and some square, were white and stood in gardens. I was taken to a large one of the square variety with a courtyard outside of it, where soon I found I was a prisoner.

"After dark a man visited me. As there was no light in the hut I could not see his face, but he told me that he was a priest of the *Engoi*. Then, in the presence of Kumpana, he cross-examined me sharply as to the reason of my visit, and affected surprise when I answered him in his own tongue—Arabic. I told him all sorts of lies; that I wished to see his country; that I was a white merchant and wanted to open trade; that I desired to learn the wisdom of the Dabanda; and I know not what besides. He replied that by rights I should be burnt alive for sacrilege, but as a white man was expected in the country and possibly I might be that man, the matter must be referred to the *Engoi*. Meanwhile I was to remain a prisoner. If I left the courtyard of the hut I should be seized and burned.

"A prisoner I did remain accordingly. For ten long days I sat about in that horrible hut and high-fenced courtyard, overeating myself, for I was supplied with plenty of excellent food, and driven nearly frantic by doubts and anxieties. I felt that I was close to her whom I had come to see, and yet in a sense farther away than I had been in London years before. No more visitors reached me, nothing happened. At last I drew near to madness. I even thought of suicide—anything to get out of that intolerable hut and courtyard, for I saw, or thought I saw, that I had been the victim of delusions.

"One evening when I was at my worst, Kumpana, my old guide,

who from something the priest said was, I discovered, a person of great importance, came to visit me for the first time for days. He asked me if I had a bold heart and was one who would dare much to satisfy the desire of his heart, and if so, what was that desire. I replied that it was to speak with a certain holy one whom already I had met in dreams, she who was called Shadow and dwelt in a lake. He did not seem in the least surprised, indeed he said he knew that this was so. Then he added:

"'When the moon appears, walk out of the hut boldly towards the darkness of the forest. There you will find those who will guide you. Go with them to the borders of the lake, where perchance "one" will meet you. After that I do not know what may happen. It may be death—understand that it may be death. If you fear this adventure I will guide you back out of the country of the Dabanda, but, then, know that never more, in dreams or otherwise, at least during this life, will you meet her whom you seek. Now choose.'

"'I have chosen,' I answered. 'I go into the forest.'

"'A certain holy one has judged you well. Speak with her if you will, yet beware that you touch her not. Again I warn you to beware,' he said, and bowing left me.

"At the appointed time I walked out of the door of the hut, my rifle in my hand, for my arms had been left to me, perhaps because my captors did not understand their use. The gate of the fence was open and the guards had gone. I went through it and, following a path, came to the edge of the forest. Here beneath the trees the darkness was intense and I stood still, not knowing which way to turn. Shadows glided up to me. Who or what they were I could not see, nor did they speak. They did not touch me, so far as I could feel, yet they seemed to push me along. Surrounded by them I walked forward.

"I confess that I was afraid. It came into my mind that my companions were not human, that they were the spirits of the forest, or ghosts of those long dead returned to their earthly habitations. Their company frightened me; I spoke to them, but there was no answer, only I thought that cold hands were laid upon my lips as though to enjoin silence. Whither was I going in pursuit of a dream that had haunted me for years? Perhaps not to find the lovely woman of that dream, but in her place some blood-stained African fetish, some evil-haunted symbol to which I should be offered as a sacrifice. My blood ran cold at the thought, and I tell you, Mr. Quatermain, that had I known which way to go, I would have turned and fled, for in this last trial my faith failed me.

"But it was too late, and now I must face that risk of death of which the old messenger had warned me.

"In dead silence I went on and on through the endless trees. My hands brushed their trunks, I stumbled over their roots, but I never struck them and I never fell. I could see nothing, could hear nothing except my own footfall. Yes, by a pressure like to that of wind, I was guided and sustained for hour after hour.

"At length we were out of the forest, for I saw the stars and the faint effulgence of the hidden moon, also the gleam of water at my feet. My guides seemed to have left me as though their task was done. I was utterly alone, and the sense of that great solitude appalled my soul.

"What was that upon the waters, just discernible, or perhaps imagined? No, for it glided forward as a canoe glides that drifts in a current, since of oars I heard no sound. It drew near, a magic boat; a white veiled figure stepped upon the shore and stood before me. The veil was drawn, I saw the outline of a face, I saw the starlight mirrored in eyes that gleamed like stars.

"'You have dared much to come, O friend of my heart,' said a sweet voice, speaking in Arabic, 'and I have dared much to bring you here that I might talk with you a little while.'

"'Who and what are you, lady?' I asked.

"'I am one whose soul spoke with you in your great city far away. Ay, and afterwards until I drew you to this land to find me in the flesh. For I know that from of old your destiny and mine have been intertwined, and so it must be till that end which is the real beginning.'

"'Yes, perhaps. Indeed, I think I feel that this is so,' I answered. 'Yet what is your office here, you who live upon a lake surrounded by savages?'

"'For my sins, O Friend, I must play the queen to these savages, and be their oracle.'

"'Are you, then, divine?'

"'Are we not all divine, spirits fallen from on high to expiate our sins and to draw upwards those against whom we have sinned?'

"'I do not know, Lady Shadow—for I suppose that you are she who in this land is known as Shadow—since on this matter the different faiths teach differently. Yet it may well be so, seeing that this world is no happy home for man, but rather a place of bondage and of tears. But let such questions be and tell me first—are you woman?'

"'I am woman,' she answered very softly.

"'Then being woman, why have you called me—a man—to your side from half across the earth?'

"'Because it was so fated, and for the sake of ancient love.'

330

"'And now having heard your call and come and found you in the place of which I dreamed, what must I do to win you?'"

"'Look on me,' she said, 'and having looked, say whether you still wish to win me, and if it is between us as it was in days you have forgotten.'

"She came a little nearer; she loosened that enveloping veil and stood before me, perfect and entrancing. The starlight gathered upon her pure and lovely face; to my fancy it was as though she herself radiated light. She was human and yet a mystery. She was a woman and yet half spirit.

"'Of the past I know nothing,' I said, hiding my eyes with my hand, 'and of the present only that I desire you more than life and all it has to give.'

"'I thank you, and I am glad,' she replied humbly. 'Yet know that I may not be lightly won. Great dangers threaten me and those over whom I rule and whom I must save before I satisfy my soul—and yours. How are you now named in the world?'

"'John Arkle,' I answered.

"'Is it so? Then, O Arkle, you must return over the lip of this mountain, and there find a white man who comes to help us and my people in the war that is at hand. When you have found him and that war is won, we will talk again. Go now. Your guides await you.'

"'I do not wish to go,' I said. 'Let me return with you to where you dwell.'

"She became agitated. I saw her tremble as she answered hurriedly:

"'It is not lawful; first all must be accomplished; that is the price. No, lay no hand upon me, for I tell you we are watched by those you cannot see, and if you touch me I shall find it hard to save you.'

"I heard, but took no heed who was seized with a kind of madness, and forgot Kumpana's warning. I had found one whom I had sought for years. Was I to lose her thus, perhaps for ever? I stretched out my arms and swept her to my breast. I kissed her brow.

"Then came a tumult; it was as though some frightful tempest had broken over us. She was wrenched away and vanished. I was seized and shaken as though by the hands of giants; my senses left me.

"When they returned again—it must have been long afterwards—I was running on the mountain side, hunted by those savages whom you met and drove away."

CHAPTER 12

Kaneke Swears an Oath

Arkle's story came to an end, and I said nothing. Luckily, he did not appear to expect me to speak, for, glancing at him, I saw that he was limping on like one in a dream, his eyes set upon the mountain lip above us as though he were looking over, or rather through it at some vision beyond, and that on his face was a faint, fixed smile such as I have seen upon those of persons under hypnotic influence while they go about the behests of the master of their will.

Evidently the man was not with me. He, or rather his mind, was fixed upon that lake and its mysterious lady, if such a woman lived. Contemplating him I came to the conclusion that he was the victim of hallucination, or to put it bluntly—mad. For years he had been haunted by this dream of a spiritualized maiden who was his twin soul, a very ancient fantasy after all, and one still believed in by thousands.

For it is interesting to imagine that somewhere, in the universe or beyond it, is hidden a counterpart, or rather a complement, of the other sex who exists for us alone and thinks of us alone, he or she from whom Fate has separated us for a while and laid upon us the need to find again in life or death.

Such a dream is always popular because it flatters our human vanity to believe that however lonesome and unappreciated we may seem to be, always somewhere waits that adoring and desiring mate who burns to welcome and to hold us everlastingly.

Without doubt Arkle was subject to this common craze, only in his case, instead of keeping it to himself, as do the more modest, he proclaimed it aloud, as might be expected of one of his robust and sanguine temperament, streaked as it was with veins of inherited mysticism. He had followed his clues, such as they were; he who had dreamed of a lake-goddess, had heard of a holy lake supposed to be presided over by some local and female spirit, and with wonderful

332

courage and resistance he had fought his way half across Africa to the neighbourhood of this place.

Here he had fallen into the hands of a tribe hostile to those who worshipped the water-fetish, or witch-doctoress, or rainmaker (nearly all these African superstitions are connected with rain). Naturally, never having seen a white man before, they seized him and kept him prisoner. Ultimately they determined to kill him, but getting warning of their kind intentions, he made a run for it, and so blundered on to us with his would-be assassins at his heels.

This, I doubted not, was the whole story, all the rest about the visit to the lady who met him on the shores of the lake being pure imagination, or rather dementia. Still it was true that Kaneke told somewhat similar tales—a puzzling fact. Oh, how I wished to heaven that I had never tied myself to this Kaneke by accepting his ivory and cash! But there it was: I had, as it were, signed the note of hand, and must honour the bill.

As a matter of fact, at this very moment an instalment was ripe for discharge.

We had stopped for a few minutes to rest and drink some water from a mountain stream, and eat a few mouthfuls of food. Just as we had finished our hasty meal, Kaneke, who was seated on higher ground fifty yards ahead, turned and beckoned to me to come to him. I went, and when I reached him, without a word he pointed to our left.

I looked, and there, advancing along a fold of the mountain at a considerably higher level than ourselves, just at the foot of the precipitous crater cliff a mile and a half, or perhaps two miles away, I caught sight of glittering specks which I knew must be the points of spears shining in the sun.

"What is it?" I said.

"The Abanda, Lord, coming to block our road, two or three hundred of them. Listen, now. There in that cliff far above us is the only pass on this side of the mountain which runs through the cleft to the crater. The Abanda know that if they can reach the cliff before us we shall be cut off and killed, every one. But if we can reach it before them, we shall win through in safety to my own country, for there they will not follow us. Now it is a race between us as to which of us will first gain the mouth of the pass. See, already I have sent on the bearers," and he pointed to the line of them scrambling up the mountain-side several hundred yards ahead of us. "Let us follow them if you would continue to live."

By this time Arkle, Hans, and the two hunters had joined me. A few words sufficed to explain the situation, and off we went. Then ensued a struggle that I can only describe as fearsome. We who had marched far with little rest were tired; moreover we must climb uphill, whereas the Abanda savages were comparatively fresh and their path though rough lay more or less upon the flat; therefore they could cover twice the distance in the same time. Lastly, Arkle, although so strong, was still stiff and footsore after his race for life upon the yesterday, which delayed his progress. The bearers who, it will be remembered, had the start of us, made wonderful time, notwithstanding their loads; doubtless too they knew the Abanda and what would happen to them if they were overtaken. As we clambered up the mountain-side—heavens! how the sun-scorched lava burned my feet—Hans gasped out:

"A lot of those fellows who were hunting the Bull-Baas, whom I wish we had never met, got away yesterday evening, Baas, and told their brothers, who have come to make us pay for those who didn't get away."

"No doubt," I grunted, "and what's more, I think they will reach the mouth of the pass—if there is one—before us."

"Yes, Baas, I think so too, for the Bull-Baas has a sore heel and walks slowly and that cliff is still some way ahead. But, Baas, the ones who escaped yesterday have told these fellows about what happened to those who didn't escape and what bullets are like. Perhaps we can hold them back with the rifles, Baas."

"Perhaps. At any rate we'll try. Look how fast Kaneke is going."

"Yes, Baas, he climbs like a baboon or a rock-rabbit. He doesn't mean to be caught by the Abanda, Baas, or his porters either, whatever happens to us. Suppose I sent a bullet after him, Baas, before he is out of shot, aiming at his legs to make him go a bit slower."

"No," I answered. "Let the brute run. We must take our chance."

At this moment Arkle, who was growing lamer, called out:

"Quatermain, get on with your servants. I'll look after myself."

"No, you won't," I replied. "We will sink or swim together."

Then I looked at Tom and Jerry and saw that they were alarmed, as well they might be. Hans saw it too, and began to fire sarcasms at them.

"Why don't you run, you brave hunters?" he asked. "Will you let yourselves be beaten by the Owl-man? If the rifles are heavy, you might leave them behind, as you remember you did when the elephants were after us."

Such were his rather bitter jests, for Hans would crack jokes at Death itself. I know that afterwards he regretted them earnestly enough, as we often regret unkind words which it is too late to recall. They stung Tom to fury, for I heard him mutter:

"I'll kill you for this afterwards, yellow man," a threat at which Hans grinned.

The more phlegmatic Jerry, however, only smiled in a sickly fashion and made no reply.

At length we were quite close to the face of the cliff, into which we saw the porters vanishing, showing us where the pass or cleft began. Unfortunately, too, the Abanda were quite close to us; indeed, their leading spearsmen had emerged from the fold in the mountain-side about three hundred yards away on to the open slope of lava, and were racing to cut off Kaneke. That active person, however, was too quick for them, as before they came within spear-cast of him he bolted into the cliff-face like a meer-cat into its hole—perhaps a snake would be a better simile.

"Now we are done," I said. "We can't get there before those brutes and it's no use trying to run down the hill, for they would overtake us. So we had better stay where we are to get our breath and make the best end we can."

"No, Baas," puffed Hans, who had been searching the scene with his hawk-like eyes. "Look. The Abanda are halting. They want to kill us, Baas, but there is a donga between them and the hole in the cliff. See, one of them is beginning to climb down it."

I looked. Although I had not observed it before, because it curved away from us, on our left there was a donga, that is a gully or crack, formed no doubt when the hot lava contracted ages before, which crack the Abanda must cross to reach us.

"Push on!" I cried. "We may beat them yet."

Forward we went, the lame Arkle resting his hand upon my shoulder. Now at last we were near the face of the cliff and, not more than sixty or seventy yards ahead of us, could see the crevice into which Kaneke and his crowd had vanished. Could we reach it? As I wondered an Abanda appeared on this side of the donga. I halted, lifted my rifle, fired, and, so blown was I, missed him. Yes, I missed him clean, for I saw the bullet strike the spear-blade three feet above his head and shatter it to pieces. This seemed to frighten him, however, for he dropped back into the donga, and we pressed on.

When we had all but reached the cleft in the precipice that once had been the lip of the extinct volcano, whence I trusted, quite vainly as it proved, that Kaneke and his people would sally forth to help us, out of the donga appeared six or seven men who rushed between us and the cliff face in which we hoped to refuge.

There they stood preparing to attack us with their spears. We opened fire on them and this time did not miss. They went down, but as they fell more appeared, brave and terrible-looking fellows, furious at the death of their companions. We fired rapidly, forcing our way forward all the while, but I saw that the game was almost hopeless, for every moment more of these Abanda crawled up some narrow ladder or pathway from the bottom of the donga.

Then it was that I heard the Abyssinian hunter Tom call out:

"Run on, Macumazahn, with the lame master. Run on. I see how to stop them."

Without waiting to reflect how he proposed to do this, for at such moments one has little time to think; with Arkle leaning on my shoulder and Hans at my side, I charged forward to the mouth of the cleft. Certain of the Abanda were between us and it, but with this we managed to deal with the help of our revolvers before they could stab us. Thus we reached the cleft and plunged into it, for, to my relief, no more Abanda appeared. Once in the mouth of the place, which was very narrow, so narrow and twisted that a few men could have held it against a thousand, as Horatius and his two companions held the bridge in the old Roman days, I stopped, for I heard firing still going on outside.

"Who is shooting?" I asked, peering about me in the gloom of that hole, and as I spoke the echoes of the last shot died away and were followed by a savage yell of triumph.

"Little Holes and Jerry, I believe, Baas," answered Hans, wiping his brow with his sleeve, "though I do not think they will shoot any more. You see, Baas, for once in their lives they behaved very nicely. Yes, they ran to the edge of that donga and stuffed themselves into the mouths of the two paths by which these Abanda are climbing up it, firing away until they were speared, thus giving you and the Bull-Baas time to get into this hole, for of course they did not care what happened to me who was their friend. So I suppose that they are now dead, although perhaps they may have been taken alive."

"Great heavens!" I exclaimed. Then after a moment's reflection, in spite of the remonstrances of Hans (at the moment Arkle was ahead of us), I crept back to the mouth of the cleft and looked out, taking the risk of being speared.

He was right. Yonder on the lava plateau lay the bodies of Tom and Jerry, dragged there by the Abanda, one of whom was engaged in cutting off poor Jerry's head with a spear.

Filled with grief and fury, I put a bullet through that savage, which caused them all to scuttle back into their donga. Then, before they could recover from their surprise, followed by Hans I rushed out, seized Tom's rifle which one of them had been carrying and let fall in his fright, and bolted back with it into the mouth of the cleft. That of Jerry unfortunately we could not recover. I suppose it was carried away.

That was the end of those two brave but ill-fated hunters who, from the first day of our journey, had seemed to walk in the shadow of approaching doom. It was a very gallant end, for without doubt they had given their lives to save us, or rather to save me.

This indeed they had done, for by blocking the two exits of the steep-sided donga for a few minutes, they had enabled us to fight our way through into the cleft. Whether their courage was spontaneous, or whether it was induced by a sense of their previous failure when they had thrown away their guns, a trivial incident that seemed to prey upon their minds, and by the gibes of Hans, I do not know. At least in this moment of trial it asserted itself, with the result that they died and we lived. All honour to their memory! One of my hopes is that in some place and time unknown I may be able to thank them face to face.

I returned into the cleft filled with sorrow and told the others what had happened. Hans, to do him justice, when he saw that his guess—it was nothing more—had come true and that Tom and Jerry were really dead, was also much distressed. He began to talk of their many virtues and to rejoice that they, like himself, were "good Christians", and therefore had nothing to fear in the "Place of Fires", his synonym for heaven, which doubtless they were now inhabiting. Perhaps also his conscience smote him a little for all the sharp things which jealousy had caused him to say about them while they remained upon earth.

Arkle's attitude was different.

"These hunters," he said, "have died doing their duty, and therefore are not to be pitied, for how can one make a better end? But what of that fellow Kaneke, who ran ahead with his men and deserted you, his companions? I say nothing of myself, for I am a stranger towards whom he had no obligations. Why did he bolt?"

"I don't know," I answered wearily, "to save his skin, I suppose. You had better ask him if we ever meet again."

"I will!" exclaimed Arkle, and as he spoke I noted that his face was white with rage.

Soon the opportunity came. We thought it unwise to remain so near to the mouth of the cleft, although none of the Abanda so far had attempted to follow us, why, I could not imagine at the time, though it is true Kaneke had said it would be so. Therefore I suggested that we had better go on and find out whither the road led.

On we went accordingly, a darksome journey at first, for little light reached us in that deep and narrow hole. Presently, however, it widened and we found ourselves upon a kind of plateau bordered by cliffs.

Here Kaneke was waiting for us seated on a rock, the bearers having gone on; at any rate I could see nothing of them. He stared at us with his sombre eyes and said to me:

"Knowing that you would be safe, Lord, I entered this passage before you and have waited for you here, where the Abanda will not follow us."

"So I see," I said sarcastically, "but pray, how did you know that we should be safe?"

"I knew it, Lord, because it is written in your stars, as I knew that the two hunters would die because I saw death in their stars; and they are dead, are they not? As for the fate of the strange white man," and he looked at Arkle—malevolently, I thought—"I knew nothing, for I have not yet had time to study it in the heavens."

Before I could answer Arkle broke in, speaking very quietly in a low, fierce voice.

"No, you knew nothing, dog that you are, but I think that you hoped much, for you believed that to save himself this white lord would desert me who am lame, as you did, and that I should be speared. Well, I can read stars better than you, and I tell you that you will die before I shall and that what you lose I shall gain. Do you understand me?—you who hope to be Chief of the Dabanda and Lord of the Lake with its Treasure, as I learned before ever I set eyes on you."

How had he learned this? I wondered. At the moment I could not guess, but it was quite obvious to me, watching him, that Kaneke understood these dark words better than I did, for their effect upon him was remarkable. First he turned pale, or rather a kind of dirty white, as though with fear, a mood that was followed at once by one of fury. His big eyes rolled, foam appeared at the corners of his mouth, the hair of his face seemed to bristle.

"I know you," he cried, pointing to Arkle, "and why you have come here. Long ago my spirit warned me concerning you and your purpose. You hope to rob me again, as once you robbed me in the past, though that you have forgotten. For this reason I bribed the white hunter Macumazahn to accompany me here, knowing that without his help I was doomed to perish. But Fate has played me an evil trick. It was revealed to me that I should reach the land before you and be ready to make an end of you; revealed falsely, for while I tarried you came—you, the white thief. Still there is time. Never again shall you look upon the Treasure of the Lake."

As he hissed out these last words, suddenly Kaneke drew knife, a hideous curved knife of the Somali sort, and sprang at Arkle. He sprang swiftly as a lion on a drinking buck, and it flashed through my mind that all was over. Standing at a little distance with Hans, I could do nothing; there was no time, not even to draw a pistol; nothing except watch the end. It came, but in a strange fashion.

Arkle must have been waiting and ready. He did not move; he only stretched out his arms. Next instant, with his left hand he gripped the right arm of Kaneke, which was raised for the blow, and twisted it with such a grasp of iron that the knife fell to the ground. With his right he seized him by the throat and shook him as a mongoose shakes a snake. Then, putting out all his strength which in truth was that of a bull, Arkle loosed Kaneke's throat, gripped him in his arms, lifted him from his feet, and hurled him away so that he fell to the rocky ground, striking it with his back, and lay there senseless.

At this moment a little withered, keen-eyed man whom I had never seen before appeared from round a corner and, running across the open space to Arkle, whispered rapidly into his ear after the fashion of one who gives instructions. For quite a long time, or so it seemed to me, he whispered thus, while now and again Arkle nodded, showing that he understood the meaning of what he heard. At last the old fellow uttered a warning exclamation and pointed to Kaneke who, I saw, was recovering from his swoon. Then he ran back across the open space towards the corner of the cleft whence he had appeared, and for a minute I lost sight of him in its shadow.

Arkle picked up the knife, and, springing forward, set his foot upon the breast of Kaneke, who was trying to rise.

"Now, dog," he said, "shall I treat you as you would have treated me? I think it would be wisest. Or will you swear an oath?"

"I will swear," muttered Kaneke, fixing his eyes upon the knife.

"Good. Kneel before me."

Kaneke scrambled stiffly to his knees, and at this moment Hans nudged me and pointed. I looked and saw that from the corner of the cleft where the old man had vanished on the farther side of the open space, were advancing a number of the Dabanda, led, I think, by some of our bearers who no doubt had summoned them. They were tall, big-eyed men of the same type as Kaneke and the Abanda who had attacked us; by no means naked savages, however, as every one of them wore a long garment, apparently of linen, for the most part white in colour, though in some instances these robes had been dyed blue.

"Keep your rifle ready," I said to Hans, and waited developments.

If these men had meant to attack us—which I do not think—the strange sight before them caused them to abandon the idea, for all their attention seemed to be concentrated upon Kaneke kneeling at the white man's feet.

Arkle saw them also and called out in his big, booming voice:

"Welcome, Kumpana, and you, men of the Dabanda, guardians of the Treasure of the Lake. You come in a good hour. Listen now, while this Kaneke who I hear is a great one among you swears an oath of allegiance to me, the white wanderer from beyond the seas. Learn that but now he tried to murder me, springing at me with this knife to take me unaware, and that I overthrew him and spared his life. I say listen to the oath—and do you, O Snake Kaneke, repeat in a loud voice the words that I shall speak, so that all may hear them and make them known to the people of the Dabanda, the guardians of the Treasure of the Lake. Repeat them, I say, for if you refuse, you die."

Then he began thus, doubtless as Kumpana had taught him, and sentence by sentence Kaneke echoed his words:

"I, Kaneke, of the people of the Dabanda, tried treacherously to murder you, the white man from beyond the seas, but, being strong, you overcame me and gave me my life. Therefore I, Kaneke, bow myself to you henceforth, as your servant. All my rights and place among the Dabanda I give over to you. Where I stood, there you stand; henceforward my blood is in your body and all that comes to me with this blood is yours. So I swear by the *Engoi*, the Shadow that rests upon the holy lake, and if I break the oath in word or deed, may the curse of the *Engoi* fall upon me."

All of this Kaneke repeated readily enough until he came to the words "So I swear by the *Engoi*", at which he jibbed, and indeed stopped dead.

"Continue," said Arkle, but he would not.

"As you will," went on Arkle, "but understand that if you refuse, you die, as a murderer deserves to do," and, bending down, he seized Kaneke by the hair with his left hand, preparing to cut off his head with the curved Somali knife.

Now Kaneke, evidently in a great fright, appealed to me.

"O Lord Macumazahn," he cried, "save my life, I pray you!"

"Why should I?" I answered. "Just now you deserted me and my people, so that my two brave hunters are dead. Had you with the bearers stayed behind to fight with us, I think that they would not have been dead—but this you can talk over with them in that land whither you are going. Again, you tried to murder the white lord for reasons which I do not understand, and after you had sworn to me that you would not harm him. By his strength he overthrew you, and now your life is justly forfeit to him. Yet out of the greatness of his heart he offers to spare you if you will swear a certain oath to him upon a certain name. You refuse to swear that oath upon that name. So what more is there to be said?"

By this time, although he had not seen them, for his back was towards them and they remained silent, watching these proceedings with a kind of fascinated stare, evidently Kaneke remembered that Arkle had addressed some of the Dabanda people, who must therefore be present. To these he made his next appeal, calling out:

"Help me, O my brothers, you over whom I have been appointed to rule. Would you see me done to death by this white wanderer who comes to our land for no good purpose? Help me, O Guardians of the Holy Lake and of the Shadow that rests upon the lake."

"Yes," said Arkle. "Come forward, you Dabanda, laying down your spears, for know that he who first lifts a spear shall be dealt with by the Lord Macumazahn. Come forward, I say, and judge between me and this man."

To my astonishment those Dabanda obeyed. They laid down their spears, every one of them, and advanced to within a few paces of us, led by the little withered old man with keen eyes, who moved as lightly and silently as does a cat, the same man who had whispered into Arkle's ear. Arkle looked at this man and said:

"Greeting, Kumpana, my friend and guide. I thank you for the counsel you gave to me but now, for I know you to be wise and great among your people and it was you who taught me all that I have learned of them and of this Kaneke. Judge now between me and him. You have heard the story. According to your custom, is not this man's life forfeit to me whom he strove to murder?"

"It is forfeit," answered Kumpana, "unless he buys it back with the oath which you have demanded of him."

"And if he swears that oath, must he not, under it, become my servant and give to me his place, his power, and his rights among the Dabanda?"

"That is so, White Lord."

"And if he swears it and breaks the oath, what then, Kumpana?"

"Then, Lord, you can loose upon him the curse of the *Engoi*, and it will surely be fulfilled. Is it not so, Dabanda?"

"It is so," they assented.

"You have heard, Kaneke; yes, out of the lips of your own people you have learned their law. Choose now. Will you swear, or will you die?"

"I swear," said Kaneke hoarsely, as the sharp knife—his own—approached his neck. "I swear," and slowly he repeated those words which before he had refused to speak, transferring all his rights and privileges to Arkle and calling down upon his own head the curse of the *Engoi* if he should break the oath. I noticed that as he invoked this fate upon himself, the man shivered, and reflected that after all there might be something in the curse of the *Engoi*, or that he believed there was. Indeed, sceptical as I am, I began to feel that all this queer story had more in it than I had hitherto imagined, and that I was coming to the heart of one of those Central African mysteries of which most white men only learn in the vaguest fashion, perhaps from prejudiced and unsympathetic sources, and then often enough but by obscure hints and symbolical fables.

The oath finished, Kaneke kissed the white man's foot, which I suppose was part of the ceremony, and strove to rise. But forcing him to his knees again, Arkle addressed the little withered old man who stood watching all.

"Tell me," he said, "who and what are you, Kumpana?"

"Lord, though I until now have hid it from you, I am the head of the Council of the Shadow, he who rules in this land when the Shadow has passed from the world and before she returns again."

"Are you then he who weds the Shadow, Kumpana?"

"Nay, Lord. He who is called Shield of the Shadow dies when the Shadow passes. I am but a minister, an executor of decrees. As such I led you to this land, whence you were hunted because you would not be obedient, but broke the law. Mighty must be the strength that guards you, or by now you would be dead."

"If I have erred, O Kumpana, I have paid the price of error. Am I, then, forgiven?"

"Lord, I think that you are forgiven, as this Kaneke, who also erred in his youth in a worse fashion, was forgiven, or rather," he added, correcting himself, "suffered to go unpunished."

"Who and what is Kaneke?" Arkle asked again.

"Kaneke is he who was destined to be the Shield of the Shadow when she appears to rule for her appointed day. For his sin against the *Engoi* he was driven from the land and lived far off, where the white lord who is called Watcher-by-Night found him. At the proper time he was ordered back that his fate might be fulfilled, and returned bringing the white lord, Watcher-by-Night, with him, as also was decreed. The rest you know."

"Kaneke tried to murder me and bought his life by a certain oath, selling to me his place and rights. Shall I then be known and named Shield of the Shadow in place of this Kaneke?"

"It would seem so, Lord," answered Kumpana, a little doubtfully as I thought. "But first the matter must be submitted to the Council of the Shadow, of which I am only one. It may be," he added after a pause, "that the Council will call upon you to buy the Shadow at a great price."

Then I, Allan, took up my parable, saying:

"Kumpana and men of the Dabanda, I, a white hunter, have been led, or trapped, into a land that is full of mysteries which as yet I do not understand. I have rescued this white lord when he was about to be killed. I have brought him here, fighting my way through warriors who seemed to be your enemies. In so doing I have lost two servants of mine, brave men whom I loved, who came to their deaths by the treachery of yonder Kaneke and therefore my heart is sore. He deserted us, hoping that in like fashion I should desert the other white lord who is lame, that thereby I might save my life. I did not desert him, and you have seen the end of that story. Now we are all weary, and sad because of the death of the two hunters who sacrificed themselves for us; hungry also, needing food and rest and sleep. The white lord whom you name Wanderer has made his bargain with you, a strange bargain which bewilders me. I would make mine, which is simpler. If I and my servant here, the yellow man, come on into your country, have we peace? Do you swear by the *Engoi*, who seems to be your goddess, and by the Shadow her priestess, that no harm shall come to us and that when I desire it in the future, I shall be helped to leave your country again, you giving me all that I may need for my journey? If you do not swear, then I turn and go back whence I came, if Heaven permits me to do so."

Kumpana spoke with some of his companions. Then he said:

"O Macumazahn, Watcher-by-Night, we swear these things to you by the *Engoi*. At least we swear that after you have finished the service, to work which we caused you to be brought hither, then you shall be sent hence in safety as you demand."

I reflected to myself that this promise was vague and qualified. Yet remembering that I should certainly extract none more favourable and being thoroughly worn out and quite unfit to face the Abanda who probably were waiting outside, I accepted it for what it was worth, and requested Kumpana to lead us to where we could eat and rest in safety.

CHAPTER 13

Before the Altar

By the time that we emerged from the pass, that really was nothing but a cleft or crack zigzagging through the lava rock of the volcano's lips, which we did in complete safety, seeing no more of the Abanda, it was drawing towards evening and the plain beneath us was flooded with the light of the westering sun. It was a very wonderful plain, though, except for its size, of a sort not uncommon in the immense wilds of Africa. Looking at it stretching away for miles and miles, it was difficult to realize that it was nothing but the crater of some huge volcano, or group of volcanoes, which millions of years ago had been a lake of seething fire. Yet undoubtedly this was the case, for all round ran the precipice of rock that once had formed the wall of the outer crater. Now this wall enclosed a vast expanse of fertile land that sloped gently down to the confines of a forest.

Nor was that all, for from this height we could see that within the ring of forest, at the bottom of the crater-pit as it were, lay a great sheet of water, the holy lake that was named Mone. It looked handsome and terrifying enough at this hour when the tall forest trees that grew around cut off from its surface the light of the sinking sun, such a place as might well be the home of mysteries.

At that time, however, I was too tired to study scenery or indulge in speculations, and glad enough I felt when we were led to a kind of rest-house, or perhaps it was a watchman's shelter, that was hidden away in a grove of mountain palms. This place consisted of a thatched roof supported upon tree-trunks and enclosed with a fence of what looked like dried bulrushes, which formed the walls of the house. It was clean, comfortable, and airy; moreover there must have been a cooking-place outside, for hot food was brought to us, of which I ate thankfully, being too exhausted to inquire its nature or whence it came.

Only one thing did I ask of Kumpana—whether it was necessary to set a guard. When he assured me that we were absolutely safe, I took him at his word and went to sleep, hoping for the best. I remember reflecting as my eyes closed that for some reason or other, humble individual as I was, I seemed too valuable to these people for them to wish to make away with me. So having ascertained that Kaneke was elsewhere, I just turned in and slept like a dog that has hunted all day, and I believe that Arkle did likewise.

When I woke the sun was high and Arkle had gone. I asked Hans what had become of him, saying that I feared foul play.

"Oh no, Baas," answered Hans. "You see that Baas Red-Bull, having conquered Kaneke, and bought his birthright from him in exchange for not sticking him like a pig—just like the man in the Bible, Baas—is now a great chief. So because he is lame those Dabanda brought a litter in which they set him and have carried him off. He told me to tell you that he did not wake you up because you were so tired, but that you would meet again at their head place, which is called Dabanda-town, Baas. Meanwhile you were to fear nothing."

"Which means that he has deserted us," I said.

"Oh no, Baas, I think not; I think he went because he was obliged, and that we shall find him later on. You see, Baas, the Baas Red-Bull has become a priest and a chief, and such people are never their own masters. They seem to rule spirits and men, but really these rule them and order them about as they like. For the rest, Kumpana stays here to guard us, and breakfast is coming, so let us eat and be happy while we may, Baas."

The advice was good and I acted upon it at once. After a wash at the spring by which the rest-house was built, I ate an excellent breakfast, a stew of kid's flesh with quails in it, I remember it was, made memorable by the fact that after it Hans produced a skin bag full of excellent tobacco. On inquiry it appeared that the Dabanda grew this herb, and what is more, smoked it in cigarettes made of the soft sheath which covers the mealie cobs. Also, like the Bantu, they took it in the form of snuff.

By the way, what an interesting study would be that of the history of tobacco in Africa. Is it indigenous there, or was it perhaps introduced from some other land by the Arabs, or later by the Portuguese? I don't know, but I remember how delighted I was to see it upon this occasion, when ours was exhausted and the spare supply a bearer carried in a box was discovered to have got wet in crossing a river and to be nothing but a mass of stinking mould. Some people inveigh against the use of tobacco, but to my mind it is one of the best gifts that Heaven has given to man.

Just as I had lit my pipe with delight and was testing the sample, which proved to be sweet and cool though rather strong, Kumpana arrived and asked if I was ready to start. I said yes, and off we went with a guard of ten Dabandas, marching downhill in the direction of the forest.

Now I saw that this vast crater was a wondrous and a most beautiful place, though it is true that its climate is hot. For the most part it was lightly timbered with large trees, a species of mahogany, many of them, mixed with cedars, growing in groups or singly, and interspersed with grassy glades after the fashion of some enormous park. Among these trees wandered great quantities of game; thus I saw eland, koodoo, sable-antelope of a very large variety, and blue wildebeest, to mention a few of them, also bush-buck of a bigger kind than I had ever found anywhere in Africa.

It seemed, however, that the elephant and the rhinoceros did not live here; nor, strange to say, were there any lions, which perhaps accounted for the great number of the various species of buck. The birds, too, were numerous and beautiful; and everywhere I noted lovely butterflies, some of which, of a brilliant blue colour, were of great size and flew high and as fast as swallows. In short, so far as its natural conditions were concerned, after the arid plains beyond the mountains, the place was a kind of earthly paradise; well watered, also, by little streams that came from springs and ran down fern-clad ravines towards the lake.

As we went I talked with Kumpana, who, outwardly at any rate, proved to be a most agreeable and candid old gentleman. From him I gathered much information, true or false. Thus I learned that his people were really star-worshippers, as were the Abanda who lived without the mountain, and knew a good deal of crude astronomy.

It seemed that originally the Abanda and the Dabanda were one race, but that "thousands of years ago", as he put it, they were ruled by two brothers, twins, who quarrelled. Then ensued a civil war, in the course of which one brother murdered the other treacherously. This angered the *Engoi* of that day, whom both of them aspired to wed; indeed, this was the cause of their difference. She called down the curse of heaven upon the murderer and those who clung to him, divorcing them from her worship and causing them to be driven (whether by force of arms or by supernatural means, I could not discover) out of the earthly paradise of the crater on to the mountain slopes and plains beyond.

From that time forward, Kumpana explained, the Abanda had sought reunion with the goddess, both because of the material benefits they believed to be in her gift, such as rain and plenty, and for some spiritual reason that had to do with the fate of their souls after death. This, however, they had never achieved, since the curse upon them continued from age to age. Indeed, the prophecy was that their desire could not be fulfilled until a high priest of the *Engoi*, the husband or the affianced of the Shadow, she who was also called "the Treasure of the Lake" came to lead them back into the land of the Dabanda and made peace between them and the *Engoi* incarnate in the priestess known from generation to generation by the name of "Shadow", who, from birth till death, dwelt on the island in the holy Lake Mone. Until that hour, went on Kumpana, none of the Abanda dared to attempt to re-enter Mone-land, as the country encircled by the crater's walls was called.

"Why not, if they are so brave and numerous?" I asked, astonished.

"Because, Lord, if they did the curse would fall upon them and they would perish miserably, I know not how. At least, so they believe, as we do; and it is for this reason that from the moment you entered the pass of the cliff yesterday, you were safe. Had it been otherwise the Abanda would have followed you and killed you in the pass, for they were many and you were few. For this reason, too, we do not so much as guard that path and certain others."

Hearing this I reflected, first that I liked not the security. For what was the sum of it? That a vast horde of savages, or semi-savages, who believed themselves to have been driven out of a kind of Garden of Eden by the flaming sword of a heavenly curse, although they were much more numerous and stronger than those who still dwelt in the Garden, and although the gates of that garden stood open, dared not enter them because they were sure that if they did so, the invisible sword of the curse that always hung over them would smite and destroy them.

Still, there seemed to be truth in the story, for otherwise why were we not followed into the unguarded cleft? Doubtless the Abanda were frightened of our firearms, but seeing that we were but three men against hundreds, this was not enough to have held them back. No, the mighty hand which restrained them must, as Kumpana declared, have been that of spiritual fear.

Oh, what a force is superstition; as I sometimes think, the greatest in the whole world, or at any rate in Africa. So mighty is it that when I contemplate its amazing power, at times I wonder whether in many of its developments it is not rooted deep in the soil of unappreciated and unknown truths.

Of these reflections of mine, however, I said nothing to my companion, because I thought it wiser to be silent. Yet I did ask him—if he felt at liberty to tell me and had the necessary knowledge—what part I and Arkle, whom he called The Wanderer, had in all this business.

To my astonishment, instead of refusing to answer the question or thrusting it aside as natives can, he replied quite frankly that he did not know, or at any rate knew very little.

"The stars guide us, Lord," he said. "We consult them, as our fathers have done from the beginning; we read their messages and obey their commands. Long ago the stars told us, speaking through the mouth of her who is named Shadow, not she who rules today, but she who went before her and has been gathered to the heavens, that in this year a great war would fall upon us—we do not know what war. More recently we were told, through the mouth of that Shadow who has faded, to call back Kaneke from the land where he dwelt because of his crime against her, that he might bring with him a certain white man whose name was your name, namely Watcher-by-Night. This command was sent to Kaneke and he obeyed it, as he must do or die; for if he disobeyed, the messenger was commanded to bring death upon him, as she was commanded, if he obeyed, to protect him from all dangers. That is all we know of the reason of your coming, though now I see that if you had not come the other white lord would have been killed."

Reflecting that this tale about myself was, with variations, much the same as that told by Kaneke, something real enough to these people, but to me a mystery, and wondering if by any chance this fate-dealing messenger was White-Mouse, I left the subject and attacked one of more immediate interest, namely that of Arkle, saying outright:

"The white lord Wanderer told me that you, Kumpana, met him beyond the country of the Abanda and guided him into your own land. Why did you do this?"

Kumpana's face changed; it was as though a veil fell over his eyes and mild, intelligent features, a veil of secrecy.

"Lord," he answered, "there are matters of which it is scarcely lawful that I should speak, even to you who have come here to be our friend. I would have you understand that we Dabanda are not as other folk. We are a small people and an ancient who live by wisdom, not by strength, and this wisdom comes to us from heaven. We worship the stars, or rather the Strength beyond the stars, and from them come spirits who teach us through the mouth of the Lake-Dweller, Shadow, or otherwise, much that is not known even to the wise of the earth, such as yourself, Lord. They give us gifts of vision also, so that at times we can see into the darkness of the past, and even look beneath its curtain into the light of the future that blinds the eyes of other men.

"Moreover we, or some of us, have certain powers over Nature. Death indeed we must suffer like all who live. Yet we know that it is not death; that it is but a door of darkness through which we pass to another house of flesh, a better or a worse house according to our deserts, that is yet inhabited by the same spirit. So, too, we have strength over beasts" (here I bethought me of Kaneke and the elephants), "which we can cause to obey us as though they were our dogs. You smile. Then, look upon those buck," and he pointed to a bunch of blue wildebeests, which I have always found wild and savage creatures, that were staring at us from among some trees about a hundred and fifty yards away. "Now I will call them, that you may believe."

Well, stepping a few paces to my right, call them he did, uttering cries in a kind of sing-song voice. The wildebeests seemed to listen. Then presently they moved slowly towards us, and soon were standing within a few yards of Kumpana, as cows might do that are waiting to be milked. There they stood, patient and submissive, until they caught my wind, when they snorted, whisked their tails, put down their heads and, to my great alarm, prepared to charge me. Just as Hans and I were about to fire to keep them off, Kumpana said something and waved his hands, as a beast-tamer does to his performing animals, whereon those gnus turned and gambolled off in their well-known lumbering fashion.

"They are no wildebeests, Baas," whispered Hans to me. "Like the elephants, they are men wearing the shape of brutes."

"Perhaps," I answered, for I was too mystified to argue; also Kumpana was speaking again, saying:

"Now mayhap you will believe me when I tell you that we have power over the animals, who are as our brothers and not to be harmed by us; so much power that we have driven those of them that can hurt men, such as lions, from our land; yes, and evil reptiles also. Search where you will here, Lord, you will find no snakes," a statement which caused me to reflect that St. Patrick must have bequeathed his mantle to the Dabanda. "Thus, too," he went on, "we control sicknesses, summon rain, and hold off tempests, which is why we are reported to be a people of wizards."

"If so," I replied, "all this does not tell me why the white man Wanderer was guided by you and why afterwards he was driven away, as it seemed, to death."

"I guided him, Macumazahn, because I was so commanded, and because he is appointed to play a great part in our history, as once

before he did in the past. He was driven away because he was diso-
bedient and suffered folly to master him, for which causes he must be
punished and learn the taste of terror. Ask me no more concerning
this lord, for I cannot answer you. Yet it may happen that before all is
done you will learn the answer for yourself."

Now I proposed, in my thirst for information, to put some questions to him concerning the wondrous woman, or sacred personage
who was said to dwell in the lake, and who, as I suspected, was an
African version of the old legend of the Water-Spirit which is to be
found in many lands. But when I mentioned her name of Shadow,
Kumpana turned upon me with so fierce a look in his eyes, hitherto
mild enough, that I grew silent.

"Lord Macumazahn," he said, "I see that you do not believe in
our priestess, the Shadow of the *Engoi* whom we worship. Though
you have never said so to me, it is written on your face. That is to be
understood, for white men, I have heard, can be very ignorant and
scornful of faiths that are not their own. Yet I pray you do not make a
mock of her to me, as I am sure you were about to do. I have answered
all your other questions as best I might, but as to her I answer none.
Nay, of her you must learn for yourself"; and before I could reply or
explain, he departed to join the guard, leaving me alone with Hans.

"Baas," said that worthy, "you are always seeking new adventures and
strange peoples, and this time I think you have found both. These folk
are all wizards, Baas, like Kaneke, and we are caught in their web, where
I expect they will suck us dry. I think the Baas Red-Bull is a wizard
also, for otherwise why was he not killed; and unless he is one of their
brothers, why are these Dabandas so glad to see him? Also, how did he
learn so quickly all that oath which he made Kaneke swear? Then there
was White-Mouse who, I am sure, was a witch, though a very pretty
one, for otherwise how could she have deceived me, Hans, as she did,
making me believe all sorts of things that were not true, such as that she
was a jealous wife of Kaneke who liked me for myself? Oh, we have
come into a land of spells where the fierce wildebeests are as dogs and
the passes are held by ghosts, and I do not think we shall ever get out of
it alive, Baas, unless indeed, for their sport they turn us into animals, like
elephants and the wildebeests and hunt us hence."

Now I remembered that Tom and Jerry had talked in this fashion,
with good reason in their case; and looked at Hans doubtfully, fearing
lest he might have caught the infection. However, this was not so, for
as is common with primitive men of mercurial nature, suddenly his
mood changed, and, grinning, he said:

"Yet, Baas, though White-Mouse did blind me for a little while, these wizards will have to be very clever if they hope to deceive Hans, who is such a good Christian that he can defy the devil and who, moreover, has the reverend predicant, your father, for his friend and guide. Cheer up, Baas, for I think I shall bring you through safely, if only you will be guided by me and not let that Shadow woman make a fool of you, as White-Mouse did. Yes, yes, everything may still be well, and after all, perhaps those wildebeests were just tame buck like some that the Scotchman kept on his farm near Durban which used to come and feed out of his hand."

"Yes," I said, "no doubt they were tame, and I don't believe in the magic. Still, I should like to know what has become of the Baas Arkle."

Well, we walked on all day through that most lovely land, until towards evening we came upon patches of cultivated ground and drew near to the edge of the forest, where I saw that there was a town.

It was a straggling place and quite unprotected; just a number of neat houses built of whitened clay and thatched with palm-leaves, or in some cases, having flat roofs of lime cement, standing, each of them, in a garden of its own on the borders of wide roads or streets. In short, this Dabanda town had nothing in common with the crowded cities, if they may be so called, which exist in Nigeria and elsewhere. It was just a sparsely populated village, such as may be seen by scores in certain districts of Eastern and Central Africa.

"If this is their big kraal, these Dabanda are but a little people, Baas," said the observant Hans.

I agreed with him. As I had noted during our march, their crater-land was wide and most fertile, but until we approached the town I saw few signs of cultivation. Here and there on the track that ran to the pass were two or three huts surrounded by gardens. Nor in these outlying districts were there many domestic animals; they were almost entirely occupied by wild game. Near the town, however, we did see herds of cattle of a small breed, also flocks of long-haired goats. Clearly the Dabanda, so far as numbers were concerned, must have been but an insignificant tribe, relying for their protection upon moral forces rather than those of arms, a fact that seemed to bear out some of Kumpana's statements as to the reason why the passes were left unfortified.

We entered the main street of the town which began nowhere in particular, and walked down it without exciting much attention. Occasionally a woman stared at us from the door-way of her house, or an old man stopped his work in a garden to see who the passers-by might be. Also from time to time a few grave-faced children, three or four perhaps, followed us for a little way, then stopped and returned whence they came. This I thought strange, for they could never before have seen a white man, except perhaps Arkle. But then everything about the Dabanda was strange; evidently they were a folk apart, one of whose characteristics was a lack of curiosity.

To tell the truth, they gave me the impression of people living in a dream, or under a spell, human in form and mind, yet lacking some of the human attributes; lotus-eaters who felt no need for energy or effort, because Nature fed them and they were, or considered themselves to be, god-guarded. Such was my first impression of these Dabanda, which in the main was confirmed by what I saw and learned of them in after days. I should add that they were all extremely good-looking, men and women together, but very like one another, as though from continual in-breeding; remarkable, too, for their fine-cut features, light-coloured skin like to that of half-castes or Persians, straight hair and large, sleepy, owl-like eyes, of which I observed the pupils seemed to grow bigger after nightfall, as do those of certain animals that seek their food by night.

The long, wide street ended in an open area that for want of a better name I will call a market-place, where the ground was levelled and trodden hard. At intervals round half this area stood houses of a larger size than those that we had passed, occupied, as I guessed rightly, by the chief men of the tribe, with their wives and children, if they had any. The other half of the area was bounded by a dense forest formed of tall and solemn trees, which forest ran down to the borders of the lake that, as I had judged from my view of it from the higher land, lay at a distance of several miles from the town. In the centre of this open space stood three curious erections; two pointed towers of rough stone, fifty or sixty feet high perhaps, with spiral stairways winding round them to their tops, and between these a large platform twenty feet or so in height, that looked like the base of an uncompleted pyramid, on which platform burned a fire.

"What are those, Baas?" asked Hans.

"Watch-towers," I answered.

"What is the good of towers whence one can see nothing except the sky?" asked Hans again.

Then I guessed their real object. They were observatories, and the truncated pyramid was a great altar where priests gathered and offered sacrifices. Of this I had little doubt, though I wondered what they sacrificed.

At the moment I had no time to make further observations, for just then we reached a house where Kumpana, who had rejoined us on the outskirts of the town, informed me I was to lodge. Though flat-roofed and somewhat larger than the rest, except one adjoining which I took to be that of the chief, like the others it was situated in a garden and had a veranda, from which a door-way led into the building. It consisted of one big, white-washed room, without windows. Such light as there was came through the open door-way, over which a mat was hung, to be used at night, for there was no door. Like the passes, the houses were undefended against attack or thieves; indeed I learned afterwards that such a crime as theft was quite unknown in Mone-land.

In this room, to my delight, I found all our goods which had been carried by the Dabanda porters for so many weary marches. There were the spare rifles, the ammunition, the medicines, the cooking-pots, the clothes, the beads and cloth for presents—everything; even the suspicious Hans could not discover that a single article was missing. While we were checking them, food that had been prepared in a cook-hut in the garden at the back of the house, was brought to us by a decently clothed old woman, who seemed to accept our presence without curiosity, also earthenware jars full of water and a tub burnt out of a block of wood in which to wash. This we did on the veranda, for the surrounding fence made the place quite private, and afterwards sat ourselves upon wooden stools which we found in the room, and ate a good meal.

By the time we had finished our food it was dark, and the old woman appeared again carrying two lighted earthenware lamps of an elegant boat-shaped pattern, filled with some kind of sweet-smelling vegetable oil in which floated wicks made of pith or fibre.

As there seemed nothing else to do and no one came near us, I began to take off my clothes in order to turn in upon one of the very comfortable-looking wooden bedsteads that had been provided for us. This bedstead was of the kind that is common in Eastern Africa, having a cartel, as the Boers call it, strung with green hide and a mattress stiffed with dried grasses that gave a scent of hay. Already my boots were off when Kumpana appeared and said that he had come to conduct us to a ceremony where we should see the other white lord who was called Wanderer. This being what I most desired, I put them on again in a hurry and away we went.

Kumpana led us to the market-or gathering-place that I have described. Here we found what I suppose was the entire adult population of the town, seated on the ground in front of the truncated pyramid of which I have spoken, the men upon one side and the women upon the other, as they might be in some high churches. They were very quiet and orderly and for the most part engaged in smoking their native cigarettes. We were conducted along a broad passage which was left between the men and the women, to the foot of the pyramid and up some twenty rough steps to the platform that proved to be quite a large place.

Here in front of a low altar, a primitive erection about twelve feet square built of blocks of black lava, upon which altar burned the fire that I have mentioned, stood three white-robed men facing the fire, whom I took to be priests, for their heads were shaved and they seemed to be engaged in prayer. To the right of this altar, seated on a stool and clothed in a white robe like a Dabanda, was none other than Arkle, who, I am bound to say, so far as the firelight revealed him to me, looked very imposing in this costume. Opposite to him, also clad in white and seated on a stool, was his enemy Kaneke. Very fierce and sullen did he appear as he glowed at Arkle with his great, round eyes. I noted at once that he was guarded, probably to prevent him from making another attack upon his rival, for behind him stood three tall men armed with spears.

A second stool was set by that of Arkle and to this I was conducted, Hans, who seemed rather uncomfortable and kept his hand upon the hilt of his revolver, being directed to stand behind me. Then Kumpana left us and took up a position facing the audience midway between Arkle and Kaneke, with his back to the altar and the priests. Here he stood silent; indeed, everyone was silent, and when I tried to whisper something to Arkle, he shook his head and laid his finger on his lips.

Very impressive was that silence. Never shall I forget the scene as I saw it by the light of the young moon which changed its quarter that day, and of the bright stars burning in the deep-blue sky. Not a breath of air was stirring. To my left the great trees of the forest stood motionless in endless rows. To my right were the dim grey roofs of the town, and between them the crouching audience of robed Dabandas, looking few and small upon that wide expanse, the glowing tips of their cigarettes marking the ordered lines in which they sat, like men and women stricken with dumbness. Then, within a few paces, the primeval altar upon which even the fire seemed to be subject to the general spell, for it burned brightly without a sound, and the three shaven priests bowing and waving their hands, but uttering no word.

I felt like one under a charm, which was not strange; for so deep was this quiet that when I shifted my foot, causing the nails in my boot to grate upon the stone platform, the noise seemed quite loud, so loud that all turned their heads and looked at me as though I had done something outrageous and indecorous. This went on for quite a long time, till at length I felt an hysterical desire to rise and make a speech, just to show that I was still alive. Indeed, I think that very soon our strained nerves would have caused either Hans or me to commit some indiscretion involving sound, when suddenly the chain of silence was broken by a melodious voice above us.

I stared to see whence it came, and for the first time observed that on the top of each of the tall columns which rose in front of the platform stood a white-robed figure, evidently engaged in observing the stars. Instantly the chanting voice on the right-hand column was answered by a similar voice upon the left-hand column. Then both of them sang something in unison, something sweet and solemn, though what it meant I could not understand, and as they sang, pointed with wands they held upwards to the heavens.

At this signal all present seemed to come to life, as in the story did the Sleeping Beauty and her court at the kiss of the Fairy Prince. The audience or congregation below us began to talk with some eagerness, men calling across the passage to women, and vice versa. Evidently they were discussing the message conveyed to them in the chant of the astrologers on the towers, telling them, I suppose, what those astrologers had read in the stars. In the same way the three priests, ceasing from dumb show, broke into open prayer, which again I could not understand, because the language was probably archaic. At any rate it differed so much from the dialect of Arabic used by these people that I could only distinguish one word, *"Engoi"*, which was their name for the Divine.

Encouraged by this change of demeanour, I asked Arkle in English what it all meant and what he was doing there dressed up like a Dabanda.

"You forget, Quatermain," he answered, "that I have become a chief or a priest, or both, by virtue of what happened yesterday between me and the gentleman opposite. At least, I fill these offices on probation, for my true position is about to be settled at this meeting. For the rest, those men on the towers have been reading omens in the stars, though exactly what they read I cannot tell you. Now I think that they are about to make prayers or offerings to the planet Venus, which you can see blazing away up there near the moon, after which my case will be tried."

He was right. Having thrown something on to the fire, what it was I could not see, the three priests turned so as to face the congregation below and, pointing to Venus, began a hymn in which the whole audience joined, also pointing at the planet with their right hands. Even the astrologers on the towers pointed with their wands and took part in this chant, which was really very fine and moving, a great volume of rhythmical sound.

Presently Kumpana, who now stood in front of the three priests, acting apparently as a master of ceremonies, waved his arms, whereon the song ceased with a crash of sound. In the silence that ensued he began to speak, but so rapidly that I could make out very little of what he said. He may have been reciting ritual, as was suggested by the strange words and forms he used. Or perhaps he was repeating passages from ancient history. At length his address became less impetuous. He spoke more slowly, and in language that was easier to understand, so that I had no difficulty in discovering that he was telling the story of what had happened between Arkle and Kaneke in the pass; of the attempted assassination of Arkle, of the overthrow of Kaneke, and of the oath that he had sworn to the victor. Finally he said:

"The stars, having been consulted by those who can read them, declare that Kaneke, who by the choice of that chief who went before him, was appointed to follow him as Chief of the Dabanda, the Holy People of the Lake and the Guardian of the Treasure of the Lake, and, after long punishment and exile, was named to be the Lord and Shield of the Shadow, is rejected from his place and stripped of his offices. They declare also that the stranger, who in this land is named Wanderer, he whom Kaneke tried to murder and to whom he swore the oath of submission and fidelity, giving up to him all rights and power in exchange for life, henceforward stands where Kaneke stood. Do you, O People of the Dabanda, to whom is revealed the secret mystery of the stranger that for ages has been hidden, accept the decree of the stars and depose Kaneke, setting up in his place the white lord, his conqueror?"

"We do," answered the audience, with such singular unanimity that I guessed all this scene to be formal and arranged.

"Kaneke," cried Kumpana, "you have heard the decrees of the stars and of the Holy People confirming your own oath. Do you obey?"

Now Kaneke sprang to his feet and answered in a great voice that seemed alive with rage:

"I do not obey. What I swore was to save my life and such oaths are binding upon no man. As for the decrees of the stars and of the people of the Dabanda, these are but tricks. I, too, am a master of the stars, and I read their writing otherwise, while the people are in the hands of the priests, who in their turn are in the hands of Kumpana and the Council who plot against me. The sin that I sinned in my youth against the Shadow, who has passed back to the Light which cast it, is purged by punishment. Moreover, was it half as great as that of this white thief, whom most justly I would have killed, he who, as I have heard, strove to do violence to the Treasure of the Lake, and for that cause was hunted from the land? But let that matter be. Who is this foreign man that you name Wanderer? What does he in our country? I know what the magicians declare, namely that, like myself, he is one long dead who has returned again; that he is the very king who fought with his brother to win the Treasure of the Lake, and drove his brother and those who clung to him over the mountain edge, where they became exiles and the fathers of the people of the Abanda. Yes, that king who, being wed to the Treasure of the Lake, was so beloved of her that when she knew death was near to her, she killed him that he might accompany her to heaven, a crime for which heaven brought woe upon her.

"So runs the tale, but I say that it is a lie told by the Council of the Shadow to favour this white wanderer, who has made great promises to them if they will give the Shadow into his keeping that he may steal her away, leaving them to rule the land."

This statement, I noticed, seemed to disturb the audience below, among whom, it appeared afterwards, Kaneke had many friends, members of his family and others who desired that he should be chief and wed the Shadow. These stirred impatiently as the meaning of the sacrilege came home to them and whispered to one another.

"Yes," went on Kaneke, "such is the accursed plot of the white stranger who is named Wanderer which has been revealed to me, a plot so wicked that the guardian spirits of the Lake and Forest cast him from our land that he might die by the spears of the Abanda. Yet he did not die, because he was saved by the other white man, the Lord Macumazahn whom I was commanded to lead to our country, doubtless that he might play his part in the plot and be rewarded of the thief his friend."

Here I remarked in a loud voice to Kaneke that he was a liar as well as a traitor, for I knew nothing of any plots, but he took no heed of me and continued:

"Therefore it was that I sought to execute justice upon this red-bearded lord who had escaped from the Abanda. Yet I was overcome not by strength, but by evil magic, and swore an oath to save my life who desired to live on that I might avenge you, the Holy People, upon him who would rob you of your Treasure and your Oracle."

At this point Arkle intervened in a businesslike and British fashion.

"You dirty dog!" he said. "You snake who spits poison at me whom you have failed to reach with your fangs. You traitor who deserted the lord Watcher-by-Night and brought about the death of his servants, because you hoped that it would mean my own death also, and afterwards tried to stab me whom you had sworn not to harm. You oath-breaker. I will not reason with you as to your falsehoods, but I am ready to fight you again, here and now and to the death. Yes, weary and lame as I am, I am ready to fight you under the stars you worship, before their altar and in the presence of your people and thus let Fate judge between us. Answer. Will you fight me again?"

"I will not fight you, Red Wanderer, that I may once more be overcome by magic and butchered," shouted Kaneke. "Nay, I appeal from you and from your fellow plotters to our Lady, the Voice of the *Engoi*. If I am justly judged, if I have spoken what is not true, let her appear here and now and pass sentence on me with her own lips. Ay, Kumpana, chief of the Council of the Shadow, summon the Shadow if you can, and let the people see her and hear her voice."

Thus he spoke in tones of triumph who, as I learned afterwards, knew well that never in their history had the Lake-dweller who was named Shadow come from the lake to the town to judge of any matter, and having spoken, sat himself down and waited.

Then in quiet tones Kumpana answered:

"O Kaneke, I will make prayer to the Shadow. Perchance she may be pleased to do as you desire, and come hither to give judgment in this cause in the presence of her people."

CHAPTER 14

Shadow

"Will she come?" I whispered to Arkle.

"Yes, I think so—that is, I hope so," he replied.

Then I guessed it was arranged that on one pretext or another the holy personage called Shadow or the Lake-Dweller, should make a public appearance that night. It might well be, and indeed probably was the case, that Kaneke's appeal to the head and source of the local law was but a happy accident which chanced to fit in with a preconceived plan. But, putting two and two together, that such a plan existed seemed to me more probable. After all there might be something in Arkle's story, which up till now I had held to spring from the illusions of a man who had suffered great hardships and had been hunted almost to death. I allude not to his dreams of a twin-soul awaiting him in some far-off place, which were of a character that has been heard of before in the case of young men and women of strong imagination and romantic nature, but to his tale of having actually met this lady on the shore of the sacred lake, after which he remembered no more until he found himself running for dear life from the spears of the Abanda.

According to this tale on that occasion his love-affair had made most satisfactory progress. The lady, it seemed, was a thorough convert to the twin-soul theory and alleged that what he had experienced were no myths but spiritual realities, or in other words that for years the two of them had been in some kind of mystical communion. Moreover the not unnatural conclusion of the matter was that he had embraced her. It was true that she protested, yet why? Not because she was personally offended, and much less shocked or pained; but for the reason that he was violating the sacred law of her country and thereby exposing himself, and possibly her also, to very terrible risks and danger, even of death—which in fact, whether from this or some other cause, nearly overtook him.

Well, always presuming that some such event took place, what was more natural than that these two young people should wish to meet again and to, so to speak, regularize their relationship? Nothing can be more dangerous to either party among savage or semi-savage peoples, than that a stranger should become extremely intimate with a sanctified lady who by the custom of ages is vowed and sealed to the ruler of her tribe. But if that stranger himself becomes the ruler, the face of the problem changes.

Now it appeared that, for reasons which I could not pretend to fathom, this was exactly what was desired by the priestess herself and by some of her most important adherents. Otherwise why did Kumpana, the Prime Minister or head of the Council of the Shadow, go to meet Arkle far away and guide him through the Abanda and into the hidden country at great risk to himself? And having done this and other things, would it be surprising if he had arranged a dramatic public appearance of that priestess, at which she was to recognize the stranger as the man of the prophecy, as chief, too, in place of one who had been given his life in exchange for his abdication of that and other offices, and consequently as her future husband? Oh, the whole business was as clear as the tall observation tower in front of me; such obvious manoeuvres could not deceive a person of my acumen for a moment—or so I thought.

Now while I was reflecting thus, Kumpana had passed between the priests and, standing with his face to the fire upon the altar, was engaged in uttering some petition in a voice which I could not hear because he spoke very low and his back was towards me. Nor could I see much of him or anything else, for the reason that the observation tower I have just spoken of as so plainly visible, vanished from my sight, being suddenly obscured by clouds which appeared upon the face of the sky. They were thick tempest clouds, for I heard the muttering of distant thunder, and a breath of cold wind passed through the forest with a moaning noise. Indeed, everything became so dark that I whispered to Arkle to look out lest Kaneke should take advantage of the gloom to attack him. He made no answer; his attention was so fixed upon other matters that he did not seem to hear me. He leaned forward, breathing heavily like a man under the stress of emotion, and stared at the fire upon the altar. I, too, stared at this fire, because in that gloom I could see little else except figures moving dimly against the background of the fire, which I took to be those of Kumpana and the priests.

The heart of the distant storm rolled away over the western cliffs of the crater, drawing the clouds after it and the half-moon appeared again. Its light falling direct upon the platform revealed a single figure standing in front of the altar, the tall figure of a woman arrayed in glittering robes, green they seemed to be, sewn with silver. Of her face I could only see that it was young, and fair-skinned like to that of a white woman, for it was shadowed by a dark veil which hung from her head, unless indeed what I took to be a veil was the mass of her black hair flowing over her shoulders. Her arms were bare except for bracelets of what looked like pearls fastened upon the wrists and above the elbows, and on her head she wore some kind of crown or fillet which added to her height and shone, but of what it was made I do not know.

The whole effect of this figure seen thus in the half-light and against a background of the altar with its flickering fire, was strangely impressive, mystic, and beautiful; so much so that I remember catching my breath at its first appearance. If I had any doubt as to who this woman might be, it was removed by the audience on the plain who, with one voice cried:

"*Engoi! Engoi!*" (a word that among them means, it seems, "Spirit" as well as "Divinity") and prostrated themselves.

Arkle, too, muttered something about "Shadow" and half rose as though to go to her, when an instinct warned me to catch him by the arm, whereon he sat down again and waited.

She fixed her fine eyes upon the face of old Kumpana, who stood in front of her but to her left, and began to speak in a very sweet low voice, that gave the suggestion of a chant learnt by heart rather than of ordinary talk, for in it was something dreamlike and rather unearthly. Indeed, it was unlike the voice and speech of any woman that I had ever heard, except one—and she was in an hypnotic trance. In fact, it reminded me forcibly of what the prophet Isaiah describes as the voice "of one that hath a familiar spirit" speaking "low out of the dust". Hearing it for the first time I felt rather frightened, because it suggested to my mind that this fair creature might be under an unholy spell, or even something more or less than mortal. Evidently Hans thought the same, for he muttered into my ear:

"Keep clear of that one, Baas, or she will bewitch you worse than White-Mouse. She is not a maiden but a spook. Yes, she is the queen of the spooks."

I hit him in the face with my elbow as a sign to be silent, though the thought did pass through my mind that there was an air about this lady which reminded me of White-Mouse, White-Mouse grown taller and more imposing. To my fancy they might well have been sisters.

Then in the midst of the deep quiet she spoke, or chanted as an oracle might do.

"I have been called. I come from where I dwell upon the water. In my secret place where I dwell with my maidens and no man may set his foot save he who is appointed to be my lord; yes, there in the ancient halls built by a people that is no more, the swift messenger has brought me the message of my priests, and I have considered of their riddle. To it I, the Oracle inspired, give answer in the hearing of my people that all may learn my will and the will of That I serve:

"One," and she pointed to Kaneke with something in her hand, it looked like a little wand or sceptre of ivory, "who sinned against the Shadow that has faded, and was driven from the land, has returned again to take the place that was sworn to him according to the ancient law and to wed the Shadow that has risen from the House of Shadows. One," and she pointed to Arkle, "called hither by the decree of Fate, a wanderer from far, has come to the hidden land and suffered many things because in ignorance he broke its customs. One," and she pointed to me, "who, like the Wanderer also called hither by the decree of Fate, rescued him, the Wanderer, from death at the hands of the Abanda, my enemies. He who should be chief of the people and Shelter of the Shadow, foully strove to murder the white Wanderer, but was overthrown of him, and to save his life swore an oath upon my name and upon that whereof I am the Voice, that in return for breath he would sell his lordship and its rights. So he was spared and not slain, and became the servant of the Wanderer whom he would have murdered. Now, the message tells me, he takes back his oath and claims the chieftainship that was his heritage, and with it the Holy Bride. Is the case thus, O Priests and Ministers and People?"

"It is thus," all answered with one voice, for even Kaneke attempted no denial.

Now she stared hard at Kumpana, as an actor might at the prompter in the wings, then seemed to catch her cue and went on:

"I, the Voice, speak the judgment that is set within my lips. Hearken. It is told, ay, and written in the secret records which are hidden yonder where I dwell, that once in a far age it chanced that he who was appointed to be the Shield of the Shadow, sought to slay another foully. But this other conquered that murderer, and in exchange for the gift of life bought from him his place and power and the Shadow of his day herself. Thence came a great war and the division of the people which endures until this hour. As it was, so let it be. I, the Voice, decree and declare that Kaneke, the murderer at heart and the oath-breaker, is no longer chief of the Dabanda and that never shall he be the Shield of the Shadow and her spouse. I decree and declare that his chieftainship has passed to the Wanderer lord whom he would have slain, and that with it passes the Shadow herself, should the Wanderer desire to clasp her for his hour. The Voice has spoken. Is the decree accepted, O Priests and Ministers and People?"

The dreamy, mysterious tones died in the silence and again in a great volume of sound came the answer:

"It is accepted!" and a priest speaking out of the darkness added, "Kaneke called upon the Shadow to appear and give the judgment of the *Engoi*. The judgment has been given; the *Engoi* has spoken by its oracle; it is finished."

"It is not finished; it is but begun," shouted Kaneke. "You who have bewitched the Shadow, call down a curse upon your souls and on her the curse of war."

Here his words came to a sudden end, for what reason I could not see, but I think that the guards threatened him with their spears, commanding his silence. Nor did she who was called Shadow seem to hear them, for once more she spoke in her cold, chirping voice like one who repeats a lesson in her sleep.

"Come hither, O Wanderer," she said, "to do me homage, and take from me the lordship of the Land of the Holy Lake, and if it be your pleasure, swear yourself to me, as I will swear myself to you. Or, do not come, if such be your will. For know, O Wanderer, that with this rule goes trouble and the dread of death. Yonder man who would have murdered you spoke truth. War is at hand, and of that war the end is not shown to me. Mayhap in it you will find nothing save doom and loss. Choose, then."

"I have chosen," said Arkle, and rising, strove to walk to her, only to find that his hurts had stiffened so that now he could scarcely stand unaided.

"Help me!" he said, and a few seconds later was limping towards the altar supporting himself upon my shoulder. It was but a little way, yet that journey seemed long to me, perhaps because of its strangeness, perhaps because the concentrated interest of every watching man and woman beat upon me with such intensity that it hampered my physical powers. At length we reached the altar and the big, golden-bearded Arkle sank on to his knees before the goddess, for so they held her.

For the first time I could see her face, though even now not too clearly because her back was to the fire. Certainly it was beautiful; the fine features, the curving lips, the large eyes, dark and tender, shining under the ivory pallor of her brows, the masses of the black hair flowing from beneath her coronal—all were beautiful, as were her arms and shapely, tapering hands. Her tall figure, too, was full of girlish grace and yet of dignity, that of one born to command, while her shimmering robes, how fashioned or of what stuff I know not, were such as might have been worn by the creature of a dream and even suggested something unfamiliar to our world.

What could this woman be, I wondered, and from what blood did she spring? Arab, Egyptian, Eastern? I never learned the answer. One thing, however, I did learn then and there, namely that when the shell was off her, at heart she was very human. Her face showed it as she bent down over this man whom in some strange fashion she had drawn to her from half across the world. It was not the face of the priestess of some ancient, secret faith welcoming a worshipper, but rather that of a woman greeting her lover won at last. The lips trembled, the eyes filled with happy tears, her figure drooped; she grew languid as though with an access of passion, her arms opened as if they would clasp him, then fell again when she remembered that eyes were on her—oh, that this man was everything to her I could not doubt!

With an evident effort of the will she recovered herself and began to speak again, but in a fuller and more natural voice than she had used when she played her part of oracle. Indeed it was so different that if her face had been hidden from me, I should not have thought the speaker to be the same.

"Wilt thou serve my people and accept lordship over them, O Wanderer?" she asked, probably in the adapted words of some ancient ritual.

"The lordship I have bought already, and I will serve them as best I may," he answered.

"Wilt thou do homage, O Wanderer, to me, Shadow, the Dweller in the Lake, the Oracle, the Priestess of the *Engoi*?"

"I will do you homage, O Shadow," he answered, and bent his head as though to kiss her sandaled feet or the hem of her robe.

She saw it and swiftly stretched out her arm, murmuring so low that only he and I could hear.

"Not my foot, my hand."

He took it and pressed it to his lips. Then with her little ivory sceptre she touched him on the brow twice, once to accept the homage, and next to give him all authority. Now she spoke for a third time, asking,

"Wilt thou swear thyself to me, that at the time appointed thou mayest take the Shadow to thee and for thine hour protect her on the path of Fate?"

This she said out loud so that all should hear, then before he could answer, made a sign to him to be silent, and added in a whisper,

"Bethink thee, O Beloved, before thou dost answer. Thou knowest the mystery and that our hearts have spoken together across the empty air, as once they spoke in an age bygone. Yet remember that I am not of thy land and race, that I am strange and secret, full of a wisdom that thou dost not understand, that my day is short and that when I die it is the law that thou diest also, so that together we may pass to another home of which thou dost not know and in which thou mayest not believe. Remember also that dangers are many, and it may be that never wilt thou hold me to thy heart. Therefore be warned ere thou tiest a cord that cannot be undone save by the sword of death. Dost thou understand?"

"I understand," he whispered back, "and on the chance that thou mayest be mine if only for an hour, I, who have risked much already, will risk the rest, I who love thee, and if need be, for love will die."

She sighed, so deeply that her whole frame shook as though with the joy of an intense relief, saying, still beneath her breath,

"So be it. Now take the oath."

Then in a loud voice he said,

"I swear myself to thee, O Shadow. Dost thou swear thyself to me?"

"I swear myself," she began, but said no more, for at that moment Kaneke leapt upon her, swiftly as a leopard leaps upon a buck. I suppose that while all watched the remarkable scene I have described, he had slipped from his guards. What he meant to do I am not sure, but I imagine that trusting to his great strength, he intended to carry her off with the help of confederates among the people. Or perhaps it was in his mind to kill her out of jealousy rather than see her give herself to another man.

The sequel was both swift and most amazing. I did nothing, to my shame be it said; I was taken too much by surprise, and before I recovered myself that sequel was accomplished. The priests did nothing either, being like myself overcome with astonishment. Arkle was on his knees and even if he understood what was passing, being lame and stiff, could not rise from them without assistance. Only from either side of the altar, or from behind it, white-draped figures seemed to flit forward. I suppose these were the virgins of the Shadow, but really I cannot say, for their appearance was so quick, so mysterious and so vague that in that light they might quite well have been shades born of imagination, or even large white-winged birds seen for a moment in the light of the fire. Nor, whatever they were, did they take any action that I could discern; they just came and presently were gone again. Further, my attention was not fixed upon these appearances which I only saw out of the corner of my eye, as it were, but on the central figures, the lady called Shadow, and on her assailant, the owl-eyed Kaneke.

Evidently she saw him come, for her face grew frightened and she uttered a little cry. Then in a twinkling her aspect changed, or so I fancied. She drew herself up to her full height, her face hardened and became stern, the fear passed from it and was replaced by a cold anger. As the man leapt on her she stretched out her arm, that in which she held the little sceptre and exclaimed.

"Be accursed!"

The effect upon Kaneke of these words, or of her mien, or of both, or of something that I could not see or appreciate, unless it were the flitting white figures, was wonderful. I have compared his rush with that of a leopard. Well, have you ever seen such a beast stopped by a bullet, not a bullet that killed it dead, but one that paralysed its nervous system with the shock of its impact, taking all the courage out of it, causing it to stop, to tremble, and finally to turn and flee for shelter? If so, you will understand what happened to Kaneke better than I can describe it in writing.

He came to a standstill, so sudden that the weight of his charge caused him to slide forward for a foot or two upon the pavement. Then he appeared to collapse; at least to my sight he looked actually smaller, I suppose because his breath left him, causing his body to shrink. Next he uttered a low cry of fear and, turning, fled like a flash, bounding down the steps that led to the altar and vanishing into the gloom.

I think that some ran after him, but of this I am not sure. If so, perhaps it was the faint indefinite figures that I have described, for I lost him in a kind of white mist that may of course have been an effect caused by the robes of those who followed.

To tell the truth I did not look long, because Arkle, who was struggling to his feet, uttered an exclamation which caused me to turn my head and perceive that the Shadow lady was no longer there.

"Where is she?" I asked.

"I don't know," he answered. "I think women came and took her away, but it was all so confused I cannot swear."

Then the gathering broke up in tumult. Kumpana and others escorted us down the steps, Arkle still leaning on my shoulder and expostulating, for naturally enough he wished to follow the Shadow, which he was not allowed to do. At the foot of the steps we were separated, he being helped off I knew not where, while I was taken back to the guest-house.

"We will meet tomorrow," he called after me, and I replied that I hoped so. Then he and his escort vanished into the darkness.

"Baas," said Hans, as I began to undress, "it is almost a pity that those Abanda did not catch the Baas Red-Bull."

"Why?" I asked wearily.

"For two reasons, Baas. If he had been killed he would have been saved a great deal of trouble, who now is caught like a fly in a spider's web. You know the sort of spider, Baas, which bites the fly and sends it to sleep for days or weeks, until it wants to eat it. The fly looks quite happy and so it is until the eating begins, when it wakes up and kicks because it can't buzz as its wings have been pulled off. Well, that is what will happen to the Red Baas. The pretty-painted spider has got him and made him drunk and he will be quite happy, not knowing that his wings have been pulled off until the time comes when he wakes up to be sacrificed, or something of that sort, Baas. That's the first reason."

Now I bethought me that as usual there was wisdom in Hans' cynical remarks and metaphors. Undoubtedly Arkle was entangled in an evil web, and what was the fate which lay before him, a white man of good birth and education and presumably a Christian? He was beloved of a beautiful and mystic woman whom he in turn adored and probably in due course would marry.

This seemed pleasant enough, and natural—if bizarre. Could he have taken the lady away to his own land perhaps the adventure might even have proved successful in a matrimonial sense. But what were the facts? Departure was impossible for her and for him also. Once he was wed to her, here he must remain to the end of the chapter.

Moreover for a bridal dower he took with her a mass of obscure and dangerous superstitions, as to which only one thing was clear, namely that, as I had heard her declare with her own lips, these would involve the pair of them in certain death, possibly quite soon, and surely at no very distant date. Of course he might maintain that he had been given fair warning and that the price he must pay was not too high for what he won. But then he was not in a state to judge with an even mind, and as an individual of his own race and standing with some experience of the world, I could not agree with this view of his case.

Such were some of the thoughts that passed through my mind but of these I said nothing to Hans, contenting myself with asking his second reason.

"Oh, Baas, it is this," he answered. "If the Red Baas were out of the way, you would have been put in his place, as I dare say will happen after all if Kaneke manages to murder him, or those priests change their minds about him."

"Thank you," I said, "and what then?"

"Then, Baas, as happy married pair always does, you would set up house on that island, which otherwise we shall never see, and find out where they keep their gold and other things that are worth money, of which I learn they have plenty hidden away on the island, although this silly people does not use them because they are a holy, ancient treasure, Baas, that has been there for hundreds or thousands of years."

"And if this treasure exists and I found it, what next Hans?"

"Why, then, Baas, of course you would steal it and get away, leaving the lady to look at the empty boxes, Baas. Perhaps you think it would be difficult, but Hans would manage it all for you. Priests can always be bought, Baas, and as for oaths and the rest," he added, springing to a very pinnacle of immorality, "good Christians like you and me wouldn't need to bother about them, Baas, because you see they have all to do with the devil. So we should get away very rich and be happy to the end of our lives. But," he went on with a sigh, "it is nothing but a nice dream, because the Red Baas stands in our way. Unless indeed"—here he brightened up—"we can make a bargain with him and go shares in everything that he gets."

I did not try to argue with Hans because his lack of moral sense, real or assumed, was, so to speak, quite out of shot of argument. So I only said:

"I should be glad enough to get out of this place without any treasure, if only I could do so with a whole skin. Did you hear all the talk about war?"

"Oh yes, Baas. From the beginning that owl-man Kaneke has said that there would be war, which was why he brought you here."

"Well, Hans, if it is to be with the Abanda, I don't see what chance these Dabanda will have, for they are but a handful."

"None, Baas, if the fight were with spears. But they don't trust to spears; they trust to magic of which there is plenty in this land. Didn't you see when the *Engoi* woman cursed Kaneke, how he curled up, just as though she had kicked him in the stomach, Baas, and ran away, although a minute before he had meant to carry her off with the help of his friends, of whom no doubt he has plenty? That was magic, Baas."

I shrugged my shoulders and answered:

"I think it was scare and a guilty conscience. But I don't understand about this Kaneke. Why, if they don't like him, was he ever brought away from the place where he was living? Why did White-Mouse insist upon our rescuing him, and a dozen other things?"

"Oh, for lots of reasons, Baas. While he was named as the Chief-to-be, no one else could take his place according to their law. That is one. Also no one else could guide you to this country. That is another. Also he had to come because the Shadow Lady said so, something to do with their fetish business, or prophecies, Baas; you will never learn what makes the minds of spook-people like these Dabanda turn this way or that."

"I dare say not. What I should like to learn is whether our friend Kaneke is alive or dead."

"Alive, I think, Baas; yes, I am almost sure that he got away by the help of his friends in the crowd below, though I dare say that the curses of the Shadow Queen went with him; indeed I thought I saw them following him like white owls. I expect we shall see and hear plenty more of Kaneke, Baas."

As usual Hans was quite right; we did.

CHAPTER 15

Lake Mone and the Forest

After this tumultuous and exciting night I spent a very quiet time at Dabanda-town, where for the next ten days or so nothing happened that could be called remarkable.

Grateful enough I was to rest thus awhile, because our long journey had tired me out and I found it delightful to enjoy repose and leisure in a climate which although hot, was on the whole delicious. Still as I am an active-minded person, I took advantage of this pause to learn all I could about the Dabanda and their enemies, the Abanda, only to find that in the end I had really learned very little. Kumpana and other members of the Council came to see me frequently and talked with great openness upon many matters, but when I came to boil down their conversation, the residuum was small enough.

I was told that Kaneke had escaped, as they said, "by making himself invisible", a feat in which no doubt the darkness helped him. Where he had gone, they were not sure. Possibly, they said, he had turned traitor and run away to the Abanda, though such a crime had never been heard of in their history. Or he might have returned towards the country where I had met him. Or possibly he was dead, killed by the curse of the *Engoi*, though they did not think this probable, for being himself a magician and one of the initiated, he knew how to fashion shields which would turn aside or delay the deadliest curses.

My inquiries upon other matters were almost equally unfruitful. I asked when the promised war would come and was informed that they did not know, but that no doubt it "would happen at the time appointed".

Nor would they tell me anything definite about the lady called Shadow, whom I had seen upon the altar platform. They were, they asserted, ignorant of what caused her to be fairer-skinned and more beautiful than other women; they only knew that for many generations the Lake-Dweller always had been so; it was a family gift. They admitted that she lived upon an island in the waters of Mone, in the company of certain virgins who dwelt with her in ancient buildings erected by an unknown and forgotten people, but of these buildings and the fashion of her life there they could say nothing, as none of them had ever visited the place, upon which it was unlawful for any man to set foot except the husband of the *Engoi* after marriage, and so on.

Thus it came about that at last I abandoned inquiries, which led to no result, for the very good reason that those whom I questioned were determined to tell me nothing, and fell back upon my own powers of observation, assisted by those of Hans. Being allowed to do so with an escort, I walked about the country, but saw nothing worthy of note.

Here and there were little villages inhabited by a handful of people, and round these some cultivated fields, also grazing grounds on which were herded cattle of a small breed and goats, but no true woolled sheep, creatures that would not thrive in so hot a district. The rest of the land, which was of extraordinary richness and could have supported ten times as many people, was given up to game of every variety except, as I have said, those that are harmful to man, which did not exist there.

The animals were wonderfully tame; indeed one could walk among them as Adam and Eve are reported to have done in the Garden of Eden. Again I asked Kumpana and others how this came about and was answered—because of the spell laid upon them, also because they were never molested or killed for food. I inquired why and was informed because they were holy, taboo in short, as Father Ambrose had heard from the slave in bygone years. Then for the first time I discovered that the Dabanda believed that after death the spirits of men, or those of certain men of their race, passed into the bodies of animals; also that sometimes this happened before birth.

It was for this reason that the beasts were not touched, since nobody likes to put a spear through his grandmother or his future child.

Next I referred to the elephants we had met outside their country, over which Kaneke seemed to have control, and inquired how this happened. The reply was that these beasts or their progenitors had once lived in Mone-land, whence they were driven, or "requested to leave" as Kumpana put it, because they did so much mischief, which accounted for the mystery.

My own view, of course, is (or, perhaps I should say, was) that the creatures were tame because no man ever harmed them, but I quote the story as an example of the superstitions of these star-worshippers. To many African tribes certain creatures are taboo, but never before or since have I heard of one to which all game was sacred, perchance because no other of small numbers has so rich a food supply that it needs to be supplemented by the flesh of wild animals. Among the Dabanda, however, this was so.

Their fertile soil, amply watered by rain and streams, needed but to be scratched to yield abundantly of corn and various roots and vegetables, while their numerous flocks and herds furnished all the milk and meat they required. Therefore there was no necessity for them to undertake the risk and toil of hunting, with the result that those beasts which they never killed, in the course of time naturally became both tame and sacred.

Having finished such investigation of the country as I was allowed to make—all approach to the lip of the crater was, I should explain, forbidden to me—I was seized with a great desire to explore the forest land and to look upon the sacred waters of the Lake Mone.

At first, when I mentioned this matter, Kumpana always turned the subject, but ultimately on the day of full moon, he said that if I so desired, he was ready to conduct me through the forest so that I might look upon the lake by moonlight, adding that it was not lawful for any man to enter this forest, much less to see the lake, in the daytime.

Of course I jumped at the offer, and shortly after moonrise we started, three of us, Kumpana, I, and Hans, whom at first Kumpana wished to leave behind. Indeed he only gave way on the point when I refused to go without him, while Hans on his part remarked, in infamous Arabic, that it has always been his custom to shoot anyone who tried to separate him from his master.

Within five minutes we found ourselves in a pit of blackness. That forest must have been dark at noonday, and at night, even when there was a full moon, it was like a coal-mine. We could only get along at all by help of some yards of the stem of a creeper of which Kumpana held one end. Then I grasped it at a distance of a few feet, and lastly came Hans holding to the other end.

It may be asked how Kumpana could see his way.

The answer is—that I do not know, but he led us quite briskly along some path that I was unable to perceive, which wound in and out through the trunks of giant trees, and skirted some that had fallen. Thus we walked for some hours, only seeing a ray of light now and then where a tree, dead and devoid of leaf, allowed it to reach the ground.

At length this forest ceased as suddenly as it had begun, and we stood upon the broad beach of the lake, most of which doubtless was covered in times of heavy rain.

Oh, how desolate was that great sheet of water glimmering in the bright moonlight, and yet how beautiful, set in its ring of forest land. Save for the soughing sound of wildfowl flighting far out of sight, and the occasional croak of a frog, it was utterly silent. Its lonesomeness was oppressive, almost terrible, for no beasts seemed to frequent it; nor did I see or hear so much as a fish stirring; well could I understand that a semi-savage race should deem it to be holy and haunted. Far away I could see the island on which the priestess Shadow was said to dwell, and noted that it was large, over a mile long as I judged, though how wide it may have been of course I did not know. What is more, I could distinguish buildings amidst the palms which grew upon this island.

Taking my glasses, very good ones of a German make which were fitted with a lens for use at night, I studied the place and saw at once that these building were large, massive, and apparently covered with sculpture. They seemed to be constructed of limestone or alabaster, or some other white rock such as marble, and before them stood gateways and towers, certain of which looked as though they were half in ruins. In architecture and style they were totally different from any that I knew of in Africa, not excepting the Zimbabwe ruins.

They had, however, a distinct resemblance to the remains of the temples of Old Egypt which at that time I had never seen except in pictures. There were what might be pylon gates; there were walls covered with great carvings; there were courts with pillars in them, for the end of one of these had fallen down or never been completed, and with the glasses I could see the columns.

The sight thrilled me. Was it possible that these mysterious buildings had been erected by people from Ancient Egypt, or even by some race that afterwards had migrated to Egypt, taking their architecture with them? Now that I come to think of it, the truncated pyramid outside the town where stood the stone altar upon which the fire burned, suggested that this might be so.

I turned to Kumpana and questioned him closely, but he could, or would, tell me very little. He repeated that he had never been on the island "in the flesh" for the reasons that he had already explained, but that he understood the buildings there to be tremendous, of a sort indeed to defy time for thousands upon thousands of years. There was no record of their construction, or of the people who had accomplished this mighty work and dwelt there. Not so much as a tradition survived. Time had eaten up their name and race, though perhaps the sculptures might tell something to anyone who learned enough to understand them. For the rest from generation to generation they had always been sacred to the *Engoi* and the home of her who for her day was known as Shadow, and her virgins.

"Can I not visit them?" I asked.

I saw a sarcastic smile upon Kumpana's wrinkled old face as he answered.

"Oh yes, Lord, if you are a very good swimmer. Only should you live to reach the island the women there will tear you to pieces."

Now since then I have often thought that this was rubbish, for surely women who lived in such an unnatural state would be glad to satisfy their curiosity by inspecting even so unfavourable a specimen of the male sex as myself, that is, if there were any truth at all in this tale of an African nunnery or Order of Virgins, like those of the Sun in Old Peru or the Vestals of Rome. At the time, however, all I thought of was the fate of the men who intruded upon the women's mysteries in ancient Greece, which was not one that I wished to share.

Today I am sorry that I did not show more pluck and have a try to reach that island, but then the adventure appalled me and our lost chances never return again. Not that I believed the story about the nuns, for I felt quite sure that if no one ever visited the island, these sometimes made a trip to the lake shore, as, according to Arkle, the Shadow herself had done. Kumpana's tale, however, was that their numbers were kept up by votaries who joined them every year from the mainland, picked girls of the age of twelve who were called "slaves of the *Engoi*".

While I was talking to him Hans, who had the sight of a vulture, said in Dutch,

"Look, Baas. The women are coming out of that big house."

Raising my glasses I saw that he was right, for a procession of white-robed figures emerged from under a gateway and walked in procession down to the water's edge. Here they must have entered boats, though, owing to the shadow of palms which grew upon the island shore, I could not see them do so, for presently three large canoes, each containing five or six women, appeared upon the tranquil bosom of the lake and were paddled slowly towards us. (Who made the canoes if no man ever visited the island? I wondered.) In much excitement I asked if they were coming to see me as I might not go to see them; but again Kumpana smiled and shook his head.

On they glided till they were within about two hundred yards from where we stood. Then they halted in a line and began a sweet and plaintive chant, of which in that great stillness the sound reached us clearly.

"What are they doing?" I asked. "Making an offering to the full moon?"

"Yes, Lord," Kumpana answered, "and I think something more."

He was right. There was "something more", for presently the women in the central canoe bent down and lifted a white draped form which they cast over the prow, so that it fell into the water with a large splash and vanished there.

"Is it a funeral?" I asked again.

"No doubt, Lord. See, they throw flowers on to the water where the body sank."

That was his reply, but something in his tone caused uncomfortable doubts to rise in my mind. What if the form wrapped in those white veils was quick—not dead? What if this rite was not one of burial but of sacrifice or execution? Here I may state that afterwards Hans swore that he saw the draped shape struggle, but as I did not, this may have been his imagination. Still the business was eerie and made me shiver; so much so that I was not sorry when the women turned the canoe-heads islandwards, and departed still singing, or even when Kumpana said it was time for us to follow their example and go home. To my mind there was something weird, even unholy, about this sacred lake and island, where rose fantastic buildings of unknown age inhabited by night-haunting women who made offerings to the full moon, as the old Egyptians might have done, and I believe did to Nut or Hathor, ominous offerings shaped like a human corpse. And if this was so with these, the forest was even worse, as I have now to tell.

We entered its shapes guided as before by Kumpana with the help of the creeper-stem. Somehow it depressed me more even than it had done upon our journey lakewards, perhaps because my nerves were jangled by all that I have described. At any rate, I suppose in an instinctive endeavour to keep up my spirits, I entered into conversation with Hans behind me, speaking perhaps rather more loudly than was necessary as a kind of challenge to that overpowering silence.

I need not repeat our conversation in detail, or further than to say that it had to do with the Dabandas, their superstitions, and their pretentions to magical powers. Speaking in Dutch, and sometimes in English, so that Kumpana might not understand me, I criticized these in no measured terms, announcing my belief that they were rubbish and that the Dabanda priests and magicians were a set of infernal humbugs. Hans, always argumentative, combated this view and gave it as his opinion that the Dabanda, from Kaneke and Kumpana down, were particular favourites of the devil.

At this point Kumpana looked back and remarked somewhat sternly that it was well not to talk so loudly in the forest lest the spirits who had their home there should be angered.

Then I lost my temper and expressed entire disbelief in these spirits, asking him too well what he meant by trying to fool a white man with talk of tree-dwelling spirits, and whether he was referring to monkeys which we knew lived in such places and were reported sometimes to pelt travellers through them with sticks or nuts.

Apparently Kumpana did not appreciate the joke, for he looked back at me (I could see him because at the moment we were wading through a little swamp where no trees grew), with an expression on his face that I thought threatening, and said with cold courtesy:

"I pray you to be silent, Lord Macumazahn, and above all not to offer insults to the masters of this place."

This made me angrier than ever. Was I, a more or less educated Christian man, to have my mouth stopped with the mud of such heathen mumbo-jumbo stuff? Certainly not. Therefore I continued my argument with Hans, speaking more loudly than before. Hans replied with sarcasm which was the more irritating because it contained a grain of truth, that the real reason I talked thus was that I was afraid and therefore made a noise to shout down my fear, as children do. Then he went on with a garbled version of the story of the Witch of Endor who, he declared, I think erroneously, also lived in a wood, and to quote absurd remarks about witchcraft, which he attributed to my poor old father, adding his devout hope that he, "the reverend Predikant" as he called him, was keeping an eye upon us at that moment.

Truly I believe that there must have been some exciting quality in the air of that forest, exhaled perhaps by the foliage or flowers of certain trees or creepers that grew there, for at this point a kind of rage possessed me which caused me to rate and objurgate Hans, begging him to be good enough not to take my father's name in vain and put words in his mouth that he had never spoken, in order to justify his low, savage beliefs in ghosts and magic.

Just then we came to a spot where a great tree had fallen, breaking down others in its descent and allowing the moonlight to reach us for a few paces. As we went round the stump of this prostrate tree Kumpana turned again, saying:

"I have warned you and you will not listen. White stranger, I shall warn you no more."

I looked at the man and it struck me that his aspect had changed. No longer did he seem the little withered old fellow with shrewd eyes and a wrinkled, rather kindly, if cunning, face to whom I was accustomed. He appeared to have grown taller and to have acquired a fierce cast of countenance, while his eyes glowed like those of a lion in a cave.

Remembering that moonlight plays strange tricks and that his added height must be due to the fact that he was standing on a root of the fallen tree, I took no heed, but continued to wrangle with Hans like one who has had too much to drink, or is half under the influence of laughing-gas. Then we proceeded as before and presently were again enveloped in the utter gloom of the forest. Suddenly I was brought to a standstill by butting into the trunk of a tree, while Hans behind ran the muzzle of his rifle into my back.

"Where are you going, Kumpana?" I asked indignantly, but there was no answer.

Then to call his attention I pulled at the vine-like creeper that served us as a rope. It flew back and flicked me in the face; no one was holding it!

"Hans!" I exclaimed. "Kumpana has given us the slip."

"Yes, Baas," he answered. "I thought something of that sort would happen, Baas, if you would keep on spitting in the faces of the forest spirits, of which probably he is one himself."

I reflected a while and had an idea.

"Let us get back to the place where there is light, and think things over," I said.

"Yes, Baas," he answered. "Lead on, Baas, for I don't know the way and can't see our spoor in the dark."

I turned and started, with the most disastrous results. Before we had gone ten paces I crashed into another tree-trunk and hurt myself considerably. Circumventing this, presently I plunged into a piece of swampy ground and sank over my knees in tenacious mud, out of which Hans pulled me with difficulty. Once more we started with my boots full of water, but before I had taken five steps I became entangled in some thorny creeper which pricked me horribly. Freeing myself at length I stepped forward again, only to catch my foot in a root and fall on my face. Then I sat down and said things which I prefer not to record.

"It is very difficult, Baas, to find one's way in a big wood when it is quite dark," remarked Hans blandly. "What does the Baas wish to do now?"

"Stop here till it grows lighter, I suppose, if it ever does in this infernal place," I answered. Then I filled my pipe and finding that I had lost my matches, probably when I fell, I asked Hans for one.

He produced his cherished box, of which we had not too many left, and having first filled his own pipe, struck a match and handed it to me. As I took it I remembered noticing how steadily the flame burned in that utterly still air. Then I lifted the match to my pipe and as I did so something blew it out.

"Why did you do that?" I asked angrily of Hans. "Are you afraid of setting the forest on fire?"

"Yes, Baas—I mean no, Baas. I mean I didn't blow it out, Baas. A monkey blew it out; I saw its ugly face," replied Hans in a voice that suggested to me that he was frightened.

"Rubbish!" I exclaimed. "Give me another match."

He obeyed rather unwillingly and the same thing happened, no doubt because there was a current of air which passed between the tree-trunks in puffs.

Well, my desire to smoke suddenly departed and I told Hans that we must not waste any more matches in such a draughty spot. He agreed and set his back firmly against mine, explaining that he was cold, a palpable lie as the heat in that stifling place was so great that we both ran with perspiration.

"Now be still and don't talk; I am going to sleep. You can wake me up at dawn," I said.

Scarcely were the words out of my mouth, when distinctly I heard laughter, of a queer sort it is true, for it was singularly mirthless, but still eerie laughter which appeared to come first from one quarter and then another.

"That old fool, Kumpana, is making fun of us all the time," I said. "He shall laugh the wrong side of his mouth—if I catch him."

"Yes, Baas, only now he seems to be laughing on all sides of his face and from everywhere at once—" Hans began, but the rest of his remarks were lost in a peal of unholy merriment.

It came, as he said, "from everywhere at once", and seemingly even from above our heads.

"What the deuce is it—hyenas?" I asked.

"No, Baas, it's spooks, very bad spooks. Oh, Baas, why would you come into this accursed forest to look at a lake where they drown people at midnight, and then sneer at the devils of the place and call them monkeys? I am going to pray to your reverend father, Baas, hoping that he will hear me in the Place of Fires. For if he can't help us, no one can."

I did not answer him, for when Hans was in this superstitious mood argument was useless. Moreover I was trying to remember a very interesting lecture I had once heard about echoes and how these are multiplied by natural causes. The laughter had died away and I was just recovering the thread of the lecture when something else happened. A great stone or clod of earth fell with a thud close to me, and was followed presently by scores of similar missiles. None of these touched us, it is true, but they struck everywhere around and even against the trees above our heads.

After that I really cannot recall what followed, for between weariness, bewilderment, and exhaustion I grew confused, so that my mind became torpid. I remember all kinds of sounds, some of them very loud as though trees were crashing at a distance, and some of them small and sharp and close at hand, like the agonizing squeals idle children can produce with a slate-pencil. I remember a feeling on my face which suggested that my ears and nose were being pulled by tiny hands.

I remember, too, Hans announcing in a voice which was full of fear that gorillas with eyes of fire were dancing round us, though if so I never saw them. Lastly I remember that he fired his rifle, I suppose at one of the nightmare gorillas, or some other dream-beast, for the sound of it reverberated through the forest as though it had been a cannon-shot. Also in its blinding flash I thought I saw queer figures round us with fantastic faces.

Then I remember nothing more of all those noises and visions, which were more appropriate to a victim of delirium tremens, than to a strictly sober man lost in a wood, till at length I heard a gentle voice say in Arabic:

"Rise, Macumazahn. You have wandered from your path and the air beneath these trees is poisonous and gives bad dreams. I have been sent to guide you and your servant back to Dabanda-town."

I obeyed in a great hurry and presently felt a soft hand leading me I knew not where. Or perhaps I should say that I thought I felt it, for I dare say this was part of the nightmare from which doubtless I was suffering, and seemed to be led forward, Hans clinging to my coat-tails like a child to its mother's skirts, for how long I cannot tell. All I know is that just as the dawn was breaking we found ourselves upon the edge of the forest, for there in front of us was the truncated pyramid upon which burned the altar fire, and beyond it the town. Here in the shadow of the last trees our guide departed, or seemed to depart. I noted vaguely in the gloom that she was a woman wrapped in white and of a graceful figure.

"Farewell," she said with a suspicion of mockery in her voice that somehow I thought familiar, adding:

"You are very wise, Macumazahn, yet, I pray you, grow a little wiser, for then you will not mock at what you do not understand, and will learn that there are powers in the world known to its ancient peoples of which even white men have not heard."

As she spoke she stepped backwards and before I could answer her had vanished, although still out of the darkness of that accursed forest I could hear her musical voice repeating:

"Farewell, Macumazahn, and mock no more at the powers of the ancient peoples."

"Baas," said Hans as we staggered into our house, "I think that missie must have been White-Mouse come to life again."

"I don't want to know if she was White-Mouse, or Black-Mouse, or Piebald-Mouse, or no Mouse at all. What I want is to get out of this accursed country," I replied savagely, as I kicked off my boots and threw myself down upon the bed.

CHAPTER 16

Kaneke's Message

It may be wondered why I have said so little about Arkle, the real hero of this story, whom Hans and the natives named Red-Bull because of his *taurine* build and great strength. The reason is that I saw little of the man. After the appearance of Shadow, "the Treasure of the Lake", that night before the altar and the disappearance of Kaneke laden with curses like the scapegoat of the ancient Jews, he was laid up for a while in the Chief's big house or hut with a sore heel. Notwithstanding their alleged mastery over diseases, this heel, which resulted from his race for life before the Abanda and his subsequent tramp to the Lake-town, defied all the skill and spells of the Dabanda doctors or magicians, for they had but one word to describe the followers of both these trades.

So I was called in and tackled the case with the help of a pot of antiseptic ointment bought originally in some chemist's shop, and lint that I made by picking a rag of linen to pieces. While visiting him for this purpose of course I talked to him, but even then with a sense of restraint. The truth was that already the man was hedged round with ceremonial. Yes, this English gentleman was, as it were, guarded by a pack of heathen priests; white-robed mystics who never left us alone. Of course they could not understand our language, but on the other hand they were preternaturally shrewd at reading our faces and what was passing in our minds, as I found out from remarks that they made now and again.

Thus I always had a sense of being spied on, and so, I think, did Arkle. If I tried to talk to him about the lady Shadow, I saw their large eyes fixed upon me and their ears, as it were, stretched out towards me, till at length I came almost to believe that after all they understood or guessed the meaning of every word I uttered. This did not tend to promote candid conversation, indeed it was paralysing, and at last reduced me to prattling about the weather or other trivial subjects.

At last I could bear no more, and taking advantage of the temporary absence of the priest on guard, for I guessed that he had only retired behind a mat curtain, I said outright, "Tell me, Mr. Arkle, if you like this kind of life. You seem to me to be a prisoner in all except name, though they call you a chief. Do you think such a position right for a white man of your upbringing?"

"No, I don't, Quatermain," he answered with vigour. "I hate the business, but I tell you that I am a man under a spell. I see you smile, yet it is true. Years ago it began with those dreams in London. Then I kissed, you know whom, down by that lake, and the spell became a madness. Lastly I swore allegiance to her and all the rest of it that night upon the platform yonder, and the madness became a fate. I am bound by chains that cannot be broken, this chieftainship is one that you can see; but there are others—and that's the end—or the beginning."

"Do you wish to break them?" I asked.

"My reason does, but my spirit, or my heart, or whatever you choose to call it, does not. I must win that woman, even if it costs me my life; if I do not I shall go mad."

"Forgive me," I answered, "but don't you think that in a way it may cost you more than your life: that is, your honour?"

"What do you mean?" he asked.

"I mean that like all of us you were brought up with certain traditions and, as you have told me, in a certain faith; in short, you are a white man. Now a love-affair with a woman who has other traditions and who is of another faith, or even a marriage is well enough sometimes—as Saint Paul points out. But this business is bigger than that, for in practice you must adopt her traditions and her faith and give the lie to your own. Further, you don't know what these are or where they will lead you. Remember, she warned you herself, for I heard her before that altar."

"No, Quatermain, I don't know, and she did warn me. But I took the oath all the same and I've got to keep it; moreover, I wish to keep it, for love sanctifies everything, doesn't it? And if ever a man was in love, I am."

"That's an old argument," I said, "and I am not sure. For love means passion and passion is a blind leader of the blind."

Here my wise remarks were cut short by the re-entry of the priest, who I was quite sure had been listening through the mat curtain and making out all he could from the tone of our voices. He was accompanied by Kumpana whom I had not seen since we parted in the forest. Remembering the trick he had played me there, and all that followed, the sight of this old fellow looking more bland and amiable than usual made me indignant, especially when he asked me how I was and if I and my servant had been taking any more walks in the dark.

"Listen, Kumpana," I said. "You played me an evil trick when you left us alone the other night in that thick wood, and still worse ones afterwards, of which I will not speak. You should be ashamed of your-self, Kumpana, seeing that I am a stranger whom you are bound to help and not to desert as you did."

"I ask your pardon," he replied very courteously, "if I say that I think it is you who should be ashamed, Lord Macumazahn, for al-though I prayed you not to do so, you reviled what I hold to be holy until I was forced to leave you to your punishment, which might have ended worse than it did. However, you are not at all to blame, because the air of that forest sometimes goes to the head, like strong drink, and takes away the judgment. Therefore let us forgive each other and say no more."

He spoke so courteously that I felt abashed and even humbled, for after all he had some reason on his side; acting under influences which I did not understand, I had offered insult to the spirits or elementals, or natural forces, which he revered. So I turned the subject by saying that Hans and I were now rested from our journey and should be glad to say good-bye to him as soon as possible, if the Council of the Shadow would be so kind as to help us to leave the country.

"You are free to go when you will, Macumazahn," he answered, "but if you attempt to do so before the time appointed, I warn you that it will be at great risk to yourself."

"I am not afraid of risks—!" I exclaimed, and that moment Arkle broke in, saying:

"For God's sake don't go, Quatermain. Stop here as long as you can, that is, until I vanish from your sight, I mean until we are sepa-rated, as I gather that we must be. For when this business is finished I have to begin a new life, but until then, don't leave me to deal with war and trouble alone."

Anxious as I had become now that my curiosity about Lake Mone was satisfied by an actual sight of its waters, to get clear of these eerie people who depressed me and of the land where even the air was so strange and unnatural that it affected the nerves and made one behave like a drunkard, I was touched by this appeal. I felt that there was a struggle in the heart of Arkle between his inherited convictions, or perhaps I should say all the impulses and associations of a man of his race and class, and the devouring passion which possessed him for a lovely and mystical woman, a priestess of some faith with which it was not healthy for one of white blood to have to do.

Perhaps if I stayed I might yet be able to save him from this snare; or circumstances might arise which would cut its claims. Whereas if I went his fate was sure. One by one the barriers of civilization and Christianity, which protected him from the inroads of primeval instincts and engulfment in the dark superstitions surviving from the ancient world that flourished here untouched by time, would be broken down. He would become in fact what already he was in name, the chief of these star-worshipping Dabanda. He would dwell upon the island with their priestess, his country would see him no more, and at last, when his part was played, there would be some unholy scene of sacrifice, mayhap such a one, if Hans were right, as we had been shown beneath the midnight moon on the waters of that lonesome mere beyond the forest.

I shuddered as a vision of it rose in my mind: the drugged man, helpless in his encircling cerements, being cast with songs and offerings of flowers into the bottomless crater-lake, there to seek the woman who, her day of power done, had preceded him to doom. Or there might be other fates yet more awful, such as madness induced by disillusionment, despair, and the impossibility of escape, or even by long-continued terrors like those of which we had tasted in the forest. Oh, the bait was rose-scented and set with jewels, but what of the hook within, I wondered, I before whose eyes it did not dangle.

All this and more that I do not remember passed swiftly through my mind with the result that I was about to say that I would stop and see the business through, when suddenly the mat which hung in the door-way of the room was thrust aside and there entered a priest conducting two men. These men, whom I recognized at once as belonging to the farming class of the Dabanda, prostrated themselves before Arkle, showing me that he was now acknowledged as Chief by all the people. Then the priest, bowing, informed him that they had a tale to tell and a message to deliver.

He bade them speak, whereon the elder of the two husbandmen said: "Last evening towards sunset, O Chief and Father of the Dabanda, to whom it is promised that he shall be the Shield of the holy Shadow and father of the Shadow that is to be, I and my son here were tracking a lost goat. We followed this goat into the western pass that leads through the lip of the mountain from the holy Land to that of the Abanda on the slopes and plains beyond.

"At length we caught sight of the goat near to the farther mouth of the cleft, and ran fast to catch it before it strayed into the country of the Abanda, whither we might not follow. The goat heard us and, being wilful, leaped ahead, so that before we could reach it, it was out of the mouth of the pass and into Abanda-land.

"Here, then, we sat on the border line, since we dared not pursue farther, and called to the goat to return to us. It knew our voices and was coming, when suddenly between us and it appeared armed men out of the bushes, and at the head of them no other than Kaneke, he who has forfeited the chieftainship and been cursed of the *Engoi*.

"'Stay still and listen,' he said, 'for if you stir we will throw spears and kill you.' So we stood still and he went on:

"'I, Kaneke, of the pure blood, the Chief of the Dabanda and the Shield of the Shadow, am now Chief of the Abanda also. Yes, I have brought together under one rule the two peoples who were divided long ago. Go you therefore to Kumpana, the first of the Council of the Shadow, and say to him that he may tell it to the Shadow, that the Abanda perish for the want of rain, which is withheld from them by the witchcraft of the priests and Council of the Dabanda. Their crops wither, their cows and goats give no milk, their springs dry up, and their children are in want and like to die.'

"'Therefore if within six days no rain falls upon their land, I, their chief and yours, will lead them in their thousands through the passes of the mountain-lip, fearing no curses such as of old have held them back, now that I, Shield to be of the Shadow, am their captain. We will kill any that oppose us; we will kill Kumpana and the Council of the Shadow who guide her ill; we will kill the priests of the Shadow who are evil wizards, practisers of black magic; we will pass the forest, not fearing the wood-dwellers; we will cross the lake, and I will take the Shadow and make her mine, and thenceforward rule over the two people become one again. Lastly, we will kill the white thief who is named Wanderer, and by the people Red-Bull. Yes, we will kill him by torture as an offering to the moon and the host of heaven, that henceforth rain may fall without the mountain as well as within its circle, giving plenty, so that all the people may increase and grow fat.'

"'With him we will kill the white hunter named Macumazahn, because now I know that I was made to buy him to come to this land, not to give me help as I believed, but to work me evil and to set in my place the thief Red-Bull; and the yellow man his servant we will also kill, burying them alive or burning them upon the altar. None of them shall escape us, for night and day all the passes are watched and any that set foot outside of them shall be hunted to death for our sport, as the thief Red-Bull would have been, had he not been saved by Macumazahn. Now go and at this same hour on the second day return with the answer to my message.'

"Then, Lords, Kaneke and those with him went away laughing together, killing our goat as they went, and my son and I came here to deliver the message."

For a while there was silence in that room. Kumpana seemed to be perplexed; the priests were speechless with indignation; I was horribly frightened at the prospect of the fate promised to me, and so was Hans who all this while had been sitting on the ground behind me, smoking and pretending to hear nothing, for he whispered:

"Oh, Baas, why did you ever come to this land of spooks? Why did you not run away after you had got Kaneke's ivory? Now we shall be buried alive. Or be grilled on that altar fire—just like buck's flesh, Baas."

"If so, it won't be Kaneke who will do the grilling, that is if ever he comes within three hundred yards of me," I answered savagely in Dutch.

Then I stopped short to consider Arkle in whom I noticed a curious change. A few minutes before he was looking troubled and unhappy, for reasons that may be guessed. Now he had brisked up and seemed quite cheerful, as is the way of some Anglo-Saxons (I am not one of them) when there is the prospect of a fight.

"When did you say I should be able to get about as usual, Quatermain? Was it tomorrow?"

"Yes, I think so, if you will keep a bandage on your heel," I said, then was silent, for Kumpana was speaking to the peasants, telling them to go away and rest until he sent for them.

When they had departed he bade the priests summon the Council of the Shadow, which they did with marvellous rapidity, for within five minutes they arrived in the room, six or seven old fellows. I suppose they were hanging about outside, having scented trouble. At any rate they appeared, bowed to Arkle and to me and sat down upon the ground. Kumpana repeated to them the tale of the two peasants which did not seem to surprise them; indeed they appeared to know it already. Next he asked them what they thought should be done, and they gave various replies which I scarcely understood, because they all talked together and very fast, using terms that were not familiar to me. Nor in fact did Kumpana appear to pay much attention to what they said, which gave me the idea that this asking of their advice was more or less of a formality. When they had finished he turned to Arkle and with much deference inquired his views.

"Oh, fight the beast—I mean Kaneke," answered Arkle with emphasis, adding, "but first ask Macumazahn there; he is a wise man and has seen many things."

So Kumpana repeated his question, inquiring of me whether I also held that we should fight.

"Certainly not, if you can do anything else," I replied, "for you are few and the Abanda are many. They say that they want rain and I have heard you declare that you, or some of you, can cause rain to fall. If this is true, do so. Give the Abanda as much water as they want and there will be no war."

This I said not because I believed that the priests or the Shadow, or anyone else, could break the drought and bring rain from the heavens upon the parched fields of the Abanda, but because I wanted to hear Kumpana's views upon the suggestion. To my surprise he accepted it with great respect, saying that the plan was good and worthy of consideration and that it should be submitted to the *Engoi*—that is to the Lady Shadow—for her decision.

"Do you mean that she can give the Abanda rain if she chooses?"

"Certainly," he answered with an air of mild astonishment, "at any time and in any quantity."

Then I collapsed, for what is the use of arguing with cranks or lunatics, although of course I knew that many natives hold similar beliefs as to the powers of their rain-makers.

Now, to my surprise Hans took up his parable. Squatted there upon the floor, he said in a brazen fashion:

"The Baas thinks himself wise, you all think yourselves wise, but Hans is much wiser than any of you. This is what you should do. Kaneke is the post that holds up the roof of the Abanda house. They dare to offer to fight you and to say that they will take away your priestess who lives in the lake, because Kaneke, whom they believe to be your real chief and high-priest with a right to the Lake Lady, has become their captain, so they are no longer afraid of you or of the curses of your *Engoi*. Kill Kaneke and once more they will be afraid of you, for without him they dare not invade your land which they have always held to be holy."

"And how are we to kill Kaneke?" asked Kumpana.

"Oh, that is easy. When those two men take your answer—unless the Baas would rather do it himself—I will go with them and hide behind a stone, or disguise myself as a Dabanda . . ."

Here Kumpana looked at Hans and shook his head.

". . . then when Kaneke comes to listen I will shoot him dead; that is all and there will be no more trouble."

On hearing this cold-blooded proposition Kumpana expressed doubts as to whether Kaneke could be disposed of in this way. It seemed to be his idea that a priest of the *Engoi* could only meet his end in certain fashions which he did not specify, and he added that had it been possible for him to die otherwise, Kaneke would have done so before, especially not long ago when he had tried to seize the Shadow, and afterwards. However, he was prepared to consider Hans' suggestion which did not seem to shock him in the least.

Having collected all our views Kumpana announced coolly that he would now lay them before the *Engoi* and learn that celestial potentate's will through the mouth of its earthly incarnation and minister, the Shadow. Of course, I thought that he meant to pay a visit to the island in the lake and remembering the riddle of those ancient buildings which I yearned to explore, I began to wonder if I could not persuade him to allow me to be his companion on the trip, though it is true that I had no liking for another midnight journey through that forest.

But not a bit of it. His methods were very different. Suddenly he commanded silence and ordered extra mats to be hung over the door-way and window-places, so that the room became almost dark. Then he sat down on the floor, the two priests kneeling on either side of him, while the Council of the Shadow, also sitting on the ground and holding one another's hands made a circle round the three of them. Hans, who, scenting spooks showed a strong disposition to bolt. I and—as I was relieved to observe—Arkle remained outside this circle playing the part for audience.

"By Jove," thought I to myself, for I did not dare open my lips, "we are in for a séance."

A séance it was. Yes, there in Central Africa a séance, or something uncommonly like it, which once more caused me to remember the saying of wise old Solomon, that there is no new thing under the sun. Doubtless for tens of thousands of years there have been séances among almost every people of the earth, civilized and savage, or at any rate similar gatherings having for their object consultation with spirits or other powers of which ordinary men know nothing.

The priests said some prayer in archaic language which I did not understand, if indeed they understood it themselves. I gathered, however, that it was an invocation. Then the circle began to sing a low and solemn hymn, Kumpana seated in the centre keeping time to the chant with motions of his hands and head. By degrees these motions grew fainter, till at last his chin sank upon his breast and he went into a deep trance or sleep.

Then I understood. Kumpana was what in spiritualistic parlance is called a medium. Doubtless, I reflected, it was because of this gift of his which enabled him to put himself in communication, real or fancied, with intelligences that are not of the earth and with human beings at a distance, also to exercise clairvoyant faculties, that he had risen to the high estate of President of the Council of the Shadow, the real governing body of the land. Afterwards I found that I was quite right in this supposition, for Kumpana was humble by birth and not a member of one of the priestly families; yet owing to his uncanny powers he outdistanced them all and in fact was the ruler of the Dabanda. The chief of the tribe was but an executive officer who acted upon the advice of the Council and in due course became the husband of the Shadow of the day, destined to the dreadful fate of dying with her when the Council so decreed.

As for the Shadow herself, she was nothing but an oracle, the Voice of some dim divinity through whom the commands of that divinity were made known to the Council, which interpreted them as it pleased, if indeed it did not inspire them as even then I suspected. The priests, by comparison, played a small part in the constitution of this State. For it was a State in miniature, the survival and remnant, I imagine, of what once had been a strong and in its way highly civilized community, whose principal gods were the moon and the planets (not the sun, so far as I could learn), one that had owed any greatness it might possess to its religious reputation and alleged magical powers, rather than to strength in war.

Therefore in the end it had gone down before the fighting peoples, as in this carnal world the spirit so often does in its struggle with the flesh, for as someone remarked, I think it was Napoleon, Providence is, or seems to be, on the side of the big battalions. These priests, I should add, in addition to attending to the religious rites and offerings before the altar, were the learned men and doctors of the tribe. It was they who studied the stars, drawing horoscopes and reading omens in them, not without some knowledge; for I have reason to believe that they could predict eclipses with tolerable accuracy. Also they kept records, though whether these were in any kind of writing, or merely by means of signs, I am sorry to say I was never able to ascertain, because on this point their secrecy was strict.

This is all I could discover, during my brief sojourn among them, as to the mystical religion of the Dabanda, if religion it can be called, of which I was now witnessing one of the manifestations.

After Kumpana had sunk into his trace the chant continued for a considerable time, growing fainter by degrees till at length it seemed to come from very far away like distant music heard across the sea. At least that was the effect it produced upon me, one as I think, of a semi-hypnotic character, for undoubtedly this hymn had a mesmeric power. At any rate, either owing to it or to the gloom and closeness of that room, I fell into a kind of bodily torpor which left my mind extremely active, as happens to us when we dream.

In my imagination I seemed to see a shadowy Kumpana standing before the beautiful woman upon whom I had looked on the altar platform, and speaking to her in some great dim hall.

She listened; then stood a while with outstretched hands and up-turned eyes, like one who waits for inspiration. At last it came, for tremblings ran up and down her limbs, a slight convulsion shook her face, her eyes rolled and grew wild; the pythoness was possessed of her spirit or familiar. Then her lips moved rapidly as though from them were pouring a flood of words, and the fancy faded.

Of course it was nothing but a dream induced by my surroundings and some heavy perfume, which I forgot to say, unseen by me, evidently the priests had sprinkled or scattered about the room. Yet probably this dream represented faithfully enough what took place when the oracle was consulted, for whether such ceremonies occurred in ancient Greece or are practised by the witch-doctors or diviners of Africa, there is much similarity in their methods.

I woke up, Kumpana woke up, everybody woke up. (Both Arkle and Hans told me afterwards that, like myself, they went to sleep and dreamed dreams.) The old seer yawned, rubbed his eyes, stretched himself and said quietly that he had received full directions from the *Engoi* as to what was to be done to meet the danger which threatened the Dabanda, but what those directions might be he declined to reveal. Then he sent for the two husbandmen and, pointing to one of the priests, said to them:

"Return to the Western pass with this man, and tomorrow at sunset, be at that spot where Kaneke spoke with you. If he comes again or sends messengers, as he will, say that his words have been delivered to the *Engoi*, and that this is the answer: 'Remember that you are accursed, O traitor Kaneke. Take what road you will, but learn that every one of them leads you to the grave.' Say also that the rain which the people of the Abanda demand shall fall upon them in plenty, for the time of drought is done. Let them be content therewith and know that if any of them dare to follow Kaneke into the land of the Holy Lake, a curse shall fall upon them also, such a curse as has not been told of among them or their fathers. Add these words: 'O Kaneke, the *Engoi* reads your heart. You do not seek rain to make fruitful the fields of the Abanda. You seek the Shadow. Kaneke, for you that Shadow has faded; for you she is dead. She whom you strove to bear away is dead and there awaits you only the fate of one who has slain the Shadow.'"

This cryptic message Kumpana caused the two peasants, also the priest who was to accompany them, to repeat twice. When he was sure that they had it by heart to the last word, he sent them away without any ceremony, as though he attached no particular importance to their mission.

Now I could no longer suppress my irritation, or rather my wrath. I was most heartily sick of the whole affair. I saw that there was going to be fighting of some sort in which no doubt I should be expected to take part, and I did not want to fight. What had I to do with this ancient quarrel between two long-separated sections of a tribe, who were at loggerheads over the possession of a priestess supposed to be gifted with powers as a rainmaker?

Moreover, the moral atmosphere of the place was unwholesome and jarred upon me. African customs of the more recondite sort and ancient superstitions are very interesting, but I could have too much of them, especially if certain, as I was, that behind their outward harmlessness, lies hid some red heart of secret cruelty. I wanted to get out of the place before that cruelty became manifest, or before something horrible happened to me—with Arkle if possible, but if he would not come, without him.

To tell the truth I was frightened. I suppose that my dreams in the forest and the occurrences of this séance, if I may so call it, had got upon my nerves, just as old Zikali used to do in the Black Kloof. I have always believed that there are forces round us which our senses do not appreciate, secret doors in the natural boundary wall of life that most of us never find, though to them some may have the key. But I also believe that it is most dangerous and unwholesome to come into touch with those forces, or to peep through those doors when they are opened by others. Here in Dabanda-land, however, they always stood ajar, or so I imagined, and through them came experiences and what Hans called "spooks", which thrust themselves upon the attention of those who did not desire their company. In short I wished to be gone back to a wholesome, everyday existence and never to see or hear anything more of Lake Mone, its priestess, or her votaries.

"Kumpana," I said, "is there to be a war between your people and the Abanda?"

"Yes," he answered with a slow and rather creepy smile, "there is to be war—of a sort."

"Then I want to have nothing to do with it. Kumpana, I want to get out of your country at once; risks or no risks, I wish to be off."

"I fear that is impossible, Lord Macumazahn," he answered. "Have you not heard the word of the *Engoi* that the drought which has endured beyond the mountain for three years is at an end? That word is true; great storms are coming up through which you could not travel. The rain would stop you even if you escaped the spears of the Abanda. Moreover," he added quickly before I could express disbelief in the arrival of these storms, and with a faint sneer, "we have been told that the Lord Macumazahn is a very brave man, one who loves fighting."

"Then you have been told a lie. Also, who told you?"

"That does not matter. We know more about you than you think, Macumazahn. Also we have been told that you accepted payment from Kaneke to come to this country and not to leave it until the object of your coming was accomplished, payment in ivory and gold; and we believed, Lord Macumazahn, that you were a very honest man who always fulfilled your promises, especially when your services had been bought."

Here Arkle, to his credit, intervened sharply, saying:

"Be silent, Kumpana. Would you insult your guest—?"

"Thank you, Arkle," I broke in in English, "but I can look after myself. He will only tell you that you are now the Chief of his people and that I am your guest, not his."

Then addressing Kumpana in his own language, I went on.

"You have been misinformed. I never pretended to great courage, especially in wars that do not concern me. For the rest my bargain was to accompany Kaneke to his country, not to fight battles there, as I could prove to you if you were able to read my language. This Kaneke who was to be your chief, said that he could not travel here without me, which is true, for had it not been for me and Hans he would never have started. Further, had it not been for us he would have been killed by the Abanda who were hunting the white lord who is now your chief. So I came, not for that reason but because he paid me, for in such fashions I earn my living. Yet I should not have come for this cause alone. I had another. It was that I had heard of your holy lake and a little of your people and their customs, and being curious in such matters I desired to look upon the one and to study the others for myself—"

"Which things you have done to your heart's content," broke in Kumpana.

"Still," I went on not heeding him, "never shall it be said that I, Macumazahn, took pay that I did not earn to the full. Therefore I will take my share in your war, doing all that is asked of me as best I can, especially as I have a score to settle with this Kaneke, who by his treachery brought my two servants to their death. Only I demand your promise and that of the Council of the Shadow and that of the white lord who has now become your chief against my counsel, that when this war is finished, I and my servant shall be allowed to depart at once in peace and with such help as you can give me."

"It is yours, Lord, we swear it by the *Engoi*!" exclaimed Kumpana in a humble voice and with the air of one who is ashamed of himself. "Pardon my words if they offended you, for know that as to your love of fighting I have but repeated what your servant Hans told me, and for the rest I learned it from Kaneke."

"Whom you have proved to be a traitor and a liar," I said angrily.

Then I turned to Arkle and asked him whether he also gave me his promise that I should be allowed to go when the war was ended.

"Of course, if you wish it," he answered in English, "though I hoped that you would stop here with us a while. The truth is, Quatermain, that I shall be very lonely without you," he added with a sigh, which I thought pathetic, knowing all it meant.

"Then why do you stay here?" I asked bluntly.

"Because I must; because it is my fate; because I am under a charm that may not be broken. Also, Quatermain, do you not understand" (this he said rapidly and in a low voice) "that if I were to break my oaths, or try to—which I cannot—I should not live another day?"

"Yes, Arkle, I understand and I am sorry," I replied, and, bowing to them all, left the house.

"Baas," said Hans outside, "do you remember that trap of willow-rods I made once to catch eels" (he meant barbel mudfish) "down on the Tugela when we could get nothing else to eat? It was a very good trap, Baas, for when the eel had pushed its way in, the willow rods shut up behind it, so that it could not get out again, and afterwards we ate it. This land is a trap like that, and the Baas Red-Bull is the eel and the Shadow lady is the bait, and by and by I think these spook people will cook and eat him."

I shivered at Hans' suggestive illustrations, and answered:

"Look out that they do not cook and eat us too."

"Oh no, Baas, they won't do that because they haven't found the right bait to catch you. Luckily there are not two Shadow-ladies, Baas, and the trap is no good without the right bait."

CHAPTER 17

The Great Storm

That evening clouds like to those of a monsoon began to bank up over lake-land and all the country round so far as the eye could see.

"That Shadow-lady is a very good rain-doctoress, Baas," said Hans. "You remember Kumpana said that she promised rain to those Abanda who have had none for three years, or very little. Now I think that they are going to get plenty."

"Then perhaps they won't make war," I answered indifferently.

Certainly the weather was very peculiar. The heat, which had been considerable for some days before, now grew intense; I should imagine that on this particular evening it must have risen to 108 or 110 degrees in the shade. Moreover it was of a most oppressive character; the air was so thick that I felt as though I were breathing cream and I could not make the slightest effort without bursting into profuse perspiration.

There I lay upon my bed stripped to the shirt in the best draught that I could find, which was none at all, and gasped like a fish out of water, praying that the storm would burst and bring coolness. In the lady Shadow's powers I had no faith. I was quite certain, however, that Kumpana and the other old men were well acquainted with the signs of the local weather, and knew that it was about to undergo a general break after the long drought. Hence the prophecy so confidently announced by the Council. This drought, for some reason which I cannot explain, never affected the crater area unduly, for the Dabanda had just gathered in an excellent harvest.

Hans, who like most Hottentots was quite indifferent to heat, went out into the town to prospect and returned saying that the people showed considerable alarm. Some were looking to the roofs of their houses, while others were driving their stock into caves and sheltered places, or carrying home the last of the harvest in baskets, even the children, of whom there were not many, being pressed into this service. The priests, too, he said, were engaged in building a kind of palm-leaf tent over the altar on the stone platform, presumably to prevent the rain from putting out the fire, which it seemed had always burned there from time immemorial.

The night came, a night of dreadful heat in which I could not sleep a wink, or do anything except swallow quantities of water mixed with the juice of a sub-acid, plum-like fruit that grew wild in the crater, which made an astringent and most refreshing drink. The dawn that followed was as dark as that of a November day in London, but as yet there was no rain nor any lifting of the heavy silence.

After eating, or pretending to eat, I crept across to the Chief's house, to be informed by a priest outside that I could not be admitted, as the lord Wanderer was engaged with the Council. I took the hint and went home again, feeling sure that the plan was to cut me off from Arkle over whom my influence was feared. It almost seemed as though Kumpana and his companions were psychological experts, if that is the right description, who could read what was passing in the minds of others. Indeed, I began to believe that although they could not understand our words when we spoke in English in their presence, they understood the drift of them, also that I wished to persuade him to shake off their shackles and get out of their clutches.

Why were they so anxious to keep him here? I wondered. I wonder still. Doubtless there was some overwhelming reason which they would not reveal. As I do today, I inclined to the view that mainly they were actuated by ambition. They, a dwindling, superstition-ridden race, desired once more to become a power in their world. To accomplish this they must add to their number, which could only be done by incorporating the thousands of the virile Abanda under the rule of a man of force and ability who understood the arts of civilization. This to my mind is why Arkle was brought to Mone-land, tempted by the bait of the beautiful woman called Shadow to whom he had been so mysteriously drawn.

That is the best explanation which I can offer; not a very satisfactory one, I admit, because it presupposes that this lady Shadow could impress her personality upon him from a great distance, as he alleged that she had done, and also some knowledge of the future on the part of her priests and advisers. Or mayhap these were only acting upon the dictates of some ancient prophecy of a sort that is common enough among the more mystical of the African peoples, although such prophecies rarely come to the knowledge of Europeans, save in forms too obscure and tangled to be understood by them. The same reason, if to a less degree, made them so anxious that I should visit their country for a while. They wanted to pick my brains as to our system of government and the rest, which indeed they did upon every opportunity, although I have not recorded their questions. They were a little, buried folk, which its astute rulers, especially that very clever man Kumpana, desired to build up again into a nation. This, I believe, was the true key to the secret of all their plottings.

When I got back I found men strengthening the roof of my house and others digging a trench round it, connecting it with a sluice or water-course not far away, which showed me what they expected in the way of a storm. I went indoors and tried to take a nap, but could not because of curious noises that I was unable to explain and felt too languid to investigate.

Towards sunset Kumpana came to see me. Although I received him somewhat coldly he was very polite. Having inspected the arrangements for the protection of the house, he apologized for having sneered at me on the previous day, saying that he did it for a reason and not because he believed that I was a coward or had taken pay for which I did not intend to give consideration. This reason, he explained frankly, was that he knew I should get angry and promise to stop with them till the end of the war, and that having once given my word I should not break it.

I sat amazed at his cunning, which showed so deep a knowledge of human nature and such insight into my character, but I really was too hot to argue with him. Then, leaving the subject quickly, he begged me not to go out, as the storm might begin at any minute, and also for another cause.

"You are wondering what the strange sounds you hear may mean," he said. "Come up to the roof of the house and I will show you."

As I have said I had heard such sounds, which I thought were like to those of the galloping of herds of cattle, mixed with grunts and bellowings. When I reached the roof I saw whence they came. On either side of the town enormous numbers of every kind of game were rushing towards the forest, doubtless to shelter there from the approaching tempest. There were elands, hartebeest, gnus, sable-antelope, oryx, buffaloes, quaggas, and a host of smaller animals, all possessed by fear and all galloping towards the trees.

"These beasts understand what is coming," said Kumpana, "and are mad with terror. They will not hurt us Dabanda because they know us, and, as you have seen, we have power over them; but if they smelt you, a stranger, they would toss and trample you."

I admitted that it was very probable, and stood a while staring at this, the strangest sight, perhaps, that I have seen in all my experience as a hunter. Presently I turned to descend, but Kumpana bade me wait a while if I would see something still more strange.

As he spoke I heard a sound which I could not mistake: that of an elephant trumpeting shrilly.

"I thought you told me that all the elephants had been driven out of Mone-land," I said, astonished.

"So I did, Lord," answered Kumpana, "but it seems that they have come back again, flying before the great storm or earthquakes for shelter to the country where some of them were bred generations ago, before we sent them away."

As he spoke, emerging from a cloud of dust to the right of the town there appeared an enormous bull elephant running rapidly, and behind it many others. I knew the beast at once by its size, the grey markings on its trunk and forehead, and certain peculiarities of its huge tusks. It was the king-elephant with which we had experienced so curious an adventure upon the mound in the midst of the plain that Kaneke had called the gathering-place of elephants; the very beast which we had seen being greeted by the countless company of its fellows, which, too, with them, had afterwards pursued us back to our camp. Its appearance here was so marvellous, so utterly unexpected even in that eerie land of strange happenings, that really I turned quite faint. As for Hans, who was beside me, he sank down in a heap, muttering:

"*Allemagter!* Baas, here is that ugly old devil which threw Little Holes and Jerry into the pool and nearly blew my stomach out. He has come after us, Baas, and all is finished."

"Not yet," I answered as quietly as I could. "Also perhaps he has come after someone else."

Then I turned and watched the majestic creature rush past the town, followed by a great number of others, between fifty and seventy, I should say; all of them, I noted, mature bulls, for not a cow or a half-grown beast could I see among them.

Kumpana seemed to understand my wonder at this circumstance and without its being explained to him, for he said:

"These elephants are the bulls that were bred in this country long years ago in our fathers' days, and have now returned to their home. The cows and all their progeny have gone elsewhere, and indeed we did not need them."

"What do you mean by that?" I asked sharply, but he pretended not to hear me, or at any rate he made no answer.

When the herd of elephants had thundered past and, following all the other creatures, had vanished into the forest, we descended from the roof into the house, where Kumpana began to say farewell, cautioning me not to leave its shelter until the coming storm was over.

"Wait a minute," I said. "Where is the white lord, your new Chief?"

"In his own place where he must stay, Macumazahn," he answered.

"I perceive that you wish to separate us," I said again.

"Perhaps for a while, Macumazahn, for the good of both of you. You, for your part, wish to separate him from us which, though it is natural enough, may not be. The white lord has sworn himself to the Dweller in the Lake and must abide with her and us. Should he try to break his oath, he would be slain; and should you tempt him to do so, you would be slain also. Therefore it is best that you should remain apart till this war is accomplished."

"Is it certain that there will be a war?" I asked, "and, if so, when?"

"Yes, Lord, I think there will be a war of men after that of heaven is finished," and he pointed towards the sky, "for Kaneke will surely strive to win back all that he has lost. In that war, Lord, you will be called upon to take your share, though perhaps it will not be such a one as you expect. When the time comes I will wait upon you, and now farewell, for the great storm is at hand and I must seek shelter while it rages."

When he had gone I talked to Hans about the arrival of the mysterious old elephant and its herd, which upset him very much, for he answered:

"I tell you, Baas, that these beasts are not elephants; they are men bewitched by the Dabanda wizards, and, Baas, there is something terrible going to happen in this accursed land."

As he spoke "something terrible" began to happen, for the dense air was filled with a moaning sound, the exact like of which I had never heard before, caused, I suppose, by wind that as yet we did not feel, stirring in the tops of the trees of the vast forest. It was as though all the misery in the wide world had gathered and was giving utterance to its pain and sorrows in prolonged, half-stifled groans.

"The ghosts are flying over us, Baas," began Hans, but he did not finish his sentence, for at that moment the solid ground began to heave beneath our feet. It heaved slowly in a sickening fashion that made my vitals writhe within me and threw to the floor articles from some rough shelves which Hans had made.

"Earthquake! Out you go before the roof comes down!" I exclaimed to Hans, quite unnecessary advice in his case, for he was already through the door-way. I followed, running across the little garden to the open space where there was nothing to fall upon us. Here I was brought to a standstill, for another prolonged heave threw me to the ground where I thought it safer to remain, praying that it would not open and swallow me.

"Look!" said Hans at my side, pointing to one of the two column-like towers whence the Dabanda astrologers observed the stars, or rather at what had been the tower, for as he spoke it bowed gracefully towards us, as did the forest trees, as though they were making an obeisance. Then down it fell with a crash—which, however, we could not hear because of the moaning sound that I have described.

The heaving ceased; that earthquake went by, and with it the moaning, which was succeeded by an intense and awful silence. It was now the hour of sunset and the air seemed to be alight with a red glow like to that of molten iron, though the sun itself could not be seen. This glow, in which everything appeared monstrous and distorted, suddenly broke up into great flakes of furious colour, which to my fancy resembled wide-winged and fantastic creatures, such as haunted the earth in the reptile age, only infinitely larger, flitting away into the darkness overhead.

These shapes departed on rainbow-tinted wings and the darkness fell, a palpable thing, a mass of solid night stretching from earth to heaven. A minute later this inky blackness ceased to be, for it was changed to fire. All space was filled with lightnings, not here and there only, but everywhere those lightnings blazed, and in the glare of them we could see for miles and miles. They seemed to be striking all about us. Thus I saw trees collapse and vanish in clouds of dust, and a great rock that lay not far off shatter to pieces. By common consent we rose and ran back to the house, and as we passed its door came the thunder.

I have listened to much thunder of the African brand during my roving life, but over it all that of Lake Mone can claim supremacy. Never have I heard its equal. Some thunder cracks, like a million rifle shots, some roars like the greatest guns, and some rolls and mutters. This did all three, and at once; moreover, the cliffs of the huge crater in which the Dabanda lived caused it to echo backwards and forwards, multiplying the volume of its sound. The general effect was fearsome and overwhelming; combined with that of simultaneous and continual lightnings it crushed the mind.

Through the tumult I was aware of Hans staring at me with a terrified countenance which the blue gleam of the flashes had turned livid, and heard him shouting out something about Judgment Day, a quite unnecessary reminder, as my own thoughts were already fixed upon that event, which almost I believed to be at hand. I do not know for how long we endured this awful demonstration of Nature at her worst, because I grew bewildered and could take no count of time, but at length the turmoil lessened somewhat and the flashes blazed at longer intervals. Then, just as I hoped that the storm was passing, the rain, or rather the water-spout, began. Seldom have I seen such rain; it fell in a sheet and with an incessant roar for hours.

Our house had stood the shakings of the earthquake, which still continued at intervals, because its walls were made of tree-trunks plastered over, and therefore being non-rigid, gave to the shock. But these had cracked the roof in two places, with the result, of course, that the water poured into the building, so that soon we were half flooded. Indeed had not the cement-like mixture, as yet not firmly set, which had been poured on to the roof that day to strengthen it, been driven into those cracks, and closed them, I think that we should have been washed out of the house. But luckily this happened and we only experienced great discomfort. Luckily, too, our beds stood upon a kind of raised platform, so that the water did not reach them and we were able to lie down, and after the earth-tremors ceased, at last to sleep.

When I woke daylight, of a sort, had come and it was raining less heavily. Throwing a skin rug over my head, I climbed to the roof, and beheld a scene of desolation. All the country was more or less under water, some of the houses of the town had been shaken down by the earthquake or washed away, and many of the forest trees were shattered by lightning.

The open place on which stood the stone platform was a lake, and the shelter which had been erected to protect the fire upon the altar was crushed or shaken flat, having as we learned afterwards, extinguished the fire, to the great consternation of the Dabanda people and especially of their priests. Moreover, although there was less rain falling within the crater-ring, over the country beyond, as the sky there showed, it was pouring as heavily as ever. Also new thunderstorms were in progress far away.

For three days this miserable weather continued, marked by constantly recurring tempests beyond the borders of Mone-land, and a few more slight shocks of earthquake. During all this time Hans and I scarcely left the house, nor were we visited by anyone, except the women who waited on us and brought us food. With great courage these women stuck to their duty through everything, and from them we learned that all the people were terrified, for no such tempest was told of in their annals.

On the fourth morning old Kumpana appeared, looking as calm as ever. He told us that, so far as they could learn, no one had been killed in Mone-land which, as the crops had been harvested, had taken little harm. Reports reached them, however, that the Abanda who lived on the outer slopes of the mountains and plains beyond had suffered terribly. Some had been drowned by the torrents which rushed down the hillsides, and some crushed in their houses that, owing to their lack of timber, were largely built of stone, and therefore were overthrown by the earthquake. Also such crops as they had, which ripened later than those in Mone-land, were flattened and destroyed.

I remarked that all these misfortunes must have taken the heart out of them, with the result that they would probably give up the idea of making war, especially as they had now got all the rain they wanted.

"Not so," answered Kumpana, "for they need food of which they know there is plenty in our country and nowhere else. Tomorrow, Lord, we shall ask you to march with us to fight them."

"Where?" I inquired.

"I am not sure, Lord. The order that we have received is that we should march to the western pass. Doubtless when we come to it, other orders will reach us, telling us what we must do."

"Whose orders?" I asked, exasperated. "Those of your new Chief?"

"No, Lord, those of the *Engoi* which come to us through the air."

"Oh," I exclaimed, "do they? And does your Chief, the Wanderer, come with us to this battle?"

"No, Lord, he stays to guard the town. Now I must bid you farewell as there is much to do. Tomorrow, when it is time to march, I will send for you."

"Well, I'm blessed!" I said as the door closed behind him.

"No, Baas," said Hans, "not blessed; another word, Baas, which your reverend father would never let me speak. As he used to say, Baas, the world is full of wonders and it is nice to see as many of them as one can before we go to the place where there is nothing but fire, like there was here the other night when the storm burst. This will be a very funny war, Baas, in which the orders reach the generals through the air and they don't know what they are going to do until they get them. That war will be a fine thing to think about afterwards, Baas, when we are back in Durban or in the Place of Fires, whichever it may be."

"Stop your ugly mouth and listen," I said. "I mean to get out of this hole. We are going to march to the western pass; well, I shall run through it and desert."

"Yes, Baas, and leave the guns and everything else behind, and be killed by the Abanda on the other side, or lose our way and starve if we escape them. Well, it will be soon over, Baas, and we shan't have a long journey to make this time."

So he went on, talking sound enough sense in his silly, topsy-turvy idioms, but I paid no more heed to him.

So sick and tired was I of the whole business that I did not care what happened. I would just go as the wind took me, hoping that it would blow me out of Mone-land as soon as possible. If it were fated otherwise I could not help it and there was nothing more to be said.

That day I made yet another effort to see Arkle, but when we had tramped through the mud to the Chief's house, it was only to find it guarded by soldiers, who politely turned us back. Then understanding that a wall had been built between him and me which I could not climb, I returned and wrote up my diary. Those pages of smudged pencil, by help of which I indite this record, are before me now and their language is so lurid that it is difficult to believe they were written by a man as temperate in all things, and especially on paper, as myself.

That night some solemn ceremony took place on the altar platform, to which I was not asked and, I think, should not have attended if I had been. I believe that it had to do with the relighting of the fire, for from our roof we saw this blaze up suddenly. It was witnessed by a great number of people, Arkle among them, for Hans caught sight of him arrayed in Dabanda dress and escorted by priests with torches.

It distressed me to think of him playing the part of a high-priest among these uncanny other-world kind of folk, but like the rest, there it was and could not be helped.

The religious function, for I supposed it to be religious, was accompanied by much melancholy music and many songs, also by drum-beating, which I had not heard before. It went on for a long while and ended with a torchlight procession back to the town.

After we had breakfasted next morning, Kumpana arrived, accompanied by a guard of thirty spearmen, and remarked casually, just as though an evening party were concerned, that if we were ready, it was time to start to the war. I replied in an airy fashion that, being impatient for battle, I had been waiting for him, for I wished to give him the impression that I was pawing the ground with eagerness, like the warhorse in the *Book of Job*.

He smiled and said he was glad to hear it and that he hoped I should remain in the same mind, adding that he knew I could run fast from the rate at which I entered Mone-land.

I reflected to myself that this would be nothing compared with the rate at which I should leave it, if I got the chance, but contented myself with inquiring who would look after our possessions while we were away. He replied that they would be removed to a hiding-place and well cared for; which left me wondering whether they would ever come out of it again.

So off we went, closely surrounded by the guard, two soldiers carrying our spare rifles, ammunition, and necessary kit. As we marched through the town where I saw women, but no men, repairing the damage done to the houses and gardens by the storm, a girl pushed through the soldiers and gave me a note. It was from Arkle and read:

My Dear Quatermain, Don't misjudge me, as I fear you must. I cannot go with you. It is impossible, for reasons you would scarcely understand. Also if I could, my foot is not well enough yet. Whatever you see, do not be astonished, for these Dabanda are not as other people and play their own game, which is dark and difficult to follow. Above all, don't try to escape. It would only mean your death and that of Hans.

That was all, except his initials, and quite enough too, as I thought. Evidently Arkle was an eel in a trap, as Hans put it, or a bull in a net, a better simile in his case. Also he or some of his confounded councillors had guessed my desire to escape, for in this country a bird of the air seemed to carry the matter even faster than it does in others, and he warned me against it, having been told what the result would be. Well, the idea must be abandoned; from the first it was madness to think that such an attempt could succeed.

About three miles away at a village, or what remained of it after the storm, we met the "army", to give it Kumpana's imposing name. It consisted of some two hundred and fifty spearmen! I asked him where the rest of it was and he replied, with his odd little smile, that it did not exist, for all the other able-bodied men had been left to defend the town and the Chief. Then I asked him what strength the Abanda could put into the field. He replied that he was not sure, but he thought from ten to twelve thousand warriors, for they were a large people accustomed to the use of arms, and sometimes they warred with other tribes and, always conquering, absorbed those who were left of them.

Lastly I inquired in mild exasperation how he expected to fight ten thousand men with two hundred and fifty. He replied blandly that he did not know, being himself a councillor and seer, not a soldier, but that doubtless it would be done somehow according to the directions he might receive; adding, I presume in a sarcastic spirit, that my presence would be worth many regiments, because Kaneke and the

Abanda were afraid of me and my white man's wisdom and weapons. Then I gave up, fearing lest more of such gibes should cause me to lose my temper and say things I might regret.

We marched on for the most of that day through the beautiful crater country where flooded rivulets—for it had no large streams, some of which we forded with difficulty—gave evidence of the great tempest, as did landslides on the slopes and lightning-shattered trees. But not one soul did we meet, although I saw a few cattle grazing, apparently unherded. The land seemed to be quite deserted, even by the game which I presumed was still hiding in the forest, and when I asked Kumpana where the people had gone, he said he did not know, but he supposed that they were in hiding fearing a return of the storm. Or perhaps, he added, as though by an after-thought, it was the Abanda that they feared, knowing that now they were under the command of Kaneke who might dare to enter the land.

At length in the afternoon we came to a village, to reach which we had to march round some deep clefts that, from their fresh appearance and great depth must, I saw, have been caused by the recent earthquakes. Here a few old men, and some women, also old, were engaged in cooking large quantities of food, evidently in preparation for our arrival.

We were now within five or six miles of the wall of cliff which surrounded the whole crater, although we could scarcely see this cliff, because the village lay in a hollow and for some time we had been passing through park-like country where tall trees grew so thickly that they cut off the view.

We ate of the food, which was excellent, and rested, because Kumpana told us that we should remain at this place until far on into the night, when we must march again, so as to reach the cliff by dawn. I asked what we were to do when we did reach it. Again he replied that he did not know; perhaps we should go through the pass and attack the Abanda, or perhaps we should wait for them to attack us, or perhaps we should retire. Then he hurried off before I could put more questions.

The last thing I saw as the sun set was the party of old men and women who had cooked the food tramping off eastwards with their bundles on their backs, which suggested that they did not mean to return. Then, in order that I might be fresh in the face of emergencies, I went to sleep, and so remained till about three on the following morning when Kumpana woke us and suggested that we should breakfast, as the army was about to start.

Having swallowed something, presently off we went, travelling by the light of the waning moon and the stars. It was so dark among those trees that had not a man led me by the hand I should not have been able to see where to go, but the gloom did not seem to incommode the Dabanda, a people who must have had the eyes of cats. On we travelled, always uphill, for we were now climbing the slope of the cliff, till at length the sky grew grey with dawn. Then we halted, waiting for the sun.

Presently with startling suddenness it appeared over the eastern edge of the crater far away, its level beams striking upon the western cliffs, although the crater itself was still shrouded in mist and gloom. Or rather, immediately in front of us, they struck upon where the cliff should have been and showed us a strange and terrible sight, which caused a gasp of astonishment to burst from the lips of even those cold, silent men. For behold, it was riven from crest to foot by the shock of earthquake, and in place of the narrow pass a few yards wide, was a vast gulf that could not have measured less than a quarter of a mile across!

The great mass of the precipice was torn asunder and hurled, I suppose, down the outer slopes; at any rate there was but little debris in the cleft itself, which suggested that the earth-waves that did the damage must have rolled from within the crater outwards towards the plain. Why it should have concentrated its terrific strength and centre of disturbance upon this particular spot I cannot say who am ignorant of the ways of earthquakes, unless it was because here the wall of cliff was thinner and weaker than elsewhere; also it may have been destroyed in other sections of the gigantic ring of precipice upon which I never looked.

The result of the cataclysm, so far as the Dabanda and their country were concerned, was obvious. They were no longer protected by a mighty natural wall pierced only with a few narrow clefts that could be held by a handful of men, for there was now, as Hans remarked, a fine open road between them and the rest of Africa, on which an army could march in safety without breaking its ranks. Their seclusion was gone and their secret land lay open to the world.

Did Kumpana understand this and all it meant? I wondered as I gazed at his impassive face. More, did he know what had happened before we reached the place, and, if so, why did he come there with his beggarly little force? Was it with some subtle hidden object? I cannot tell, though in view of what happened afterwards I have my own opinion of the matter.

Chapter 18

Allan Runs Away

"If you intended to hold the pass with these, Kumpana," I said, pointing to the redoubtable two hundred and fifty, "now that it has grown so wide, that cannot be done."

"No, Lord," he answered, "it is not possible by strength alone; even charging cattle could sweep us away with their horns if there were enough of them."

"Then what do you mean to do, Kumpana? Return home again?"

"I cannot say, Lord. Let us go forward and look through the gap in the cliff, for then perhaps we shall learn what we must do. It may be that the Abanda, frightened by its fall, have run away, or that they are afraid to enter lest another earthquake should come out of Mone-land and swallow them up living."

"Perhaps," I answered, but to myself I thought that unless I were mistaken, it would take more than this to frighten the furious and desperate Kaneke.

Kumpana issued an order to his men who, with a kind of stolid indifference which suggested fatalism or a knowledge that they were protected by unseen forces, instantly marched forward towards the new pass.

"Baas," said Hans to me, "we are not captains here, but only 'luck-charms', so let us keep behind. I don't like the look of that place, Baas."

As usual there was practical wisdom in Hans' suggestion, for if there should happen to be an ambush, or anything of the sort, I did not see why we should be its first victims. So, taking my chance of again being sneered at by Kumpana, I kept well to the rear of the little column, among the carriers indeed.

Well, there was an ambush, in fact a first-class specimen of that stratagem of war. In one of Scott's poems I remember a description of how a highland hillside which seemed to be quite deserted, suddenly bristled with men springing up from behind every bush and fern-brake. Substituting rocks, of which thousands lay about in the newly opened pass, for bushes and bracken, the scene repeated itself in that Central African gorge.

Indeed, unless their *Engoi* had developed wonderful spiritual activity for their protection, I suppose that every Dabanda spears-man would have been killed, had not some donkey among their enemies made the mistake of blowing a horn before they had advanced into the mouth of the pass, thereby giving a premature signal to attack. At the sound of this horn the rocks became alive with Abanda warriors who rushed to the onslaught with a savage yell. Our heroes gave one look, then turned and bolted in a solid mass, I presume without waiting for orders. Or perhaps their orders were to bolt at this critical moment, which had been foreseen. Really I neither know nor care.

"Run, Baas," said Hans, wheeling round and giving me the example, and off I went back upon our spoor. Never a shot did I fire, or do anything except foot it as hard as I was able.

I think I have told how Kumpana remarked at the beginning of this expedition that he believed I was a good runner, which is, or was, true, for in those days I was very light and wiry with an excellent pair of lungs. Now I determined to show him that he had not over-estimated my powers. In fact, for quite a long way I led the field with Hans, who also knew how to step out when needful, immediately at my heels.

"Baas," puffed that worthy when we had done a mile or two down the slope, "if we did not lead these dogs to battle, at least we are leading them out of it."

So we were, but just then some of the most active of them got ahead of us.

Well, to cut a long story short, we ran all day, with short intervals for repose and refreshment. Looking back just as we entered the more densely wooded country where we had camped the night before, I saw that this strategical retreat was quite necessary, for at a distance followed the Abanda army by the hundred, or, unless my fears multiplied their number, by the thousand. But they could not run as we did, though once they made a spurt and pressed us hard. Or perhaps they feared lest they too were being led into an ambush and therefore advanced with caution, sending scouts ahead. At any rate, after this rush from which we escaped with difficulty, they fell back again, and when we reached Dabanda-town, which we did before evening, for we returned at about twice the rate of our outward journey, they were not in sight.

Some of the Council and a few others were waiting for us in the town. Evidently they knew we were coming, how I cannot say, but there they were with watchmen set upon the altar platform. Also most fortunately they had prepared food and native beer for the consumption of their retiring heroes. Good heavens! how we fell upon it, especially upon the drink, of which Hans swallowed so much that at last I was obliged to knock the pot out of his hand.

Whilst we were devouring this meal, with anxious eyes fixed upon the route we had followed, I realized the fact that except for the few people I have mentioned, the town was quite deserted; nobody could be seen.

"Where have they gone?" I said to Hans.

"Into the forest to join the spook-elephants, I expect, Baas," he replied, stuffing a lump of meat into his mouth, "and that is where we shall have to follow them."

So it was, for just then Kumpana arrived, quite calm but looking a little the worse for wear. Having congratulated me upon "the strength of my legs", he remarked that we must take refuge by the lake at once, and that as the forest was a difficult place in which to find one's way, we should do well to keep close to him.

"Certainly," I replied, "and I hope that this time you, Kumpana, will keep close to us."

So we started, wearily enough, and without an opportunity being given to us to visit our house, as I wished to do. As we reached the first of the trees, looking back I saw the Abanda hordes running into the town, which was quite undefended. They did not stay to plunder or to burn it; they simply ran through it on our tracks. When they reached the stone platform, however, they stopped, and one of them, I think it was Kaneke himself, rushed up the steps followed by some others, and scattered the sacred fire, extinguishing it for the second time.

Kumpana, at my side, shuddered at the sight.

"He shall pay. Oh, certainly he shall pay!" he muttered, adding, "Come on, you fools, come on. The *Engoi* awaits you!"

Then we plunged into the thick of the forest and lost sight of them.

This happened while it was still afternoon, some time before nightfall, so that light of a sort befriended us until we were well into the wood. Just before the perennial gloom of the place, deepened by the advance of evening, turned to darkness, we reached a spot where few trees grew because of the swampy nature of the soil. Here, on the shore of a shallow lake formed by flood water, Kumpana announced that we must camp till the following morning, as so many men ignorant of its paths could not travel through the forest before the sun rose.

"What if the Abanda overtake us here?" I asked.

"They will not overtake us," he answered. "They dare not enter the trees until there is light, and then I think that only the boldest will come, because they know this place to be holy, one forbidden to them."

As I was too tired to inquire further about this or any other matter, I accepted the explanation and just lay down to sleep, hoping that Kumpana would not give us the slip for the second time. To tell the truth I was so exhausted after racing along all day in a hot climate, that I was ready to trust to luck, not caring much what happened.

On the whole I rested well, which is not always the case when one is over-weary with mental and physical exertion, and without suffering from any of the unpleasant experiences which had afflicted Hans and myself on our return from our visit to the lake. Once I did wake up, however; I think it was after midnight, for the moon, now in its last quarter, shone brightly overhead and was reflected in the flood-water. By its light I saw a long line of shadowy and gigantic forms marching between the trees upon the farther side of this water, and for a moment wondered what they were, or whether I was dreaming. Then I remembered the elephants that we had seen fleeing before the storm and earth-tremblings to refuge in this forest, where doubtless they still remained with the other wild beasts.

After this I went to sleep again, nor did I wake until the sun was up. We rose and ate of food that was given to us. Whether the soldiers carried it with them from the town, or whether it was brought to them during the night, I do not know, but both then and afterwards there was plenty for us all.

Our meal finished, Kumpana gave the order to march, and off we went, walking slowly round the stretch of flood-water which I have mentioned into the dense woodland beyond. While we crossed this patch of comparatively open ground, I observed that our numbers were now much diminished. We had entered the forest over two hundred and fifty strong. Now I could not count more than five and twenty men, the rest had vanished.

I asked Kumpana where they had gone.

"Oh," he answered, "this way and that to talk to the wild beasts, of which the wood is full after the storm, and tell them that we are friends whom they must not harm," a reply I thought so crazy that I did not continue the conversation.

When I discussed the matter with Hans, however, he took another view.

"They are spook-beasts, as I have told you before, Baas," he said, "especially the elephants. These wizards have command over them, as we have seen with our eyes, and doubtless have gone to order them out of our path, as Kumpana says. It is as well, Baas," he added meaningly, "seeing that we are without rifles."

"Have you not been able to find that man to whom I gave mine to carry?" I asked, colouring.

"No, Baas. He is not to be found; perhaps he is dead or perhaps he has stolen it, or hidden it away. Nor are those who carried the spare guns to be found."

"And where is yours?" I asked sharply.

"Baas," he answered in a dejected voice, "I threw it away. Yes, when I thought those Abanda were going to catch us, I threw it away that I might run the faster."

We looked at each other.

"Hans," I said, "do you remember that Tom and Jerry did this same thing when we were hunted by the elephants, and how I told them that this we should never do, whereon they said that if they were not Christians they would hang themselves for very shame? And do you remember that only just before they died so bravely to save us, you taunted them about that business, bidding them throw away their guns again if they were too heavy to carry?"

"Yes, Baas, I have been thinking of it all night."

"And yet, Hans, we have done worse than they did, for they were only being hunted by beasts, while we fled from men, so that now when presently we may have to fight, we have no rifles."

"I know it all, Baas, and I am so ashamed that almost I could hang myself as Little Holes and Jerry wished to do."

"Then we ought to hang together, for what you did I did. At least I gave my rifle to a savage, knowing that very likely I should never see it again, so that we shall be defenceless before the enemy and these Dabanda will make a mock of me, the white man who has promised to serve them."

Here Hans became so deeply affected that I saw him draw the back of his hand over his flat little face to wipe away the tears of shame.

For a while we trudged on in silence, then he said in a broken voice:

"Baas, it was quite right of you to give your rifle to a black man to carry, as it is the custom of white masters to do, and if he stole it or was killed, it cannot be helped. But it is different with me. Baas, I am a yellow cur, but even curs can learn a lesson, as I have."

"What lesson, Hans?"

"That we shouldn't judge each other, Baas, as I did when I mocked

410

Tom and Jerry, because you see we may always do the same things or worse ones. Baas, if ever we get back to Zanzibar I will give all the money I earn upon this journey to Jerry's daughter, who is in a school; yes, and my share of that which Kaneke gave you, and not spend one shilling upon gin or new clothes."

"That shows a good spirit," I said, "but what should I do?"

Now all this requires a little explanation. When writing about our flight before the Abanda hordes, I was ashamed to tell what after all I have been obliged to record because of this talk between Hans and myself, and what happened afterwards. As I have said, there was a time during that flight when the Abanda, rushing forward, pressed us very hard, and because of the heavy rifles and ammunition which we carried, Hans and I were dropping behind and likely to be speared. Then it was that I gave my gun and cartridges to a long-legged soldier who bore nothing except his spear, and Hans, seeing me do so, bettered my bad example by throwing his away, which enabled us to put on the pace and again draw out of danger.

It may be argued that we were justified by the circumstances, and, so far as Hans was concerned, doubtless this is true. But I was not justified, I, the white man to whom all these people looked up as one braver and superior to themselves, and at whom now doubtless they jeered as Hans had done at Tom and Jerry. There is nothing more to say, except that I look upon this incident as one of the greatest humiliations of my career. Not only to Hans did it teach a lesson as to loose and easy criticism of others, for from it I learned one which I shall never forget throughout my life.

For most of that day, stopping now and again at the command of Kumpana, we marched on slowly and with caution through the forest, of which the dense gloom did not tend to raise our spirits, that were already low enough. From time to time I caught sight of elephants and other wild game, which stared at us as we went by, but neither ran away nor attempted to attack. It was as though they knew these Dabanda, to whom they were taboo, to be their friends. Indeed, during that march I grew quite convinced that Kumpana's story as to the mastery of his people over the beasts of the field was true, for, as will be seen, they were savage enough where others were concerned, whom, I suppose, they recognized to be different by their smell. Of course, as I have said, Hans had another explanation, for he was, and always remained, convinced that these animals had the spirits of men in them, which is absurd.

At length towards evening we emerged from the forest and saw the great lake in front of us. Also we saw that on its shores were gathered several hundreds of the Dabanda, a sight that gladdened my eyes, and in the midst of them Arkle himself, easy to recognize by his great height and size and red beard, although he wore Dabanda dress and carried a long spear.

Presently we were among them and I was shaking Arkle by the hand.

"I see that you look depressed," he said, "and I fear that you have had a bad time."

"Very bad," I answered. "I have run from enemies faster than ever I ran before, and I have lost my arms, which a soldier should not do—they were heavy to carry, you see. Nor indeed did I want to shoot people with whom I had no quarrel."

"I don't wonder you threw them away, Quatermain. I did the same when the Abanda hunted me. I had rather live without a rifle than stick to it and die."

"The point could be argued," I answered, "but there isn't time. Tell me, what the devil does all this play-acting mean? Why was I dragged out with two hundred and fifty men to fight thousands of Abanda, which, of course, was impossible?"

"I am not sure. You see, Quatermain, I am only a figurehead in this country, and figureheads are not told everything. But if you ask me, I believe you were sent to be a bait. You see, Kaneke thinks you a very great man, and it seems he had announced that if he could capture you, or, failing this, if he could kill you, the Abandas must win, he would get all he wanted—you know what it is—and they would grow into a mighty people, never lacking rain or anything else. Also the Dabanda would become their slaves and the power and wisdom of the *Engoi* would go with them ever more."

"Still I don't understand why we went out to fight," I said, "without the ghost of a chance of winning, or doing anything except run away."

"Because you were meant to run away, Quatermain, in order that you might draw the Abanda after you. Unless you had run they would not have followed, for not even Kaneke could make them enter the Land of the Holy Lake. You see the ruse has succeeded, for presently they will be here. Don't look at me angrily, for on my honour I had nothing to do with the business."

"I should hope not!" I exclaimed. "For if I thought you could play such a trick upon a white man who has done his best to help you, I would never speak to you again. Besides, what is the object of it all? Why have the Abanda been tempted to take possession of this country, from which you will never be able to drive them out again?"

"I cannot tell you," he answered in a low voice, "but I think in order that their fighting men may be destroyed. Quatermain, I believe that something terrible awaits those unfortunate people, but I swear to you that I do not know what it is; those priests will not tell me."

At this moment Hans nudged me.

"Look," he said, pointing towards the edge of the forest.

I did so and perceived a great body of men, a thousand or more of them, emerging from its shadows, drawn up in companies. The Abanda were upon us with Kaneke at the head of them. Arkle saw them also, for I heard him utter an exclamation.

"Well," I said, "we can't run away this time, so I suppose that we must fight until we are killed. Have you your rifle? If so, give it me and I will shoot that Kaneke."

"It has been taken from me," he answered, shaking his head. "When I protested they told me that the white man's weapons were unlawful for me, and would not be needed."

As he spoke a number of Dabanda priests ran up and surrounded Arkle, so that for the time I saw no more of him. Confusion ensued while Kumpana and other officers tried to marshal their men into a double rank. Hans and I found ourselves pushed into a place in the centre of the first line. There we stood, unarmed, except for our revolvers and a few cartridges, which fortunately we had preserved. Arkle, still surrounded by priests and others, was kept at the back of the second rank in such a position and with such precautions as to give me the idea that the business of this force was to act as a bodyguard and safeguard him, rather than to fight the Abanda. Yet it seemed that fight it must, for the lake, into which retreat was impossible, was behind it and the enemy was in front.

The Abanda marched on. Scrutinizing their faces as they came, it struck me that there was something the matter with these men. Of course they were tired, which was not strange, seeing that after enduring the terror of the earthquake and the storm, they had pursued us all the way from their own boundary and through the forest. But their aspect suggested more than weariness; terror was written on their faces. Why? I wondered; since although they must have left most of their army behind, perhaps in occupation of Dabanda-town, they still outnumbered our force by three or four to one.

Had they perhaps met with strange adventures in the forest, as once Hans and I had done? Or were they overcome by a sense of their sacrilege in violating the forbidden land, upon whose soil for generations none of them had set a foot, except their leader, the renegade

Kaneke, and were fearful of some supernatural vengeance? I could not tell, but certainly they had a frightened air, very different from that of the bold fellows whom we had met hunting Arkle and who had tried to cut us off from the mountain pass.

Still they advanced in good order, as I supposed to attack and make an end of us. Yet this was not so, for at a little distance they formed themselves into three sides of a square and halted. Now, while I marvelled what was going to happen (had I been in command of the Dabanda I should have rushed at them), Kaneke emerged from their ranks and walked to within fifty paces of us, which he was quite safe in doing, for the Dabanda had no bows, being armed only with long and heavy spears that could not be thrown.

"Men of the Dabanda," he cried in his big voice, "though you ran fast, I have caught you at length, and with nothing but water behind you, you are in my power, for I see that the white man, Macumazahn, has lost the weapon with which he is so skilled." (Here I was minded to see whether I could not reach him with a pistol shot, but remembering that the quarrel was none of mine and that I had very few cartridges, I refrained from trying.)

"Yet, men of the Dabanda," went on Kaneke, "I do not wish to kill you among whom I was bred and who I hope will live on to be my subjects. I do not even wish to kill Macumazahn and his servant, because once they saved me from murderers, and we have been companions upon a long journey. There is only one whom I will kill, and that is the white thief, whom I see skulking yonder behind your lines, who has stolen my place and heritage, and would steal the Shadow, my appointed wife. Therefore give him up to me that I may make an end of him before your faces and submit yourselves to me, who will harm no other man among you; no, not even that cunning jackal, Kumpana."

Now Kumpana stepped forward and said clearly but quietly:

"Cease from your boastful talk, Kaneke, wizard and traitor, who sold your birthright to save your life, you who did violence to the *Engoi* before her altar, you who but yesterday scattered the holy fire of the altar and stamped it out, you who are accursed. Hear me, men of the Abanda," he went on, raising his voice, "what is the quarrel with us? You asked for rain. Has not rain been sent to you in plenty? Do not your lands run with water? Give us this man who has beguiled you and depart in peace—or keep him and be destroyed.

"Has not the ancient prophecy been handed down to you by your fathers, that the very rocks will hurl themselves upon those of your

414

people who dare to set foot within the forest and to look upon the holy lake, and that the wild beasts will rend them, and that those who escape the rocks and the beasts will be seized with madness? And have not the rocks already hurled themselves upon you, killing many who dwelt beneath them? Will you wait till all the curse fulfils itself, or will you give up this man and depart in peace unharmed? Answer while you may, for by sunset it will be too late."

Now I could see that the Abanda soldiers were much disturbed. They whispered one to another, and some of their captains began to consult together. How it would have ended I do not know, though I doubt whether these Abanda, who seemed to me to be brave and loyal savages, would have consented to surrender the man whom they had chosen as their general in the attempt to possess themselves of Dabanda-land, with its material riches and the boon of what they believed to be an especial spiritual protection. This matter, however, remained undecided, for Kaneke, who doubtless feared the worst, cried out:

"Men of the Abanda, am I not the appointed Shield of the Shadow, a greater wizard than yonder low-born Kumpana, the son of a slave? When the mountain heaved did I not open a roadway through it, making the two lands one, and as for the beasts, are they not also at my command? If you doubt it, ask the white lord, Watcher-by-Night, and the yellow man, his servant, to whom I showed my power over them. And remember that but now I have led you unharmed through a host of elephants that fled at my word. Ho! you white thief"—and he pointed at Arkle with his spear—"I have an offer to make to you. If you are not a coward, come out and fight me man to man, and let the conqueror take the Shadow. Come out and fight me, I say! Or go tell the Shadow that he who woos her and has come from far to win her, is but a coward with a heart whiter than his face."

Arkle heard him; with a roar of rage he shook off the priests who held him and charged through our lines straight at Kaneke. To my horror I saw as he passed me that he was quite unarmed, for either he had dropped his spear or it had been taken from him by the priests; yes, he was attacking the man with nothing but his naked hands.

"Let none come between us!" he shouted as he went.

Kaneke lifted his spear to pierce him, but somehow Arkle avoided the thrust and, rushing in, gripped its haft and snapped it like a twig, so that the broad blade fell between them. Then he threw his arms round Kaneke and they wrestled. They were mighty men, both of them, but once that spear was gone I had little doubt of the issue. Still, the end came sooner than I expected, for Arkle seemed to lift Kaneke from his feet and dash him to the ground, where he lay half stunned. Then, before the Abanda could come to the help of their captain, he picked him up as though he were a child, carried him to the ranks of the Dabanda and through them, and cast him down at the feet of the priests!

CHAPTER 19

The Bridal and the Curse

The torrential rains which fell during the storm had reached the lake by many streams, with the result that its waters had enlarged themselves. The old shore-line, fringed with tall reeds, where I had stood on my first visit, was quite a hundred yards away. Thus the reeds, or rather the upper halves of them, now stood like a thicket at that distance from the shore, cutting off the view from the stretch of water that was beyond but near to them, while the rest of the lake and the distant island were turned to a dazzle of gold by the fierce rays of the sinking sun.

Out of these reeds, at the exact moment when Arkle cast down the great form of Kaneke before the priests, suddenly emerged a large canoe, or rather a barge, for its stern was square. It was paddled by white-robed women, quite thirty of them, I should say, seated upon either side of the craft, which had a gangway running down its centre. Upon the broad poop was a curious carved seat, large enough, I noted, to accommodate two persons, and in the centre of this seat sat a woman whom I knew must be she who was called the *Engoi*, or Shadow, a tall and beautiful young woman whose gauzy robes glittered in the sunlight as though they were sewn with gold and gems, which perhaps they were. She wore a high head-dress with wings, not unlike to those of a Viking's helm, from which, half hiding her face, flowed down a veil spangled with stars.

On came the boat, so gently that one could not hear the paddles' dip, and as its prow touched the shore, priests sprang forward and held it fast. The regal-looking woman rose to her feet, while there went up a great shout of:

"*Engoi! Engoi!*"

Clothed, as it were, with burning light, she stood above us on the high poop, gazing at the prostrate form of Kaneke, at the man who had cast him there, at the tall, white-robed, large-eyed Dabanda spearsmen, and at the Abanda warriors beyond. Then she spoke in a clear, flute-like voice, which in that silence could be heard by all.

"I, the Treasure of the Lake, greet you, servants of the *Engoi*; I greet you, White Lord from far away" (this was addressed to Arkle; of me she took no notice). "I greet you all. Tell me, O Kumpana, Father of my Council, what host is this that threatens you with spears?"

"That of the Abanda, O *Engoi*, who, breaking the oath sworn by their forefathers and braving the curse, have dared to enter the holy land of Mone to slay us and to give you, the divine Shadow, to be the wife of this dog." Here he pointed to Kaneke, who, I noted, had recovered his senses, for he raised himself upon his arm and listened.

"Take him and judge him, the accursed, according to your law," she said, "for on him I will never look again." Then added in louder tones that trembled with cold anger: "Men of the Abanda, the curse with which Kaneke is cursed, clings to you also and the mercy that you would not take departs from you. Begone to the beasts for judgment and become as beasts, till Heaven lifts its wrath from off you and creep to my feet as slaves to pray pardon for your sins."

The Abanda heard. They stared at the priestess clothed with light, they spoke together, as I supposed making ready to attack us. But it was not so, for, of a sudden, panic seemed to seize them. I saw it pass from face to face, I saw them tremble and cover their eyes with their hands. Then without a word they turned and ran back to the shelter of the forest, an army that had become a terror-stricken mob.

They were gone, the thunder of a thousand feet died away into silence; not one of them could be seen; they were lost among the darksome trees. The beautiful maiden called Shadow, whose eyes had been fixed upon the water, lifted her head and looked at Arkle, saying softly:

"White Lord from afar, our dream is fulfilled and once more we meet, as was foretold, and I am yours and you are mine. Yet if you would depart with your companion"—here for the first time she glanced at me—"still the road lies open. Go, then, if it pleases you; only if you go, learn that henceforth for this life and all that are to come we separate for ever. Learn, too, that if you stay, there is no power in heaven or in earth that shall part us while time endures and the star we follow shines in the sky. Choose, then, and have done."

Arkle stared at the ground, like to one who is lost in doubt. Then he lifted his eyes and met hers that were fixed upon him, till the radiance which shone upon her face seemed to pass to his, and I knew that she had conquered. He turned and spoke to me, saying:

"Farewell, my friend whom I shall see no more. I know you believe me mad, even wicked perhaps, and so I am according to your judgment and that of the world we know. Yet my heart tells me that love can do no wrong and that in my madness is the truest wisdom, for yonder stands my destiny, she whom I was born to win, she who was lost and is found again. Farewell once more, and think of me at times as we shall of you, until perchance elsewhere"—and he pointed upwards—"we meet again, and you too understand all that I cannot speak."

He took my hand and pressed it, then very slowly stepped on to the prow of the boat, and passing down its length between the two lines of women who sat like statues, came to her who stood upon its poop. As he came she opened her arms and received him in her arms, and there they kissed before us all. For thus was the shadow wed in the presence of her people.

Side by side they sat themselves upon the throne-like seat. The priests thrust the boat out into the water, the paddlers turned its prow towards the reeds and the island that lay beyond them, and the sun sank.

The sun sank, the waters of the holy lake grew dark, and these strange travellers departed into gloom. Once more only did I see them after they had passed through the reeds out on to the darkened bosom of the lake. Some cloud above caught the last rays of the sun that had vanished behind the crater cliffs, and reflected them in a shaft of light on to the water and the boat that floated there, turning those it bore to shapes of glory. Then the ray passed and the shadows hid them.

"That's a good omen for the Red Baas and the pretty spook-lady who has carried him off," remarked Hans reflectively, "for you see after the sun seemed to be dead, it came to life again to wish them luck, Baas."

"I hope so," I replied, turning my back upon that melancholy lake and not in the best of spirits. Arkle at least had won the lady whom he so passionately desired, but I, who had won nothing and nobody, felt very much alone. My part in all this business had been to do everybody's dirty work—that of White-Mouse, of Kaneke, of Arkle, and of Kumpana—and to tell the truth I did not like it. No one really enjoys the humble office of a tool which is thrown aside when done with.

That night we camped by the lake, and I have seldom passed one that was more disturbed. From its solemn and mysterious depths came the mournful cries of wildfowl and the drear sighing of the wind among the reeds. But these were as nothing compared with the sounds which proceeded from the forest. Fierce trumpeting of infuriated elephants, bellowing of other beasts, and, worst of all, what sounded like the screams of terrified and tortured men, which were so loud and persistent that if I had known where he was sleeping I would have gone to Kumpana and asked their cause. But I did not know and probably if I had found him he would have told me nothing. At length, too, these noises ceased, and I got some rest.

Before sunrise, when the sky grew grey and the night mist still hid the face of the lonesome lake, Kumpana appeared, bringing us some food and saying that we must eat it as we marched, because it was time to be gone. So off we went, and entered that hateful forest just as the sun rose. Before I had gone three hundred paces between the trees, I stumbled over something soft and, looking down, to my horror discovered that it was the mutilated body of an Abanda warrior, who from various signs I knew must have been killed by an elephant.

"See here, Hans!" I said, pointing to the dreadful thing.

"I have seen, Baas," he answered, "and there are plenty more of them about. Didn't you hear those spook elephants hunting them last night as the Dabanda wizards brought them here to do?"

"I heard something," I answered faintly, remembering as I spoke the words of Shadow when she told the Abanda "to begone to the beasts for judgment"! Great God, this was the judgment!

Hans was quite right. There were plenty more of the poor creatures lying about, indeed I imagine that some hundreds of them must have been killed. What an end! To be hunted in the darkness of night and when caught, stamped flat or torn to pieces by these maddened animals which probably tracked them by their scent. If this were the fate of his tools, what, I wondered, was that reserved for Kaneke, who by the way, as I supposed, had been taken on ahead of us for I saw nothing of him?

Until then I had merely disliked the Dabanda, now I hated them and desired nothing so much as to get out of this land of cruelty and African witchcraft. For although I had tried to find other explanations, such as the fact that all game was taboo to them, what but witchcraft or some force which we white men do not understand, could account for the dominion of these people over wild animals? It may be thought that the attack upon these Abanda by the elephants was an accident resulting from their breaking into the herd in their terrified retreat after they fled from the presence of one whom they believed to be almost a goddess. But this could scarcely be so seeing that when, following on our footsteps, the Abanda passed through the forest to the lake, the elephants must have been all round them, for as I have said, I saw the great beasts watching us from between the trees.

Why, then, were they not attacked upon this outward journey? I can only suggest one explanation. At that time Kaneke was with them whom the beasts knew and obeyed, as they did other leaders of his tribe, for had he not shown his power over these very elephants long before we entered Dabanda-land? When the Abanda soldiers were deprived of his protection the case was different, for then they were fallen upon, trampled and torn to pieces as Hans and I should have been if we had been alone.

As a matter of fact, however, we should have had nothing to fear on this return journey, for we never saw these beasts again. Indeed, I heard afterwards that when they had wreaked vengeance on the Abanda, led by the ancient bull, they marched solemnly out of the forest and across the crater-land to the pass through which they had appeared. What became of them I do not know, but I suppose that they departed back to their own haunts where we had first met them.

After sundry halts, of which I was not told the reason, towards evening we emerged from that awful forest, only to be confronted with more terrors. On the open space which surrounded the altar platform and in the streets of the town beyond, hundreds of men of the Abanda army were running to and fro, some with torn robes and some stark naked, shrieking and staring about them with eyes that were full of fear. A mob of raving maniacs who seemed hardly human, they foamed at the mouth, they rolled upon the ground, they tore their hair and bit each other's flesh.

"They are all mad, Baas," said Hans, getting behind me, for as is common with African natives, he had a great horror of the insane and supposed them to be inspired by heaven. "Don't touch them, Baas, or we shall go mad too."

His exhortation was needless, for my one desire was to get as far as possible from the hideous sight of these poor creatures. What could have brought them to such a pass, I marvelled, as I do today. I can only suppose that when the survivors of the regiments which had followed us to the lake arrived among the army that awaited them at the town, they communicated to their brothers the terror which had driven them crazy.

Or perhaps now that Kaneke had disappeared, the superstitions he had kept in check broke out among them with a force so irresistible that they lost their minds, remembering the ancient curse which was said to overtake any of their people who set foot in the land of Lake Mone, whence they had been driven in past ages. I cannot tell, but certainly they had "become as beasts", as the priestess Shadow foretold. It was shocking, it was terrible, and thankful indeed was I when, on catching sight of us, with howls and lamentations they drew together and fled away, I suppose back to their own land.

Soon they were gone into the gathering darkness, thousands of them, and quiet fell upon the town, which was quite unharmed. Hans and I made our way to our own house where we found a lamp lit and food prepared, I presume by the women who waited upon us, who all this while had remained faithfully at their post. The first thing that we saw were our lost rifles and ammunition, carefully laid upon our beds.

"Allemagter!" exclaimed Hans, pointing first to the lamp and food next to the rifles. "We have met many strange peoples in our journeys, Baas, but never any like these. But, Baas, they are not men and women, they are witches and wizards, every one of them, whose master is the devil, as those Abanda will think when they get their minds again."

Then, quite overcome, he sank on to a stool and began to devour his meal in silence. I, too, collapsed; no other word describes my state, brought about by physical fatigue and mental astonishment. At that moment I was almost inclined to agree with Hans, though now of course I know that these events which at the time seemed so strange were quite susceptible of a natural interpretation. It was not wonderful that the Abanda soldier should have been attacked in the forest by a herd of elephants whose tempers were upset by storm and earthquake, or that the survivors of them and their fellows should have been crazed by the experience, added to the effect of their inherited superstitions.

Nor was it wonderful that an ardent man like Arkle should have succumbed to the charm of a beautiful priestess, whose personal attractions were enhanced by the mystery with which she was surrounded, though I admit that I do not understand the tale of his previous telepathic intercourse with her, if it may be so described. Very possibly, however, this existed only in his imagination, and the real romance began, on his part at any rate, when he first saw her upon the borders of the lake.

Still, the cumulative effect of so many eerie happenings, reinforced by the legends with which my ears were filled, and the constant ceremonies and experiences of an abnormal and unwholesome nature in which I had been forced to take a part, together with the vanishing away of Arkle into what I understood to be a kind of Eastern *houri* paradise, was crushing; at least this was its effect upon a tired and puzzled man.

So I went to bed with an attack of fever and low spirits that kept me there for a week, after which I took another week to recover my strength.

During all this time very little happened, for Hans reported that everything in the town went on as it used to do before the great storm. The people were cultivating their gardens; the sacred fire was re-lit upon the altar and the priests had rebuilt their fallen observation tower, whence they watched the stars nightly as of old. To judge from the aspect of the people, indeed one might have thought that nothing unusual had occurred, or at any rate that it was quite forgotten.

Now, being filled with nervous apprehensions and extremely anxious to escape from this country as soon as I was well enough to face the journey, I tried several times to get into touch with Kumpana, the only man in the place who seemed to have any real authority, but was always told that he was absent.

At length he came, bland and smiling as ever, and apologized for not having done so before, "For then," he added, "I, who am a doctor, should have been able to cure you more quickly."

I replied that it did not matter, as I was now quite recovered who never suffered from serious illness. Then I asked him the news.

"There is little, Lord," he answered. "From the lake we hear that the *Engoi* and her husband, the Shield of the Shadow, are well and most happy. The Abanda, now that they have reached their own land and found their wits again—for only about two hundred of them were killed by the elephants—are very humble and have sent to make their submission, promising henceforth to be our faithful servants and to live with us as one people."

"So you have got what you want," I said.

"Yes, Lord, for now we shall become a great tribe, a nation, indeed, as once we were hundreds of years ago, because these Abanda are brave fighting men and their women have many children, whereas ours bear few or none at all. Never again will they threaten us, but, directed by our wisdom, will do all that we command."

"Which was your object throughout, I suppose, Kumpana?"

"Yes, Lord, it was our object, which explains much that you have never been able to understand, amongst other things, why you were brought to Mone-land. Without you Kaneke could not have been saved from the Arabs, and the White Lord, Shield of the Shadow, could not have been saved from the Abanda after his madness had caused him to be cast out of our country, which even I was unable to prevent."

"But why did you want Kaneke back, Kumpana, seeing that at once you took away his chieftainship and made him an outlaw?"

"Because, amongst other reasons, if he had not returned and been driven out again, he would not have fled to the Abanda and led them to attack us, as we wished that he should do, knowing the fate that would overtake them. Even then I do not think that the Abanda, who fear the *Engoi* and her servants, would have followed him, had they not seen you, the great white lord whose fame is everywhere, running before them like a hunted jackal, which was why we took you with us to the pass, telling you that it was to fight them."

Now controlling my wrath as best I could, for it was useless to argue with Kumpana about this disgraceful episode of my career, I said with sarcasm: "So you foresaw all these things, Kumpana, and arranged accordingly?"

"Of course, Lord, for we have that gift," he replied in the mild, protesting voice of one who humours an ignorant fool.

This amazing lie took away my breath, but again feeling it useless to argue, I changed the subject, by asking:

"And why did you bring him who is now her husband here to marry the Shadow, instead of giving her to Kaneke, to whom she was promised, or to some other man of your people?"

"Because, Lord, our men are—" and he used an Arabic word which I can only translate by the English phrase *played out*. "The race has grown too ancient and too interbred. Therefore it was necessary that she who is now the *Engoi* upon earth should wed one of a different stock who has knowledge of the arts and laws of the great white races. For, Lord, from this marriage will spring a woman, the *Engoi* to be, who will be very great of heart. It is she," he went on with a ring of triumph in his voice, "who will once more make the Dabanda mighty among the peoples of Africa, not the lady who now rules over us, or the white wanderer who is her spouse."

"So that is another of your prophecies, Kumpana?"

"Yes, Lord, and one which most certainly will be fulfilled," he answered in the same triumphant tone. Then, as though the matter were one which he declined to discuss, he said in his ordinary voice:

"This is the night of full moon, and there is a ceremony before the altar which we pray you to attend. For tomorrow doubtless you will wish to bid us farewell as it has been arranged that you should do."

"I am glad to hear that," I exclaimed, "but I don't want to be present at any more of your ceremonies."

"Yet, Lord," he answered with his queer little smile, "I am sure you will do what we wish, now, as always before."

"Which means that I must come."

"Oh, Lord, I never said so. Still I am certain that you will come and shall send an escort to attend upon you, that you may fear no harm."

Then he rose and bowed himself out.

Not until he was gone did I remember that I had never asked him what had become of Kaneke.

"Baas," said Hans, "I always thought you clever in your way, but this Kumpana is much cleverer than you, or even than I am, because you see in the end he always makes us do, not what we want but what he wants, and then laughs at us about it afterwards. We shall have to go to that fetish business tonight, because if we won't walk, we shall be carried there, quite nicely, of course, by the men he is sending to protect us. I wonder what we shall see, Baas."

"How do I know?" I snapped, for the gibes of Hans irritated me. "Perhaps the lady Shadow and her husband will come to visit us."

"I don't think so, Baas. I think that they are sitting holding each other's hands and making faces at each other, and saying silly things about the moon. If it were six months later when they want to hold other people's hands and to look into new faces and have forgotten all about the moon, then they would come, Baas, but not now. But perhaps Kaneke will visit us, unless he is dead, which we haven't heard, and I'd much rather see him, Baas, than two people who keep saying 'Sweetie-Sweet' and 'there's no one else in the world, Pretty'."

"Would you, you ugly little sinner?" I replied, and walked away.

As it happened, Hans, who could smell out the truth like any witch-doctor, had made no mistake, for when, conducted by our promised escort, a strong one by the way, we reached the altar platform that night, it was to find that the centre of interest proved to be Kaneke and no one else, and that for the second time it was our lot to see him tried for his life. What is more, even among that undemonstrative people, made apathetic by the passage of many ages of plenty, and by iron priestly rule, the event excited keen and universal interest.

This might be seen from the fact that every creature from the town who could walk or be carried, was gathered upon the marketplace beneath the platform, and with them a great number of people from the villages and farms beyond its borders. The priests too were present in force; the astrologers watched the heavens from their towers and shouted out the messages of the stars; a choir hidden behind the altar sang solemn chants at intervals; and the sacred fire blazed like a signal beacon upon a mountain, as though to make up for the fact that very recently it had twice been extinguished. Indeed it was a veritable furnace.

In front of it, its fierce light playing on him, stood Kaneke, bound and closely guarded, while on either side sat the white-robed Council of the Shadow, whose office seemed to be that of judge or jury, or both. Near to them, so placed that he could be heard from the audience below as well as by all upon the platform, stood Kumpana, who in this drama played the part of the prosecuting counsel.

When I arrived with Hans and had been given a seat not far from Kumpana and facing Kaneke, the proceedings began. I need not detail them further than to say that they consisted of a recitation of all his crimes, starting with a long account of the act of sacrilege he had committed in his youth against a former *Engoi*, that apparently was much worse than he had intimated to me, and had resulted in his banishment or flight, and going on to those offences with which I had some acquaintance.

At length the tale was finished, and Kaneke was called upon to answer. This he did with a certain dignity, pleading that his judges had no jurisdiction over him, that he was their lawful chief and could not be tried by any court. The crimes alleged against him he made no attempt to deny or explain, perhaps because they were too flagrant to admit of defence.

When he had finished speaking, Kumpana said to the Council and the priests:

"What say you?"

Whereupon they answered all together:

"We say that he is guilty!" and the people gathered in the marketplace beneath echoed the words in a roar of sounds.

Then Kumpana cried aloud to the astrologers upon their towers, asking:

"What reward is appointed to this traitor Kaneke, the accursed of the *Engoi*, for his sins against the Shadow and against the people?"

The diviners on the towers stared at the stars, making a pretence of consulting them, then spoke together in a secret language I did not understand. At last one of them, he on the right, called out:

"Hear the voice of Heaven! Let him who quenched the fire, feed the fire."

I contemplated the leaping flames upon which the priests had just hurled more wood, and not understanding all that these words meant, remarked to Hans that it did not seem to want feeding.

"Oh, Baas," he replied, "why are you so stupid? Don't you see that they are going to burn this owl-man as an offering? The woman in the hut told me that it is what they always do to anyone who has tried to lay hands upon the Shadow of the *Engoi*, and sometimes to her husband also if she gets tired of him."

"Great heavens!" I exclaimed, turning quite faint. Then, before I could get out another word, Kaneke, who was a coward at heart, as he had shown when he bartered his birthright to Arkle in exchange for his life, with ashen face and bulging eyes began an impassioned appeal to me to save him.

I did try to say something on his behalf, I forget what it was, but at once Kumpana cut me short with the remark that there was plenty of room for two upon that altar. He added in explanation that in his country under an ancient law, he who tried to save a criminal condemned to death must share his punishment.

Hearing this, as I was helpless and could not stop there to see a man burned alive, however great a blackguard he might be, I rose and with the best dignity I could command, walked down the platform steps and through the people at the foot of them, back to our house. As I passed him Kaneke shouted out:

"Farewell, Macumazahn, whom I met in an evil hour. If, before you leave this land, you see your friend, the white thief who has stolen her that was mine, tell him that in a day to come, instead of her lips he too shall kiss the altar flames."

Now all my pity departed, for I knew well that these cruel words had been spoken to create baseless fears and doubts in my mind and in that of Arkle also, should they reach him.

"Cease from lying and die like a man," I said.

If he answered me I did not hear him, for just then the priests set up a song, a very savage song, which prevented his words from reaching me. At the edge of the market-place some impulse caused me to look back, just in time to see the great shape of Kaneke outlined against the flames into which he was being tossed whilst the people around, who till now had remained silent, uttered a shout of joy.

A while later Hans joined me.

"Baas," he said, "I am glad they burned that beast Kaneke."

"Why?" I asked, for I thought the remark pitiless.

"For two reasons, Baas. First because he left Little Holes and Jerry to be killed when we were running for the pass, being a coward who could desert his friends; and secondly because he called out after you that if he had won, he would have burned you and the Red Baas and me, Hans, as well. That is why I stopped to see the end of him, Baas."

"Let us pack up," I said, "for tomorrow we start."

"Yes, Baas, but where to, Baas?"

"I don't know and I don't care," I answered, "so long as it is out of this accursed country. Why on earth they ever brought me into it I can't understand even now."

"That you might bring Kaneke, Baas."

"But why did they want Kaneke? They would have got on quite as well without him."

"To burn him, Baas. He had sinned against another Shadow who is dead and ran away, and the priests, who never forget, brought him back that he might be killed for his sin. That is why White-Mouse was sent to tempt him from home, telling him that he was to marry the new Shadow, and that is why she was so much afraid lest he should be killed by the Arabs and cheat the fire on the altar. Oh, they had thought it all out quite nicely, Baas, as Kaneke has learned."

"Perhaps. Well, they won't tempt me back," I said.

CHAPTER 20

Farewell

Now with the execution of Kaneke in the savage fashion that I have described, the story of my visit to the sacred lake called Mone, and the people who dwelt there comes to an end. Perhaps, however, there are one or two things that I should mention.

All the day following the horrible scene upon the altar platform, Hans and I spent in getting ready, tying up loads for the bearers who, we were informed, would be provided on the next morning, superintending the cooking of food to take with us, seeing to our boots that were much the worse for wear, and so forth. In our spare time I tried also to think out the great problem as to the route that we should take. Were we to return by that which we had followed into the Lake-country, or to strike out on a desperate journey for the West Coast? Upon my soul I did not know, and all that Hans would do was to point out the difficulties and dangers of either course.

When I lay down that night I was still quite unable to make up my mind, and went to sleep determined to postpone further consideration till the morrow, hoping that meanwhile some inspiration might come to me. As a matter of fact it did, and in a curious fashion.

About midnight I woke up and saw, by the light of the lamp which I kept burning, the white-draped form of a woman, standing at the foot of the bed, who appeared to be looking at me.

"What the dickens—" I began in a hurry, when she stopped me with a motion of her hand.

Then she drew her veil aside so that I could see her face. It was that of White-Mouse!

Surely I could not be mistaken, although I had only seen her twice or thrice upon a single night. There was the same delicate shape, the same pleading, dark eyes, the same curling hair, and the same sweet, plaintive face so suggestive of mystery and acquaintance with secret things.

"White-Mouse!" I murmured beneath my breath, for to tell the truth I was half afraid to speak aloud, fearing lest what I saw before me was a ghost, or at the best a dream.

"Yes, Lord Macumazahn; at least once I bore that name far away among the Arabs."

"But you are dead! They killed you there in the courtyard of Kaneke's house."

"No, Lord, they could not kill me. I escaped out of their hands and returned to this country before you, making your road smooth and easy."

"Before us! How did you do that?"

"It is one of the secrets which I may not reveal, Lord, nor does it matter. Also we have met since then when you were in trouble yonder with the 'dwellers in the forest' and one came to guide you."

"I thought it!" I exclaimed; "but before I could make sure you were gone, so that almost I believed you to be—not a woman but—well—one of the dwellers in the forest."

"I knew it," she replied with a sweet little smile, "and for the rest, even now are you sure that I am a woman?"

"No, I am not," I answered.

"Nor am I quite sure, Lord Macumazahn, but that is another of the secrets, and it does not matter. See, I am a messenger tonight whatever else I may be and I have brought you a letter which you can read when I am gone, for I think that to it there is no answer. Or if there should be an answer, shape it in your mind and I shall learn it there and deliver it word for word."

"Again I begin to think that you are a ghost, White-Mouse, for women do not talk thus," I said as I took the little roll of paper which she handed to me and laid it down upon the bed.

The truth was that at the moment I was more interested in White-Mouse than in what might be written in the roll.

"Although some do not know it, we are all of us ghosts, are we not, Lord Macumazahn? Though often if the veil of flesh be gross, the light of the ghost-lamp that shines within you cannot be seen. Lord, my time is short and I have something to say to you. Will it please you to listen?"

"When you speak, what could please me better, especially in this land, White-Mouse?"

Again there flitted across her face a quick smile so strangely sweet that it thrilled the nerves, as do certain notes of music we hear upon a violin. At least for some indefinable reason I always connect that smile of hers with such vibrating notes.

"Yet it would not please you in other lands, Lord, for there among your own people nothing would delight you less than to hear the voice of a ghost-woman, the dweller in a spell-bound, haunted place. Were it otherwise, perchance I should accompany you, as, although you will not see me, I may do yet."

"What do you mean?" I asked rather anxiously.

"Nothing that you need fear, Lord, except that I like you well, and both ghosts and women are pleased to be with those whom they like. Oh, I have watched you from the first and noted how you have borne many troubles that were not of your seeking, and read your heart and found it worthy to be praised. In this land, Lord, such are not found."

"I am glad to hear it," I said, who had little admiration for the Da-banda. Then to change the subject which I found somewhat personal and embarrassing, especially to a modest man who could neither rise nor escape, I added, "Will you do something for me, White-Mouse, and before you go? Tell me, why I was ever brought to your land?"

"You wished to come, Lord; and if they be real, wishes always fulfil themselves soon or late. Moreover, besides those you know which Kumpana has set out to you, there are other reasons, which, even if I might explain them, you would not understand."

"Why not?"

"Because they have to do with things which you have forgotten; yes, with other lives that lie buried in the past, when you and I and two great ones who dwell in the midst of Lake Mone, and Kumpana and Kaneke knew each other, as we do today. Man's life is a long story, Lord, of which we read but one mad chapter at a time, thinking that it is all the book, and not knowing what went before, nor what shall follow after."

Now I reflected that many wise men, of all epochs, such as Plato and others, as I have heard, were of this opinion—one that it is not impossible though difficult to accept at any rate in the West, whatever the East may hold. Not wishing, however, to enter upon so vast a subject, I merely said:

"And do you know, White-Mouse?"

"I know something, Lord, and I guess more. For the Dwellers in the Lake, whom doubtless you believe to be savages blinded by the teachings of a false faith, yet have the wisdom of our race."

"Yes," I answered sharply, "wisdom of which I saw the fruits last night when a man was burned living upon your altar fire."

"You are wrong, Lord. In our wisdom of the Lake, cruelty has no place, and with it she who rules the Lake has naught to do, though the Dabanda be given to her for servants, and in a fashion, for masters. When she learned what had chanced to Kaneke and to those whom he led astray, she wept, though she knew that these things must come and uttered the decree of death. Yes, we women of the Lake renounce the world and fix our thoughts on heaven, which is our home. Therefore do not judge us hardly, Lord, or measure us with the Dabanda rule. Now I have done, who may say no more, save this: Have no fear upon your journey, for we know that you will accomplish it safely and live on for many years. Go where fortune seems to lead you and all will succeed with you. So farewell, Lord Macumazahn. Think kindly of us of the Lake, although we be women, for as you have learned, or will learn, women, with all their faults, are better and wiser than men, for sometimes to them is shown the light that is hidden from the eyes of men."

Then she bent down, took my hand, kissed it, and turning lifted the curtain of the door-way of the house and glided away into the darkness, leaving me glad that I had found one person whom I could like in Mone-land, one, too, who liked me!

From the bed on the other side of the room came the stifled voice of Hans, whom all this while I had quite forgotten, saying:

"Is that the last kiss, Baas, and if so, may I put out my head? It is very hot here under this skin rug, where I have hidden my eyes for so long without being able to breathe, Baas."

"Well, you haven't hidden your ears," I said, "so stop talking rubbish and tell me what you think of White-Mouse."

"Oh, Baas," he said, sitting up, "I think that she is a spook, more so than all the rest of them. But I think also that she is a nice spook, although she did deceive me yonder in the Arab town, making me believe that she was a jealous wife of the Owl-man Kaneke, and that she liked me much more than she did him. Also I am happy now, Baas, because she, who being a spook knows all about it, said that we shall come safely to the end of our journey. But of course you are very unhappy because you have seen the last of one of whom you think so much, that you have even forgotten to read the letter she brought you, for reading letters is much duller than being kissed, Baas."

"Bring me the lamp," I said as I loosened the string of scented grass with which it was bound and undid the little roll.

It was of paper cut from a note-book, and, as I expected, from Arkle. It ran thus:

> Dear Quatermain, We know that you are going, and I send you this by a sure hand to bid you farewell. Do not think badly

of me, Quatermain, because I have forsaken my country and put aside all the traditions in which I was brought up, in order to marry the priestess of a strange faith, here in Central Africa. Love is stronger than are the ties of country or of tradition, and in our case it is a force which will not be denied: a destiny indeed. Probably you put little faith in the stories I have told you of how I came to be drawn to my wife, thinking them the harmless imaginations of a romantic mind. Therefore of them I will only say that to me they seemed real enough and to be justified by the event, though of course here coincidence might have played its part. Probably, too, you set little store by the occult powers and superstitions of this secret and ancient people, finding for all, or most of them, a natural explanation.

For many reasons I wish that I could share this view, but alas! I believe those powers to be very real. And here I want to make one thing clear: they do not reside in the spirit of her who amongst other titles is given that of the *Engoi* or rather of the Shadow of the *Engoi*! She is but the medium. The strength lies with others, in the present case principally with the head of the Council, Kumpana.

Did you notice the voice with which she spoke when first you saw her upon the altar platform, and again in the boat on the day of our marriage, and that it was not natural? At least to me it seemed very different from that which she used when addressing me directly, as a woman addresses the man she loves. For example she seemed to pass sentence upon the Abanda giving them into the power of the beasts, over which undoubtedly the Dabanda have command, and to the fate of madness, which I learn fell upon them afterwards.

Yet I assure you that she never knew she had spoken these words, any more than she knew that the rascal, Kaneke, was doomed to be burned alive, in short they were uttered by her under an obscure, hypnotic influence. Further, it seems that these mediumistic gifts pass away in the course of years, and that is why the Dabanda priests kill their *Engoi* at a certain age, and her husband with her and choose another Shadow to fill her place.

You will say that for her and for me the prospect therefore is terrible enough. But I want you to understand, Quatermain, that I have no intention of sitting still and allowing such a fate to overtake us. I mean to match myself against those priests and the Council and to overthrow them—how I do not know— and to establish in their place a pure and kindly rule. If I find that this is not possible, then I mean to escape from this country with my wife. So do not look upon us as lost, or on me as wholly a renegade and an apostate, but rather as one who is hidden for awhile.

Meanwhile, I assure you that I am intensely happy and that the book of an ancient wisdom which I thought lost to the world, is being opened to my eyes. I would that you could see this place and the buildings on it, and the old writings it contains in a language I have not yet learned to decipher. But that cannot be, for any such attempt would certainly cost you your life. So you must go your way while I go mine, hoping that our paths may cross again, even in this world.

Meanwhile, I thank you for all you have done for me, and trust that your strange experiences may bring you some reward for your work and the dangers you have run. God bless you, my friend, if I may call you so, and farewell! I beg you and Hans to talk as little as possible about me or the Dabanda and Mone, the Holy Lake. Above all, do not try to return, or to send other white men to explore, or to search me out, for such attempts would certainly end in death. Let me vanish away as many a white man does in Africa, and my story with me.

Again farewell, *J. T. Arkle*

P.S.—I enclose a note addressed to the captain of the hunters whom I left in charge of stores and equipment at a place to which you will be guided. He can read more or less, and it commands him to hand these over to you absolutely, and with them a sealed box that contains a sum in gold, which I hope you will find useful. I recommend you to head for the West Coast, as the hunters can guide you on that road, at any rate for part of the way till you come into touch with white men.

J. T. A.

Such was this strange letter, which I was most glad to receive. For did it not give me hope that one day Arkle would escape from this accursed country, either with or without the woman whom fate had appointed to him as his wife? Further, did it not explain much, or at any rate something, of mysteries that hitherto had been as black as night to me? I think so.

Here I will stop this tale, for to describe all my adventures and experiences on my way to the West Coast would take another book, which I have neither the time nor the inclination to write. Suffice it to say that all went well. I was guided to Arkle's camp, and by help of the outfit I found there, to say nothing of the money, of which there was much, ultimately I came to the sea and took ship back to South Africa, where I gave it out that I had been for a long hunting-trip in Portuguese territory.

"Baas," said Hans to me one day when we had been talking over Arkle and his great passion, "what are the 'twin hearts' of which you talk?"

I explained as best I could, and he replied:

"Baas, you remember that Kaneke said just before they put him on the fire, that the Red Baas would follow him there one day. If that is what must be paid for having a 'twin heart', I am glad I haven't got one—unless it is for you, Baas!"

I should add that of Arkle, if this was his real name (which I doubt), I have heard no more. Nor until now, when after many years I write it down, have I ever told his story.

LEONAUR

ALSO FROM LEONAUR

TROS OF SAMOTHRACE 1: WOLVES OF THE TIBER by *Talbot Mundy*—When his ship is taken and his crew slaughtered Tros of Samothrace is captured by Imperial Rome.

TROS OF SAMOTHRACE 2: DRAGONS OF THE NORTH by *Talbot Mundy*—Tros of Samothrace burns for vengeance and has declared himself the implacable enemy of Rome.

TROS OF SAMOTHRACE 3: SERPENT OF THE WAVES by *Talbot Mundy*—Tros, his allies and the forces of Rome have drawn apart to prepare for the conflict to come.

TROS OF SAMOTHRACE 4: CITY OF THE EAGLES by *Talbot Mundy*—As Tros of Samothrace continues in his attempts to confound Caesar's plans for the invasion of Britain, he journeys to the Eternal City to seek the aid of its great leaders—and Caesar's opponents—Cato, Pompey and the Vestal Virgins themselves!

TROS OF SAMOTHRACE 5: CLEOPATRA by *Talbot Mundy*—Cleopatra—Queen of Egypt—is a formidable character ever ready to play the game of intrigue, betrayal and shifting loyalties to suit her own objectives. Blood will surely be spilt and once again Tros finds himself inexorably caught up in monumental events that threaten his life and those he loves.

TROS OF SAMOTHRACE 6: THE PURPLE PIRATE by *Talbot Mundy*—The epic saga of the ancient world—Tros of Samothrace—draws to a conclusion in this sixth—and final—volume. Julius Caesar has been assassinated and Queen Cleopatra of Egypt finds herself in a perilous position and desperate for allies to secure her power.

THE ILLUSTRATED & COMPLETE BRIGADIER GERARD by *Sir Arthur Conan Doyle*—These are the adventures of Conan Doyle's incomparable French hero-the finest swordsman in the Light Cavalry-Etienne Gerard. Arranged for the first time in historical chronological order, his many enthusiasts can now properly appreciate his colourful career as he fights, loves and blunders his way through the Napoleonic epoch-from his earliest adventure as a young blade determined to reach his lady love despite the unwelcome attention of her fathers bull-through many campaigns and special missions-to the bloody field of Waterloo, the downfall of his beloved Emperor and beyond. This is the complete collection of these classic stories. What makes this edition exceptional is the inclusion of nearly 140 illustrations-mostly by the famed military artist William Barnes Wollen-which accurately portray the spirit of the stories and the uniforms and scenes of the events they portray.

LEONAUR

ALSO FROM LEONAUR
AVAILABLE IN SOFTCOVER OR HARDCOVER WITH DUST JACKET

GARRETT P. SERVISS' SCIENCE FICTION by *Garrett P. Serviss*—Three Interplanetary Adventures including the unauthorised sequel to H. G. Wells' *War of the Worlds--Edison's Conquest of Mars, A Columbus of Space, The Moon Metal.*

JUNK DAY by *Arthur Sellings*—". . . . his finest novel was his last, *Junk Day,* a post-holocaust tale set in the ruins of his native London and peopled with engrossing character types . . . . perhaps grimmer than his previous work but pointedly more energetic." *The Encyclopedia of Science Fiction.*

KIPLING'S SCIENCE FICTION by *Rudyard Kipling*—Science Fiction & Fantasy stories by a Master Storyteller including 'As East As A,B,C' 'With The Night Mail'.

THE COLLECTED SCIENCE FICTION AND FANTASY OF STANLEY G. WEINBAUM: THE BLACK HEART by *Stanley G. Weinbaum*—Classic Strange Tales Including: the Complete Novel The Dark Other, Plus Proteus Island and Others Stories included in this Volume The Dark Other (novel) Proteus Island The Adaptive Ultimate Pymalion's Spectacles.

THE COLLECTED SCIENCE FICTION AND FANTASY OF STANLEY G. WEINBAUM: STRANGE GENIUS by *Stanley G. Weinbaum*—Classic Tales of the Human Mind at Work Including the Complete Novel The New Adam, the 'van Manderpootz' Stories and Others Stories included in this Volume The New Adam (novel) The Brink of Infinity The Circle of Zero Graph The Worlds of If The Ideal The Point of View.

THE COLLECTED SCIENCE FICTION AND FANTASY OF STANLEY G. WEINBAUM OTHER EARTHS by *Stanley G. Weinbaum*—Classic Futuristic Tales Including: Dawn of Flame & its Sequel The Black Flame, plus The Revolution of 1960 & Others.

THE COLLECTED SCIENCE FICTION AND FANTASY OF STANLEY G. WEINBAUM INTERPLANETARY ODYSSEYS by *Stanley G. Weinbaum*—Classic Tales of Interplanetary Adventure Including: A Martian Odyssey, its Sequel Valley of Dreams, the Complete 'Ham' Hammond Stories and Others Stories included in this Volume Mars A Martian Odyssey Valley of Dreams Venus Parasite Planet The Lotus Eaters Uranus The Planet of Doubt Titan Flight on Titan Pluto The Red Peri Io The Mad Moon Europa Redemption Cairn Ganymede Tidal Moon.

SUPERNATURAL BUCHAN by *John Buchan*—Stories of Ancient Spirits, Uncanny Places & Strange Creatures.